TROPIC OF FEAR

ALSO BY RON TERPENING

SUSPENSE

League of Shadows

Storm Track

YOUNG ADULT

The Turning

In Light's Delay

TROPIC

STUYVESANT & HOAGLAND   ·   NEW YORK

OF FEAR

RON TERPENING

Stuyvesant & Hoagland
1133 Broadway, Suite 706
New York, NY 10010

Library of Congress Cataloging-in-Publication Data

Terpening, Ron.
    Tropic of fear / Ron Terpening.
        p. cm.
    ISBN-13: 978-0-9755761-9-9 (hardcover : acid-free paper)
    ISBN-10: 0-9755761-9-4 (hardcover : acid-free paper)
    1. Americans--Paraguay--Fiction. 2. Conspiracies--Fiction.
    3. Paraguay--Fiction. I. Title.
    PS3570.E6767T76 2006
    813'.54--dc22

                                    2005004450

    Printed in the United States of America on acid-free paper. ∞
    Dust jacket and title page illustration © 2005 by Edward Miller.
        Dust jacket design by Robert Aulicino.
    Visit the publisher's web site at http://www.suspensepub.com
        and the author's web site at http://www.ronterpening.com

Dedicated to Howard and Darlene Herman and Myrna Hargrove,
in honor of three masters of the Latin American thriller
Joseph Conrad (*Nostromo*, 1904)
Graham Greene (*The Power and the Glory*, 1940)
and Robert Stone (*A Flag for Sunrise*, 1980)

"The horror is past…The good life is just beyond the next banana tree."

— U.S. STATE DEPARTMENT ON LATIN AMERICA

Ecco il don dei tiranni: pensando la morte non dar di dar la vita.

Chapter One

By the time the plane landed at the international airport outside Asunción, Diane Lang had a massive headache that threatened to go migraine; four Nuprin and two Maxalt in the last three hours had failed to diminish the pain. The penalty for having light-colored eyes, she thought: Everyone said they were her best feature—pale blue with specks of gray—but she paid for that with headaches.

As she waited in line for customs, the cigarette smoke in the arrival hall nauseated her. The heat and humidity weighed down on her head like a lead cloak. Far ahead, two customs agents were methodically ransacking the suitcases of returning Paraguayans, looking for smugglers apparently, and the press of anxious passengers was suffocating.

She shut her eyes for a moment, head tilted, viscous waves sliding in slow, sickening motion to the left side of her skull. *Just let me through to a bathroom.* Dizzy, afraid she might fall, she opened her eyes and was startled to find a uniformed policeman standing in front of her.

He reached for her elbow, said, "*Señora* Lang," waited for her nod, then added, "Come with me, please."

Finally—out of this mob! Had someone arranged to meet her?

The policeman escorted her past a sign reading *Bienvenidos al Aeropuerto Silvio Pettirossi* to a small room off to one side. The nameplate read *Ibarras.*

She didn't recognize the name but assumed someone from the *Universidad Católica* had prepared the way for her. An assistant professor of German at Yale, just a year away from tenure at the age of thirty-two, she was due to read a paper at an international conference of German scholars on Monday of the following week. One more invited paper to add to her *Vita.*

But it wasn't a colleague. Instead, as the policeman ushered her into the room, he said, "*El señor Jefe de Investigaciones* would like to speak with you." He nodded to an officer sitting behind a glass-topped, mahogany desk. "*Coronel, Señora* Lang."

The colonel looked up from a file he was reading, his face expressionless, then pointed to a straight-backed wood chair against the far wall.

Breathing heavily in the unexpected heat, slightly alarmed, Diane took a seat and waited while the officer continued to peruse the file. Her anxiety was repressing the headache, but she knew it would be back when this was over.

She wondered how the policeman had identified her. No one was meeting her at the airport. She hadn't told anyone in Asunción what she looked like. Had a flight attendant pointed her out after collecting the transit cards?

She knew summer was just beginning in the southern hemisphere and had dressed accordingly in beige cotton slacks and a white blouse, but she was still uncomfortably hot. Her thick, shoulder-length black hair, naturally wavy, had been pulled back into a pony tail held loosely by a barrette, but the bangs on her forehead were damp. The only jewelry she wore were hoop earrings of peach-colored enamel.

She thought about freshening her lipstick, then decided not to. She didn't want to suggest she was attempting to sway the colonel with her looks.

God, her head hurt. *Deep inside now, waiting to explode.* She wished the colonel would finish so she could get to the hotel and rest.

She stared at the officer, who continued to ignore her. He did not look like a man who would take kindly to interruption.

The colonel was a thin man, almost emaciated, with dark shadows in the pockets below his eyes. His lips were compressed so tight they were bloodless, and the well-trimmed mustache he sported lent a touch of cruelty to his face. He gripped the file with long, bony fingers, the nails in need of cutting, thick and slightly curved.

Looking away with a barely repressed shudder, she glanced around the room, trying to calm herself with an observation of detail—but there was little of interest to attract her attention. In fact, other than the one desk and three straight chairs, the room was empty. No filing cabinets, no wastebaskets, no typewriter, no coat hanger, nothing. Apart from the one file in the colonel's hands and a black telephone, the desk was bare. The only decoration in the room was a color portrait of the current president, General Enrique Zancon, in full military regalia, on the wall behind the desk.

Her headache was shifting from the center of her skull to a spot behind her left eye. The light in the room hurt: Sunlight stabbed in from a series of grilled windows high up on the wall. She shut her eyes and took a deep breath, then exhaled with her mouth open to hide the sound. A vein throbbed in her left temple, each pulse a painful hammer blow.

I haven't done anything, she thought. No drugs, no contraband, no prohibited books, no computers or electronic gadgets, nothing to be nervous about. Sit and wait …

The colonel's voice startled her, the tone knife-sharp: *"Señora, ¿quién le formuló la invitación para venir a Asunción?"*

Her eyes fluttered open and she cleared her throat, feeling a sudden constriction. Why should she need an invitation to the city?

"The authorities of the Catholic University—I was invited to read a paper. And then I'll be conducting research on the Mennonite settlements in the Chaco." She took a deep breath to calm the quaver in her voice. "I'm a professor of German at Yale University. I have the invitation with me in my briefcase." She fumbled for the case at her feet.

The *Jefe de Investigaciones* waved aside the proffered letter when she finally found it. "You are a professor of German, yet you speak Spanish very well. Why is that?"

"Why not?" Her voice was clipped, a touch of aggravation creeping in despite herself. "I also speak French and some Italian. And I've studied Latin and ancient Greek."

His eyes hardened. *"Señora*, what is the topic of your essay?"

He emphasized the term *señora* and she knew why; he was refusing to dignify her with the title *profesora*.

"I'm a specialist in the Protestant Reformation. I'll be speaking on Menno Simons. The Brotherhood of the Believers—*die Nachfolger.*"

The colonel stared at her a moment and then extended his hand. "The essay, please."

She hesitated. "I— I don't have a written copy. I usually improvise when I speak; I've been teaching courses on Mennonite culture for at least ten years."

Which wasn't quite the truth. She had mailed a copy of the paper to the conference organizers, who had advised her not to carry it with her. Now she understood why. But she couldn't comprehend why something so innocuous would be subject to seizure by the authorities.

She tried to meet the colonel's eyes, but his black, piercing stare un-nerved her. Her throat had gone cottony and she licked her lips, catching the bottom one in her teeth and pulling at it.

The colonel lifted the folder in one hand. "We have a file here provided by your State Department that shows you have been involved in several questionable—possibly even subversive—activities."

Her heart beat accelerated. "Impossible." She frowned as the implication settled in. "Subversive to whom?"

"It says, for example, that you visited Yugoslavia in 1991 to read a paper in Belgrade. You had contacts with communist scholars—two professors from the Soviet Union."

She stared back at the man's dark, impenetrable eyes, her own reflecting anger. She wondered who reported the conversation. She had talked to the Soviet scholars about Jakob Hutter, a sixteenth-century Swiss minister who had proposed a community of goods for the Brotherhood of Believ-ers, claiming that private property was a major obstacle to Christian love. Most of the Hutterian Brethren now lived in Canada. The Soviets had wanted to know if the authorities considered them communists. Who cared about the communists now?

"Does that make me a threat to the state?" she asked, a note of bel-ligerence in her voice.

"In 1996, you arranged for a delegation of Cubans to take part in a conference in Munich. And in 99, you chaired a session at a congress on agrarian reform and indigenous peoples."

"Those— All those activities were university-related. The congress on indigenous peoples was co-sponsored by the government. We received grants from federal agencies. There was nothing subversive about it."

"*Señora* Lang, you offend me, you piece of cockroach shit."

Her mouth dropped open. Had she misunderstood him? Had he reverted to Guaraní—used a word that sounded like Spanish? Paraguay-ans were bilingual, proud of their Indian heritage, even if most were of

European origin. But still, his tone …

The colonel got to his feet and walked around the desk.

She straightened, unsure of the man's intentions, her eyes wary. Was that it? Now that she'd been insulted, was she free to go?

Despite her concentration, the slap caught her by surprise. Stunned, she found herself on the floor, ears ringing, the chair on its side at her feet. One of her earrings had broken and rolled lazily under the desk.

Shocked and disoriented, her first reflex was to protect her stomach. She crossed her arms in front of her, the letter from the Catholic University still in her right hand. She did not try to get up. Her cheek stung from the blow and her eyes were watery, as much from humiliation as pain.

"*Señora* Lang, we do not like people like you in our country." The colonel stood over her, his voice harsh, every *s* a sibilant hiss. "I advise you to leave. If you insist on staying, we will follow you every step of the way. We will investigate anyone who contacts you. In Paraguay, *señora* Lang, no two stones can come together without me hearing the click. Remember that. If my men find you alone in the streets late at night, who knows what might happen? A pretty woman—a *yanqui* …" He smiled thinly. "*¿Comprende?*"

Anger flowed through her, driving out the fear, headache forgotten. She sat up, her eyes flashing as she waved the crumpled letter.

"I have an invitation from the *decano* of the Universidad Católica Nuestra Señora de la Asunción. I am a scholar with an international reputation. After I read my paper, my government will hear about your behavior. And if your men accost me while I'm here—or hurt me in any manner—you will have an international incident on your hands. Is that what you want? I know about your violations of human rights. If you violate mine—" She stopped, her jaws clenched.

The colonel laughed. "Go tell it to the Marines. I'm not through with you yet." He kicked the chair at her side and sneered when he saw her flinch. "Wait here, *puta*." He turned and left the room.

Chapter Two

Adrenaline-shock ... disbelief ... anger ... fear ...

The surge of conflicting emotions left Diane feeling weak. The colonel had called her a whore; there was no mistaking his language this time.

Shakily, she got to her feet and righted the chair, then retrieved her broken earring. After dabbing at her eyes, she straightened the letter, put it in her briefcase, and sat down, numbly rubbing her cheek where Ibarras had hit her. Why her? What had she done to antagonize him?

The colonel had told her to wait. Were they going to take her to police headquarters? A shiver ran up her back and sweat broke out under her arms and on her forehead. She had no real gauge to measure the extent of the danger, but she'd heard what the secret police did to women. She didn't want to think about that.

Minutes passed, an eternity of waiting. Her headache was back, the tension making it worse; if she didn't get out of the light and lie down soon, she would vomit.

She looked toward the door, wondering if Ibarras was standing outside, waiting for her to make a move so he could arrest her.

Oh, Kim, she thought. What would you do if I didn't come back?

The sudden realization that she might die left her breathless. She tried to tell herself she was exaggerating the danger. She had no connection to any revolutionary movements in Paraguay; her talk had nothing to do with politics. Yes, she was studying the Mennonites—and, yes, they espoused a doctrine of non-resistance and, yes, by law they did not have to serve in the military. Still—

She stopped, willing her mind to calm down. It did no good to question why. The only thing that mattered was survival. Her daughter—

A vision of Kim in the parking lot of the marina came to mind, waving the letter now in Diane's briefcase. It was a Saturday, in the middle of October. When the mail with the Paraguayan stamps came, Kim had begged her grandmother to drive to Lighthouse Point Park, where they could watch for the sloop's return. Kim was only twelve, but she knew how much the news meant to her mother. For two years, Diane had worked through the State Department to establish a relationship with the Catholic University in Asunción. Now, with a formal invitation in hand, her research would be that much easier. And Kim would get to stay with her grandmother, where she was pampered, for a week or two.

That Saturday in New Haven, after a clear morning, clouds had scuttled across the sky in the afternoon, pushed by a stiff breeze that snapped the sails and rattled the lines of her twenty-six foot Orion sloop, a family boat, inherited from her father, who'd been a banker. Her boyfriend Russ had tried to convince her they shouldn't go out. It was too late in the season. But she had wanted one last day on the water before dry-docking the sloop for the winter.

And it was a good day for sailing, with just the right amount of danger to make it exhilarating, especially when sailing to windward, close-hauled, the jib sheet trimmed in flat and the boat heeled well over. Seas foaming past the lee rail. The invigorating sting of spray in the face.

By the time they returned to the harbor, the waves in Long Island Sound were cresting at over five feet, the wind was whipping froth across the troughs, and Russ was sick. At the harbor master's office, a red pennant was flying—the small-craft warning—and a squall hit while they were still at the slipway, getting the boat winched out of the water. All of which added to Russ's foul humor.

A good day and a bad day. There was the letter but also the fight with Russ. He'd been out with her before, but the storm had frightened him. He'd complained about everything she did, including the speed of the boat on the way back in.

"I'm racing that squall back," she'd said. "The sooner we get there, the better you'll feel."

"If you were any good, you could keep the boat even."

"Christ, Russ!"

"I'm sick."

Not as sick as he claimed. Most seasick people clammed up and froze, their eyes locked on some far-off point of land for stability. She had warned Russ to take two Bonine tablets before they cast off, but he'd refused.

And then at the dock, he said he'd never go out again—at least *not with a woman*. And that had angered her; she handled the boat as well as any man: Her ex-husband—Kim's father—had taught her well.

"Rich bitch," she heard Russ mutter.

She was tired of his constant harping, tired of his feelings of financial inferiority. Russ was a staff accountant in the bursar's office at Yale, but he earned half of what she did. Could she help it that women were courted with high salaries? Besides, she had a Ph.D. She got what she deserved and by managing her money she could afford to keep the boat. It had

11

nothing to do with him and she had told him so.

Fine, he said, he wanted nothing to do with her. He'd find someone who wasn't so self-centered. And with that he stormed off, not bothering to say good-bye.

Afterwards (Kim had stayed at the beach with her grandmother to ride the carousel) Diane drove to Richter's bar on Chapel Street for a cup of coffee. She needed to wash the acrid taste from her mouth.

The sidewalks were littered with leaves from the tattered elms, copper beeches, and maples. In the street, traffic was thick as fans left the stadium following the football game. This week's opponent was Lehigh, if she remembered right. Had the Bulldogs won? Apparently so, the bar was noisy with jubilant fans. Not the quiet haven she'd hoped for. Not the place to sort out conflicting emotions.

Sad about Russ, but elated at the chance to visit Paraguay, she left soon after, stopping by her office on the third floor of Harkness Hall to pick up some books before returning home.

Fate, she thought. An ending … a new beginning. Both on the same day. Maybe it had been coming for some time. She'd lost a boyfriend but gained a chance for adventure.

The door behind her flew open, startling her as it banged against the wall. Colonel Ibarras strode across the room, tossed some photo enlargements on the desktop, and sat down. Without looking at her, he picked up the photos and began to lay them out on the desk, turning them to face her.

"Come here," he said, beckoning abruptly with his head. "Recognize her?"

Diane looked at one of the photos and then averted her head. A sick feeling passed through the pit of her stomach. The colonel knew she wouldn't be able to identify the person; she was battered beyond recognition. What was this? A veiled threat? Showing her what the police could do?

"Well?"

Diane shook her head. "I've never seen her before."

"Look again."

"Why?"

"I think you know her."

She stared at the colonel, hating the man's smugness. "Who is it?"

"You don't recognize her? She's a former graduate student of yours. She came here to study and got involved with revolutionaries. She was arrested by the secret police. Your name came up during one of the inter-rogation sessions."

"Who the hell is it?"

The colonel's thin lips parted into a half-smile. "Rosemarie Krupp, recently deceased."

Diane closed her eyes for a moment, hand touching the desk to steady herself. Not her. Not Rose. She opened her eyes and looked at another photo. Swollen features ... badly bruised.

The colonel tapped a photo. "That's what she looked like after just three days. Most people last at least a week."

He picked up a small notebook. "We recovered a diary she kept in confinement. It's her version of what happened to her. Of course, if she had managed to smuggle the diary out, we would deny what she says." He held it out to her. "Here, have a look."

She didn't want to know.

Ibarras opened the diary. "She says our agents blindfolded her and tied her to a bed. Six men raped her repeatedly. When they gave her water or food, still blindfolded, they slapped or pinched her, or hit her with their fists. They burned her feet, they carved *¡Viva El Tigre!* on her stomach, they pierced her—"

"*That's enough!* I can see what they did to her."

Ibarras shook his head, his eyes narrowed to thin slits. "I've only covered the first paragraph of the first day. There are eight pages." He snorted. "Now you see why she's unrecognizable. She became another person the second she was blindfolded. She lost her personality. She lost her independence. She became an object. A horribly mistreated object. No longer a human. What was done to her—"

"Shut up," Diane screamed. "I've heard enough."

Ibarras stared at her, breathing evenly. He raised a finger. "Good, then listen to this. It's the last thing I'm going to tell you. If you complain to any other authorities about—" he gestured around the room—"about this, you will be arrested under the accusation of *querer atentar contra la paz y la seguridad de la Republica*. The same accusation lodged against your friend here. Do you know what that means?"

"I speak Spanish." She didn't like being threatened.

"You may understand the words, but not the meaning." His voice hardened. "Anyone who disturbs the peace and security of the Republic is charged as an international terrorist, *un agente provocador*. And in this country, *señora* Lang, we execute terrorists."

In the taxi, with the smell of acrid exhaust strong in the air, Diane closed her eyes and tried to blot out what had just happened to her. The driver was speaking—something about the city having 153 plazas—but she was oblivious to the view, his words washing over her, drumming on her head like rain beating down on tin. She had vomited in a restroom at the airport and couldn't control her shaking. Tomorrow, she told herself, she would laugh about this. With her migraine she had exaggerated everything. They were just trying to intimidate her. They—

No. The pictures … She wouldn't forget and she sure as hell wouldn't laugh.

Oh, Kim, what have I gotten into?

Chapter Three

At first Walter Stanek thought the trouble began in Asunción. On the night of his arrival, the envelope he was supposed to deliver to a Samcon representative was stolen when he was distracted by an American woman at the bar of the Club Bahia Negra, a middle-class dining establishment located off the Avenida Artigas just south of the Jardin Botánico. But no— On reflection, he realized the deception had begun nearly a week earlier, late one night in Tucson, Arizona …

If there was one thing Walter Stanek hated during his sabbatical it was being caught in his office by a student wanting help. It was the ambivalence that bothered him—his desire to help tangling with his desire to be left alone. The sign on his door in the Mines and Metallurgy Building on North Campus Drive—"Dr. Stanek is on sabbatical—here, but *not here*"—did absolutely no good. Either the students failed to read it, or if they did they didn't understand it or assumed the words didn't apply to them; after all, they were *his* students; *they* knew him personally. And once the door was open he was usually too kind to say no to their requests.

Finally, he had taken to working at home, checking books out of the Science Library early in the morning when former students and colleagues were in classes—or still in bed; and then, late at night, he would drive in to the university when you could park anywhere on campus without a permit, including in the concrete parking structure next to the Administration Building, and get what he needed from his office, usually a reference work or a file with notes, occasionally an article in one of the engineering or hydrology journals he subscribed to.

So, on the last Friday in October, when someone knocked on the door at two a.m., he was startled. The janitors, who usually worked late, had already been through his office; the wastebasket was empty. At that hour, the building was locked: Only teaching assistants and faculty had keys. There should be no students in the building.

Still, his first vision, before opening the door, was of a disgruntled student standing on the other side with a shotgun in hand, someone with a grudge at an F received in an upper-division course on hydrogeology or upset with a C in a graduate seminar on geological engineering. Few people considered teaching a hazardous profession; little did they know, he thought: Engineering students would kill for an A.

Stanek took his time and made sure he had a sheaf of papers in his left hand when he opened the door. Light cascaded from behind him into the dim hall. Due to the state-mandated budget cuts, only one light fixture was in operation down at the end of the hall near the door to the stairwell, where it gleamed softly on the recently waxed floor. He blocked the opening with his body, his right foot wedged behind the door; the message was clear: *No access now. I'm busy. Do not disturb.*

He didn't recognize the man, a guy in his early thirties, maybe ten years younger, dressed in slacks and a striped, short-sleeved sport shirt with buttoned-down collars. A sliver of light glinted off a fancy gold wristwatch. Probably drove a BMW with vanity plates reading *HOT BMR*, thought Stanek. The type who made sure they addressed him by name after class and touched him on the shoulder when they said, "Great lecture, Doc!"

"What can I do for you?" Stanek asked, not bothering to smile. The tone of his voice held no invitation.

"Dr. Stanek? May I come in? I'd like to talk to you in private." A New England accent, faintly aristocratic to Stanek's ear.

"In private?" Stanek looked up and down the hall. It was as private as you could get on a university campus.

The fellow persisted. "May I come in and sit down?"

Begrudgingly, feeling guilty at his uncustomary surliness, Stanek stepped back and motioned for the fellow to take a chair. With an inaudible sigh, he walked around behind his desk, sat down in the swivel chair. He placed the sheaf of papers in an open file, closed it, and then leaned back, elbows on the thin, scuffed leather arm rests of his chair, hands steepled in front of his chest.

"I don't believe I recognize you," he said. "And as you saw from my note on the door, I'm on sabbatical and not available right now. So I'm afraid I really can't help you with any extended project."

Hit them before the request—and again afterwards, if necessary. The eager usually needed a double dose of negativity. Everyone else in the department told him he was too amenable, and now—*by God, it was two a.m.!*—he was resolved to stand fast.

"Sorry for contacting you this way," the man said, "but I'm not a student. I called your home and got your machine, so I thought I'd stop by here to see if you might be in. I was told you often work late."

Told? By the office no doubt. Stanek had asked them not to refer people to him while he was on sabbatical, but the secretaries and administrative assistant never remembered—or simply found it easier to pass problems on to him: He had a knack for working things out.

He sighed, squared his shoulders, and ran a hand through his tousled brown hair. Stanek was a muscular, compact man, an inch short of six feet. At the age of forty-three, he still weighed the 175 pounds he had in high school. He had a strong face, with a broad forehead, forceful nose, and rugged chin. Dressed in brown cords, a light blue T-shirt, and with an unbuttoned flannel shirt for a jacket, he looked as if he'd be more comfortable wearing a hard hat and boots on a construction project than sitting behind a desk in an office. At the moment, he set his jaw like a linebacker waiting to make a tackle, and said nothing, his eyes boring into those of the fellow across the desk.

The young man leaned forward, smiling pleasantly, and stuck out a hand. "I'm Greg Brown, by the way. I represent Samcon Engineering. Perhaps you've heard of us."

Stanek frowned. "I don't believe so. A new company?" This was not what he'd expected.

"We've been active in South America for quite a few years. We used to be called South American Continental." Brown grinned. "The hotshots in the head office in Houston thought Samcon was slicker. Shorter URL, you know. Anyway, among our other services, we supply engineering consultants for hydroelectric projects in Latin America. Our latest job was Itaipú and now we're involved with its two sister dams downriver, Yacyretá, which is under construction, and Corpus, still in the planning stage."

"In Paraguay?"

Brown's eyes brightened and he nodded cheerfully. "You've heard of the project then?"

"I'm familiar with it. Vaguely." Stanek, trying to be civil, gestured off to one corner of the small room. "I just came back from Alaska myself. Spent two months this summer working for the Alaska Energy Authority on the Bradley Lake Hydroelectric Project." Stanek never taught during the summers; that was a time for research or outside consultation.

Brown looked thoughtful. "Yes, the people who recommended you to us mentioned that. What was it you did exactly?"

Stanek hesitated, running a forefinger behind one ear. Oh, what the hell; the guy wasn't going to ask him to supervise an independent study, didn't have a problem getting into a class, wasn't going to complain about how unfair the system was, didn't want him to sign a petition so he could get into an already full class, wasn't going to ask for help with a paper. Be nice and get the guy out of here. Besides, he liked talking about his work.

He cleared his throat. "The project managers had several environmental concerns." He shrugged. "Bradley Lake is on the Kenai Peninsula—near a state park, a national wildlife refuge, and two critical habitats. I was the consulting hydrologist. We had to redesign a tailrace channel to minimize excavation near one of the habitats. And we set the lower portion of the power tunnel deep in the mountain. Minimized the visual impact of the penstocks from Kachemak Bay."

Eyes blank, the man nodded as if he understood, then said, "I've heard of your work, though I must admit I'm not an engineer myself. I'm in personnel—which is why I've come to talk to you."

Stanek leaned forward. "You should talk to the university's placement office. I don't have any graduate students finishing their degrees right now, and, as I told you, I'm on sabbatical—for the entire academic year."

Brown nodded. "I talked to your department head and the dean before approaching you." He made a deprecatory gesture. "They've approved a postponement of your sabbatical—if you're willing."

"Yeah, well—"

"We'd like to offer you a one-month position as a consultant with our Risk Control Management division. You'd take part in a disaster prevention and response project in Asunción, and then you'd be advising the contractors on environmental problems at the Corpus site. The Paraguayan government is concerned about the effect of the dams on the ecology of the Paraná river downstream. We're willing to pay sixty thousand for the month, plus travel and all expenses."

Stanek raised his eyebrows, but said nothing. He hadn't liked hearing that Brown had approached the department before talking to him: He should have been the one to ask for a postponement if there was to be one—but sixty thousand bucks for one month's work … at Arizona, that was close to half a year's salary for an associate professor of engineering.

"Have you ever been to Paraguay?" Brown asked.

Stanek shook his head. "Never worked south of Mexico."

Brown removed a sheet of paper from a folder. "The Itaipú and its sister dams are a twenty-six billion dollar project. Itaipú took twelve of that. Sixty stories high with twelve million cubic meters of concrete in her, and sixteen turbine and generator units. Puts out 12,600 megawatts of electricity. They tell me it's the world's largest." He handed the page to Stanek. "Here, you can keep this. It lists the specifications. Itaipú beats out Grand Coulee Dam, by the way."

Stanek shrugged. Both his father and grandfather had worked on Grand Coulee, and he was born and raised in the city itself, before his father moved the family to Wenatchee and then back to the family homestead in Ferndale. But no reason to tell Brown that. Or did he already know?

Brown's eyes flitted around the room, falling on an amateurish painting of a farm scene. "Where you grew up?" he asked, nodding toward the painting.

Stanek responded with a noncommittal gesture: He didn't like people prying into his past. His grandparent's farm. His sister had painted the scene when she was still in high school. *Randi*. She lived and worked on the farm now.

Brown pulled at the skin on his neck. "As I said, your first few days would be spent in the capital playing 'war games.' That's what they call these things." He rolled his eyes as if to say boys will be boys. "You'd be part of a team advising the government on how to react to man-made and natural disasters."

Stanek's eyes narrowed. "Man-made? You mean—"

"Anything from massive chemical disasters—like Bhopal—to isolated incidents of terrorism."

Stanek frowned. "What's this have to do with dams? I'm no expert in responses to terrorism."

"As I said, you'll be part of a team, each with his or her own area of expertise. It all ties in. What if a terrorist group threatened to bomb Itaipú? You'd be able to suggest ways to thwart that."

Stanek looked doubtful. "I don't know … it's really not my field."

Brown leaned forward, his expression earnest. "You come highly recommended. Not many people have your training and experience in environmental risk control."

Stanek had a master's in hydrology and water resources and a doctorate in geological engineering with a thesis on earthquake engineering. He'd studied the bolster embankments behind Pinopolis West Dam at Lake Moultrie on the Cooper River, thirty miles north of Charleston, South Carolina. And he been a consultant on numerous other flood control projects. But still—hey, they were offering sixty-thousand.

"How soon do you need an answer?"

Brown hesitated. "We're short on hydrogeologists right now. The fellow we had on the project disappeared on us just before we could get started on the war games."

Stanek looked askance. That didn't sound so good—and neither did Brown's use of the phrase 'war games' for a disaster prevention program. "Disappeared?"

Brown pursed his cheeks and wagged his head as if they were talking about a recalcitrant child. "Well, he left without telling anyone. We got a letter of resignation in the mail a week later. Never heard from him after that."

"What was the problem?"

"Problem?" Brown's eyes blinked in surprise. "Oh, with Rodriguez. Nothing to do with the job. Carlos got involved with the wrong people." Brown shrugged. "Hit the bottle too often, if you ask me. Burnt out. He'd been working pretty hard."

"Well, for sixty thousand a month—you'd better expect to work."

"That's the attitude. Couldn't have said it better myself." A fake smile, a glance at his watch. "I'll be in town until five tomorrow evening." He grinned. "Halloween. Trick or treat. Give me a call. I'm staying at the campus Marriott. If you're willing, I already have a ticket for you from Tucson to Miami with a connection to Asunción. You have a passport, right?"

Stanek nodded.

"We'd need you out of here by next Wednesday. The fourth. Disaster prevention project starts on the sixth. That's a Friday. You should arrive sometime Thursday. It won't give you much time to get acclimated, but it's the best I can do. We'd be very happy to have you on board."

When he was alone again, Stanek stared absentmindedly at the specification sheet for the Itaipú project. Charts, diagrams, rows of figures. A list of the world's ten largest hydroelectric projects.

Brown was damned sure of himself, he thought. First that patronizing comment about the right attitude and then the smug look on his face—like some smooth-talking frat boy who'd just gotten into the pants of the head cheerleader. Made Stanek feel like turning the guy down on principle alone.

November 6—that was only a week away. But sixty thousand, gee … and for one month—at that rate, he might consider going into business for himself. Forget sabbaticals!

Chapter Four

Randi, this is Walter. Happy Halloween!"

He could hear her voice pick up. "How you doing, Wally? Looking forward to seeing you. Only four weeks now."

"Uh, listen, Randi—"

"Wally, what now? You've been promising to come up for two years."

Stanek sighed. His sister had just broken up with her live-in boyfriend of five years and had been pestering him—a little emotional manipulation added to the normal pressure—to come up for a week at Thanksgiving. She lived on the family farm near Ferndale, just outside Bellingham. It wasn't that he didn't like his sister; they were best friends. It was just . . .

"Randi, I know I promised, but something's come up. I'm going to be out of the States for at least a month. Down in Paraguay. Why don't I come at Christmas? We can roast a turkey and the works—just for the two of us."

"I'll be tired of cooking by Christmas."

He could hear the hurt in her voice. "I'll cook," he said. "You know I like cooking turkey and dressing."

"For two people?"

"Invite some friends over. The dog can eat the leftovers."

"Turkey and dressing are for Thanksgiving, not Christmas."

"We used to have it at both."

"That was when mom and dad and grandma were alive."

Walter sighed. He could imagine her in the kitchen, plaid shirt and jeans, sleeves rolled up just beyond the elbow, blonde hair in a pony tail, brown eyes downcast. Her telephone was on the wall by the refrigerator and he thought he could hear its soft hum. And far off in the background the barking of a dog. That would be Buck, Randi's golden retriever.

"How's your love life?" he asked, hoping to change the subject.

"I already told you Jeff moved out, right? I've been too busy to worry about men. I've been trying to reroof that old shed behind the barn by myself. I got an extra cutting of hay this year. The bales are sitting outside under plastic sheeting." She paused. "Damn it, Wally. I was looking forward to seeing you."

He nodded, and then, realizing she couldn't see him, said a belated, "Me too."

After a moment she asked, "Who you seeing now?"

" No one."

"No one! What happened to Shirley? And that girl that played the piano?"

Stanek grinned. "Linda. She didn't like my taste in music." He took a deep breath. "And Shirley ... well, that's over. She kept trying to mother me—inviting me over for milk and cookies."

"Wally, what's wrong with that? They're not too many woman like that around anymore."

"She was smothering me. I felt like an infant in a cradle."

"We make a fine pair, don't we?"

"Whaddya mean?" Randi had a way of making him feel defensive.

"Our success with relationships."

He paused, shifting the receiver. "We owe dad for that, I guess. Our legacy from an anal-retentive tyrant. But what about you and me? We did pretty good there."

"Yeah," she said dryly, "we survived."

"And we love each other, right? You're my favorite sister."

"Your *only* sister—and you beat me up when we were kids."

"That's 'cause you were always smarter."

She sniggered. "Right. I should've been the prof."

"And I the farmer."

"You wouldn't like what I had to do yesterday."

"What's that?"

"Remember Grandma Wilson and Noodles?"

That wild cat they could never catch. "What about them?"

"I've got another one like Noodles around here. She just had her second litter and the place is being overrun. Thank God, I found where she'd hidden them. The first bunch has been killing chickens."

"What'd you do with the second litter?"

"What Grandma used to do."

"Not that."

There was a moment of silence. "Does how you do it matter?" she said. "They're dead."

"But drowning defenseless kittens in a bucket ..." He took a deep breath. "Was it hard?"

"I cried before, during, and after. What would you have done? Hit them over the head with a board like dad?"

"Dad did that to rabbits, not cats."

He could *hear* Randi's shrug over the phone. "Nature's a cruel step-mother, Walter. She does it slow. We kill 'em fast."

He thought of all the animals he'd seen butchered. Chickens with their heads cut off running around spouting blood from the neck and urine from the butt, pigs with their throats slit from ear to ear, a steer felled by a sledge-hammer blow to the skull, deer hung up from a rafter in the barn, drowned kittens.

"Wally, I thought you hated Latin America."

"That was Mexico," he said.

"What makes you think Paraguay will be any different? Wally, I'm worried. I've been reading bad things about South America."

"Hey, who hasn't? But you're thinking of Bolivia or Columbia—or one of those cocaine countries."

"What's Paraguay?"

"Right! That's the question. You never hear of it, so how bad can it be?"

"You don't *know*? You're going to the country and you don't even *know* what's going on there? You didn't *check*?"

Walter sighed. "Randi, my bladder's full. I'll talk to you another time."

"Wally, you're the only person I know who talks about their bladder when they have to pee."

He laughed. "I could've mentioned my kidneys. Anyway, I—"

"Forget your kidneys. So what'll you be doing in Paraguay?"

"Working for an outfit called Samcon. It's a good contract. Sixty thousand for a month. I just found out about it yesterday. I'll be advising the government on a hydroelectric project."

"You don't need the money that bad, do you?"

"Randi, I thought I could help you out. Give you the down payment for a new tractor. That old John Deere's ready for the graveyard. Besides, I need a change."

"A change. Wally, you just got back from Alaska two months ago."

"I haven't been sleeping well. Twelve hours a night now. I go to bed at one or two in the morning and can't get out of bed till noon."

"Well, if I was free, I'd probably sleep twelve hours, too. Like Buck. Another old dog in the family." Her voice was dry.

"Only it's not really sleeping, Randi. It's lying in bed trying to come awake but not making it. It's being weighed down—it's being fifty feet down in the ocean with all that pressure on you and not having the air to rise to the surface. It's like being drugged."

"Wally, maybe you're sick. What is that illness they get out there in the desert? Valley Fever? Doesn't that make you sleepy?"

"I don't have the other symptoms. It's this sabbatical. I can't get used to not having a schedule. It's not like me to be so tired all the time. I'm in a daze. I saw a book advertised in the paper—*Cut Your Balls in Half*—and just about jumped out of my skin. I had to read it twice before I saw it said *Cut Your Bills in Half*."

Randi's peal of laughter was contagious. When they both stopped laughing she said, "You're mentally exhausted, Wally, ever think about that? That's what a sabbatical's for. To refresh yourself."

"I'm supposed to be working on a book. Haven't felt much like writing. I outlined the thing and then gave up."

"So what are you doing?"

"Reading. Trying to keep up with the field. But I can't understand why I'm so tired. The doctor asked me if I was depressed. Hell, I don't know. I told him I wasn't."

"So you're bored and you took this job for a change of pace. You think it'll pep you up." It was a statement, not a question.

"I guess," he said. "And maybe I can do some good for the country."

"Some good for the country? Wally, this is a job, right? They're not hiring you to be a hero. Just do your job and get back here."

"Right," he said. "That's all I plan on doing."

• • •

27

Stanek was not an avid collector of stamps, but he did tear off foreign issues and commemoratives whenever he found them, storing the stamps in a cubbyhole of his rolltop desk until he had enough to fill a number ten envelope. And then the sealed envelopes were stuffed in a desk drawer for the day he retired and had time to steam them free and mount them in a stamp book.

Later that night, at his second meeting with Greg Brown, after signing Samcon's requisite personnel forms, including a free life insurance policy in the amount of one hundred thousand dollars (for which he listed his sister Randi as beneficiary), Stanek was given a stamped manila envelope to deliver to Raymond Kohlbert, a Samcon representative in Asunción. Kohlbert would meet Stanek for dinner on the night of his arrival, Brown said. Thursday, November the fifth, eight p.m. at the Club Bahia Negra. Take a taxi, everyone knew where the Club was. Until then, keep the envelope in his possession at all times. Brown had intended to mail the envelope, he'd said, until he realized it would be safer to have it hand-delivered.

When Stanek saw the colorful stamps on the envelope—three large commemoratives depicting World War I posters from the National Archives, he couldn't help exclaiming. "Gee, I hate to see such beautiful stamps go to waste."

"Hey, what's three stamps?" Brown said, then smiled broadly. "We can afford it."

His face had the same amiable cast Stanek had seen earlier—a look that reminded him of a slick salesman, both patronizing and false. Brown needed a scar on his chin, he thought, or some other defect to add a little character to his face.

"And with you hand-delivering the material, well,"—Brown shrugged in eloquent condescension—"it'll just get there quicker and safer, won't it?"

Stanek wanted to say, "I doubt it," or a blunt, "No, it won't"—anything to turn those cherubic cheeks sour—but resisted the temptation. For sixty thousand bucks he'd be happy to deliver the letter in person, and he'd even treat Kohlbert to dinner while he was at it.

After the meeting with Brown, when he was at home—a modest two-bedroom bungalow in the Sam Hughes neighborhood not far from campus—temptation reared its ugly head. Stanek had dropped the envelope on the kitchen table and over coffee, eyeing the series of stamps, he felt the first twinge of desire building somewhere deep inside.

He hadn't seen the stamps before, each dedicated, he noticed, to the war efforts of women. One showed a youthful, armorclad girl, sword in hand, and read at the top "Joan of Arc Saved France" and at the bottom "Women of America, Save Your Country, Buy War Savings Stamps." Another showed a jaunty woman in uniform, with the phrase, "If You Want To Fight! Join the Marines." And then there was one with three women, all rather dowdy by modern standards, under the heading "Feminine Patriotism"—a maid with a broom in hand ("Domestic Economy"), a Wac in jacket and skirt standing with rifle at parade rest against a backdrop of the flag ("Home Defense"), and a nurse ("Aid to the Suffering"). Nicely done, he thought. The stamps were worth saving all right.

When he finished his coffee, he looked through his supplies for a matching manila envelope. Fortunately, Brown had not used company stationery—the envelope was addressed by hand, each letter of Raymond Kohlbert's name and Samcon's company address on Calle Iturbe carefully printed. Stanek copied it twice before he was satisfied that the recipient, even if a longtime correspondent of Greg Brown, would not notice the difference.

Only then did he slit the original manila envelope, remove Brown's letter—a brief note accompanying the photocopy of a technical document, and transfer the material to the new envelope. Finally, in case Kohlbert talked to Brown in the near future, Stanek attached three of his own commemoratives to the new packet.

And then he tore off the corner of the old envelope with the stamps he wanted and set them to soaking in a bowl of warm water. It was not the preferred method, he knew, but was quick and didn't seem to harm the stamps.

Just before tossing the water away, while the stamps were drying on a kitchen towel, Stanek noticed several black specks floating in the bowl. Pepper, he thought. How'd that get in there? And then, entranced by the stamps, he washed the specks down the drain, failing to observe that each one was a perfect square.

Chapter Five

The brilliant white light, which had hit her eyes like a hammer shattering diamonds, was finally receding to a rosy hue, tapering down in intensity along with her migraine. It was just after six in the evening and for an hour, as her stomach settled from the medication she'd taken earlier, Diane Lang sat on the bed and watched the sky change outside the westward-facing windows of her hotel room.

The city of Asunción sat astride the twenty-fifth parallel. The Tropic of Capricorn. The torrid zone. And in early November summer was just beginning. A smoky conflagration had flared briefly across the sky leaving behind a scarlet glow that now tinged the far horizon, while overhead whisps of clouds dissolved into tendrils of pink and gray.

She was still shaky, and didn't know if that was caused by the migraine or the confrontation with Colonel Ibarras at the airport.

After checking into the hotel and getting her room, she'd gone through the usual curative procedures, moving like an automaton in an attempt to block out the pain, each act a mindless routine: an Imitrex injection—the third and final use of sumatriptans for the day, hot water to the hands and feet, ice to the head, finger pressure on the left eye socket (the pressure a form of home-grown shiatsu), then fingernails in the scalp, thumbnails in the temples. And, finally, Xanax to induce sleep, which was at best a dazed state that left her drenched with sweat when she awoke.

Near seven, feeling better, she rose to prepare for a light dinner out.

The sky had turned a uniform gray and the first few city lights were hazy pinpoints of mother-of-pearl against dark velvet—soft and easy to bear after the harsher brilliance of the day.

Beyond the few high rises between her and the horizon, she could still make out, though faintly, the dark broad bay of Asunción, and beyond that, a narrow strip of lights, and then the black, flat ribbon of the Paraguay river. The river angled away, disappearing in the distance like an eel struggling upstream through a swampy estuary.

A strange land, divided by the river. To the west lay the Chaco—a semiarid green hell of dense scrub, seasonal marshland, and barren terrain. If all went well, in a few days she would be out there, at the Mennonite settlements, far removed from the capital. Only three percent of the population managed to survive in the Chaco. The rest lived to the east, in the forests, wooded hills, and grassy plains of the Paraná Plateau that stretched between the Paraguay river and the Paraná, with its massive hydroelectric projects.

The darkness out there made her feel lonely ... and so far, her contacts with the people filled her with foreboding. She needed to get out into a more cheerful crowd.

After washing and reapplying her make-up, Diane unpacked her suitcase, hanging the clothes in an antique walnut armoire à deux corps.

Other than the ornate wardrobe, the room was rather plain—tall-ceilinged with white stucco walls, no paintings, a crucifix over the headboard of the double bed, and a small nightstand with a reading lamp. In the bathroom, the sink was chipped and the drain rusty, and the toilet bowl stained from age. Not your typical luxury hotel, but she'd chosen one of the less-expensive offerings listed in the conference brochure.

For the moment, her books and papers were strewn over the bed: a guidebook, two paperback novels, an airline magazine with an article on neighboring Brazil, file folders and papers.

Nothing academic. She was trying to forget Yale. Two of her colleagues would teach her classes while she was gone, and she had resolved, once she'd read her paper, to do all her research on the Mennonite settlements *in situ*, at Colonia Neuland and the town of Filadelfia, the latter founded by a group of immigrants who had fled religious persecution in the Soviet Union in the 1930s. Both settlements were located in the central Chaco, to the west of Concepción. The two weeks she had free would be part research time, part vacation.

And tonight was still vacation.

Diane glanced through the guidebook for restaurants and then decided to ask for a recommendation at the desk. The guidebook seemed suddenly inadequate for what faced her. What could it divulge to explain what had happened to her at the airport? Could any book prepare one for that? You could read about the most horrible methods of torturing political prisoners and still be unprepared for a simple interrogation.

Before coming, she had immersed herself in books about Paraguay. Books were her sanctuary, her attempt to understand the world. She had given herself a crash course in the country's history and culture. She was not naïve, not the typical tourist. She knew there were political problems, she was familiar with the country's traditions—with its coups d'état and military dictators, with its wars and civil turmoil, with its oppression and poverty.

The first Nazi Party branch in South America had been founded in

Paraguay in 1931, and during World War II the country had provided a haven for Axis spies and agents, and after the war a refuge for ex-Nazis, fascists, and terrorists. Nothing should have shocked her. It was only when it became personal that she saw that reading about something was not the same as experiencing it.

And now, last in a long series of *caudillos*, came General Enrique Zancon, another strong authoritarian leader kept in power by thugs like Colonel Ibarras.

Would the cycle of repression and violence never end?

"*Señora,* you like very much the Club Bahia Negra. Casual, as you say, but very good dining. And the distance is not far. Shall I call for you a taxi?"

The man behind the desk was unctious, eager to help, his greasy, bald head shining with zeal. Despite the fact that she spoke to him in Spanish, he insisted on practicing his English.

"I think I'll walk," she said. "The fresh air will do me good."

The deskman, fumbling through a sheaf of papers, seemed not to have heard.

Waiting for him to take her key, Diane felt almost giddy with happiness. A cathartic release after her migraine. It was almost as if she'd been elevated to a state of grace. A lost sheep readmitted to the fold. The absence of pain produced a sort of euphoria, a heightened feeling of well-being, as if she were floating. And talking to Kim had raised her spirits yet higher. She'd telephoned from a phone booth in the lobby, catching Kim at her homework. Grandma had fixed goulash for dinner, Kim's favorite.

Diane hadn't mentioned her ordeal at the airport.

The deskman looked up, took the key from her hand, and shrugged. "Taxi best. At this hour it very hot for you. Traffic is bad, air is bad. Not so good for *los pulmones*." He tapped his chest.

When she hesitated, he added, "Coming dark soon."

She looked across the lobby toward the double front doors, where interior lights reflected off the glass. Outside, the sky had lost all color. A dusky haze hugged the pavement. She could hear the rumble of traffic, the sharp blasts of horns from impatient drivers. A surge of pedestrians.

"Perhaps you're right."

For a moment, she had forgotten what Colonel Ibarras had said—that he would have her followed, that she was in danger if she went out alone. Would his men really have orders to harm her? A taxi would be safer.

She felt a flash of anger at the loss of independence. She didn't like people telling her what to do. But she couldn't take a chance. Not until she talked to the faculty members who had organized the conference. They would know what was going on.

She looked at her watch. Perhaps she should have called someone before going out. It was getting late. She really didn't like to impose on others … and she'd hoped to see some of the city before she got too involved with the university. As soon as she read her paper, she'd be taking a bus to Filadelfia, four hundred and fifty kilometers into the Chaco. No more chances to see Asunción. And you couldn't see a city unless you walked it.

Damn.

"There's a taxi right outside," the deskman said. "Five, ten minutes you be there. I call and make a reservation for you."

She took a deep breath to hide her frustration. "Thank you," she said, trying to appreciate his concern. "You're very kind."

Colonel Hector Ibarras wiped the tears from his cheeks as the credits scrolled across the screen. Another episode of *El día sin fin* and this time the orphan had stood up to the bully in the *asilo's* dirt playground, catching the attention of a businessman and his wife, who decided to adopt the boy and give him a good home.

The colonel dabbed at his eyes and then realized he had gone the whole hour without urinating, this despite beginning the show with an overfull bladder that now ached.

The colonel's office, in the building closest to the circular tower on the compound of the Regimiento Escolta Presidential just off the Avenida General Maximo Santos, was the only one with an adjoining private toilet and wash basin. The water closet was a narrow cubicle to the left of his desk, small enough that he could sit on the toilet when drunk and vomit into the sink, or when constipated, dig himself out and wash his fingers under the single faucet.

Once, on a bet, he had gouged out and eaten the eyes of a political prisoner, and later, sitting on his toilet, had spewed thready rot from both ends at the same time. Thinking of the moment now, he smiled. That had to be one of life's greatest pleasures—to vomit and crap in concert. Like the orphan, he, too, for his stage in life, was fortunate. But soon, when things turned out as planned, life would be even better.

All he had to do now was find Francisco Rojas de Alquijana. The rebel leader, even though under the control of the 1st Army Corps, was still a threat. The Corps' commander, General Bernardo Paredes, was a deceptive man. The Army did not trust the police. Paredes refused to tell anyone other than the President where Alquijana was located. But Ibarras's men would ferret him out—and then kill him.

And after that? After that would come his own boss, *El Tigre*, General Zancon, the president. And who would care? The man was another dictator—oh sure, elected, but in an election without opposition.

Dictators—that was all the masses knew in Paraguay. The more corrupt, the better for the people. *El Tigre* just wouldn't do. He had promised free elections within the year, had even permitted the return of exiles and the reopening of banned newspapers and magazines and radio stations. Opposition political parties, with the exception of the communists, had been legalized. General Zancon needed Alquijana alive. When the time was right, close enough to the elections to have an effect, *El Tigre* would free him in a magnanimous gesture of liberality. The general would be assured of a new term in office.

And that was something Ibarras did not want. He did all the dirty work for the general—suppressed the opposition, murdered their leaders, shook down smugglers, extorted funds from businesses, laundered the profits from the drug cartels in Bolivia—why shouldn't he sit in the general's seat? He deserved the job.

Yes, the title had a nice ring to it.

President of the Republic.

Colonel Hector Ibarras smiled. Not long now.

Chapter Six

Uniformed policemen were painting over the graffiti on a low wall running along an elevated, cobblestoned sidewalk in central Asunción when Walter Stanek passed in a taxi. In the dim light, *Abajo la dictadura* was still visible and what looked like *Por la libertad de los presos politicos*.

Great, he thought. Greg Brown had told him Paraguay was a peaceful nation with an elected president friendly to the United States. General Enrique Zancon. *El Tigre*. Zancon was scheduled to open the disaster prevention "war games" the following day.

Stanek should have known there'd be trouble. This was Latin America.

A traffic jam. Plaza Uruguaya.

The porticoed train station sat off to the left. In the right curb lane a kid struggled to push a two-wheeled cart with a sign reading *MOSTO—HELADO*. Ice cream. Have to avoid that. Frozen tap water.

An old bus huffed at the taxi's rear bumper. *Linea 19*, it looked like. Going to Lambaré, wherever that was.

God, it reminded him of Mexico. Too many bad memories there.

Stanek glanced at his watch and shook his head. He was running late. His flight, which was supposed to have been direct from Miami on, had been diverted to Belize with engine trouble. Two hours on the steamy tarmac before they fixed the problem. In Asunción, he'd barely had time to drop his suitcase off at the Paraná Hotel's front desk before leaving for the Club Bahia Negra. Hadn't even seen his room.

Calle 25 de Mayo. A children's hospital. Defaced posters visible out the window. *Paz y Bienestar con Zancon.* Peace and Prosperity with Zancon. On some of the posters, the name had been changed to Zambo.

"What's Zambo mean?" he asked the driver.

"Zambo? Where you see Zambo? Eets a little monkey."

"I meet him tomorrow," Stanek said.

"¿Qué dice?"

Stanek laughed, then switched to Spanish. *"Mañana voy a encontrar el Presidente."* Did that make sense? He hadn't had much time to refresh his Spanish before the trip.

The driver glanced in the rearview mirror. A quick look and then away.

Stanek saw the expression on his face. The guy thought he was crazy. Stanek grinned. Should tell him the president was his friend. That he was a new member of the cabinet. Make the guy really think he was out of his mind.

But hey, in a way, it was true, even if only temporary.

Before leaving Arizona, Greg Brown had told him he was to be a minister in the "cabinet." The war games, as he explained them, consisted of three components: central control, a cabinet, and the opposition.

The control group, a trinity of three, represented God. They determined the weather, chance, unforeseen events, the response of the masses. Control would publish a daily newspaper with the results of the actions between the opposition and the cabinet. As part of the challenge, this particular trinity, composed of ex-government and military figures, would throw an occasional club between the spokes of the cabinet wheel.

"You'll meet them Friday," Brown had told him. "God the Father, God the Son, and God the Holy Ghost." He'd laughed. "God the Father is the head of the First Army Corps, General Bernardo Paredes, a good friend of ours. Samcon has funneled a lot of money his way. And the Son is the head of the Army's intelligence service, Major General Alberto Campos. A real bulldog. The Holy Ghost is the ex-president of the *Banco Central*, Francisco Gonzalez. An intellectual they tell me."

"I'll never keep the names straight," Stanek said.

"It doesn't matter. Once the games start you'll never see them. Forget names."

"Who's the opposition?"

"Think-tank experts," Brown said, and then grinned again, lopsided this time. "Some from Rand. Terrorists at heart. They can't do it in the real world, so they do it in games."

Stanek snorted. "They have the easy job. How many members in the cabinet?"

"Eleven. You're the Minister of Public Works. I'll ask another fellow to keep an eye out for you. He's done this before. A professor of surgery—Dr. D. Benjamin Harrington. He'll be the Minister of Public Health and Social Welfare. Don't be surprised by his accent. He was born a British national, but he's been an American for close to forty years now."

"What's the D stand for?"

"What? Oh—" Brown looked disconcerted for a moment. "Disraeli, I think." He laughed. "But don't tell him I told you. He doesn't like anyone knowing."

Brown paused and then said, "Harrington will probably find you at the Club Bahia Negra on the night of your arrival. You'll meet the other cabinet members at the first session on the sixth. Americans, Europeans, Japanese, a Canadian—this is an international operation."

"Why is everyone worried about Paraguay?" Stanek had wanted to know. "Does the U.S. have any strategic interests in the area?"

Brown shrugged. "Some. Paraguay lies right in the center of South America. Between the two biggies—Brazil and Argentina. It's at the top of what's called the Southern Cone. Their former president, guy named General Alfredo Stroessner? One of the U.S.'s staunchest supporters. Hell, back in '58, vice-president Nixon called him the world's greatest anticommunist. Now the country's a major transit point for illegal drugs. They're being overrun by cocaine traffickers from Bolivia and Peru. And their internal stability has been threatened by outside forces—mostly left-wing extremists. General Zancon has asked for our help and we're happy to give it."

Sure, Stanek thought. As long as there's a profit. Wait till the general threatened to nationalize foreign companies. These guys never thought about that.

They had turned twice and were on Avenida Artigas, skirting the Parque Caballero, when Diane Lang asked the taxi driver if they were being followed. She'd kept her eyes trained out the back window and thought a car with yellow headlights had turned with them.

"Followed? No, *señora*. Who would follow us?"

"Someone's been bothering me," she said. "A man. I told him I wasn't interested, but he keeps following me."

"*¿Un lisonjero?*" The driver shrugged. "It's harmless. A little flattery." He waved his hand. "It's best to ignore him. No one will bother you. I drop you off at the door."

Yeah, she thought. So they'd know right where she was.

Chapter Seven

The Club Bahia Negra was located a half mile to the west of the Avenida Artigas near a soccer field and an army commissary, just south of the Jardin Botánico. Built on a knoll overlooking a lagoon, rather than a bay as the name implied, the colonial style building had a long narrow dining room, with floor-to-ceiling windows facing the reed-choked marshy shallows. Hand-carved log beams supported the roof and stuffed trophies lined the north wall. It had been a hunting lodge in the old days, and was now a restaurant and bar.

At the back of the building to the east, encroaching on the club's playing fields, lay a barrio of tin-roofed shacks and dusty, unpaved roads. Every few blocks, a streetlight illuminated a corner. Under most, Walter Stanek had seen dark-skinned kids in ragged clothes kicking soccer balls.

Stanek was talking to the maître d' in Spanish, struggling to make himself understood, when a woman burst through the entryway and came up the steps to the landing, which led past a row of potted palmettos to the dining room and the bar.

The maître d' turned to watch her, a smile on his face. "Can I help you, *señora?*" he said in English, bending his body so he could speak around Stanek, who was impatiently flapping Samcon's manila envelope against his leg.

Stanek glared at the man. The asshole. Making him flounder around to communicate, pretending not to know English, and then when a woman arrives he's suddenly a linguist. Stanek had been awake too long, was too damn tired, to be polite.

"Hey," he said roughly. "I'm late for an appointment and I'm next. I asked you about a table for Raymond Kohlbert."

"Just a minute, sir," the maître d' said, pushing him gently but firmly to the side. "The lady has a reservation if I'm not mistaken."

The man smiled and dipped his head. "It's *señora* Lang, isn't it?"

"Diane Lang."

"Yes, I thought so. Miguel at the hotel called and said you would be arriving for dinner. He said I would recognize you because you were very beautiful, but—" He paused, his eyebrows lifting dramatically. "I thought he was exaggerating, but I see he was too modest on your behalf. You look very radiant this evening."

Stanek scowled. She was just another person, like anyone else. "If you had any manners, you'd wait your turn," he muttered.

The woman seemed momentarily flustered, then angry. "I've had enough trouble with assholes today," she said, glaring at Stanek before turning to the maître d'. "Go ahead and take him first." Her voice was icy. "Apparently he's in a hurry."

The maître d' ran a jaundiced eye over Stanek, then took the woman by the arm and said, "I'm sorry, *señora*. You'll both have to wait at the bar. But just for a few minutes. I'll call you when your table is ready."

"What about Kohlbert?" Stanek asked over the man's shoulder. "Isn't he here yet?"

"Sir, you'll just have to wait. No one by that name has arrived yet tonight."

Damn. Busted his ass to get here by eight and the guy hadn't shown up yet.

The bar, at the southern end of the dining room, was demarcated by a wall with open semicircular arches, and had a long, curved mahogany counter and padded leather seats on tall metal stools. There were no tables in the narrow room. A long strip of bright crimson neon ran along the top of the mirror behind the bar and provided most of the illumination, a ruddled light that made the goateed bartender seem devilish, despite his white shirt and tie.

After the woman was seated at the far right, Stanek took the next to last seat on the left, just inside the door, then caught the maître d' on his way out and said, "You can forget dinner for me. I've lost my appetite. When a man named Kohlbert comes, tell him I'm in here."

The maître d' gave him a curt nod. *"Muy bien, señor."*

The bar was not crowded. There had to be at least fifteen empty stools between the two Americans. Stanek ordered a beer and saw that the woman, off to his right, had asked for a mixed drink. Gin and tonic.

Attractive, but not his type. Wearing a summer dress, white, with a floral print. Trying to run roughshod over everyone else just because she had a reservation—although the maître d' was partly to blame for that, sucking up to her as if she were the last woman on earth.

And what had put the burr up her butt anyway? Calling him an asshole. He was the one who'd had a hard day. He was the one who'd got there first.

Fifteen minutes later, he was hunched over the bar on his second beer, still grumbling to himself, when someone tapped him on the shoulder.

He turned to see an angular, splotchy-faced man wearing a rumpled sport coat of Donegal tweed and a polka-dotted bow tie that called attention to the slack skin at his neck. He was an older man who'd once been fat. He had big, bony knuckles on his hands.

"You must be Stanek," the man said.

"Raymond Kohlbert?"

"Sorry, old chap, D. Benjamin Harrington here. Another Samcon flunky. I wanted to meet you before we start working together tomorrow. Kohlbert said to tell you another half-hour by the way. He's tied up with the boffins at headquarters or something like that. I do say, my good fellow, he was rather accurate in your description. Do you always wear corduroy pants and flannel shirts? Rather hot in this climate, I should say."

Stanek grinned. "They look better than bow ties." Apparently Greg Brown had informed them of his taste in clothes.

"I should say not, old chap." Harrington fingered his tie. "This is the height of fashion in my crowd."

"I thought you were a surgeon," Stanek said, a bemused look on his face. He reached out to shake hands.

"Jolly good of you to notice. Of course you thought I'd be wearing a mask and gown. Let's have a drink, shall we?"

Harrington took the seat to Stanek's right, waved at the waiter, then ordered a double Martini.

Stanek couldn't help grinning. Harrington reminded him of a professor of classics he'd had as an undergraduate. A visiting scholar from Oxford, sharp-eyed and sharp-tongued. Like him, Harrington had short hair that jutted out in front, once sandy-blond in color but now turning dishwater gray, trimmed high off the ears. He had a yellow cast to his brown eyes, and hands that were liver-spotted. He looked to be in his late fifties.

"Kohlbert's just back from São Paulo," Harrington said after taking a sip of his drink. "I say, with Samcon's help it won't be long now before the Brazilians have the A bomb."

"The A bomb?" Stanek's head jerked to the right. "What do they want that for? I thought South America was free of nuclear weapons."

Harrington shrugged. "Can't let the Argentineans beat them to it. They're working just as hard on their own." Harrington looked around, then gestured toward the manila envelope. "What's in the package?"

The envelope was lying to Stanek's left, on the bar where he wouldn't forget it. "Material for Kohlbert. Greg Brown asked me to give it to him."

"Using you for his spy work, eh?"

Stanek glanced at the man to see if he were joking. "Just some engineering article, I think."

Harrington laughed once at the back of his throat, a thin smile on his lips. "Don't be a ruddy fool, lad."

Stanek's brows were knitted as he swiveled to face the older man. Harrington was serious. "Are you saying Samcon's into industrial espionage?"

Harrington snorted. "Samcon's into everything. And so's Kohlbert— the bloody Kraut. Hard to believe we defeated those blokes and now they've damn near taken over the world. Them and the Japs."

Stanek shrugged. "I guess defeat's a great motivator," he said, wondering if he had a jingoistic bigot on his hands. He was tired of hearing people complain about the Germans and the Japanese. He figured they got what they earned—through hard work. The kids he was teaching in school now wanted it all and right away—and they expected to get it sitting behind a desk. The paper plan syndrome. They'd rather let a computer do the work than get out in the field and see what was going on. Didn't want dirt under their fingernails.

And if Samcon was getting by with industrial espionage that was just as bad—worse actually. Living off other people's work.

"Does this have anything to do with the war games?" he asked. "Is Paraguay getting involved in something tricky?"

"Best to keep quiet about that." Harrington nodded toward the barman, who was standing a few feet away with his back to them, fiddling with the bottles on a rack along the wall. "Secret police hear you talking about a government project and you're in trouble. Bloody Gestapo."

"Aren't they in on this?"

"You never know. Anyway, it doesn't matter. If it gets back to *El Tigre*—if someone says you've been blabbering ..." He shrugged and then ran a finger across his throat. "It doesn't pay to talk about this sort of thing in public, not in Paraguay. Kohlbert's always spouting off about how German they are." Harrington laughed dryly. "Now there's an ex-Nazi for you."

"Kohlbert?" Stanek stopped, beer bottle halfway to his mouth. "He was a Nazi?"

"No, no, just joking." Harrington pulled at the skin on his neck, scrutinizing the taller man out of the corner of his eyes. "I say, old chap, first time in the big city? Don't be too gullible. A fellow has to resort to a little sardonic humor to survive down here. What happened to your sense of irony?"

Stanek didn't reply. He usually believed people when they told him something. Okay, maybe he was naïve, but, hey, in his view that was the great American virtue.

Harrington drained his double Martini, wiped his lips on the back of his hand, and gestured for another. "Another beer?"

Stanek shook his head. "This is my second."

"Your second! Well, golly, another drunk. Don't expect me to carry you home."

Sarcastic bastard when he had a little booze in him. He seemed to have arrived with a head start in the liquor department.

"To be honest," Stanek said, "I *am* feeling a little tipsy. Stomach's empty—and I've been up for what seems a day and a half. I've had enough take-offs and landings to satisfy me for a while."

"Then don't let Kohlbert get a hold of you. He flies his own plane. Upside down half the time." Harrington rolled his eyes, his right hand jerking back and forth on an imaginary stick. "Likes to do rolls and loop-de-loops. Wears an old Luftwaffe jacket and aviator's cap when he goes up. Heil Hitler and all that."

"Thanks for the warning. So—" Stanek looked around and then dipped his head—"*is* he an ex-Nazi?"

Harrington hacked out a dry laugh. "We're all an ex-something, aren't we? I'm an ex-Brit, Kohlbert's an ex-paratrooper, and you—I suppose you're an ex-pert." Harrington chuckled, drumming his fingers on the bar and shaking his head as if marveling at his own wit.

After a moment, he said, "The Luftwaffe. That's all Kohlbert can talk about. Claims to have been a friend of Himmler and Schellenberg, knows all about them. Stick with him and you'll meet a few ex-SS members living as Paraguayan citizens in the hinterlands of this glorious country. I say, you have heard of Joseph Mengele, haven't you? Stroessner, the former dictator, gave him an honorary officer's commission and a passport."

"Mengele—didn't they catch him? Was that here in Paraguay?"

Harrington just lifted his eyebrows, as if the question didn't deserve a response, then took another sip of his drink and smacked his lips.

"Yes, this is the place to be all right." His face had a shrewd look. "You know, at the start of the big war, the military here were gung-ho over the Axis." Harrington nodded with broad strokes as if someone had questioned his veracity, then scratched pensively at one of the splotches on his forehead.

"Listen to this, the bloody gall: The chief of the national police force named his son Adolfo Hirohito. His cadets displayed swastikas on their uniforms. The director of the police academy was an active member of the Fascist party. He worshipped Mussolini. Gave speeches from a balcony like the Duce. And the head of the secret police belonged to a Nazi underground group called the Ring of Sacrifice. My dear friend Kohlbert will tell you all about it."

"Isn't that all kind of old stuff now?" Stanek rubbed his jaw and then yawned; the beer was making him sleepy. "Who cares anymore?"

Harrington stabbed a finger toward Stanek's bottle, a wry look creasing the loose skin on his cheeks. "Hey, isn't that *German* beer you're drinking?"

Son of a gun. Imported from Hamburg. Stanek grinned his appreciation. Even in his cups the old guy was alert. He was getting dizzy himself, best to stop soon. He didn't want to be drunk when Kohlbert arrived. Had the maître d' taken the woman to a table yet?

He leaned forward and looked beyond Harrington. No, she was still there, with one other guy between them now, two seats away from her. He was a dark-skinned fellow with black hair cropped just short of his eyes. An Indio. He had a stocky build and broad, flat facial features. A rough-looking hombre. He reminded Stanek of some of the Eskimos who'd worked on the dam in Alaska.

Harrington rubbed his nose as if he'd finally absorbed what Stanek had said, then raised a finger in admonition. "And it's not all *old* stuff, as you put it. This is a right-wing regime if there ever was one." He paused. "Ever hear of Stefano Cirillo?"

"Sounds Italian."

"He is Italian, old chap. A right-wing, neofascist terrorist. He's been seen in Paraguay. Working with the secret police, they say. He's the bloke who tracked down Alquijana for General Zancon."

"Who's Alquijana?"

"The last of the revolutionaries. He's the only one who really had a chance to rally the people. Funny thing is, the secret police would like to see him dead and Zancon has him hidden away somewhere."

"I told you, I'm not interested."

The voice was loud and angry, a woman's.

Both men turned to look. The Indio Stanek had seen earlier was hanging on to the American, his right arm draped around her neck as if he were trying to embrace her. She was struggling to free herself.

No sign of the barman. He'd been coming and going out a side door, carrying in boxes of liquor that were stacked beneath the counter top.

And where in hell was the maître d'? Letting a drunk into the place.

A kid was standing by the door to the dining room. Nut-brown face, lean body, ragged clothes. He had a pair of sandals tied on a string around his neck. The Indio's son? No one else was in sight. The diners at the other end of the club seemed oblivious to what was going on in the bar.

Oh shit. The man was pulling her by the hair now.

Stanek slid off the stool, adrenaline pumping through him. Damn! He was going to have to do something. Okay, so she'd called him an asshole. But she was a woman and if there was one thing he didn't like it was men hitting women. His dad had done enough of that.

Harrington was stumbling to his feet.

"Stay here and watch my back," Stanek said. "I'm going to help her."

Chapter Eight

Diane Lang had just started to calm down from her earlier hassle with the American, who'd been joined by his friend—a weird-looking guy with a bow tie—at the far end of the bar, when things went crazy.

The Indio to her left, either drunk or *loco*, began muttering to himself—short, harsh, angry words, the language Guaraní.

Just what I needed, she thought. What else can go wrong today?

Then suddenly the Indio stopped, and the brooding silence that followed was almost more frightening than his muttering.

A moment later, when she glanced at him out of the corner of her eye, she saw that he had turned toward her.

He had a dead stare, his mouth half open, slobber on his lips. He was mouthing something repulsive. She turned away, trying to ignore him, a sick feeling pooling at the bottom of her stomach.

What was he doing in the bar? She'd seen at a glance he didn't belong. His loose fitting white shirt—open at the neck—was filthy, and he wore no socks below dark, ragged pants. On his feet were rope-braided sandals, the soles cut from tire rubber.

He was speaking to her, but she refused to look. He raised his voice, repeated the request in guttural Spanish. "American friend, you buy me drink."

"No," she said. She shook her head forcefully and then stared straight ahead. She was not going to let him bother her. If he said another word, she was going to stand up and leave. She hadn't liked it when he sat so close to her in the first place. The bar was nearly empty.

The Indio pushed himself away from the counter and lurched to his feet, standing in the aisle facing her.

"You want to buy?" He held out a small wood carving of a lizard, polishing it with a colored handkerchief extracted from a back pocket. His belt, she saw, was a piece of twine, and the fly of his pants hung open.

She shook her head, and then looked away, jaws clenched. Her fingernails dug into the palms of her hands.

She should have moved earlier. Now he'd blocked her way out, and the barman was nowhere to be seen. The two guys at the far end hadn't noticed what was going on. But in a minute, if the Indio persisted, she would call for help. In normal circumstances, she might have felt sympathetic. He was clearly poor, but tonight, after the interrogation by Colonel Ibarras, she wanted only to be left alone.

The Indio's face grew sullen. He took a step towards her. "You buy."

"No." She refused to look at him.

"You buy!"

"I said, *no!* I told you, *I'm not interested.*"

She felt a hand on her shoulder, hard fingers digging into the flesh.

"Leave me alone!" She tried to twist away, but he dropped the wood carving into her lap and began pawing at her with his other hand.

She pushed at his arm and then grimaced as he yanked at her hair. For a moment, because of the pain, she was not able to react. He was stronger than she'd expected and his left hand was digging at her throat, his fingernails sharp. She flailed back with an elbow, trying to free herself, but the man's grip only tightened. A gurgle escaped from her mouth as she fought for breath. Panic took over. *He'd cut off her wind!*

And then suddenly a release of pressure. A roar in her ears—whether inside or outside her head she couldn't tell.

She stumbled away, gasping for breath as her head cleared.

The noise—it wasn't just her ears ringing: A terrible growl rushed out of the throat of the taller American as he slammed the Indio into the bar and then stood facing him, his feet planted, legs bent, fists ready for action.

In the dim light of the bar's crimson neon, Diane saw a flash of metal.

"A knife!" she screamed, her voice scratchy. "He's got a knife!"

Moving swiftly, Stanek had crossed the bar, an unexpected surge of anger rising deep from within him—a glimpse of kids around him as he lay flat on his back, the knife at his neck, his own switchblade half-opened in his right hand, Mexico City, late at night, the attack from behind near the corner of Aguascalientes and Medellín, his feeble attempts to tell them in Spanish that they could have his wallet, just spare his life ... his humiliation as they ran off laughing, waving his money in their hands. In the grip of emotions from the past, he attacked the Indio with blind force—unaware of danger, no conscious thought of what he was doing, rage directing the course of his actions—until the woman's scream penetrated the haze that darkened his mind ... and he caught a glint of light on silver slicing through the air.

A knife!

Stanek jumped back, flinging his arms to shoulder height, as the blade slashed across his chest, catching the loose front placket of his flannel shirt and ripping away a button. In the heat of the moment he didn't know if he'd been cut, a sudden awareness of danger flooding in.

"Get back!" he yelled at the woman. He stepped away in the opposite direction, eyes alert for another attack, fear making him cautious now. He hoped the Indio came for him and not the woman—and that the guy was drunk.

He could hear a scuffle behind him, another voice being raised.

What in hell was Harrington doing? Just don't trip him up from behind.

The Indio broke into a horrible grin, chipped teeth visible, his nose flattening out on his face. Spittle dribbled down his chin. He raised the knife and brandished it in a small, circular motion.

Stanek went into a crouch, his left hand groping for a bar stool. He needed to get something between himself and the other man. And then, from behind the bar, just as the Indio was about to lunge forward, a bottle crashed down on the man's skull. In the explosion, shards of glass and liquor splattered in Stanek's direction. The Indio's face went slack and he collapsed to the floor.

The barman! Thank God someone was thinking.

Stanek turned to see what Harrington was doing.

The old man was untangling himself from one of the bar stools.

"The envelope," Harrington gasped. "The damn kid took the envelope!"

Oh shit! The dark-skinned boy he'd seen at the door. Greg Brown had told him to hang on to the envelope and now he'd lost it. Damn it, this was all the woman's fault. Stanek cast an angry glance in her direction and then turned back to Harrington, crossing the room to his side.

"Where'd he go?"

Harrington got to his feet shakily. "I tried to grab him." He was breathing heavily. "Slippery little bastard. Couldn't have gotten far."

"Stay here and watch these two," Stanek said. "I'm going after him."

Chapter Nine

Diane wanted to say, *No, don't go; it's dangerous out there*—but the guy who'd tried to help her was already running for the landing and the front door.

Everything was falling apart.

She looked around, expecting to see a crowd of diners, but no one at the other end of the building seemed to have noticed the ruckus. The barman was coming around the counter to help and the weird-looking guy in the bow tie was standing in the aisle, staring at her as if this was all her fault.

A shudder passed over her as she looked at the man sprawled at her feet. At the Indio. His hair, drenched in whiskey, had turned an oily black. She couldn't tell if he was bleeding.

Ibarras ... Was this thug one of his?

The taller American was going out there alone, unarmed—a mistake in the dark. If the secret police saw him chasing a boy, they might jump to the wrong conclusion. They might shoot and ask questions later.

A taxi—get a taxi and follow him. He'd tried to help her. She owed him as much.

She hesitated for just a moment as a cold hand of fear squeezed her heart and sweat broke out on her forehead.

What if the American was working with them? What if this was a set-up, all part of a plot to get her alone in the dark?

She couldn't let their threats intimidate her, could she? Was she going to be afraid of everything? Living in paranoia the whole time she was in the country?

"Stay here," she said to the older fellow, who tried to grab her arm as she slipped by him, a surprised look in his eyes. "I'm going after your friend."

Behind her, she heard him cry, "Wait!" And then, when she didn't stop, a feeble, "I do say, this is rather irregular."

But no one was going to stop her now.

The kid was barely fifty feet up the road when Stanek charged through the front door of the club. Heading toward the barrio.

"Hey!" he shouted at the top of his lungs."¡Alto! Stop, you little brat!"

The kid looked back quickly, saw Stanek coming in his direction, and kicked it into high gear.

The single arc lamp in the club's parking lot caught the boy from behind, puffs of dust rising with each footfall. The kid's sandals, still tied together by a piece of string hanging around his neck, bounced on his chest as he ran. Stanek could see the manila envelope in the boy's left hand.

Why wasn't he wearing the sandals?

Within the first few feet, lunging after the kid, Stanek felt a slight pull in his groin and had to ease off to keep from tearing the muscle. He tried to relax and move loosely, lengthening his stride as his muscles warmed up.

Damn! A forty-three year old chasing a kid. He'd have to catch him fast or he'd run out of breath. He was already sucking for air.

In Tucson, when the spirit moved him, he worked out on the Nautilus machines at Mid-Valley Athletic Club, but aerobic conditioning was never his favorite form of exercise. Still, he was gaining on the kid.

As Stanek's heavy tread drew nearer, the boy looked over his shoulder, his eyes widening. He put on a renewed burst of speed.

Get the little bastard!

Stanek lunged forward and caught the kid by the shoulders. The boy spun around in fright and flung his arm up to defend himself. One of his sandals, propelled by the momentum, swung up and slapped Stanek in the face.

Stunned by the blow, he stumbled and the kid slipped from his grasp, the envelope still clutched in one hand. It took Stanek a moment to realize what had happened. His nose was bleeding.

Shit! Should have grabbed for the envelope!

Stanek reached for his handkerchief as he ran and without unfolding it tried to hold it to his nose. The effort slowed him down. It was harder now to breathe. Blood blocked the passage of air.

Hell, let it bleed. He tucked the handkerchief in his shirt pocket and tried to pick up the distance between him and the kid. Farther away now.

White stuccoed houses with barred windows and iron-grill fences flashed by to his left—homes of the rich who lived near the club—their exterior lights providing some illumination.

He'd have to catch the kid before he disappeared into the night. Just ahead was the barrio, where most of the lights died out.

Palm trees loomed into the sky. The dark shadows of citrus trees in full bloom. The warm, night air was heavy with the scent of flowers.

Footlights along a flagstone path illuminated the climbing vines of clematis and the red clusters of bougainvillea. Then the febrile rays of one goose-neck streetlamp appeared to his right. He dashed by a fig tree and a somber row of stately Italian cypresses, gray-green and funereal in the artificial light. The kid was still in sight and seemed to be tiring.

And then darkness. The shantytown. A lightless cluster of huts hunkered down in the gloom like cow byres or dog kennels.

Despite the blood blocking one nostril, the strong smell of garbage wafted to him, and then, along with that stench, came the odors of cooking—some kind of meat, and onions, and pungent spices he couldn't identify.

Twenty feet ahead of him, the kid disappeared between two dark mounds of rubbish. A path through a bulldozed dump.

Hurry! Don't lose him now!

Just beyond, he could make out a distant road with a streetlight and a row of shacks. The kid was just a shadow now, the air much darker, large gaps to each side of the road. Swamp land? Fields of refuse? The stench grew stronger. A mixture of sewage, stagnant water, and rotting garbage. He gagged, but kept after the boy.

Scattered habitations appeared to each side, weakly illuminated from within. He ran by hovels of scrap wood and corrugated tin, mud-and-stick ranchos, lean-to sheds, cardboard shacks.

And then the boy left the dirt lane, which was rutted from storm runoffs, and slipped down a narrow path to the right, away from the bay, heading deeper into the barrio.

Stanek, hot on his heels, gulped in lungfuls of air.

A branch slapped him in the cheek, momentarily stunning him. His head snapped back and he felt the branch scrape across his face, but he kept after the kid, struggling to see in the dark, his eyes watering from the blow.

A back yard. A clothesline stretched between two poles. *Watch out*! He'd wind up decapitating himself.

Damn. Where was the kid?

Pitch black … no flickering shadows. Had he lost him?

He stopped and listened for sounds, heard something to his right, and moved around a dark mass and into a streak of dim light that spilled out the open door of a rancho.

No sign of the kid.

Stanek had lost all sense of direction. He trotted beyond the rancho into the darkness, letting his eyes readjust to the gloom.

To his left, in the distance, he could make out a faint glow. Another streetlight apparently. The sound of a vehicle.

He moved in that direction, picking his way around dark objects, stumbling over loose boards and other debris, crossing a ditch that smelled like a sewer. He went through a dirt yard with a brazero full of glowing coals. No one attended the dying flames.

Shit. He'd lost the kid. He'd never find him now.

An alley. A dark line stretching across the barrio. He picked up his pace, running down the alley toward the light in the distance.

A taxi down there. He could see the illuminated sign on the vehicle's rooftop. Moving slowly.

"Hey," he yelled. *"¡Espereme!"*

The vehicle's lights disappeared as it crossed the road and continued on its way.

Dejected, Stanek slowed to a walk, still breathing heavily. His shirt was soaked with sweat. What in hell was he running for? He'd lost the kid. He wasn't going to find him in this maze of paths and alleys and lanes, of unpaved and unmarked streets.

Samcon wasn't going to be happy about the envelope. But what could he do? He'd kept it on him the whole time—at least until that woman distracted him.

For a moment, he was angry that Greg Brown had asked him to deliver the letter in person in the first place. What was so damn important? It could have gone through the mail like anything else.

He stopped, sensing someone behind him. A quick glance over the shoulder. Thoughts of Mexico again. He'd been taken once, but not again—

Nothing.

He waited a few seconds, then moved on toward the corner, listening carefully now.

Another glance behind.

When he turned back to the front, he saw them: three kids standing in the alley blocking his path, angular forms haloed by the streetlight in the distance. Could they see him in the dark?

He hesitated. He could hear noises behind him now. They had him pinned between them.

No time to sit and think. *Move!*

He took off running, heading straight toward the boys in front. If he was lucky, he'd get by before they knew what was coming. And if he could get to the corner where he'd seen the taxi, maybe he could flag someone down.

But the boys were ready. As he charged by them, they lashed out with sticks, beating him on his arms and back. His fist caught one of them in the shoulder. He could hear grunts of exertion, muffled cries.

As he tried to run away, he felt a slash from behind, the shock of quick blood wetting the shirt at his neck. A club on his back.

Fear put extra speed in his legs. Adrenaline pumped through his body. No one had said anything. His shirt was ripped open down the front. He could feel the sweat streaming down his body, hear feet pounding behind him, each sensation sharp and clear despite the thudding of his heart.

When he came into the pool of light at the crossroads and swung around to face them—(there were no cars in sight, but he was too exhausted to run any farther)—he saw what they were carrying. Two had sticks with razor blades taped to the ends, the other a thick, knotted club.

They'd sliced open his left sleeve and he could feel warm, sticky blood dripping from a cut on his biceps. From there, his right hand moved to his neck, found the other wound. They hadn't got an artery, thank God. His neck was slippery with sweat and blood but nothing was spurting.

He stood there panting for breath, waiting to see what they would do.

And then four other boys stepped into the light and joined the three who'd assaulted him—scrawny kids with bare feet and filthy hair. They were all mean-looking street urchins dressed in tattered discards: a striped soccer shirt, a dingy T-shirt with no sleeves, ragged sport shirts, cut-offs with the pockets ripped out. Hard to tell their age—teenagers maybe, a couple even younger.

"*¿Que quieres?*" he asked.

No one responded.

Without having said a word they were moving to encircle him. Kids all right, but armed with sticks and homemade weapons. He saw a rusty meat skewer. A knife cut from a tin can with a strip of cloth twisted around the shaft. A board with nails protruding from one end.

"You can have my money," he said, shifting around to keep the larger boys in sight. *A distorted sense of* déjà vu, *things not quite the same, buried memories jangling.* The tallest wore a plaid sport shirt, stained with grime and torn open down the front. He had the makeshift knife. A skinny kid with a hairless chest, not much muscle on the bones. By himself no big threat perhaps but dangerous in a group.

Stanek reached into his back pocket and pulled out his wallet. "Here, take this." He grabbed a wad of guaranies and flung them into the street, notes ranging in amount from five hundred to ten thousand—all told, less than a hundred dollars, which was all he'd been able to buy in Tucson before leaving. He had his credit cards in the wallet and a money belt around his hips and traveler's checks in his briefcase in the hotel room. He didn't need the cash.

The boys made no move to pick up the money.

"What do you want?" he asked. "You can have whatever you want."

"*¿Es verdad?*" one said, "Even your life?"

Several laughed. Stanek didn't say anything in response.

Another spoke in broken English. "American man, we take your *vida* and your *denaro.*"

"*¿Por que?* I haven't done anything to you."

A few of them snickered and a boy in a tattered green shirt said mockingly, "The gringo wants to know why. He chases one of us and he wants to know why."

The kid in the sleeveless T-shirt hit Stanek in the arm with a stick. "This is our territory. You come on our territory and we kill you."

Stanek struggled to find the words in Spanish to explain. "I had an envelope," he said. "A boy stole it."

"And now we steal your life," said the kid who'd hit him.

God, what had he gotten into? They were serious. He was going to have to fight if he expected to get out of this alive.

He shifted his weight, glancing quickly over one shoulder and then the other, trying to keep the more dangerous weapons in sight, waiting for the first move. He cracked his jaw, then flexed his fingers, trying to relax, to be ready. Every muscle in his body was tense, his senses attuned.

The boys began to taunt him, the little kid in the striped soccer shirt going first, speaking in Guaraní. Rough words ... unintelligible ... the tone harsh. Building their courage for the attack. Closing in for the kill.

By God, he wasn't going to go easy. The next time someone swung at him, he was going to take his weapon away.

They wanted his life, *fine*, let them try to take it.

Chapter Ten

They were on the return trip when Diane Lang saw the cluster of boys under the streetlight, half a block away to the left. The American from the bar loomed above them, his back to her. The driver glanced that way quickly and then began to pull away.

"Wait," she said to the driver. "That's the man I told you about—the Anglo. I need to go back to that corner."

The driver, an overweight man with tattoos on both biceps, hesitated a moment and then brought the taxi to a stop. He looked over his shoulder at her and shook his head.

"No sirve," he said. "It's no good. A gang from the slums. Too dangerous. You said the Anglo was alone."

"That man's in trouble."

"Lo siento mucho"—he waved both hands—"but … it's none of my

---

concern."

"Then let me out here and wait for me. I'll be right back."

"No, you pay first."

"Wait for me. I'll pay you when I get back."

She was out of the cab before he could protest.

Swearing to himself, the driver watched her in the rearview mirror until she disappeared from sight around the corner, then looked in the back seat to see if she'd left her purse. It wasn't there. *Chingada la madre que te parió.*

He shook his head. If he knew those *mozos* back there—outcasts who fought over scraps, boys old before their time—neither of the Americans would come back with money. A lost cause.

And the woman. *¡Loca!* Wearing a skirt and high heels and running off into the barrio by herself. Carrying a purse. *¡Jesucristo!* Talk about a gringa.

Well, he wasn't her guardian. *En boca cerrada no entran moscas.*

He eased his foot off the brake and onto the accelerator. Too risky to hang around. The last time he'd been in this shantytown, someone had tossed a rock through his back windshield. Sit here for five minutes and they'd strip the car—with him inside! Besides, those damn fool gringos were asking for it. Wandering around in the barrio at night.

Look for the devil and he's bound to show up.

Two minutes into the fight, Stanek could see that the boys were startled by the scream—a shrill, hysterical shriek that sent shivers down his spine. Ignoring its source, he whirled around and lashed out for the kid wearing the tattered green shirt, striking him in the face with a broken stick he'd taken from one of the others. The kid let out a cry and backed away, then took to his heels.

There were only two boys left who were still trying to fight—a one-eyed kid with a club and the boy with the skewer.

The tallest boy with the knife had been his first target—a backwards kick to the clavicle. Stanek had heard—almost as one sound—the audible snap of the bone and the horrible scream that burst from the kid's mouth before he collapsed in the dirt.

The shock had slowed the others just enough for Stanek to grab and break one of the razor-bladed sticks. The razor was somewhere in the dust. His initial attack had demoralized others; they'd fled without striking a blow. But he'd still had to deal with the rest. Kicking and hitting, jabbing with the broken stick, grabbing a handful of dirt and tossing it in their eyes, pulling hair, punching and warding off blows.

Two to go now.

The woman who'd screamed came running into the light.

God damn if it wasn't the American from the bar!

Stanek straightened, was about to shout for her to back off. If these kids got her—

Diane saw the blow—a skinny kid in a striped soccer shirt clubbed the man on the side of his head as he turned to shout at her. She flinched, saw him go down in a heap, and then began screaming again—a high, piercing sound that rent the night air. Unnerved, the two boys took off running, leaving the American lying motionless in the cone of light cast by the streetlight.

Diane ran to him, knelt over his body and felt for a pulse at his neck. He was unconscious and bleeding but his pulse was strong.

She looked back for the taxi.

Nothing in sight.

They needed to get out of the barrio before the boys regrouped. If they saw she was alone they might attack again. She had nothing with which to defend herself—except for her scream.

Diane was embarrassed by that. A moment of hysteria that made her feel she'd been weak. A reversion to an atavistic response to danger. Like a shrieking baboon. But it had worked.

Headlights.

She looked up the dirt road as a vehicle approached from the opposite direction, light beams swaying as the car bounced over the ruts.

She stood and waved her arms. The American was lying in the middle of the street. They would have to stop or swerve around him.

The car came to a stop fifteen feet from her. A moment later the driver's door opened a crack and a man said, "What is it, *señorita?*"

"Sosa, Renato," the man said. "And this is my wife Pina."

"Pleased to meet you," Diane said.

She was in the back seat with the American, who was just beginning to stir, and with one of the two kids, a young boy. From the middle of the front seat, the girl said, "I'm Eliana. Today's my birthday."

The mother, a stocky woman taller than her husband, said, "Hush, Eliana. We can talk later. Renato, let's go."

"To the clinic?"

She shook her head. "Home first. We can call Dr. Prio from the house if need be." She turned around. "Is your husband badly hurt? What happened to him?"

Diane hadn't had time to explain. "He's not my husband," she said. "He was hit in the head. A group of boys attacked him." She hesitated. "Do you live in this area?"

The father cleared his throat. "A shortcut," he said. "We're coming from the river. We spent the day on a steamer to Concepción and back."

"There was a brass band and a big party," the girl said, still excited. "For my birthday. I'm fifteen today."

So they weren't poor, Diane thought. Did they live near the club?

As if reading her mind the mother said, "We live in the Santísima Trinidad area. Five minutes more." She turned around and looked back, her eyes squinting. "This is a dangerous barrio for Americans."

Diane nodded. "We were at the Club Bahia Negra. A boy stole something from this man. I followed him."

"He is your friend then?"

"No, we'd just met in passing in the club. I'm not sure who he is. An American." She shrugged.

"And you followed him here?" The señora was clearly surprised.

"I know it was stupid but—" Diane hesitated. She didn't want to tell them about the Indio who'd molested her. "He helped me earlier," she said. "I had to do something."

"Well, you sit back and relax. When we get to the house, we'll put some ice on his head and see how he is."

They had left the barrio, had crossed the Avenida Artigas, and were in a nicer neighborhood of stucco and wood houses. Most of the streets were paved, with streetlights at corners, and orange trees along the curb. Hot air wafted in through the open windows, carrying the scent of their blossoms.

"Santísima Trinidad," the father said.

Stanek stirred, a moan easing from his lips. For the last minute he'd heard voices but couldn't place what was happening. Where was he? His mind was foggy. He couldn't remember if he'd left his office at the university or not. Had he been in an accident?

He opened his eyes and saw a woman—a faint glimmer of recognition—long black hair, a pale face, dark eyelashes, a soft, warm feeling to her touch—did he know her?—and then a young boy. The back seat of a car. Three people in front he'd never seen before.

"Where am I?" he asked. "What happened?"

Everyone turned to look at him.

The woman sitting beside him said, "We're in a car. We're going to get help for you. You were hit in the head." An eastern accent. Delicate red lips fit for an angel in a dream.

"In the head?" Stanek lifted a hand and felt a knot over his left temple.

His hair was soaked.

"Am I bleeding?"

"It's stopped now. You were cut on the neck."

Cut on the neck. Everything she said seemed foreign to him. "How?"

"Friends of the boy you were chasing."

He was chasing a boy? "A student?" he asked, confused by it all. Why was he chasing a student?

"No," she said. "You were chasing the boy who stole your package."

He was still groggy. Nothing made sense. "Who are you?"

"I'm Diane Lang. What's your name?"

He paused for a second, groping to find his name, surprised at how difficult it was. "I—I have some amnesia," he said. "I can't remember what happened. My name's ... Walter Stanek. I teach at the university."

"What university?"

The question surprised him. The only one in town—or did she think he was visiting from Arizona State? Down from Tempe. "The University of Arizona," he said. "Here in Tucson."

There was a pause, a startled look on her face.

"We're in Asunción," she said. "In Paraguay."

He took a deep breath and slowly it came back to him—Paraguay ... the bar ... Greg Brown and the manila envelope ... the woman who'd called him an asshole. She was no angel. He sat up and grew dizzy.

"Kohlbert," he said. "I've got to talk to him."

"He's back at the bar," she said. "You told him to wait."

"No." He shook his head. "Another man. He hadn't arrived yet."

They'd been speaking in English, the Sosa family listening raptly. Diane switched to Spanish. "He's an American professor."

"We speak English," the father said. "Eliana's been an exchange student in Oregon, just outside Portland. Twice now. The whole family visited your country last year. What are you doing in Paraguay?"

"Research," she said. "I'm a professor at Yale University. I'm here to read a paper at the Catholic University and then I'm going to the Chaco."

Pina Sosa said, "The Chaco! Why out there? It's a wasteland."

"The Mennonite settlements. I teach German."

"Ah, yes." She turned to Stanek. "What about you, señor?"

Walter opened his eyes. The car was easing into a porticoed driveway. The glare of the headlights on white stucco blinded him.

"I'm a hydrogeologist," he said. "An engineer." It was all coming back now. "I'm down here to work on the Corpus hydroelectric project."

The car had rolled to a stop and the boy sitting next to Diane jumped out and ran across a flagstone path to a gate in a tall wall topped with broken bits of glass. Behind the wall and surrounded by native trees stood a two-story stucco house with a gabled tile roof.

Stanek moved to follow and felt something on the floor blocking his way.

"What's this?" he asked, his hand running over an object with a rough texture.

"Oh, my Mexican piñata," the girl said. "It's a bull, but only his belly is broken. I'm saving it."

"I hope I didn't get blood on it."

She giggled. "That's okay. It's red crepe paper."

Another vision of Mexico … ten years earlier … a Christmas party in the street, a piñata, the blindfold that he could see under as he tipped his head back, the crowd laughing as he swung the stick, piñata bobbing out of reach as they pulled on the string, saving it for a kid. But he could see and they didn't know that. He'd jumped then, giving a tremendous whack at the stuffed bull, scattering candy, surprising them. He'd spoiled it for the kids, but what did he care? He didn't like any of them. They'd only invited him to the party because of his American girlfriend.

"Let me help." The voice came from far away and then his eyes focused. The driver—Renato Sosa. He'd opened the back door on Diane Lang's side, was offering his hand.

Stanek slid out of the car. His head was aching but he had to think. He'd lost the envelope. He reached out and grabbed Sosa by the arm. "Can you call us a taxi?" he asked. "I have to get back to the club." Kohlbert would be there. Have to explain about the package. Face his wrath and get it over with.

"Let's go inside," the *señora* said, moving up to help. "It will take some time for a taxi to get here. I can clean your cuts while we wait."

On the veranda, while *señor* Sosa unlocked a security alarm and a series of bolts and locks on the double doors, Stanek turned to Diane Lang. "How did you find me?"

"I took a taxi," she said. "You were already gone by the time I found one. The driver didn't want to enter the barrio. He said it was a real slum."

Stanek nodded. His neck was beginning to sting and a dull pain throbbed through the knot on the side of his head. "What happened to the taxi driver?"

"He left."

He stared at her with renewed appreciation. "Thanks," he said, then couldn't help adding, "But if you hadn't gotten involved with that drunk, none of this would've happened."

"Yeah, it was all my fault," she said, her voice sharp.

Stanek bit his tongue. His frustration with events only made his head hurt worse. Let her be sarcastic; he had better things to do than waste his time in a frivolous argument. The first order of business was to get a taxi and get back to the club. Explain it all to Harrington and Kohlbert. They would have the Indio; maybe the old man could lead them to the boy.

Renato Sosa was a lawyer and the family's home was a villa constructed around a central patio. There was a gallery running around the second level, with a floor of large red tiles, and the *corredor* was lined with large and small pots filled with exotic flowering plants, some bearing fruit—figs, tangerines, and pomegranates. The ironwork of the balustrade itself, running between white pilasters, was draped with a leafy green screen of ferns and cascading lileacea. Below, in the center of the quadrangle, sat an octagonal cistern with a rope and bucket on a pulley.

The boy, José, was sent to bed, but Eliana watched while her mother washed the blood from Stanek and then bandaged his arm and neck. He had refused to see a doctor. They had tied an ice pack to his head with a shawl, covering his left eye, and the girl laughed at the sight.

"I'm sorry," she said, when her mother remonstrated with her. "You look like a pirate, *señor* Stanek."

"Profesor Stanek," the mother said. "What happened to your manners, Eliana?"

"And the young woman is also a professor," Renato Sosa reminded his daughter. He was sitting in a plush wing chair, smoking a pipe while his wife worked on Stanek. His feet rested on an antique European footstool, low and cushioned, looking like an armadillo whose bony back was stuffed with steel springs and horse hair. Across the room—they were in the family room on the first floor—a fire blazed in a massive stone fireplace.

"I heard," Eliana said. She looked at Diane Lang, who was standing at the side of the mantle near the wood carrier and the bellows. "I've been studying English in school for over five years, *profesora*. When I finish I'm going back to Oregon. I have a *novio* there."

"Hush," her mother said. "Don't wear them out with your chatter; you're just a girl. No talk of *novios*. Robert's your American *hermano*."

The girl giggled again. "The first summer I went he was my brother. The second time no more. For a year we were sweethearts. Some day Robert wants to marry me."

Renato Sosa took the pipe from his mouth and said, "Eliana ... let our guests rest."

"It's okay," Stanek said. He was sitting at a table in a straight-backed Spanish chair of brown wood with a thinly padded leather seat, dark and abraded with wear. He turned to the girl standing behind him. "Eliana, you remind me of my sister when she was your age."

"How old is she now?"

Stanek tried to grin, wincing at the pain. "She's four years younger than me," he said, one arm leaning on the table. "Thirty-nine."

"She's old."

Pina Sosa put her hands on her hips. "Eliana! What's gotten into you?" She washed the last of the blood from Stanek's chin. "Thirty-nine is not old and neither is forty-three. The professor is younger than your father."

Across the room, his head wreathed in lunt, Renato Sosa raised his eyebrows but said nothing.

In this family, Stanek thought, the women would always have the last word.

Chapter Eleven

By the time a taxi arrived at the Sosa residence, it was too late to return to the Club Bahia Negra. The club, like most restaurants in Asunción, closed at midnight and it was already nearly one o'clock in the morning. Kohlbert, Stanek decided, would have to wait until later to learn what had happened. And if he and Harrington had taken the Indio to a police station, Stanek would find out about it at the first session of the war games that afternoon. He was too tired and too sore to do anything else at the moment.

Before leaving the Sosas, Stanek had invited the family to have dinner with him the following evening, Friday, at the Restaurant Zodiac—at his expense in gratitude for their help. According to his guidebook, perused on the flight down, the restaurant had a terrace for outdoor dining on the thirteenth floor of a building with a good view of the city.

Pina Sosa had tried to say no, embarrassed that he should feel obliged to repay them for an act of human kindness, but Stanek had insisted.

"Then all of us should meet," Renato Sosa said, gesturing around the living room, his gaze including Diane Lang. "But I have a suggestion. Let us show you another place where you can experience fine, native dining in an atmosphere that is more typical of the people—the Parrillada Aregua, which means 'grill from the past.' And it will be less expensive."

"Renato," his wife said. "You should let the professor choose."

"That's okay," Stanek said. "Anywhere is fine. And I'd be happy to treat everyone, including—" he glanced carelessly in her direction—"Professor Lang."

"I'm sorry," she said immediately, a touch of reserve in her voice. "I have other plans." She wasn't going to force him to do anything. Him and his ridiculous accusations. He still blamed her for the loss of his stupid envelope. She didn't like men who had to whine about everything. Besides, it was clear; neither one of them liked the other. They'd clashed from the first moment.

But again, Renato and Pina Sosa had protested, and when she wasn't able to think of a good excuse, she'd finally consented to join them.

Now, she had to ride back into the city with Stanek.

It was a short ride made long by their silence. Neither one said a word to the other and the taxi driver ignored them, intent on a program broadcast by *Radio Ñandutí*.

The first thing Stanek saw when he unlocked the door and stepped into his room at the Hotel Paraná was a large manila envelope lying on the floor. *Come on, what is this?* He found the light switch to the left, a button that had to be pushed into the outlet, and examined the envelope under the weak overhead light. An eerie sensation came over him—it was Greg Brown's letter all right. The flap was torn open, but nothing, as far as he could tell, was missing.

Strange.

He sat down on the bed and wondered why the clerk at the front desk hadn't mentioned the envelope. They'd talked for five minutes, Stanek trying to explain how his shirt had been ripped to shreds and why he looked the worse for wear. But there'd been no mention of anyone dropping off a package for him or asking for his room number. Earlier, the hotel's bellboys had carried his luggage to a stand near the closet. Had they also delivered the letter?

He turned out the light, bent down and looked under the door. A thin sliver of light from the hall was visible. Whoever delivered the envelope could have slipped it under the door, but that meant they had to have asked for his room number.

Whoever they *were.*

He stared again at the envelope. No indication of who *he* was and where *he* was staying. For a return address it had Greg Brown's name and the company location in Houston and was addressed to Kohlbert at Samcon's office on Calle Iturbe.

So how did whoever found it—or stole it—know where to return it?

He picked up the phone and dialed the front desk, inquired if anyone had asked for him, and was told no.

With the hotel operator's help, he dialed Samcon's office but at that hour of the night no one answered. Kohlbert's name was not in the local directory.

Too exhausted to ponder the situation at greater length, Stanek turned on the air conditioner, took a quick shower and—for the first time in a month or more—fell asleep the minute his head hit the pillow.

He was awakened at eight the next morning by an insistent pounding on the door. He rolled over in bed, feeling groggy, swearing at the intrusion. He hadn't bothered to leave a wake-up call since the "war games" session didn't start until midday. Who in hell was bothering him now?

"*¿Quien es?*"

"*Policía.*"

He came awake quicker when he heard that, his feet sliding out of bed and finding the floor. For a moment he grabbed his head as the pressure inside made it seem his brain was swaying back and forth like the action of an ocean wave caught between narrow straits.

The pounding on the door hit his ears with renewed vigor. Voices pitched more insistent now.

"*Vengo, vengo,*" he shouted, then looked around the room for his pants. He'd left them on a chair by the bathroom.

He answered the door without a shirt, blinking in the sudden infusion of bright light. The windows in the hallway let in the morning sun and the glare on the white walls and polished wood floor was unbearable.

"What is it?" he asked in English. There were two men in the hall, neither one in uniform, a short fellow with a surly look, stony-eyed and unshaven, straight black hair hanging over his ears and forehead like a wig, and a heavyset man with puffy eyes, a well-nourished face, and a quality of indolence in his gaze.

The corpulent one said, "Señor Walter Stanek?"

He nodded, looking from one to the other. Harrington must have turned the Indio in the night before and now the cops were here to question him.

The two men stepped into the room, the shorter one shoving the door open before Stanek could step away. For a fraction of a second, surprised by the brusque move, Stanek resisted his pressure—they could have asked if they could come in—then gave way. He shut the door behind them, then walked to his suitcase, found a dress shirt and put it on.

"We're with the *Comisaria Seccional Decimotercia,*" the fat man said. The thirteenth police precinct. "*Santísima Trinidad.*" He spoke in a slow, hypnotic voice, the tone languid. "The hotel manager told us of your incident last night. Why did you not report this crime to us?" He smiled wearily.

Stanek cleared his throat. His tongue felt like balsa wood pasted to the top of his mouth. "It was late and I was tired. I just arrived yesterday." And I didn't think it would do any good, he wanted to say, but thought better of it. There was a trickiness about this cop, the voice which came and went like the swaying of a cobra. He noticed he hadn't told them the letter had been returned. Innate caution taking over around policemen. Let them work for it.

The short, surly fellow said, "In our country, *señor*, it is a crime for a foreigner *not* to report a crime. Only criminals are afraid of the police." He looked around the room, his eyes cold. "Do you like beating little boys?"

Stanek's eyes widened and he had to clear his throat again. "No." He didn't like the question.

"So do we," the cop said. The fat man sniggered.

"Look," Stanek said, "I didn't intentionally break the law." Oh hell, what was the use trying to reason with a cop? The letter of the law—not common sense—was all that mattered to most. Forget it. Use what they understood best—political connections, influence. He said, "I'm here as a guest of your country."

The two men looked at each other and the porker smiled. "A guest of our country?" His tone blended incredulity and derision.

Stanek's jaw line tightened. "That's right. I've been invited here to take part in a disaster prevention program. I'm working for a company called Samcon on a project to help your government."

The shorter mean-looking fellow shrugged. "And who is this Samcon?"

"Look, they have an office in the city. You can call them. President Zancon will be speaking at today's inaugural session."

There was a moment of silence. Both cops were looking around the room as if they thought it was bugged.

The cop with the indolent gaze pulled at the rolls of fat at his neck and said, "This woman who helped you—Diane Lang. Why did she get involved? Is she an acquaintance of yours?"

Stanek sighed. He would just as soon forget her. "She's a professor from Yale University in the United States," he said, his voice a monotone. "I just met her last night. She was trying to help a fellow American." He was reluctant to mention the Indio. The next thing they'd do would be to hassle Professor Lang for not reporting a crime. Or had she reported it? he wondered. The police knew her name.

But perhaps the Sosa family had filed a report.

"We should inform you that she is under suspicion. You would do better to avoid her in the future."

"Under suspicion?" Stanek snorted. "Of what?"

"Avoid her. Get the message?"

They were staring at him expectantly so Stanek nodded, repressing a frown, then remembered the dinner that evening. He'd invited the Sosa family and they'd invited Professor Lang. Renato Sosa had promised to pick her up first and then him. Tell the cops?

But they were already moving toward the door and it seemed easier to forget the whole thing. He'd expected more questions, perhaps even the necessity of a visit to the police station. *Don't call them back now.* He'd just get in more trouble.

At the door, the thin fellow turned and stared at him for a moment, his hand on the latch. "Remember what we said," he warned. "Stay away from the woman." And with that he shut the door behind them.

When they were gone and he had time to think, Stanek wondered about the purpose of the visit. They hadn't really questioned him about what had happened; they weren't interested in the crime. They'd joked about beating kids and then warned him off Diane Lang.

Under suspicion. The words had an ominous tone. What in hell was she involved with?

Chapter Twelve

Diane Lang spent Friday morning touring Asunción. She had no intention of letting Colonel Ibarras's threats keep her from seeing what she wanted and as far as she could tell no one was following her.

Professor Aguirre of the Catholic University had left a message for her the evening before, volunteering to send a student to show her around before the conference started, but she had decided to call later in the morning and decline his offer. The University had planned several cultural events and excursions beginning Saturday, to go along with the lecture sessions on Monday and Tuesday of the following week. She would be busy enough once those started, and on Wednesday she would leave for the Chaco. In the meantime, she preferred being alone and freer to absorb the sights.

Despite the late night, she was up early and out of the hotel by six, taking a taxi out Avenida Mariscal Lopez to the residential district around the Escuela de Bellas Artes and the Biblioteca Nacional. At that hour, both buildings were deserted.

As the sky turned from oyster-gray to a high, thin blue and the air began to take on a tropical warmth, she moved back and forth from broad paved avenues to narrow residential streets with grass-grown cobbles, sauntering under mauve jaracanda and palacha trees, by green tipas and lapacho with their brilliant violet flowers spread across the stones.

Many of the finer homes were old Spanish-colonial houses, some with overhanging Andalucian-style balconies and rejas. White, pillared, porticoed, with shutters on their windows, they had lawns with palm and mango trees. She was surprised at the number of trees and flowers in the city and pleased to see an occasional brilliant green parakeet along with the swallows, hummingbirds, and sparrows.

The warm air, the palms and flowering trees, the tropical birds and high sky brought home to her how far away she was from her daughter. Kim would just be rising from a warm bed into the cold air of her grandmother's upstairs bedroom. She would get ready for school while the skies were still dark outside, and frost covered the ground.

Diane missed her already. They grow up too fast, she told herself, then cringed at the hackneyed thought. Still ... it had its own kernel of truth. In six more years, Kim would be ready for the university. She'd already declared she didn't want to go to Yale, despite the reduced tuition fees for faculty family members. No, for her it was Berkeley. That was the only place Kim wanted to go, which meant she would be leaving home.

Diane shook her head. Talking about college and she hadn't even started high school yet. Was that the result of running around with the children of other academics? Diane had been nowhere near so precocious—or so pressured; she'd never even thought about college until her senior year in high school.

Berkeley was a city she knew well—she'd received her Masters there—but what enamored Kim of the place was already in Diane's time only a distant memory—the Vietnam war protests, the crazy antics of the hippies, the psychedelic craze. In the nineties, when Diane was a graduate student, the campus was quiet. For her, what had happened twenty-five years earlier was of no interest; she wasn't even alive in '68 when the movement began and in her youth news of those wild days had swept over her as if nonexistent—a ruckus that left her untouched. But for Kim it was different. Kim was studying the sixties in school; for her, it was history—and she wanted to attend one of the hotbeds of revolution from those fabled days.

Diane took a deep breath and resolved that when she got back to New Haven, she would spend more time with her daughter—while she could. Six years would pass all too soon.

As the sun rose higher and the heat built up and the streets grew more congested, Diane shook off thoughts of home and caught a bus with a crowd of *Asunceros*, finding a seat by good fortune, and taking the bus all the way to its terminal—the Terminal La Immaculada—in order to rest her tired legs.

On the street again, with people brushing quickly past her as they set about their chores, she found the bus station on her map, saw that it was just to the east of the main campus of the National University, and walked that way. In a few moments, she was surrounded by students, who milled about chattering animatedly with one another. Below the campus, she had a view of the Paraguay river as its broad expanse swept around a bend to the south. From there, thinking of her classes at Yale and wondering how her students were doing without her, she headed back toward the port area near the bay.

Stevedores with rags tied around their foreheads roamed the wharves, and modern cranes were busy loading and unloading cargo from several freighters docked at the three *depósitos* to the left of the Port Authority

and Customs buildings. The sight of the activity brought back her tiredness; she had overestimated her energy, she realized. The interrogation
by Colonel Ibarras, the migraine that lasted all afternoon, the confrontation with Walter Stanek, the late night and the chase, all had sapped
her strength.

Food, she thought. She'd skipped breakfast. It was time to eat. She
hadn't minded missing dinner the night before—too much was happening
to make her think about her stomach—but now she was famished.

She stopped in front of a street vendor, a wizened man with a baseball
cap, selling hand-sized pancakes slathered with what looked like straw-
berry jam and then served folded in a V. She ordered two, eating them
with such obvious relish that the vendor began laughing and jabbering
at her in Guaraní. She didn't understand a word he said but nodded her
head at his enthusiasm.

Feeling better, thinking briefly of Walter Stanek, the Sosa family, and
the dinner planned for that night, she worked her way eastward away from
the river. She took a zig-zag route, up and down the city's central district,
turning corners as the whim seized her, not looking at her map.

As the day advanced, the crowds of pedestrians, the excited jabbering
of friends, the jangle of traffic made her feel suddenly lonely—and that
surprised her. She had always considered herself a self-sufficient woman.
Was it her fight with Russ? The realization that another relationship was
down the tubes?

God knew starting fresh was hard enough for her. Soon after her di-
vorce, when Kim was three, Diane's father had died of a heart attack at
his office in the bank, an attack caused in part by the stress of what was
happening to her, she thought. She'd taken his death hard, feeling that
she hadn't really had a chance to say good-bye.

And then, when she was finally ready to date again, the first guy who'd
asked her out died a month later in an automobile accident on the Connecticut Turnpike. For a reason she still couldn't fathom, his death (he

was three years younger than her) had affected her so deeply that she'd refused to go out again for over two years.

She knew it wasn't her fault, but still …

At least now she'd *saved* someone from dying. Walter Stanek didn't think so, of course, but who knew? Those kids might have cut his throat if she hadn't followed him in the taxi.

Diane shrugged. She didn't care who took the credit. All that mattered was that they were alive. When the Sosas picked her up and she met Walter Stanek again, *she* would be the first one to extend the olive branch. They weren't at war; there was no reason to be so prickly with each other. Life was too short for that.

When she looked up and saw where she was, she realized she had walked two blocks without being aware of her surroundings. To her right stood a large Volkswagen garage and the street in front of her had the marvelous name of Juan E. O'Leary. She looked at her map and turned left, moving north toward the bay and the Government Palace.

Soon she was wandering past helmeted soldiers on guard duty, up to the entrance hall of the palace itself, a dazzlingly white, bracket-shaped, two-story edifice set back from the traffic behind lawns, flower beds, and ornamental shrubs. Its central pinnacled tower, flying the tricolored Paraguayan flag, each side different—national coat of arms on the front, treasury seal on the reverse—rose above a Greek temple facade. At the back of the palace lay the bay.

She was surprised at the ease of approach—the president's office was in there somewhere. After what Ibarras had done to her, she'd expected to see armed soldiers everywhere—a state of siege. But maybe, she thought, a more effective siege was that of men in plainclothes—the secret police. That was where real terror lay: the call at three o'clock in the morning, the threat of torture, the knife in the back. And underlying it all, the realization that you had no control over your life—that the police could pull the strings whenever they wanted.

———

It was hard to enjoy the city when thoughts like that were nagging at her. And that made her angry, too. Colonel Ibarras was going to ruin her trip if she let him.

She stopped and took a deep breath, imagining herself on the crest of a steep mountain. *Take your anger,* she told herself, visualizing the action in her mind, *pack it up inside a ball, and roll it downhill, far, far away.*

But when she tried that, breathing deeply to relax, the ball, after tumbling down the slope, shattered on rocks at the base of the hill and the anger came swarming back like an attack of virulent bees.

Marveling at her topsy-turvy emotions, she realized that the only way to forget Ibarras and the interrogation was to keep busy. If she saw enough sights, if she tried hard to learn what she could about the city, if she occupied her mind with facts, perhaps that would do the trick.

Near ten, as the heat grew and sweat stood out on her neck and temples, she passed the former Colegio Militar on Calle 14 de Mayo. The street ran along one side of Plaza Constitución, an immense square that overlooked the bay, with important buildings on each side—to the north across the busy Avenida República, Parliament; to the south, the *Departamento Central de Policía* and the main post office, both on Paraguayo Independiente with its trolley lines, and to the east, the *Catedral Metropolitana.*

A fascinating city, once just a sprawling cow town built on seven low hills, now a metropolis, with miniature skyscrapers scattered about, fancy shops, and impressive monuments attesting to its violent past and its great dictators.

Dr. José Gaspar Rodriguez de Francia, *El Supremo*—he built a strong, prosperous nation, then imposed an authoritarian police state on it based on espionage and corruption.

Carlos Antonio Lopez, *El Excelentísimo*—an obese lawyer who ran the country like a personal fiefdom.

Francisco Solano Lopez, pampered son, a brigadier general at eighteen—he used priests as agents to report on subversion, then executed countless numbers of citizens, including two of his brothers, several relatives, the bishop of Asunción, thousands of military officers, and over five hundred foreigners.

And in this century, after more than thirty unstable dictatorships in just fifty years, the authoritarian banner had been carried for an awe-inspiring thirty-five years by General Alfredo Stroessner, *El Gran Líder*, and then for a short time by General Andres Rodriguez, *El Benévolo*, and from him it had been assumed—rather seized—by General Zancon, *El Tigre*. From all indications, Zancon would live up to his nickname.

Tired of history and politics, she ate an early lunch at a hole-in-the-wall restaurant—the Tuyuyú Guasú. The giant stork. On the cracked plaster of the back wall someone had painted a solitary stork standing tall in thick clumps of reeds and cortadera grass. She ordered the house specialty—*locro*, a stew of meat, maize, marrow, and vegetables, chased down with a bottle of Coca-Cola. Outside, vintage yellow tramcars clattered down the street.

From there, she walked to the Plaza de la Independencia, surprised to see the square and the adjacent Plaza de los Héroes jammed with people apparently attending a political rally. In one corner, along Calle Palma, rose a tall structure that reminded Diane of Les Invalides in Paris. The Pantheon of Heroes. As good a place to rest as any, she thought. She would listen and watch.

As the crowd grew, she stood to the side, watching the faces of the *Asunceros* as they listened with rapt attention to the speakers. She was not aware of it, but she, too, was being watched. She had tried to forget Colonel Ibarras—and for the moment had succeeded—but he had not forgotten her.

Chapter Thirteen

When the rally started, Elbert "Dink" Denton was sitting on a bench in the park facing the Pantheon of Heroes, pretending to read a Spanish translation of a Mack Bolan novel—*Encuentro in Kabul*. The book was in Dink's left hand, a bottle of beer in his right.

A flatbed truck bearing Paraguayan and Church flags and with two loudspeakers set up in back pulled to a stop near the monument itself. Almost immediately an amplified voice echoed over the plaza. Apparently the truck was expected. A crowd of what must have been nearly two thousand people formed with astonishing rapidity.

Dink Denton did not get caught up in the crowd. An American citizen and a Special Agent in the employ of the Drug Enforcement Administration, he was following a reputed *narcotraficante* who had brought his family to the park for what looked like a picnic lunch. The father, mother, and six-year-old boy sat on a park bench with napkins on their laps and food in their hands.

Intelligence had reported that the family planned to attend a comic bullfight that afternoon at the Estadio Comuneros. When Dink had asked, "What's a comic bullfight?" he was told the matadors were blindfolded and wore red pants. Most wound up with the bull's head between their legs and their arms around his withers.

"A sport for eunuchs," Dink had said, flexing his muscles in disdain.

A former marine (which meant he'd been trained twice at Quantico, once for the Corps and once for the DEA), Dink was only five feet seven but he had massive arms and legs, a neck the size of an elephant's foot, and enough hair on his chest and back to clothe a bald ape. He had a cleat scar on his chin from his days as a defensive tackle with a high school football team in Gary, Indiana. His teammates had called Dink the village smithy; he'd pretty much hammered anyone who'd faced him across the line.

When the rally started, the first thing Dink noticed was a man in a black shirt standing under a tree with a two-way radio in his hand, eyes scanning the crowd as he spoke softly into the transmitter. He had a pinched face and a receding hairline.

Undercover cop was his first thought, although he briefly considered the possibility that the man might be a bodyguard for the *narcotrafi-cante*—and thus someone to worry about.

But not likely. The man with the radio had the furtive look of the secret police—already on the scene for the rally, which meant an informer had squealed.

And then something else caught Dink's attention and made him sit up, suddenly alert. It was not the undercover cop, not the crowd in the Plaza de los Héroes, and not the family he was watching. They weren't going to move, not with food in their laps. No, what he noticed right off was the woman. And it was not just that she was some hot chick and, by the way she looked and dressed, probably an American.

She was under surveillance.

The guy with the radio was tracking her; the political commotion in the background was just an annoyance. And then Dink saw the tracker's accomplice—another guy in a sport coat, moving in from the side, both of them hard-faced men, with the air of hired killers.

Damn, what had she done? Slept with one of the opposition's top honchos?

For Dink, everything came down to sex in one form or another—even revolution. The opposition leaders wanted to fuck with the people just like everyone else. That's what politicians did—they got into bed with whoever had the money to keep them in power. Fuck idealism. That was probably what got the chick in trouble—although she looked a little too mature to have been suckered by some rinky-dink, wild-eyed revolutionary.

He looked at the two men again, at how they moved. Secret police all right. He'd already had a run-in or two with their type in Paraguay. Tried to make you think they could kill with their eyes alone, but answer them in kind and they soon lost their bluster—unless they were in a crowd.

Pussies, he thought. If they fucked up his own surveillance—

Dink stiffened. The guy in the sport coat was heading toward him, approaching the bench, his radio stuffed in a pocket. Eyes that were over-alert, nervous.

Dink tried to bury his head in the Mack Bolan novel. Had the guy recognized him from somewhere?

No words passed between them.

The man sat to his left, pulled his slacks up an inch or two for comfort and then leaned forward, both hands resting on the front slat of the bench. He looked around carefully, surveying the area as a whole and then Dink himself. Dink glanced his way quickly, caught the guy's eye, and looked back down. Damn. Had they met before? He didn't think he recognized the guy.

Five minutes passed while voices boomed out of the loudspeakers. Dink had trouble understanding what was going on. He spoke what he called "pigskin" (for pidgin) Spanish, but it wasn't good enough to make out the words through the sonic distortion of the microphones. He could see that the final speaker was a priest.

"A chaplain of bandits, that one. Every time I see a priest I touch my belt buckle."

Dink looked up, eyes narrowing. The guy to his left was talking to him—*in English*. Dink had bought his clothes in Asunción—from his shoes to his shirt—trying to look more like a native, but something had given him away.

Still, he shrugged his shoulders as if he hadn't understood, his eyes sweeping casually from the family of the *narcotraficante* to the woman. The cop in the black shirt was leaning against a tree less than fifteen feet from where she stood.

Dink took a sip of his beer—getting warm, damn it—and went back to reading. His eyes swept over the lines without absorbing the words. He had enough trouble with Spanish as it was.

"A parish priest," the cop continued, shaking his head and gesturing toward the truck. "He should stick to the gospel. He makes the people restless."

What was it with this guy? Gabby bastard. Did he think they were friends? Dink cleared his throat. Hell, he'd better say something back or the guy would get suspicious. "Who is he?"

"Ramon Ibañez. An agitator. You get up close and you can see it in his face." The man laughed, but there was no mirth in the sound. "You can see the dots of white cartilage on the tip of his nose. You can see his eyes." He looked at Dink, pointing at his own face and running his finger around in a circle. "Rimmed in red—the eyes of a fanatic."

Dink made a noncommittal gesture, then casually made sure that both the *narcotraficante* and the American woman hadn't moved. For all he knew this was a ploy to distract him. Maybe the police were working *with* the drug smuggler. But what in hell did the woman have to do with it?

The cop nodded with conviction. "The bishop assured us just yesterday—Ibañez has no authority to speak for the Church. I am afraid *El Tigre* will soon lose his patience with these priests." He snorted. "They have no political *reason*, just political *passion*; they erupt like volcanos. They spit in church and then claim to worship God."

"Yeah," Dink said, with a cynical shrug of his shoulders, "I worship God, too—only my God's the bottle." He hefted the beer he was holding, then drained it. "For me, the rivers of heaven—and the pee of every decent *hombre* and *mujer* on earth—run yellow with booze. My motto is—suck it dry."

The other guy was intent on the woman, who had left the sidewalk and was moving toward one of the trees. After a moment, he said, "Suck what dry?"

"Life, man."

The woman had stopped; she was leaning into the tree, both hands behind her to keep her skirt clean. The ground around her feet was covered with pink petals, recently fallen.

Now that was some sight, Dink thought, licking his lips. His local girlfriend, a sweet little *Asuncera*, was going to like what she got tonight.

The cop's lips twisted in scorn. "Life is a fat whore flopped on a mattress." He spit between his legs. "On her hands and knees with her ass in the air."

"Yeah, maybe so, but not everybody's man enough to take advantage of that."

When the other guy just shrugged, Dink said, "Pussies sit back and *enjoy* life. That's no way to live. Hell, you pursue life—you seize and plunder and consume it."

The cop stared at him, a glitter in his dark eyes. "Until death grabs you by the balls," he said.

"Only pussies fear death," Dink said. "I chase the grim fucker away. Every time I wake up I say, 'Come and get me, you lily-livered coward—but you better bring more than a fuckin' scythe.'"

The cop laughed and then looked away. After a minute he snorted. "Listen to him. Calling for a crusade *para salvar al país*. As if the country needed saving."

The words came louder and clearer now. The priest was shouting something about the time being ripe—Dink caught the words *"la hora de la dignidad paraguaya ha llegado."* Whatever "Paraguayan dignity" meant. The crowd seemed to like it. The priest's words echoed over their heads, bouncing off the drab buildings that surrounded the plaza.

A list of demands followed. The cop was silent now as they listened together. Words easy to understand: a general amnesty ... freedom of speech ... no more repression ... *libertad.*

And then, in a harsh voice, the priest changed course. He criticized the waste of *"milliones"* in military affairs while *"la gente del campo muere de hambre"* and urged the people to stand up against tyranny and the willful thievery perpetrated by foreign corporations.

The enthusiastic crowd interrupted with shouts of *"Viva la libertad,"* *"Viva la democracia,"* and *"Abajo la tiranía."*

The dual-toned warble of sirens cut through the loudspeakers and the roar of the crowd.

"Finally," the cop said in a soft voice. *"Las perreras."* He got to his feet.

The dog wagons. Is that what they called them? Dink could see the trucks coming from at least two directions—the red paddy wagons used by the police for mass arrests.

The cop walked away from him, toward the woman. The *narcotraficante* and his family were hurriedly packing their food, wrapping everything in paper and stuffing the packages into a straw hamper.

The crowd was breaking up, people beginning to run in every direction. A man fell in the roadway and scrambled painfully to his feet to avoid being trampled. His pants were torn and blood showed at his knee. The crowd pushed him along. Sweat pouring down their faces. The sun high overhead and hot, the morning breeze dead.

Dink jumped up on a two-foot-wide concrete barricade protecting a clump of elevated trees. He knew what was going to happen now. In the crush of people, in the confusion, he was going to lose the *narcotraficante* and his family.

And the American woman, would she lose the men following her?

Hell, he thought, she's going to lose her *life*. The guy in the black shirt had drawn a knife from an ankle sheath. He was moving in on her in the confusion, the blade held flat against his leg.

An awful sensation came over Dink. The guy was ten feet away from the woman. Could he get there in time? The second cop, the talky one, was moving toward his partner, right hand in the pocket of his sport coat.

Shit! No time to wait.

Dink ran by the second cop, delivering a fierce judo chop to the guy's neck. The cop collapsed like an old bull in a slaughter house; he wouldn't be getting up for a while. But his partner had seen the blow, was turning to face Dink, a look of surprise flickering over his face only to be replaced by deadly purpose.

Dink saw the kick coming—one of those fancy, pivoting, roundhouse moves. Karate or kung fu.

Fuck this shit. He stepped into the blow, parrying it with one massive arm while slamming the fist of his other hand into the guy's unprotected balls. The cop passed out in the middle of his scream.

Must not have paid his due homage to Santa Rosa de Lima, Dink thought, a grin creasing his face. He'd been in Asunción on August 30, when the police celebrated the day of their patron saint. Bunch of malarky as far as he was concerned. Like the karate. He didn't have time for shit like that. When he hit someone, it didn't much matter if the move was fancy or not, they went down.

The woman had caught sight of him, saw the men on the ground. Before he could say anything, she took off running, but she was funneling down a corridor where the cops were waiting with their clubs and police trucks.

Let her go or chase her and loose the *narcotraficante*?

Hell, he could always find the guy later. He'd be at the bullfight all afternoon. And back home that night. And once Dink got the woman out of there he could find a phone and call for assistance. Hand the drug trafficker over to a buddy.

Yeah, see what the chick was up to. His buddies would say he was thinking with his pecker but his pecker was a damn sight smarter than their pea-brains.

Diane Lang felt the fist close over her arm as she stumbled forward through the press of the screaming crowd.

"This way," the man shouted. "Too many cops ahead."

An American, the guy she'd seen take out the man with the knife. She hesitated, feeling the panic of the mob as the *Asunceros* swirled around them. The man trying to help her had his legs planted like pylons on a bridge.

"Come on." He tugged at her arm and then let go when he sensed her resistance. "We can't stand here. We'll be trampled."

He turned and she followed him as they battled against the flow. In a moment, they were able to break away from the mass of bodies and work their way toward a side street, past the Banco Paraguayo de Comercio. The man took a circuitous route, checking over his shoulder as they moved from street to alley to street.

When he finally stopped, they were standing in front of the Jordanian

Consulate on Oliva Street.

"You okay?" he asked. "You're American, right?"

Diane nodded, trying to catch her breath.

"What happened back there? You had a guy coming at you with a knife."

Diane glanced around with an air of distraction. "He was coming after me?"

"Damn right. And he had a partner. A blabbermouth. He'll have a stiff neck for a week." The man paused and then grinned. "Course I'd rather be in his position than in his partner's. That guy'll be walking bowlegged for a month or two."

"Fudge," she said, her voice a whisper.

"What's that?"

"Oh, never mind." She shook her head in frustration. "It was an expletive."

The man laughed and then cocked his head. "Hear that?"

A crackling sound came from the from the direction of the plaza.

"Shots," he said, growing serious. "They're fucking shooting at their own people."

They listened to the sound in the distance, small and unreal. Police sirens again. Scattered groups of people were moving quickly down the street.

The man said, "What's your name?"

"Who are you?"

"Dink Denton. Wherever you're staying, you'd better change hotels."

"Is anyone following us?"

"Not now."

She took that in. "Thanks for helping me," she said. "I'm Diane Lang."

"My pleasure," he said. "Glad I was there. It's not hard down here to recognize the secret police. They had you under surveillance. What'd you do anyway?"

"I don't know." She looked around, feeling the rise of panic again. "I just got here yesterday. They stopped me at the airport." She took a deep breath in an attempt to calm herself. "They think I'm involved with a subversive element."

"Are you?"

"How in hell should I know?"

He grinned. "Good to hear you can swear. A few moments ago you reminded me of my mother."

"Listen, Mr. Denton—"

"Call me Dink. Everybody else does."

"Are you free tonight?" She had to trust someone—and the guy had risked his life for her. She needed protection.

"Tonight?" He shrugged. "Depends. What for?"

She looked at him, saw what he was thinking. "Oh, no ..."

"No what?"

"This isn't a proposition. Thanks for saving my life, but I don't pay off that way." She could feel the flush in her cheeks. "I'm having dinner with some friends—acquaintances really. I just met them last night. I'd like to treat you to a meal if I could. To thank you."

Stanek could thank the Sosas, she thought, while she thanked Dink Denton. She owed him more than words of gratitude.

And maybe he could help her. Get rid of Ibarras's thugs once and for all.

But that could wait.

She could see he was thinking about the meal. "You could meet us at the Parrillada Aregua," she said. "Or we could pick you up. Are you familiar with Asunción?"

"I'll be there," he said. "What time?"

Chapter Fourteen

Raymond Kohlbert hefted the manila envelope and said, "Harrington told me you lost this and then up and disappeared into the night."

"I was lucky," Stanek said. "I got it back." He decided not to tell Kohlbert how. Hell, might have been the cops. "I had to chase down the kid who stole it. Where is Harrington anyway? I left him in the bar at the club watching this drunk."

"Yes, he told me. He couldn't stay there forever. The guy finally just walked out of the place. Harrington said he couldn't do anything about it. But that's over now." Kohlbert held out his hand. "Thanks for delivering this. Greg Brown had only good things to say about you."

Stanek winced—not at the words but at the crushing pressure of Kohlbert's handshake.

Kohlbert looked to be in his sixties, with grizzled hair cut military style above stubby boxer's ears, but he was a big, strong man with a barrel chest, a powerful handshake, and a booming voice that carried up and down the hallway. The two men were standing outside an open double door that led to an auditorium with a steeply slanted floor, located in the Colegio Militar.

"That's quite some grip you have," Stanek said, massaging his fingers.

"A plumber's hands," Kohlbert said, spreading his fingers and admiring them. He grinned. "You know what Himmler told the SS. Best preparation in the world for a choke hold."

"When'd you do the plumbing?" Stanek asked, ignoring the Nazi reference.

Kohlbert looked happy to talk about the old days. "Did my apprenticeship in Germany right after the war and then worked for five years in New York. Journeyman plumber."

"What'd you handle? Cast iron?"

Kohlbert unleashed a crooked grin. "There weren't any specialties in those days. We did it all—cast iron, copper, gas lines, fixtures, canning out. That's what I liked best. I was a young Turk then. Nothing scared me. I followed the Mohawks up with the steel—best guys in the world at topping out. They'd be ninety-five stories up and I'd be right there with them, tying empty cans to the rebar."

"Things haven't changed much have they?"

Kohlbert shook his head. "No, it's always the young ones who do the stupid things. The older plumbers would come along later when the concrete was poured and everything was safe, knock the cans out, and lay the plumbing. I never lasted long enough to have that luxury. Got into other things."

"Harrington said you had something to do with nuclear energy."

Kohlbert laughed, showing large white teeth. "You can't believe everything you hear from Harrington. He likes to pull your leg. Samcon's working with a lot of different industries."

A voice hailed Stanek from up the hall. "Stanek old chap, fervent salutations. I do say, I thought we'd never see you again."

It was D. Benjamin Harrington, padding up the hallway in soft leather shoes, in his baggy suit and wrinkled white shirt, with his bow tie askew. His hair was mussed, as if he'd forgotten to comb it, and his skin had an unhealthy sheen, with the broken stitchery of red veins standing out on pale cheeks.

Stanek acknowledged the greeting with a brief nod, then said, "Took some doing but I made it here with the package." His voice was loud and he smiled at the older fellow's involuntary grimace. A hangover. "How you doing?" he asked, then couldn't quite catch what Harrington mumbled in response. "Say again?"

Harrington cleared his throat. "I said, 'Staying sober.'"

"Oh, I thought you said, 'it's over.' Quite a difference there."

"I'll say." All three men laughed.

Harrington rubbed his forehead. "Every day I accept one new challenge to prove I'm still alive. Today it was peeing and brushing my teeth at the same time. Damn hard to keep the spittle from hitting one's stomach, you know." He tugged at his bow tie. "But what happened to you, old chap?"

Stanek told him about chasing the boy and the confrontation with the street urchins. He didn't mention Diane Lang and Harrington didn't ask about her.

When he finished, Harrington said, "Your evening was more exciting than mine—although for a while there I thought I might be in the middle of a terrorist attack."

A bemused look appeared on Stanek's face. "What happened?"

Harrington shrugged. "Oh, it was nothing. I met an American lady in the club. Quite batty really. She came over and asked me if I knew Arabic."

"That's an original line."

"Yes, well, when I asked her if I looked like Lawrence of Arabia and why she wanted to know, she said she thought someone had made a death threat against her. In Arabic."

"Here in Paraguay? What does she think this is, Bagdad?"

"Apparently. I asked if the threat was verbal. 'No, sir,' she said, 'it's on the back of my car.' So I go over to the parking lot and take a look. What do I find? Some kid has squeezed a tube of toothpaste all over the trunk of her car." Harrington laughed, a wheezy sound from deep in his chest. "That's all it was. Swirls of toothpaste."

"And she thought it was a death threat? In Arabic?"

"Yes, well, everyone's paranoid here after a while. You wait. You'll start seeing spies behind the bushes soon enough—especially if you hang around Kohlbert." He twisted his face around to look up at the bigger man.

Kohlbert shrugged. "No spies today. Sorry to disappoint you but I must be off. I'm flying a technician back to São Paulo this afternoon. I'll leave you two fellows to your own devices now. Don't bite off more than you can chew."

Harrington grinned. "Hey, if it's a great mouthful and we can't chew it, we'll just make sure we suck or gum it to death." He squinted up at Kohlbert, the wrinkles on his forehead deepening. "But don't you want to greet our great leader, *El Tigre*?" A touch of sarcasm in his voice.

Kohlbert snorted. "That *cachorro*. I just saw him last night. You do it for me, Benjamin."

"You're going to miss a good match tomorrow—Cerro Porteño against Olimpia."

"Didn't they tell you?" Kolbert said. "You'll miss it, too. They're going to run these sessions straight through the weekend."

Harrington's face turned sour. "What's the damn hurry? I wanted to see that match."

"The spinning wheels of progress wait for no man," Kohlbert said. "Anyway, it's just a soccer game. You'll have more fun matching wits with General Paredes."

"Paredes—I hate that bastard. What's his role? He's not a cabinet member, is he?"

Kohlbert grinned. "He'll be running Control. God the Father. And don't forget, Benjamin. He hates you, too."

They were seated in the auditorium when an Army major with the insignia of the Presidential Escort Service stepped on stage and in a loud voice said, *"El Excelentísimo Señor Presidente de la República y Comandante en Jefe de las Fuerzas Armadas de la Nación, General de Ejército Don Enrique Zancon."*

"He forgot *todopoderoso*," Harrington whispered in a mocking voice.

Stanek's mouth took on the beginnings of a slight grin as the General, dressed in a civilian suit rather than his uniform, entered the room and walked down the aisle with two guards at his heels. Zancon did not look all-powerful. A short man with a well-tanned face, arched black eyebrows and a shriveled up mouth and nose, he cut a rather unprepossessing figure, with an inconsequential appearance that belied his nickname as The Tiger.

"Bloody mestizo," Harrington muttered.

When the general was halfway down the aisle, the audience rose and began clapping. Stanek looked around and saw that the room was filled with Paraguayan observers, some in military uniform.

When the crowd had settled down and the general opened his mouth to speak, Stanek was so distracted by the sight of a row of decaying teeth—jagged tips of black jutting up like the corroded maw of a bottom-feeder in a polluted lagoon—that he missed the first few phrases. The general spoke in heavily accented English, and by the time Stanek had tuned in to the words, Zancon had reached the conclusion of his short speech, ending on a lofty note.

"Gentlemen, your role in bringing about an era of peace and material prosperity as the country emerges from this last struggle is deeply appreciated in Paraguay. The necessity of unremitting effort to secure the lasting welfare of our nation is evident to all. I speak with the authority of self-sacrifice, since I am willing to give my life to safeguard our national honor. I thank you in advance, for I know that what you accomplish in these sessions will guarantee the security of our Republic in the uncharted byways of the future."

Harrington leaned over to Stanek and said, "That's what they always say—the country doesn't matter—Asia, the Middle East, Africa, the Caribbean. In Latin America, it's usually something like *los problemas están para ser resueltos*." He shook his head mournfully. "Treat me to a drink every time someone says that and I'll treat you every time they mention security, peace, and democracy in the same breath. You watch, we'll be drunk before nightfall."

And then the experts took over. A brief presentation on the nature of the disaster-prevention program. A run-down on the structure of the sessions for the next five days, with an analysis of the role of Control, the Cabinet, and the Opposition, and an introduction of the participants. As each name was read and the individual stood, Harrington whispered a word or two.

From the Rand Corporation. Japanese businessman. Jewish arms merchant. From the Pentagon. The State Department. Italian scientist. Consultant—probably an agent for the CIA. Terrorism expert from South Africa. Professor of Sociology, from Holland. Former instructor of Hazardous Incident Training for the Saudi Petroleum Institute, a German national. Mercenary—former member of the Army Aviation Task Force, the "Night Stalkers." Retired ambassador to Honduras. French Journalist. Senior analyst for the Institute for Food and Development Policy. Risk analyst—heavy into game theory, a Canadian. And on and on. With rare exceptions, Harrington seemed to know everyone.

"This is not the first time we've done this," he whispered, by way of explanation.

When his own name was called, Harrington elevated himself a few feet and then sank back down. "Clinical Professor of Trauma Surgery," he said.

And then, after several more names, it was Stanek's turn and as he sat down, he leaned over before Harrington could speak and in his best British accent said, "Bloody *dam* fool," pleased with himself at the pun.

Following the introductions and a ten-minute break, there came a series of twenty-minute speeches by local experts who discussed everything one might ever want to know about Paraguay—the history and geography of the country, its society and environment, the effect of migration and urbanization, the role of minority groups and religion in the life of the country, education, health and welfare, the economy (including, as sub-topics, labor, industry, agriculture, energy, and services), and finally in a single presentation the governmental system, the armed forces, public order, and internal security, all covered by a judge with a staccato voice that grated on Stanek's nerves.

Each participant also received a handbook detailing Paraguay's techni-cal and natural resources, its infrastructure, administrative organization, and military assets.

By the time the afternoon session came to a conclusion, Stanek was exhausted, his head ringing with assorted facts and details. He'd hoped to take a brief nap before meeting the Sosas, but now, given the late hour, it appeared out of the question.

To make matters worse, before anyone could leave, General Bernardo Paredes, head of Control, corralled the eleven members of the Cabinet and informed them that each should be prepared to speak for a few minutes the next morning on his or her area of expertise. And then he invited both the Cabinet and the Opposition to a cocktail hour at the Ministry of Foreign Affairs. Shuttle busses, he said, were waiting to transport the participants to the Ministry, or, if they wished to walk, the Ministry was located just a few blocks away on Calle Montevideo near the corner with Calle Presidente Franco.

As they were shuffling out of the auditorium, Stanek caught Harrington by the arm. "Listen, Benjamin, I'm skipping out. No one'll miss me. I have another appointment tonight and I need to get back to my room first. I promised my sister I'd call her and I haven't got around to it yet."

Eyebrows cocked, Harrington turned a jaundiced eye toward him. "An appointment tonight? With the female variety?"

Stanek shook his head. "Just some people I met."

Harrington's voice changed. "Well, I'd be careful about fraternizing with the natives and all that. Might get you in a spot of trouble—and Kohlbert's not around to dig you out, you know."

Stanek hesitated, then said, "Nothing to worry about. I'll see you here bright and early tomorrow morning."

Chapter Fifteen

Padre Pedro Guzman, a priest from the parish of Santísima Trinidad, descended from the truck—a yellow Mercedes Benz ten-wheeler with a load of cotton—within walking distance of the Penitenciaria Nacional de Tacumbú off Calle Mejico in the southern outskirts of the capital. As the vehicle pulled away, leaving a trail of dust in the air, the padre smiled at the names engraved in silver over the two mudflaps at the rear of the vehicle: Patricia and Gabriela.

The driver's wife and mistress, he thought, and then felt guilty at his presumption of moral turpitude. Perhaps, God willing, they were the man's two daughters.

Fixing his biretta squarely on his head, Padre Guzman walked south toward the penitentiary, eyes downcast but spirits soaring. The late afternoon sun, still high in the sky, beat down upon his shoulders—a trifling burden; in a few moments he would be in the presence of the Church's martyrs, good men who had committed no crime other than loving, perhaps too much, their country. On earth they dwelt in the company of murders and thieves, in heaven they would sit on the right hand of God. In the kingdom of God the tyrant.

He blinked in shock. What was he thinking? *Blasphemy!* Was even his own brain becoming perverted by the propaganda of General Zancon? The president, the man his soldiers called *El Tigre*, ordained by God to rule, God's agent on earth. No, he refused to accept that! Padre Guzman had learned long ago never to trust those who claimed to have God on their side. They usually had God on their lips, but the devil in their hearts and minds.

Christ as King. Christ as Lord. Christ as tyrant.

Why did these evil thoughts spring unbidden to his mind? Was the devil mocking his devotion? He crossed himself and said an *Ave Maria*.

A horn blast from behind startled him and he stepped suddenly to the side of the road, slipping into a mossy ditch. He heard laughter and looked up to see a man leaning out of the front passenger window of a Ford Fairlane. The other windows were darkly tinted and reflected the sun's glare, hiding the interior from view.

"Padre, may we offer you a ride?"

A mocking tone. The devil's voice.

He shook his head. Thugs. What did they want with him? "Thank you. I need the exercise."

He stepped back onto the roadway and began to walk, his eyes fixed on the reedy verge, but the car followed along at his own pace. In the late afternoon air, he could hear the hum of insects and the occasional croak of a swamp frog. The air vibrated with light and color.

"Padre Guzman, we have a message for you."

He stopped and faced the vehicle, feeling suddenly dizzy. "Do I know you?" he asked.

The man chuckled. "We know you. We have a message for you."

"For me?" He did not know what else to say, fear tightening his vocal cords.

"A message for you to pass on to one of your flock." The man gestured forward toward the penitentiary in the distance. "One of your lost sheep."

The priest straightened, trying to present a brave front. "I am a messenger of God, not of men." If they were government agents, he refused to take the bait.

The man laughed again. "This *is* a message from God."

The priest said nothing.

"You know, a message like those in the Bible: The day of judgement is approaching, prepare to meet your redeemer, something like that."

Padre Guzman shook his head, then turned away and began to walk toward the penitentiary, head bowed. He mumbled a prayer, fingers fumbling for his rosary.

The Ford crept along beside him. "Give the message to Francisco."

The priest's heart leapt into his throat.

"To Francisco Rojas de Alquijana." As he spoke the name, for emphasis, the man whacked the priest across the back with a stick.

Padre Guzman stumbled, eyes opening in shock, ears ringing from the blow. Alquijana was under heavy guard by elite troops loyal only to the president. The day before, the army had moved him to a secret military base. None of the prison guards knew where. The police must not find Alquijana before he could be liberated by the people.

The padre heard laughter ... the sound of doors opening ... the soft padding of feet in the dirt ...

Another blow across the back. Tears sprang to his eyes. His legs turned weak and he fell to his knees.

Mother of God, no!

A lash across his legs. A kick to the ribs. He covered his head and whimpered, eyes shut, as the blows continued to rain down.

My God, what did they want? *Francisco* ... Francisco was no longer at Tacumbú. If he told them that, would they stop the beating?

A blow to the neck, another at the base of his spine. He twitched in agony, stabs of pain wiping out conscious thought.

He knew they were still beating him, knew he would die if they didn't soon stop. Deep inside he could hear words. Knew he was screaming.

Do not tell them. Do not tell them where Francisco is.

Words—were they theirs or his? Was he crying out? Was he confessing the truth? But how could he? He knew nothing. Only that Alquijana was no longer there.

A babble of voices ... threats mingled with shouts ... cries confused with words of horror ... screams of pain.

Dear God, help me!

Francisco Rojas de Alquijana ... they mustn't find him.

Chapter Sixteen

Colonel Hector Ibarras slammed the white handset into its cradle and swore. "That tight-lipped *hijo de puta*."

The telephone's bell vibrated from the blow, its tinny sound setting his nerves yet further on edge. Maybe one of these day's Antelco would upgrade its equipment.

He'd just gotten off the line with the *Jefe del Servicio de la Inteligencia del Ejército*, Major General Alberto Campos, his military counterpart, head of the Army's intelligence service. Campos, a stump of a man with the nasty temperament of a spoiled child, had refused to reveal the location of the rebel leader Alquijana, despite Ibarras's protestations that the police needed to interrogate the man.

How could he maintain internal security, he'd asked, if he couldn't question the opposition's leaders? Just the week before, after grilling a member of the underground who'd been in contact with *Sendero Luminoso* guerrillas in Lima, his agents had foiled a plot to bomb the oil refinery at Villa Elisa, the only one set up for Saharan-blend oil, imported from Algeria. The government owned sixty percent of Petropar and their facilities were a common target of those wishing to foment discord.

"That's 7,500 barrels a day we would have lost," he yelled. Who knew what Alquijana was planning through his emissaries? The rebel leader had methods of contacting his followers, even while in prison. Next they'd go after a power plant, or the cement factory at Vallemí, or one of Acepar's steel mills, or the new port at Villeta. Did Campos want to bear the responsibility for that?

But the major general had been adamant, a blustery stream of objections pouring from his mouth. Alquijana's present location was a presidential secret. Only General Zancon could release that information. He himself had nothing more to say. They'd rung off without exchanging courtesies.

Staring at the telephone in frustration, Colonel Ibarras stroked his mustache and then ran his hand through his cropped black hair. Damn generals. He should have been promoted to the rank himself long ago. For public purposes, Ibarras was nominally assigned to the Presidential Escort Service, under army command, but in reality he was head of the Department of Investigations under the Ministry of the Interior, which meant the secret police. Senior army officers, members of the "Old Guard," blocked the promotions of the younger officers whenever possible, especially those assigned to the police, with whom they competed for power. It was only one of the many reasons for harboring resentment.

He snorted. *A presidential secret.* What self-respecting leader kept secrets from his police?

Nothing else to do then but talk to *El Tigre* himself.

The colonel picked up the phone, punched a button, and spoke to the regiment's operator, telling her to try the President's office in the Government Palace first and then, if he wasn't there, his home.

Better to telephone than to stop by, even though the President's residence was located less than a kilometer away on Avenida Mariscal Lopez, not far from the United States Embassy compound and the Policlinico Policial Rigoberto Caballero, the police hospital, where political prisoners were sometimes taken for interrogation. But the President's staff did not like people appearing unannounced, not even members of the government.

Ibarras switched on the radio in his office and tuned in to "La Voz del Coloradismo," a program broadcast daily on a government-owned station by the leading Partito Colorado. With the volume turned low, he perused the latest reports of his field agents, concentrating on those dealing with the rally in the Plaza de los Heroes that afternoon.

A half-hour later, when the operator had still not been able to track down the President, Ibarras told her he was going to the Policlínico and that if she reached Zancon, she was to patch the call through to the command post in the basement.

He had been informed of the arrest of the afternoon rally's main speaker—Padre Ramon Ibañez, a meddlesome priest who only recently had taken on the mantle of political messiah. Best to deal with his sort immediately, he thought, before they became well-known, especially in the international community. If the police were lucky, that piece of cockroach shit might know the whereabouts of Alquijana. The Church would not admit it, but they had their own network of agents—priests who were allowed in the jails and penitentiaries to confess the thieves and murders and rapists. The more astute of the common criminals usually knew the location of political prisoners, even those kept in solitary confinement.

Colonel Ibarras was in the basement of the police clinic when the call came through. The President's assistant was on the line but in a few moments Ibarras was speaking to *El Tigre* himself.

After his report on the unauthorized rally in the Plaza de los Héroes, the colonel told the general about the arrest of Padre Ramon Ibañez. "We will interrogate him throughout this weekend, your Excellency. I expect we will have to use the whole range of techniques available to us to learn anything useful."

The message was clear: the priest would be tortured and—if that didn't work—drugged. One way or the other, they would extract whatever information he carried around in his head.

"Fine," the general said. "I spoke to the Archbishop just this evening. He said nothing about this priest. I suspect the Church will be happy if we hear no more about him."

Encouraged by this, Ibarras moved on to the real reason for his call. "I spoke to General Campos about interrogating another prisoner currently in military hands. He requested that I contact you first for permission."

"Who's the prisoner?"

"Alquijana."

There was a pause on the other end of the line, then the general cleared his throat. "I have my own plans for Alquijana," he said. "We must move carefully in these matters. Ambassador Compton has been applying pressure recently. Threatening to cut off aid from the United States if violations of human rights continue."

"Forgive my words, your Excellency, but those assholes are going to stick their dicks out so far that one of these days we're going to cut them off."

The general laughed. "Yes, well, for now, I don't want to hear anything about Alquijana. He has a following in the United States. The Comité de Iglesias is starting to pressure their government on his behalf. Before we know it, Amnistía Internacional will try to stick its nose in."

"Your Excellency, the turd is a threat to our stability. There are many who would like to see him free—even if only in exile."

"Don't worry about him, Colonel. Alquijana is in good hands. General Paredes will take care of him."

"And you trust Paredes? The 1st Army Corps?" There was a touch of incredulity in Ibarras's voice, tempered just short of disrespect. The implication was clear—the last two coups d'état had been carried out by generals of the army's most powerful corps; it was how General Zancon himself had come to power. "Forgive my frank speech, your Excellency."

The President's voice remained mellow. "For the time being, Colonel, General Paredes is happy with the fourth gold star on his shoulder boards." Paredes had recently been promoted from *General de Division* to *General de Ejército*.

Ibarras repressed a snort but couldn't help saying, "And the Church is happy the Virgin of Asunción is an honorary marshal in the army, but that hasn't kept their priests from joining forces with the opposition."

The colonel paused. He did not want to suggest that Paredes was conspiring against the President. Dangerous waters there. Better to change the subject—and quickly. He might as well make sure he had a free hand with Padre Ibañez and that he hadn't misunderstood the President.

"Are you content, your Excellency, that I do what is necessary with this priest we've arrested?"

"Do what you have to. If the Archbishop complains—well, we can handle that." The President spoke to someone in the background and then came on the line again. "My assistant was reminding me about your promotion, Colonel. How does *General de Brigada* sound to you? That should make it easier to deal with the army generals."

"Thank you, your Excellency." His voice held joy, but he did not yet feel it in his heart.

Was there a suggestion of suspicion in *El Tigre*'s action? The President had talked about satisfying Paredes with a fourth star. Soon Ibarras's own shoulder boards would change from three stars above a chevron to two stars above a wreath. A pay-off for a job well-done? Or a bribe to keep his ambition in check?

If the latter, *El Tigre* had underestimated him. His ambition was not limited to rank insignia. His goal was the very top and nothing short of that would satisfy him.

And no one—native or foreigner, American ambassador or army commander—was going to stand in his way.

Chapter Seventeen

The street in front of the Parrillada Aregua was unpaved and heavily rutted and the passing traffic, though forced to a crawl, threw up a fine layer of red dust that coated the cars parked just off the roadway and drifted in as far as the iron railing around the restaurant's outdoor dining section.

At first, there was a steady stream of traffic—motor scooters, ox-drawn carts, large trucks with wood-stave sidewalls, four-door sedans, battered pickups, bicycles, pedestrians—*Asunceros* heading home from work. Once darkness fell, however, the traffic thinned out.

Renato Sosa parked the family car, a Toyota station wagon, at the end of a row of vehicles and the passengers disgorged and stretched their legs. There were seven of them—Renato and his wife Pina, their two children, Eliana and Jose, and then the Americans—Diane Lang, Walter

Stanek, and Dink Denton, who at the last minute had asked to be picked up. Stanek had been squeezed in next to Dink, with José on his lap and Eliana to his right against the window.

On the restaurant's patio, each table was protected from the elements by a separate thatched canopy that did little, however, to cut the heat and humidity. White Christmas tree lights were strung on poles for illumination, and in one corner near the kitchen, which was a low concrete block building with a pantiled roof and gaps where windows should have been, stood the one concession to modernity—an electrified bug zapper. What the bug zapper didn't catch was hunted down by the swallows that nested under the tiles.

Behind the restaurant stood a row of tung trees, their lustrous white blossoms glowing eerily in the twilight, and to each side lay kilns and small factories—mostly tanneries according to Renato Sosa, and between them scattered stands of eucalyptus trees.

The clientele, Stanek saw, was mixed—lower class workers, mostly Indians and mestizos, several wearing wide-brimmed straw hats and baseball caps and sipping *yerba maté* through metal straws, and middle class families from the city, the women in print dresses, the men in slacks and white shirts. All were talking animatedly as they sipped their tea or drank from cold bottles of beer.

As the Sosas found their places around a large rectangular table, Stanek sat down across from Diane Lang, even though there was an empty seat beside her. She was a woman who stood out in a crowd, drawing the eyes of all the men and most of the women. She wore a simple skirt and blouse, open at the neck, with a necklace of black tourmaline and matching earrings. A hint of kohl around her eyes, pale cheeks, and red lipstick. An underlip that begged to be sucked.

Whoa! What was he thinking? God he was getting horny. Just the day before she'd come across as a pain in the ass. Time to get laid if she was already starting to look good. Not that she wasn't attractive, just the opposite—it was just that she hadn't liked him and he hadn't liked her.

"Anything controversial we can discuss?" he asked.

She looked at him, her eyes narrowing. "Why do you say that?"

"After what happened last night, I just assumed we'd disagree on most things."

Dink Denton took the empty seat by Diane. "What happened last night?"

"On most things?" she said, ignoring Dink. She was peeved at Stanek's attitude. She'd already tried to apologize to him in the car for her brusqueness of the night before. "We've only talked together once."

"Yeah, and you called me an asshole."

"Hey, I thought you guys were friends," Dink said.

Diane shook her head. "Acquaintances." She stared at Stanek. "Maybe you were an asshole."

"That's a dirty word," Eliana said.

Stanek laughed. "You're not supposed to understand it. Did they teach you that in school?"

"On the streets in the States," she said. "Lesson number one for any foreigner."

Renato Sosa interrupted to ask if they minded if he ordered for everyone.

"Not at all," Stanek said. "Just make sure it's a feast. We have some hungry people here."

"Yeah," Dink said, "my stomach's been carrying on a conversation with itself for the last hour or two."

"Well, I hope it doesn't grumble as much as Mr. Stanek," Diane said.

Stanek grinned. She was one prickly pear. "Call me Walter," he said.

While Renato Sosa talked to the waiter, Stanek turned to Dink Denton. "Apparently you repaid my debt to Dr. Lang. She says she saved my life last night and it sounds like you saved hers." On the drive to the restaurant, Dink had told them about the incident in the park that afternoon.

Diane glared at him. "I didn't say I saved your life. I said I helped you. And so did the Sosas."

"I'm very grateful."

She wondered if he was being sarcastic. Last night he'd blamed her for everything, and it didn't look like he was prepared to forget.

Pina Sosa said, "So what are the three of you doing in Paraguay?"

For a moment as they traded glances no one responded.

"I'm a professor of German," Diane finally said. "I'm here to read a paper at a convention." She took a deep breath. "The International Association for the Study of German Language and Literature has an international meeting every three years, each time in some place different. This year it's here in Asunción at the Catholic University."

"What's the topic of your paper?"

"You're not the first to ask that," Diane said, looking into Pina Sosa's attentive eyes. She was a woman of medium height with short black hair and dark eyes, well-dressed but not quite as thin as her husband. "I was grilled by a policeman at the airport before they let me in. He didn't seem to like my topic. I'm going to be talking about a Dutch priest named Menno Simons, the founder of the Mennonites."

José perked up. "We're studying them in school now." He swung his feet, which didn't quite reach the floor, his voice high and excited. "We had a minister from Fernheim come to speak to us. And next week we visit the Iglesia Evangélica de los Hermanos Mennonitas in Vista Alegre."

Diane was impressed. "Where's Vista Alegre?"

The boy shrugged his shoulders and looked at his mother.

"It's a suburb," she said. "An area just south of the Avenida Eusebio Ayala, which runs east toward Fernando de la Mora."

Diane nodded, even though she wasn't familiar with the area. "After I read my paper I'm going to visit the Mennonite settlements in the Chaco." She addressed the boy. "Have you ever been there?"

José shook his head. "No, but I know what it is. We call it the Infierno

Verde," he said, proud of his knowledge. "The Green Hell."

"Good for you," she said.

In the gathering darkness, a breeze gusted across the soft night, coming from the inky expanse of the bay, cradling the smell of swamp grass and stagnant water, with an occasional waft of scented trees and flowers. On the way to the restaurant, Diane had seen lush vegetation—wild oranges, limes, grapefruit, and tangerines, papaya and guava, hibiscus, scarlet verbena, and a blue flower no one in the car could identify with the fragrance of fresh-crushed peaches. At dusk, in the outskirts of the city, the scents swirled into a heady perfume.

There was a lull in the conversation as two waiters arrived with the first course—a large plate of appetizers: *croquetas* of chicken and beef, *empanadas* stuffed with cheese, large green olives, hot *chipa guazú*, a type of corn bread, followed a few minutes later by *bori-bori*, a vegetable soup with meat, cheese and corn balls. While they ate, Stanek told them what he did for a living in the States.

"We have a lot of dams in our country," Eliana said when he finished. "We export electricity. A clean energy. General Zancon is very proud of that."

"It doesn't come without its faults," her father said. "Don't believe all the propaganda you hear from the government."

"What do you think, *señor* Stanek?" the girl asked.

Walter shrugged. "To get electricity you have to build dams. And dams have numerous effects on the environment."

She continued to press him. "Like what?"

Stanek grinned. "You want my lecture on dams? Come to the University of Arizona some day."

"Hey, professor," Dink said, "we can't all be students, if you catch what I'm saying. Clue us in."

"If he keeps talking," Diane said, "he won't get to eat." She pointed at Stanek's bowl. "You haven't touched a drop. It'll get cold."

"Thank you, mother," he said, and she bristled but said nothing in response.

Oh hell, he hadn't meant to snap at her. Stanek took a bite by way of appeasement, wiped his lips with a paper napkin, then placed it on the table beneath his knife. The breeze ruffled the thatched canopy overhead.

"When you build a dam, you have to consider several factors. First of all, people will have to emigrate out of the flood plain. Sometimes even wild animals have to be captured and carried to high ground. Otherwise, as the water rises, they wind up starving to death on little islands and in trees—or they drown, if they last that long.

"Then you have to consider the loss of products like wood—all the trees that aren't logged, agricultural goods if there are any farms in the area—beef, for example, and any rural industries that might be lost.

"Along with the loss of natural vegetation, you face several possibly negative factors—things like the alteration of rainfall, the evaporation of water in the reservoir, the proliferation of sick animals, the loss of fauna, occasionally even some unexpected flooding because of the water that's held back. And then you have the changes in velocity of water in the rivers. That affects aquatic life. There's usually an accumulation of sediment, with a modification in the turbidity of the water."

He took a breath and grinned. "Am I boring you?"

"Not at all," Pina Sosa said.

"Yeah, to death," Dink said. "Sorry I asked." But he was grinning. "Go on, professor. Tell us more." He reached for an *empanada*. "Leaves more food for the rest of us hungry bears."

Stanek drained the last of his first bottle of beer. He was going to have a hard time keeping up with Dink, who appeared to be a voracious eater and drinker.

"Here in Paraguay, once Yacyretá and Corpus are added to Itaipú, there'll be three dams within five hundred kilometers of each other." He looked at Eliana. "That's going to destroy an entire aquatic ecosystem and replace it with another. It'll affect the movement of fish and the aquatic life in tributaries, streams, and lagoons. It may even cause the proliferation of more aggressive carnivorous fish. And then you have the effect of electrical transmissions—the line routes and the electricity itself. It's a form of radioelectric contamination, with electromagnetic effects as well."

He looked around the table. "I'll stop there. It starts getting a little technical."

"Is that why you're in Paraguay?" Renato Sosa wanted to know. He'd loosened his tie and looked more relaxed. The waiters had arrived with the *asado*—platters of grilled meat—and with plastic paniers of *mandioca*, a form of cassava bread. In a moment, more plates arrived—vegetables and *pirayú*, a yellow fish, for those who didn't want meat.

Stanek shoved aside his bowl of soup, half-eaten, and considered the question. "I'm here to advise the government on the Corpus project, but I'm also taking part in a disaster-prevention program. We're going to be doing a risk assessment—analyzing the probabilities of man-made and natural disasters and their effects on the country's infrastructure."

Renato Sosa leaned forward, legs tucked under his chair. "Is that a government project, too?"

"Not really." Stanek hesitated. "It's run by an engineering company in Texas called Samcon—their risk management section."

"Risk management. That sounds political."

"I wouldn't know," Stanek said. He grinned. "I'm apolitical myself. I say the individual comes before the state."

Diane shook her head in amazement. "You're apolitical. That's a great statement. You come to a country, you help the ruling party solidify their position, and you say you're not political?"

"Who says I'm helping anyone solidify their position?"

"You'd have to be blind not to see that," she said. "Risk management can just as easily be used to oppress the people. Revolution's a risk, right? You're helping the current government stay in power."

Stanek didn't reply. He was thinking about Greg Brown's reference to man-made disasters and to terrorists.

Renato Sosa spoke, his voice calm. "So you have no politics, *señor* Stanek, and yet you say the individual comes before the state."

Walter grinned. "I'm an individualist but I vote Democratic."

"Now that's a miracle," Diane said. "I had you pegged for a Republican."

Dink swallowed a chunk of roast beef. "Women don't peg men," he said loudly. He'd already gone through four bottles of beer, the empties clustered in front of his plate. His mouth curled into a crooked grin. "Men peg women."

The Sosas appeared not to understand and no one else said anything.

"So," Pina Sosa said, "why are you visiting our country, *señor* Denton?"

Dink licked his lips. He'd just stripped a chicken leg of its meat and took a swallow of his fifth beer before answering; the waiters were keeping him well-stocked. "Just bumming around."

"What do you do for a living?" Diane asked.

"Oh," Dink paused and looked thoughtful. "I've worked as a mechanic, done a little carpentry, spent a year or two in the oil fields, mostly as a roughneck, worked on a cement gang for a big construction company, drove a Hyster in a cannery, odd jobs here and there. I fly cargo occasionally. Used to be a helicopter pilot."

"In Vietnam?"

Dink snorted. "Do I look that old? In Panama and Kuwait."

"What'd you fly?" Stanek asked. "Transport?"

"Hell, no. I flew the Apache. Wore that AH64A patch with *Hounds From Hell* on it. Got the Purple Heart. Took a hit from a 23mm shell and survived. After that anything's easy."

"Sounds like you can do a bit of everything," Stanek said.

"Yeah, and if I had tits on my back I'd be fun to dance with."

Diane didn't hear the coarse comment, her mind elsewhere, stuck on something Dink had said. So he flew cargo, she was thinking. Did that mean drugs? She was having great luck this trip. Who was she going to get involved with next? "Were you shot down behind the lines?" she asked.

"Hey, the Apache took a shell and I wound up with a few fragments here and there but she didn't go down. That chopper's built to take a shitload of hits and make it back to base. Hell, I've been closer to death working in construction. Could've died three or four times." He gestured in Stanek's direction. "You know what that's like."

Stanek nodded. "Especially if you're young and foolhardy." He was thinking of Kohlbert, the former plumber, canning out on the skyscrapers of New York.

"Hell, that's what I was all right." Dink's voice had grown rough and he'd hunched down so his head seemed to rest on his massive shoulders. "But I ain't afraid of dying. Wasn't afraid then, ain't afraid now."

Stanek said, "Sometimes when I think about the reality of dying, I freeze with panic. You know, when you consider that it *has* to happen one day ... to us all ... that every single one of us some day is going to die—" He paused, eyes locked in a middle distance. "When I was younger, I never thought it would happen to me. Now that I'm forty-three I see the reality of death. It can be pretty scary—that abyss, the moment of crossing over."

Not many men in their forties would admit that, Diane thought, but she admired him for saying it. To her, the thought of death sometimes came as a relief. She leaned toward him across the table. "But you can also think that every single person who lived before us died. You won't be the only one. Everyone else has had to face it, too."

He pursed his cheeks. "Sometimes that helps, sometimes it doesn't."

"Hell," Dink said. "It's as natural to die as to be born—and who's to say the one is any worse than the other? I say just go with the flow. You're alive, so enjoy the moment. The moment is as beautiful as all eternity."

"I didn't know you were so profound, Dink," Diane said.

He grinned. "Read that somewhere," he said. "I'm about as deep as a cow pie on a Kansas prairie. Hey, but it don't take brains to say enjoy what you got."

There were grunts of acknowledgment. Eliana plucked at her blouse, which was open at the neck where a gold chain with a medallion of the Virgin Mary hung. At fifteen, her body had reached maturity and she was taller and prettier than her mother. While he ate, Dink's eyes had wandered to her breasts and then up to her full lips and dark eyes, both lightly made-up. Half his age but already a real enchantress. Probably still a virgin, too. She'd been hanging on his words ever since he'd talked about getting shot in Iraq.

"How'd you almost die working in construction?" she wanted to know.

Dink shrugged. He'd had his scrapes in life. Construction work was just one of them. There was a lot he could tell her about.

He wiped his lips and raised a finger. "I was working in a cement gang in Chicago once. Got knocked off the thirteenth-floor of a high-rise. Big steel-frame apartment complex. Crane operator fell asleep and swung a quarter-ton bucket of wet concrete into me."

"Were you hurt badly?"

"Hell, no. I wasn't hurt at all. I reached around in midair, grabbed the rim of the bucket, swung out about fifty fuckin' feet, came back in with the bucket and dropped smack dab in the middle of a fresh patch of wet concrete."

Her eyes widened.

"That was nothing," Dink said, winking at her. "I had me a sixty-pound bucket of clip-ties in my arms once and fell three stories. Stepped on a plank that only went about halfway between two scaffolds."

"That time you were hurt," she said, laughing.

He shook his head. "That weren't no hurt, girl." Playing with her, emphasizing the jive talk. Most of the people he'd worked with in Chicago were Blacks. "I landed on the bucket, dented the side, cracked two ribs, lost consciousness for about a minute when my head hit the floor, then got up and went back to work. That's how you had to do it or you'd get your pink slip."

"What's a pink slip?"

"Well, it ain't what you're wearing under that skirt." He bent down, pretending to look under her skirt and she blushed. "No, they'd fire your ass. You'd be SOL."

He could see that threw her, too. He grinned. "Shit out of luck, as we say."

He swallowed a piece of bread, washed it down with a swig of beer and said, "'Nother time, I was going down a ladder on some forms we'd just poured for the wall of a gymnasium. Had this damn heavy tool box on a strap over my shoulder. There was another guy right below me and the ladder was one of these makeshift jobs with a rung missing. The other guy didn't see it and slipped and fell. Never uttered a sound. No scream, no nothing. Just whoosh and he was gone."

"It could've been you," Eliana said. "If you were first, right?"

"Hey, it was me," Dink said. "Soon enough. I never paid no attention to the sound he made. Didn't see him. I slipped at the same spot and fell fifty feet or so myself. Still hanging on to the tool box. Hell, I broke *seven* rungs with my left arm before one rung finally held. I climbed down the rest of the way. Found out my buddy was dead." He snapped his fingers. "It can happen like that. That's why I don't save any money."

He shook his head vigorously. "Suck it dry, that's my motto. Wisest words you're ever gonna hear is spend, don't save. Money should slip through your fingers like mercury from a broken thermometer. Don't even *try* to grasp it. Don't do you no good to die rich."

"My daddy's rich," Eliana said. "He's a lawyer."

"Is that what you do?" Dink asked, raising his voice. Several other diners lifted their heads and looked in their direction. He screwed up his face in a puzzled look. "Excuse my Latin, but I always said the only person dumber than a lawyer's a doctor. I didn't figure you for either."

There was a moment of silence and Dink said, "No offense. Just a joke." He leaned back in the chair and spread his arms in a gesture of submission. A big grin creased his face. "If we didn't have lawyers, there'd be no courts." He guffawed noisily, slapping his belly with both hands.

Diane cleared her throat. Dink was her guest and he was getting drunk—no, he was *already* drunk. Renato Sosa had a tight smile on his face, but she could sense his discomfort. She pushed her plate away and said, "Are you in private practice?"

Sosa shook his head. "Have you heard of the MIT?"

"The university?"

He looked startled. "No, here in Asunción. It stands for the Movimiento Intersindical de Trabajadores."

"Sounds like a union," Stanek said. He was trying to signal the waiter for a glass of water. Dink had twisted around and was staring at the other parties as if he'd lost interest in the conversation.

Renato Sosa nodded. "The Inter-Union Workers Movement. I was one of the founding members back in '85. Today I represent the workers. The government has been arresting and harassing many of our members."

Diane said, "Why's that?"

"We're usually in conflict with the CPT—that's the Confederación Paraguaya de Trabajadores, another union. But their leaders are all appointed by General Zancon. They do not stand up for the peasants. Until we came along, the Church was their only voice. I'm trying to get one of our representatives on the Council of State." He shrugged. "Right now the Council is an assembly of trained monkeys."

Diane was listening intently. "I read somewhere that the Church has supported much of the opposition to the regime. Is that true?"

Renato Sosa pondered that for a moment, head waggling. "The Church has done what it can but …" He waved his hands. "The Archbishop is on the Council. He's failed to play the political role we hoped he would. He feels he has to protect the Church's interests in Paraguay."

Pina Sosa said, "You have to understand the distinction. It's the parish priests who protect the interests of the Paraguayan people—their parishoners. That is different from protecting the Church."

José piped up. "Did you tell them about Padre Guzman?"

Dink seemed to come awake again, swinging around to join in. "Is he the one we heard speaking at the rally today?"

Pina Sosa shook her head. "I don't think so. He's our parish priest in Santísima Trinidad. I went to mass this evening and we had a substitute priest. He said Padre Guzman had been badly beaten and was in the Policlínico Cristo Rey."

"Who did it?" Stanek asked.

The Sosas traded glances. "The police, we think."

"Do you have death squads in Paraguay?"

"We have a dictatorship that calls itself a Republic with an elected President," Renato Sosa said. "Only no one runs against him. The opposition parties are usually outlawed until a few days before elections. There is no time to organize. Our candidates always lose."

Pina Sosa put her hand on her husband's, her eyes alarmed. "Renato—"

He shrugged. "They're Americans, Pina. I'm tired of hiding my politics." He paused while the waiter approached with a dessert of flan. Another man carried a tray with a bottle of *caña*, a local rum, and small glasses. Renato Sosa waited until they were alone again before speaking.

"In Paraguay, the government allows its senior military officers to participate in very profitable smuggling activities. Our country is famous for it. Goods from all around the world are smuggled in. Our banks are used to launder the money of drug cartels from other nations. The Bolivians use us as a transit point for some of their coca. And now we have our own production in the Chaco—laboratories operated with military collaboration. If you talk to the government, we produce cotton, soybeans, tobacco, coffee, sugarcane, and oilseeds. They will tell you they have nothing to do with drugs. They will say the country is one of the largest oilseed exporters in the world—cottonseed oil, soybean, peanut, coconut, palm, castor bean, flaxseed, sunflower-seed oil, petit-grain oil, tung oil. But coca? No. And when the opposition speaks, when we try to tell the truth, we are silenced. Our newspapers are confiscated on the streets. Our people disappear. Paraguay has one of the worst records in Latin America for violations of human rights. And to be honest, in part, it's you Americans who are responsible."

Stanek sighed. "Conspiracy theories—that's why I prefer to be naïve."

Diane opened her mouth to speak, frowning, but Renato Sosa responded before she could.

"Your naïveté is symptomatic of your culture. The United States loves to play dumb when it deals with its repressive clients. Your government sends in massive military aid—not just to us but all around the world—and invests money in training Paraguayan police forces—and then sees no connection between that and the resulting political imprisonments, the torture, the disappearances." He paused for a breath, visibly trying to calm himself.

"If the training and arms were traced to the Cubans or the Soviets or Qaddafi, you would be outraged."

"That's what I was about to say," Diane interjected. "No one ever asks why the liberation movements always depend on the Soviet Union or China for aid—or even on Libya."

Dink leaned back, crossing his massive arms over his chest, biceps bulging. "What's your theory?"

"It's simple when you consider it. The West refuses to support them, so who do they have to turn to? The East. And who do we always align ourselves with? With regimes of terror like those of Argentina, Chile, El Salvador, Guatemala, South Africa."

"I thought you were a professor of German," Stanek said.

Diane's eyes flashed. "My minor was Spanish, not that it matters. It doesn't take much to be interested in your own hemisphere."

"I have trouble getting beyond continents," Stanek said, smiling. "North America has its share of problems."

Renato Sosa gestured around the enclosed patio. "Most of these people are opposed to Zancon," he said. "This restaurant is a popular hang-out for leftists. Why? Because most of us have our stories of oppression." He paused for a moment, his eyes sweeping the crowd and finding a tall figure leaning on a timbered door jamb near the kitchen.

"Take the owner there. His brother was tortured to death at Emboscada. The government calls it a correctional institute but it is a concentration camp. In Minas-Cué." He raised his left hand, which Stanek for the first time noticed was deformed. "The police did this to me in the Comisaria Tercera here in Asunción. The Third Precinct. We call it the *sepulcro de los vivos*. You feel lucky if you come out alive."

"Renato—" Pina Sosa reached for her husband's arm. "Not so loud." A man at a nearby table had been staring at them. "Others are listening."

"I am tired of silence," he said. "When they beat our priests—" His voice fell away.

In the quiet they could hear the sound of a helicopter, the on-again off-again thump of the rotor blades.

Renato Sosa sat up, alarm visible in his face. The sudden noise of car engines came to them, motors revved high. A cloud of dust.

"What is it, Renato?" Pina asked, her voice quavering. Other people were getting to their feet and the waiters were scurrying for the kitchen. Dink's chair had fallen over backward and he was pulling Diane to her feet.

"A raid," Renato said. "Go, *señor* Stanek."

Dink was already moving toward an exit with Diane at his heels.

"They'll try to arrest everyone." Sosa shoved Stanek in the back, then turned to his wife. "Get the kids, Pina. We'll make a run for it."

Chapter Eighteen

The raid came down hard and fast with commando-like precision. Eight vehicles hit the scene, cutting off all avenues of escape while overhead a police chopper lit up the area with dazzling light. Overpowering force with maximum noise and light for shock effect. The shouts of the troopers as they charged the restaurant's patio gave way to shot gun blasts that shook the air—volleys fired over the heads of the diners to intimidate and quash any thoughts of flight.

In the confusion, amidst cries and screams, could be heard the shouted commands—"Get down!" "On your face!" "Shut those eyes, *cabrón*!" Feet kicked those who were too slow or who tried to look around. "Hit the dirt, *puta*!" "Face down!" "Hands out to the side, *flaco*! Now!"

Those who resisted were clubbed to the ground by men wearing military fatigues with bandanas over their faces. A youth who scaled the railing and tried to run was shot down in the back.

The panic was slowly quelled and the only shouts were those of the police. The diners were stretched out on the ground between the tables, burrowing their heads into the ground.

The police were looking for people they knew, turning them over one by one, photos in hand. They asked for identification, compared IDs with faces. They let some go, others they manacled and shoved into vans.

When they found Renato Sosa, they said, "Take him," and Eliana jumped to her feet and screamed, "No, he's done nothing … *Papá*!"

One of the policemen slapped her in the mouth and tried to shove her back to the ground, but she struggled to her feet and grabbed for her father's legs.

"Take the *vaca machorra*, too," one of the men yelled. "We'll teach her how whores are treated."

Renato Sosa turned and looked beseechingly at his wife. They'd bound a strip of cloth through his mouth and he choked as he tried to speak.

But the girl was already being hustled away toward one of the vans. When Pina Sosa protested, they leveled a pistol at her head and told her to shut up and get out of there.

Renato jerked his head, trying to tell her to leave, and Pina ran for the road, pulling José behind her.

Fifteen feet away, where they'd been forced to the ground, the three Americans were surrounded by militiamen. Dink was the first to be pulled to his feet and he showed some ID that set the men to talking.

"Immunity," Diane heard them say. "A colleague." What was that all about?

Dink gestured to the two of them. *"Son amigos míos."*

"Get the hell out of here, then. Fast!"

"Come on," Dink said, reaching for Diane's hands. "We can go. Get up, Stanek."

"What about the Sosas?" Diane asked.

"Just shut up and follow me. We can't do anything now or we'll get arrested along with the others."

Outside they flagged down a car with an older couple who were fleeing the scene. Dink had to step into the road and literally block the vehicle. "We're Americans," he said in Spanish. "Just take us up the road a ways."

They piled into the back seat and in a minute they were easing their way through people running up the road toward the city, the car's headlights picking up white shirts and blouses, people scattering for the underbrush at the verge of the road as the car approached.

"Just a minute," Diane said. "Wasn't that Pina and Jose?"

"We're not stopping," the driver said. A gray-haired man with bushy eyebrows. "No more room."

Dink leaned over the back seat and gripped the man around the neck with his hand. "Stop the car and let us out," he said, his voice a rough growl.

The driver jammed on his brakes and the three of them piled out and slammed the doors. The driver tore off the minute their feet hit the dirt, raising clouds of dust that shone briefly in the red taillights and then disappeared as the darkness closed in around them. They moved back down the road, calling for Pina, and in a minute she rose from a crouch and said, "*Estoy aquí.* They've taken Renato and Eliana."

Headlights were approaching from the direction of the restaurant, the sound that of a truck motor.

"Get down," Dink said. "Let them pass."

When the police wagon had gone by, they scrambled out of the marsh grass and briers at the side of the road. Stanek had fallen into a patch of thistles and he swore as he carefully extricated himself. On the road again he asked about the Sosa's car.

"I don't have the keys," Pina said. "Renato had them. If we can get home, I can come back tomorrow with my own set."

"If they haven't ripped off the car by then," Dink said. "Why don't we hightail it to your house and I'll come back for the car tonight?"

Pina quickly agreed and they discussed the best way to find a taxi. The restaurant was in the outskirts of the city and the few ranchos, widely scattered and set back from the road, were not likely to have telephones.

"We can walk," Diane said. "When we get to some lights, we'll look for a place with a telephone."

As they moved up the road in the darkness, the sky bright with stars, Stanek turned to Dink. "What'd you show them anyway? Got us out of there pretty quick."

Dink laughed. "My passport and a hundred dollar bill. Those hombres recognized the greenback right off. Guaranteed immunity."

"They called you a colleague," Diane said, her voice sharp.

Dink chuckled. "For a hundred bucks I'd say you were my sister. Those bastards know a bribe when they see one. Makes you an instant *compañero*."

Pina Sosa looked at him but said nothing. In the dark it was impossible to see each other's faces.

"None of the natives tried to bribe them," Diane said.

Stanek jumped to Dink's defense. "How do you know? They were letting some of them go, too."

No one said anything in response.

An hour later, they had managed to find a man who agreed to drive them to the Sosa's residence in exchange for ten thousand guaranies, just over ten dollars.

At the house, Diane went in to comfort Pina and Jose, while the two men returned with the driver, who let them off near the restaurant.

The police vans were gone and the area was dark, the restaurant closed down. They found the Toyota station wagon by moonlight.

"No damage that I can see," Dink said. "Time for us mudchuckers to vamoose. I'll take the wheel."

They drove with the windows down, the night silent, the only sound the car's springs as they bounced over ruts in the dirt roads before finally finding a stretch of pavement. The car's headlights stabbed into the darkness, blinded them to all but the thin ribbon of asphalt.

Stanek tried to lick his lips. His mouth was caked with dust and when he swallowed he felt grit between his teeth. The hot wind sucked at his clothes, drying the perspiration under his arms. Getting dehydrated, he thought, skin stretched tight over his skull, eyes losing their moisture. His forehead felt chalky with dust, a prickly dryness that left his skin as taut as baked glaze.

The whine of the car's tires was hypnotic. Exhaustion settled in as the minutes passed. Before he knew it, they had reached the Sosa residence.

Inside, Dink and Stanek washed up. The water felt cool and refreshing. Pina had prepared hot tea, busying herself to lessen the shock. By the time the tea was ready, she had steeled herself for what lay ahead.

"Renato will know what to do," Pina said. "It's Eliana I'm worried about. She's just a girl."

They could see the worry in her eyes and knew what she was thinking. Eliana was just a girl in years, but she was old enough for the soldiers to rape and brutalize her. It had happened to girls much younger than fifteen.

"Where will they take them?" Diane wanted to know.

The cup in Pina's hand rattled as she set it back in the saucer. She took a deep breath to compose herself before speaking. "The *Departamento de Investigaciones* is in the Comisaria Primera in the center of the city. They might have taken Renato there. He's a well-known lawyer. They will accuse him of conspiring against *la granítica unidad del Partito Colorado.* This is not the first time. They will torture him for information on rebel leaders, and then they will let him go with a warning." She swallowed hard. "But sometimes they keep them for months—or years ... and sometimes they disappear. With Eliana—" Pina bit her lip, trying to still a quiver.

"She's just a girl," Diane said. "What can she have done to harm them?"

Pina Sosa stared at her, a panicked look on her face, unable to repress the unbearable scenes of torture conjured up by her imagination.

"They don't need an excuse," Dink said. "They do what they want."

"I'm sure she'll be okay," Stanek said. "Maybe they've already let her go—and if not we can go to the American Embassy in the morning. We can ask them to pressure the government for your daughter's release."

"If I know the Embassy," Dink said. "They'll do diddly squat."

"Well, we can try," Diane said.

"And I have another disaster-prevention session today," Stanek said. "There'll be government officials there. I'll try to get help from them—and from Samcon. They should have some voice, they're working with the government on this program."

Diane set her empty cup and saucer on a credenza across the room and then turned to face the two men, her right hand finding her necklace beneath the open collar of her blouse, fingers tracing the outlines of the faceted tourmaline as if each stone were a worry bead. The blouse's silky fabric clung to the soft curve of her breasts.

"Why don't you two take a taxi back to the city?" she said. "It'll be morning soon. I'll stay with Pina and we'll see what we can find out when the government offices open."

"Don't forget, it's Saturday," Stanek said.

Diane nodded, her eyes finding his, a measuring look. "We'll do what we can. Once your session's over, you can reach us here to tell us what you've learned."

"Lang, you're damn lucky you got your ass out of the hotel without being seen," Dink said to Diane. That afternoon he'd helped her find a guest house near the Cine Paris on Calle Francisco Depuys, making sure she wasn't followed. "If your name's in secret police files they won't take kindly to you fraternizing with leftists."

"I don't care," she said. "I have a daughter, too. I'd want someone to help me if she disappeared."

"Well, you'd better watch your own butt while you're helping others. Otherwise your daughter may wind up with a missing mother."

Outside, the night was giving way to first light.

As Stanek and Dink Denton returned to the city by taxi, the air slowly took on a peculiar quality of stillness. The calm before the storm, Stanek thought. The birds were quiet, the hot breeze had died to a whisper, the rooms behind windows in the houses along the street were still shuttered and dark.

In a moment, as the taxi motored to their destination, houses, buildings, streets, trees, parked cars and trucks, trolley lines, all gained a soft yet distinct clarity of outline, with separate contours and self-defining angles—the advent of multiplicity, intersecting planes, and tangled lines—a premonition of noise and congestion to come. Objects were suddenly imbued with hidden being, as if waiting for their chance to spring into life, coming out of the gloom, Stanek thought, like the catcher out of the rye.

A new day, ripe for the plucking. His second day in Asunción. His second night with little or no sleep. He was beginning to wonder if sixty thousand for the month was worth it.

Chapter Nineteen

For Walter Stanek, Saturday morning passed in a daze. After a night of no sleep, he found it difficult to concentrate. At the disaster-prevention session in the Colegio Militar, mind-numbing talks followed one after the other. Fragments of speech stitched themselves together into a patchwork quilt of dizzying design.

The talks began in ambiguity and progressed to hard-line inflammatory rhetoric.

The Japanese businessman spoke first, focusing on the role of multinational corporations in the development of Paraguay. Stanek had a hard time keeping his eyes open. Within a few minutes, he drifted off, head tipped to the side.

Ten minutes into the speech, he jerked awake when the businessman smacked the podium with an open palm to make a point.

"What threatens foreign investments?" he was asking. "Nationalistic regimes unduly responsive to popular demands for immediate improvement in the low living standards of the masses."

What was he advocating anyway? Revolution or a stronger government? Stanek couldn't figure it out. Apparently he'd missed too much. The man went on to discuss the survival instincts of multinational corporations and how such corporations, less ideological and more pragmatic and flexible in their approach to operations, could be used to strengthen the host country's internal security.

Stanek still didn't get what he was trying to prove. He gave up and fell asleep ...

"Assault troops must be medically trained. In a hostage situation, such as the retaking of a hijacked plane, you have only six to nine minutes to save the hostages. Triage, the sorting and treatment of the injured, is the key to mass casualty management but it must begin immediately, even before emergency personnel arrive on the scene."

That was Harrington speaking. The trauma surgeon, going on to talk about fear—"Once fear is imprinted on the brain, it is there forever"—and victims—"The most likely victims of a disaster are the innocents—those with the greatest degree of vulnerability."

Stanek tried to listen with greater attentiveness, hoping to judge Harrington's political orientation—yesterday he'd been irreverent as far as the participants went—but Stanek learned nothing of significance. Harrington had arrived late that morning. At the first break, Stanek intended to ask for his aid. It shouldn't matter what side of the political spectrum Harrington came from. This was a humanitarian issue. Perhaps someone in Samcon's hierarchy could help the Sosas, especially Eliana.

When Harrington finished speaking Stanek waved at him, but the man appeared not to notice, taking a seat in the front row.

Next came the man from the Pentagon.

"What was the lesson of Vietnam? General Maxwell Taylor said that it was the need to create a strong police force and a strong police intelligence system to identify and repress incipient subversive situations.

"A restive underclass creates rebels, and both groups—the rebels and the underclass—are enemies of the State. The military and other elite elements of the government must be prepared to seize power and use whatever force is necessary to subjugate restive populations before damage is done. To justify the confrontation, the State needs data. Risk management begins with an analysis of capacities and vulnerabilities, passes through strategic planning, and ends, not with principles and policies, but with intervention, implementation, and action.

"In the case of a declared emergency, either the police or the military must be able to institute martial law, seize private property, assume control of the means of production, and manage the banking and communication systems."

Stanek shook his head. Did he belong with these people?

Who was next? A short, beady-eyed guy with a crewcut took the podium and began to rant about leftist subversion, droplets of spit flying from his mouth as he spoke. Despite the speaker's vehemence, Stanek nodded off, tuning in every five minutes to see where the guy was heading.

"Once a terrorist, always a terrorist. Once a victim, always a victim. As Sun Tzu said, 'Kill one, frighten ten thousand' …

"These criminals and psychopaths try to use philosophy to justify their atrocities, but it is a philosophy of nihilism, one that seeks to impart guilt to the West for our past colonial exploitation, which was in reality, as we all know, a valiant attempt to bring lesser-developed countries up to the level of our thriving capitalist economies. These criminals who have made a mystique out of violence expect us to expiate the crime of having become rich …

"When these Maoist guerrillas failed to win the support of the farmers and peasants, they came to the city and found enthusiastic converts among the students, the media, and the so-called intellectuals. Why? Because these groups were weak enough to feel guilty for being so well provided with comfort and luxury. As if worldly goods were a sin. This is where our efforts at countersubversion must be directed. This is where the battle is to be fought."

So the beady-eyed guy with the crewcut was the terrorism expert, proud to be a former member of the Nathan Hale Institute and a fellow at the Foreign Policy Research Institute of the University of Pennsylvania.

Stanek hadn't heard of either group. He dozed off again, wondering if Renato and Eliana would find each other.

". . . Microwave radiation has proved particularly effective to stun, kill, or create perceptual distortions . . ."

What? Who was this and what was he talking about? Stanek tried to focus his bleary eyes on the stage. A man in military fatigues stood behind the podium. Wasn't he the mercenary? What had Harrington said? One of the "Nightstalkers." Some type of commando.

"Warm relations should continue between the military, the police, and CAUSA—the Confederation of Associations for the Unification of the Americas—and with the World Anti-Communist League in order to negate insurgency and to counter subversion from destabilizing influences. Paraguay's role in the promotion of a global strategic plan for internal security is essential. The military has long been a firm advocate of low-intensity conflict and preemptive retaliation against terrorists and other groups suspected of working to undermine the government. Paraguayan officers have undergone training in the U.S. Army Special Forces camps at Fort Bragg, North Carolina, Fort Benning, Georgia, and Fort Lewis, Washington."

Stanek looked around the room, wondering who the people were. They seemed intent on everything that was said as if their lives depended on it. Had he been dropped into a pit in darkest hell?

"Security must be increased in the state's prisons and penitentiaries.

Recently, for example, a political prisoner was able to reveal his whereabouts by writing a message on the inside of an empty pack of cigarettes using a phosphorus matchstick and blood from his big toe. He crumpled up the pack, left one cigarette sticking half out, and then tossed the pack out the window of the prison. A worker found it and was about to pass the message on to a local priest when he was stopped by the police on a separate matter. Only luck prevented the disclosure of the prisoner's location. Greater vigilance is essential."

Was this Samcon's idea of risk control management?

A short, dapper man in a three-piece suit strode to the stage and adjusted the microphone. Tight curly hair. The second he opened his mouth, Stanek remembered who he was—the Italian scientist. Apparently a computer specialist. Speaking about technical advances in access control and personal security. A squeaky voice with an accent.

As an engineer, technical material interested Stanek. He listened as long as he could, marveling at human ingenuity and wondering why it had to be directed to such egoistic ends. The rich and the powerful wouldn't need protection if they would only share—if their interests were directed less to the self and more to the community.

Greed—that was something Stanek would never understand. All his life, as long as he could remember, he'd disdained the mere accumulation of wealth. His heroes had all lived and died in poverty. Their riches were riches of the spirit.

Then what in hell was he doing here in South America? Hadn't he in effect been bribed?

But he wanted the money for his sister, didn't he? He'd already told her he'd help buy a new tractor. But look who was paying him and what they were doing. The thought made him uncomfortable.

He shook his head to banish the feeling, trying to concentrate on the talk.

The Italian, who'd been discussing hologram key cards and electronic locks when Stanek's mind first wandered, was now commenting on the use of invisible reading-heads built into walls by doorways to scan identity badges with their own built-in microprocessors. Stanek heard something about "active identity cards that transmit their own signals and process signals received" and then the scientist was off on another topic—machine-readable passports.

Stanek frowned. What did that have to do with personal security?

The Italian turned a page without pausing, reading from a script. "When inserted into a computer terminal at the point of entry, they can directly activate the memory of the national police intelligence computer. The vehicles of suspected terrorists can then be tagged. The preferred method is by a type of bar code on the underside of the car. The vehicle can then be tracked either by surveillance beams or by coils buried in the roadways."

That was quite some leap, Stanek thought. What next? The Italian appeared to be weaving together two separate issues—personal protection and the detection of terrorists and criminals. Somehow he even got on to the use of chemical agents to tag suspected terrorists themselves! He mentioned one man, a particularly vain Lebanese with shoulder-length locks who was tagged when a gift bottle of shampoo was injected with color-coded chemical agents that were invisible to human sight but could be read by a scanner. The police tracked him from Beirut to Athens, where he was captured with plastic explosives in his possession.

More descriptions of technical equipment followed—measures to unmask impersonators and spot would-be infiltrators, thermal scanners that not only read fingerprints but verified that blood was flowing so terrorists couldn't cut off the finger of the person with access, transducers that projected infrared light to read the unique vein pattern under the skin, biometrically active cards with photo-diode arrays that read patterns and then matched them to those prerecorded in its microprocessor.

And then it was Stanek's turn and he stood before the assembled crowd, most of the seats in the auditorium full of spectators, feeling like the one cherry in a jar of olives. He hadn't had time to prepare notes and he found himself wandering from topic to topic in ways he hadn't planned, apologizing finally for his confusion.

At one point, for some reason he couldn't remember halfway through, he told them about the great floods in world history in which hundreds of thousands of people had died. He talked about Holland in 1228 when a sea flood in Friesland killed a hundred thousand, about the three hundred thousand who died in China in 1642 when the Kaifeng seawall collapsed, about the nine hundred thousand who drowned in Honan, China, in 1887 when the Yellow River overflowed, about the million deaths from drowning and starvation in the north China floods of 1939.

He tried to think of disasters in which dams had collapsed. In 1959, in Frejus, France, a dam collapsed, killing four hundred and twelve people. The Vaiont Dam in Northern Italy collapsed in 1963. Two thousand dead there. The numbers, he realized, were too small to make much of an impression. He should have mentioned the typhoons in Japan and China, or the tidal wave that killed ten thousand in East Pakistan in 1960, or even the fifty thousand left homeless in Rio de Janeiro following the floods and landslides of 1966, or better yet the cyclone in Bangladesh in 1970 when a half million died or in 1991 when over a hundred thousand were swept away.

But what did that have to do with anything? He could see the people in the audience shifting about awkwardly, whispering to each other, exchanging looks of incredulity, one rotating his finger near his ear as if Stanek were an idiot.

A fleeting thought brought a smile to his face—he could have used some disaster prevention himself. He tried to say that as a joke, but the words came out flat. No one in the audience cracked a smile. Finally, embarrassed, feeling as lame as he must have looked, he used the excuse that he'd recently been in an accident, that he was still on medication. It was a lie, but only Harrington would know. And then he stumbled back to his seat, cheeks flushed, wondering how soon he could get out of there.

These people weren't interested in dams and flood control and managing the environment; no, their worries were entirely different. They were worried about guerrillas blowing up power plants and sabotaging substations, cutting power lines to disrupt the country, seizing dams and darkening cities to make a political statement. That was what mattered. That was the disaster they were here to prevent. That was what he should have talked about.

Stanek wanted out of it. They could have their sixty thousand bucks. Let them find some other sucker.

Harrington said, "Let me talk to Kohlbert, old chap. I'm sure he can do something. Connections with the government and all that. No need to despair. Raymond's got a line into General Zancon—mutual love of the Luftwaffe or some such thing, I suspect. Let me handle it. I'll give him a ring this afternoon and I'm sure he'll get to it as soon as he returns from São Paulo."

"But when's he coming back? This is an innocent fifteen-year-old girl and her father."

Harrington ran a hand over his gray hair, slicking down an unruly curl, then lifted his head and adjusted his bow tie.

"No reason for alarm, lad. Kohlbert's due back at headquarters by Monday."

"But that's two days from now. They torture people in this country."

Harrington scoffed. "Let's not exaggerate. They won't be tortured if they're innocent. We couldn't get them out today anyway, and nothing happens on Sunday, so ... best to be patient. It's not really two days."

"You can't do anything?"

Harrington looked at him for a moment. "I say, this really matters to you, doesn't it?"

"They helped me when I was attacked by those kids. I'm just trying to return the favor. I thought you had contacts in Asunción."

"Did I say that?" Harrington frowned. "No, I don't think so."

He lifted his head, scratching at his neck, his face contorted. "Look, Stanek. I'll do the best I can." Begrudgingly. "He won't like it on a Sunday, but I'll drop by to see a judge I know."

"Is he the one who talked about security yesterday? Why not call him now?"

"Stanek, old chap, don't press your luck. These things take time—and we have another session this afternoon."

Stanek cleared his throat. "Uh, about this afternoon, I'm not going to be able to stay. I have some things to take care of."

Harrington frowned. "We start the war games tomorrow, you know. Samcon's not going to be happy."

"Then I'll go by the office and talk to them. Maybe someone there can help."

"I wouldn't bother," Harrington said. "You'll just find a locked door, and if you telephone it'll be an answering machine. Kohlbert's the one to talk to and he's out of the country. Oh, and whatever you do, you'd better be here tomorrow morning. Control finds you gone and it'll not just be Samcon who's upset. General Paredes—" he raised his eyebrows—"rather, God the Father, will not take kindly if a member of the Cabinet is absent. I believe his motto is 'Better dead than absent,' if you get what I mean."

Stanek met Dink Denton at a restaurant on Calle Palma. According to Dink, Diane Lang had gone off with Pina Sosa to talk to the Sosa's parish priest, Padre Guzman, to see if Church officials could help obtain the release of Eliana on humanitarian grounds.

"What'd you learn this morning?" Stanek asked, after he'd nearly drained a cup of coffee in one long swallow. He was roasting but he needed the caffeine to stay alert. His sport coat was draped over the back of his chair and his shirt sleeves were rolled up, but he could feel the wetness under his arms and on his forehead. The day was hot, the air humid, suffocating.

Dink was wearing a muscle shirt and looked like one of the city's manual laborers, a native from a lower-class barrio. He flexed his arms and cracked his neck, then said, "I talked to a counselor at the Embassy. Guy named Conrad Kleemer. One of the few people in on Saturday. The Ambassador's off in Concepción to dedicate some library. Kleemer'll see what he can do."

"That's it? He'll see what he can do? What's that mean?"

"Hey, who you jerking, man? I didn't press the dolt. I was lucky I got that far. And while I was there, Kleemer called the military attaché at home and talked to him. Apparently the attaché's a good friend of the honcho in charge of the army's intelligence service. They'll pursue that angle, too."

Stanek nodded. That was more like it. Diane Lang was covering the Church, Dink had hit the American Embassy, which would contact the Paraguayan military and the correct governmental officials, he himself would get Samcon to do its part, and Harrington would suggest that Kohlbert contact General Zancon. Talk about covering all the bases. And if Kohlbert got through to the general, they'd be starting at the top.

It was beginning to look better already.

Chapter Twenty

barras—" The priest shook his head, his eyes shut against the clinic's bright fluorescent lights. "He is a heathen—no, worse than a heathen; not even a miracle could save him."

Padre Guzman, his head wrapped in white bandages, lay strapped in a hospital bed in a small room on the second floor of the Policlínico Cristo Rey, a narrow building on Avenida Colón opposite the grounds of the Colegio Cristo Rey. The parish priest of Santísima Trinidad was in far worse shape than Pina Sosa had imagined—at times speaking in what seemed to be a delirium.

Diane and Pina had stepped away from the bed and were talking to each other in Spanish, unsure of what to do next. Padre Guzman was in no shape to help them. He appeared to have drifted off after listening to Pina's plea for help. And when he spoke, always after long intervals of silence, he talked with his eyes closed or opened them to stare vacantly at the ceiling, as if he had forgotten their presence.

"I know Ibarras," Diane told Pina. "He's the colonel who interrogated me at the airport."

Pina nodded. "Renato used to speak of him. He's the head of the secret police—the Department of Investigations. You should be careful. Even the government fears his agents. Our presidents always create a separate force to protect themselves. They don't trust the army or the secret police. General Zancon himself hand-picked the men who protect him. But Renato says Colonel Ibarras is smart—he made sure he has two offices, one in the central police station and the other in the compound of the Presidential Escort Regiment. His hand is everywhere."

She gestured toward Padre Guzman. "And this is typical of his work. His agents are thugs."

The priest raised his right hand and waved it in a gesture of despair. "I have a heavy heart, my child."

Pina Sosa moved closer to the bed, dropping to her knees to pray. The priest's hand found her head and then patted her shoulder in a gesture of consolation. "Pray for us all, my child."

He was silent for a moment, breathing raggedly, and when he spoke again, his voice had fallen to a whisper.

"Sometimes I feel that God is far away, so very far away … high, high above us. I reach up, I strain to touch the hem of his garment … and it is beyond reach—beyond even the reach of faith."

"Do not say this, Father." Pina dabbed at her eyes with a lace-trimmed handkerchief. She had never heard such sadness in his voice. Padre Guzman was not the dour sort, like some priests she'd known. He was a cheerful man of God, always a smile on his face, a good word, a warm hand. His heart was with the people he served.

The priest's head sank deeper into the pillow. "And then I despair—not of God's forgiveness, for that would be an unforgiveable sin, but of man, of human goodness … I see evil and I am infected by it. It is a disease of the genes … buried deep in the dark, impenetrable recesses of the brain. I try to eradicate this root of corruption"—his hand fluttered over his chest—"and it snaps off at the surface."

"Father, what are you saying?"

Diane stepped forward and put her hand on Pina's shoulder. "Get up, Pina. He's delirious. He won't be able to help us. We have to find someone else."

The priest tried to elevate himself, panting at the exertion. "It sprouts again at the first sign of rain," he said.

"Lie down, Father, rest." Pina leaned over and straightened the priest's pillow. In a minute, the nurse would tell them it was time to leave. "You'll feel better tomorrow."

The priest's eyes sprang open and the expression on his face was one of horror. He opened his mouth, but no words came at first. His chest rose and fell as he struggled for breath. "For me—I fear for me there are—there are many snakes in the gardens of Paradise … a treason of fate."

"Come, Pina. He's not making sense." Diane felt uncomfortable, as if they were somehow responsible for the priest's despair.

But Pina lingered, her hand touching the padre's brow, hot with fever. "What have they done to him?" she whispered.

The priest's head fell back and he closed his eyes again, going inward in silence. And then, just as they were about to leave, he said, "Every death … every death of an innocent one takes a little bit of truth out of the world."

Diane hoped that was not a premonition. Renato might not be innocent—from what Pina had said he was active in the opposition—but Eliana surely was. And innocent or not, neither one deserved to die.

"Dink, what are you going to do now?" Stanek asked.

The three Americans stood outside the Nunciatura Apostólica, the

Vatican's Embassy, located on Avenida Mariscal Lopez just outside the U.S. Embassy compound to the west. Pina Sosa had just left for home in the Toyota wagon to see about Jose. They had all agreed to meet at ten Sunday morning in the Plaza Constitución on the steps of the Metropolitan Cathedral, a huge, square building flanked by two bell towers. Archbishop Mario Mendez would be celebrating mass and Pina hoped to be granted an audience with the prelate.

"What am I going to be doing?" Dink turned his back to Diane and poked a finger through a circle made by his other thumb and forefinger, moving it back and forth, grinning the while.

"You're kidding."

"Nope. Got me a little mestiza in La Chacarita. Probably will have a hot meal waiting for me when I arrive. Amada makes a great *puchero* stew." He grinned again. "Has a little kerosene refrigerator for beer. Don't you wish you were so lucky?"

Diane rubbed her eyes wearily. It was seven p.m. and, other than for brief naps, none of them had slept for two days. "What are you going to do, Walter?"

He looked at her for a moment, feeling an unwanted stirring at the sight of her figure, the damp strands of hair at her neck. "Go on back to the hotel and crash, I guess. I'm dead tired."

"Me too. Do you want to get something to eat first?"

Stanek's eyes widened. "Just the two of us?" Now why had he said that?

An aggravated look crossed her face, her eyes flashing. "What is it with you? You hate women or something?"

"I've been burned a few times." This conversation wasn't going the way he wanted it to.

"Who hasn't?"

"Yeah." He paused and looked around, as if seeking a means of escape.

151

It was rapidly growing darker, but the streets were still filled with pedestrians. Buses and trolleys rumbled down the avenue in both directions
and traffic in general was thick—sleek Mercedes and fancy American
imports riding the tails of old Volkswagen vans, battered trucks, smaller
European and Japanese cars, and microbuses made in Brazil. A horse-
drawn taxi with bald tires picked its way down the curb lane.

"Actually," he said, "I like women. A lot."

"Then it's just me—"

"No." He shook his head. "Look, it's no big deal. You want to eat, let's
go eat."

She raised her eyebrows in exasperation, but said nothing in response.
They caught a bus with a hardwood floor and took it in as far as the railroad
station on Plaza Uruguaya and then walked back a block to the corner of
Eligio Ayala and Tacuarí where they had seen a restaurant.

San Roque. Ceiling fans and waiters in black tie and white jacket. A
relic from days gone by. They sat at a small table in the back room, which
was air-conditioned, and ordered palm hearts and charcoal-broiled filets
and drank *tereré*, a cold *maté* that tasted like alfalfa to Stanek. Both
switched to a local beer when the main entree arrived. For dessert they
had chilled papaya in sugarcane syrup.

They were silent during most of the meal, too tired to talk. The only
conversation of note came near the end, when both were sitting pensive,
waiting for the check to arrive.

"Why are you doing this, anyway?" Diane asked. "You don't strike me
as the type. You said yourself you were apolitical."

"Helping the Sosas has nothing to do with politics."

"So you're just a good Samaritan. You don't believe in their cause but
you want to help. Is that it?"

He considered the question for a while, then said, "Deep down I think
it comes to this: we Americans have a myth that we're the good guys.
And like all myths there's some truth in it—a lot of truth if you really

analyze motivation. We don't always get the results we hope for and we don't always foresee complications that devolve but our intentions are good. I think you can say the same thing here. I'm doing this because I think it's the right thing to do. I believe in helping the victims of a state that is oppressing them. I—"

"Aha!" she said. "So you are political."

"I believe in individual freedom," he said. "Simple as that. Of course, freedom's a word we use rather glibly at times." He paused and thought some more while she stared at him intently.

"Who knows, maybe for me it comes down to a rebellion against authority. Isn't that what we Americans are famous for?"

"James Boswell told Samuel Johnson that we were a race of convicts, and ought to be thankful for anything the British allowed us short of hanging."

Stanek laughed.

Diane sat back, smiling herself, enjoying the look on his face. His grin brightened up his face, and with his tousled hair and rugged features he looked like an outdoorsman, handsome in a refreshing way. At Yale, her colleagues were all intellectuals, usually thin and shriveled up, hopping about like nervous grasshoppers—or they were fat toads with dirty hair and greasy foreheads. Stanek had a solidity that attracted her—more than she'd realized. "You have a nice smile," she said.

A look passed between them, a moment of silence, and then Diane went on, "But back to what you were saying: you don't look like a rebel to me. You look like those hard hats who're always waving the flag at construction sites."

He laughed again. "I'm a liberal in sheep's clothing. Don't forget, I'm older than you. I lived through the sixties. Okay, I was just a baby, but I grew up hating authority—especially the police. I'm an individualist. I don't believe in submitting to the control of others. That's why I'm a teacher. I can do my own thing."

She leaned forward, both hands under her chin. "Rugged individualism, is that it? The code of the old West."

She was mocking him, but Stanek shrugged it off. "Laugh all you want," he said, "but yes, that's it exactly. Stand on your own two feet and help the innocent." It was time to turn the tables. "But what about you?" he asked. "You owe the Sosas less than I do. Why your involvement?"

"I'm not helping them out of a sense of obligation. I don't feel I owe them anything—that I have to pay them back."

"That's not what I meant about me either."

"You believe in standing on your own two feet, you said. You don't like being indebted. I bet you don't loan your tools—and never borrow from your neighbor. You'd be too afraid you owed him something in return."

He grinned. "How'd you guess? But that doesn't mean I'm not generous."

"No ... perhaps you like other people being indebted to you."

"Why do you always have to turn every thing into a fight?"

Diane's eyes had a mischievous glint. "I thought that's what *you* did."

"Forget it. We're arguing like an old married couple and I don't even know you."

"Maybe that's part of the problem," she said. "I'm sure we're both rather charming under normal circumstances."

He didn't know if she was being sarcastic or not and later, thinking about their conversation, he realized she never did answer his question. What was her stake in the Sosa's fate?

On the walk from the restaurant to the Plaza Hotel where Diane was going to catch a taxi to the guest house Dink had helped her find, Stanek was surprised when she slipped her arm through his. Just Latin American courtesy, he thought. Down here, people walked arm in arm, even men. Nothing new. He'd seen it often enough in Mexico. She didn't want to be bothered by the young guys hanging out around the shoeshine stands in the plaza.

Whatever the reason, it felt good.

As they crossed the plaza on a paved sidewalk under flowering trees and metal lampstands, Stanek was aware of the appraising glances cast her way by men seated on benches. He saw clear appreciation in their looks, a trace of envy, and was suddenly aware of how stunningly beautiful she was. He had seen it every time he looked at her but he hadn't felt it deep inside—he hadn't *let* himself feel it.

At the hotel, outside the main entrance, where a row of taxis waited, she stood on her tiptoes and kissed his cheek.

"Thanks for the company and good-night," she said. "You made me feel less alone."

He stood there, unsure what to say, mouth opening and closing as three or four different responses ran through his mind. By the time he'd settled on one, she had turned away and slid into the taxi, shutting the door behind her.

He watched as the taxi disappeared in a stream of other vehicles, the night dark about him, then turned and headed for his own hotel and bed.

The streets were still bright, the angles and projections sharply delineated as if by a scalpel, the crowd still full, but as he worked his way through the throng of jostling bodies, Saturday night revelers, noisy and cheerful, he felt suddenly alone.

To hide the screams the police played Brazilian music at full volume: usually the bossa nova or samba or something snappy out of Curitiba—*la musica popular brasileira*, the rhythm vibrant with throbbing drums, jangling tambourines, lusty guitars and brassy trumpets.

The music was played even when there were no screams—it never hurt to let the people know the threat was there.

The "Rigoberto Caballero" police hospital was located near the corner of two avenues—Mariscal Lopez and Juscelino Kubitscheck, midway between the U.S. Embassy compound and the presidential palace. The hospital had two wings joined by a smaller connecting building, all set at a diagonal to the corner. The torture went on in the basement.

Despite the incessant din and the pain from his broken nose and teeth, Padre Ramon Ibañez imagined he heard the screams anyway. Anything was possible after standing thirty-eight hours in a subterranean corridor of the Policlínico Policial tied hand and foot with his face to the wall.

The priest knew what was waiting for him. Payment for his speech Friday afternoon in the Plaza de los Héroes.

Among the revolutionaries, the mocking names used by the secret police for their instruments of torture were well known. After he passed out from standing on his feet, they would revive him with drugs—the *director general* gave the injections himself—and then they would whip him with a braided leather strap—*el látigo*, interspersing that game, for variety, with karate blows to the neck ("Let's give him some *democracia*," they would say) and kicks to the testicles and kidneys. For fun, they would pull out chunks of his hair, talking about *libertad*.

When they tired of that, they would switch to what they laughingly called the *"Constitución Nacional"*—wire entwined with small metal balls, and then maybe they would attach electrodes to his testicles (*"Presidente General Zancon"*) or dunk him in a bath of fecal matter and urine (*"derechos humanos tipo Jimmy Carter"*), or, if he was lucky, in water (*"derechos humanos tipo Clinton"*).

In the United States, meddling administrations with their talk of human rights followed one after the other like ants marching into fire, but no one—not even the do-gooders—could stop the torture. Reagan and Bush hadn't even tried. And neither did the cowboy, for all his talk of freedom.

As for the dunkings in fetid tubs of diarrheal excrement, the priest had heard that the interrogators held you under until you choked. If *los verdugos* didn't kill you themselves, you died of dysentery.

At first, despite his nudity and the wire cord cutting into his hands, Padre Ibañez had tried to hide his fear.

"Can I speak?" he'd asked the guard, a burly man in civilian clothes sitting behind a desk five meters up the corridor.

Thick black eyebrows arched in a frown. "*Hijo de puta*, no speaking allowed."

A peasant, his voice guttural.

Five hours later, the priest asked for a book to read.

"*Curepí de mierda*, that is prohibited."

Eighteen hours later, when the same guard was back on duty, Padre Ibañez said, "Then how about you reading to me?"

"*¡A la puta!*" The guard pounded his desk, screamed another series of epithets (ending with "*criminal*" and "*bandido*"), but didn't rise from his padded chair. "Absolutely forbidden," he thundered.

Padre Ibañez waited at least another six hours before he said, "Well then, can I think?"

Enraged, the guard got to his feet, kicked the priest in the butt and then smashed his face against the wall, breaking his nose and shattering his top front teeth.

When the guard spoke, each word was chiseled in cold steel: "*En una institución policial está prohibido hablar, prohibido leer, y sobre todo, prohibido pensar.*" At each command, for emphasis, he slammed the priest's head into the wall's tiled surface. "And the next time you forget, *flaco*, you will find yourself in the cemetery of Capiatá."

Dazed, spitting out blood and bits of teeth, Padre Ibañez tried to laugh. They would not break him.

Forbidden to speak, to read, and finally to think.

That was the caliber of mind of his torturers. The padre had heard of the student arrested by the secret police for carrying a book with the title

La revolución en la arquitectura contemporánea. For reading *that* subversive book—they wanted no word of revolution in Paraguay!—the student spent six months in prison.

And if your *thoughts* were subversive, what then?

Then they killed you.

He had heard of one weekend where the police killed twenty-seven detainees. Gasoline was in heavy supply. The thugs used a funnel to pour the fuel into both ears of prisoners, then ignited the fumes. They wanted to see if they could make a human firecracker, to see if the head would explode like a bomb. A woman died when they poured gas into her vagina and lit it. "A red-hot woman," they joked.

To enliven the proceedings, they poured the liquid on the feet of others, then lit it and howled at the frantic dancing of the victims, who slowly bled to death. Iron bars were heated in hot coals and thrust up the anuses of teenage boys. Others were electrocuted or had their skulls crushed in vises. The police lined up five men outside the cells of the Comisaria Primera and forced each one to kill the next man in line by bashing in his head with an iron club, then they shot the last survivor.

Brutality that had sickened him at the news. The utter lack of human compassion. He had railed against it from the pulpit, to no effect. The killings continued.

Fine, he was resigned to death. Only a fool thought he would live forever. Let it be now, rather than later. End the pain.

When he could catch his breath, he began to speak, spitting out the words one after the other, not stopping despite the blows that soon rained down: *"Asesino ... criminal ... fascista ... testaferro de la dictadura ... agente del imperialismo norteamericano ... agente de la CIA ... cobarde ... homosexual ..."* until finally his skull was shattered and the words died away for good.

• • •

Three hours later, when Renato Sosa was prodded up the corridor to one of the interrogation cells, the body of Padre Ramon Ibañez was still lying face up on the floor. But it was only twenty minutes into his own torture, trying to distract himself with other thoughts, that Renato realized who he'd seen lying in the corridor.

Father Ibañez—the man who'd baptized Eliana when the Sosas still lived in the Barrio Obrero. Fifteen years ago, at the altar of the church of the Santísimo Redentor.

My poor baby, he thought, what will happen to her now?

ting down Asunción's old port and burning one of the three *depósitos* there, thus destroying a refrigerated supply of beef that had been shipped in from Concepción. The new port at Villeta, thirty-seven kilometers to the south, was under siege by guerrillas.

That put the Minister of Commerce and Industry to work.

Flomeres, the Flota Mercante del Estado, a merchant marine under government control, which usually handled only twenty-five percent of the country's annual cargo, had to assume responsibility for all transportation of goods by river when foreign freighters (according to Control) stopped either at Corrientes, Argentina, or farther south at the Rio de la Plata estuary, due to Paraguay's unsettled political climate.

When the Minister of Defense mobilized the army's three helicopters to help, Control said the guerrillas had shot down two of them, using Soviet-supplied SAM 7 Strelas, a hand-held surface-to-air missile (supplied, they joked, by the Opposition's Jewish arms merchant by way of Nicaragua).

When the Minister of Agriculture (the Senior Analyst for the Institute for Food and Development Policy) tried to use the country's air force to transport food to Asunción, Control shut down the all-weather airport at Mariscal Estigarribia due to a collision on the runway (caused, they said, when the rebellious Sixth Infantry Division attacked one of the air force's Brazilian-made EMB-326 Xavantes, a counterinsurgency aircraft, which then collided with a Chilean-made T-25 Universal), thus grounding a fair-sized contingent of the Transporte Aereo Militar.

The two military men on Control, Stanek saw, were having fun with technical details. They also closed several other grass airstrips in the north due to bad weather.

On an irascible impulse, Stanek flipped to the section of the handbook covering the military and considered wiping out Control with one of the artillery battalions garrisoned at Paraguarí. Could a 105mm M-101 howitzer take out God? This perverse inversion of the Trinity?

As far as he could tell, Control seemed to favor the Opposition rather than the Cabinet.

A water treatment plant at Coronel Oviedo, run by the state-owned Corporación de Obras Sanitarias (Corposana), was sabotaged by guerrillas, who toppled the tower of the water-storage tank, a structure that looked (from the photos supplied to Harrington, the Minister of Public Health and Social Welfare) like an inverted dog dish with lids top and bottom.

Harrington also had to deal with an outbreak of typhoid and the threat of a cholera epidemic in several of Asunción's shantytowns, taxing the city's emergency services and hospitals. Control told him the clinics were running out of antibiotics and dextrose solutions, so Harrington arranged for a fifteen-ton donation of medicines from Argentina.

The Interior Minister had to cope with the Opposition's newspapers (which he ordered seized) and, when riots broke out, asked for army tanks to roll into the streets to help the police maintain order and protect important government buildings.

Stanek was particularly aggravated when the only minister without portfolio—the German who worked as a Hazardous Incident specialist for the Saudi Petroleum Institute—asked him about the feasibility of flooding out a major guerrilla encampment along the Paraná river near Encarnación by raising the rectangular lift gates on Itaipu dam. Would a massive spillway discharge do the trick?

"Sure," Stanek said sarcastically, "if you don't mind drowning thirty-five thousand innocent citizens in Encarnación."

"Go ahead," the German said. "I'll take responsibility."

By day's end, Stanek could see why they called it a war. The situation had so deteriorated that the Minister of Foreign Affairs was considering calling in foreign forces, including those of the United States, to reestablish order.

Control, of course, was not happy with this and closed the session, saying that the next day's first order of business would be a joint conference to analyze preventive measures that might have been taken to avert most of the day's catastrophes.

Outside, on the street again, Stanek was filled with a sense of imbalance. Normal life seemed hallucinatory. That none of the day's events had actually taken place filled him with marvel. There were no tanks in the streets, no soldiers with submachine guns, no rioting crowds. An unnatural quiet ...

He felt a distance between himself and the events of the last few days. Diane Lang, Dink Denton, the Sosas—all belonged to another world. But that was the real world, he thought. What had gone on in the Military College was only a dream.

What had the others done all day?

Earlier that morning, before Stanek had to leave for his session, Pina Sosa had met him, Diane, and Dink on the steps of the Metropolitan Cathedral. Pina had a distraught look on her face. She had been to the Central Police station, where an officer had informed her that, yes, they had initially arrested Renato Sosa, but that he had been released late the night before. They denied ever having Eliana in custody.

But neither of them had shown up at the family residence, she said, her eyes filling with the shadows of fear. They were both missing and she was frightened. The archbishop would do nothing since the police claimed her husband had been freed. If he didn't show up at home, the implication was that he had gone underground or fled to Buenos Aires.

Dink had advised her to return home and wait. "Maybe it's true," he said. "Maybe Renato will show up later—and Eliana, too. I talked to a guy I know at the Embassy. He might have pulled the right cords."

Pina looked doubtful.

Dink said he was off to attend to some business, but gave Diane a telephone number where a message could be left for him. She, herself, had told Pina she would contact a professor she knew at the Catholic

University and see what he advised. In the meantime, she was at a loss. She didn't know what else could be done.

Stanek had promised her that he would report on Harrington's efforts to contact a prominent judge he knew. But now. . . if the police had freed Renato and Eliana—

"I know," Pina said, a hint of sarcasm joining the resignation in her voice. "What can *he* do?" She bit her lip. "If the archbishop will not help me, I'm going to the MCP." When they looked at her with questions in their eyes, she said, "The Movimento Campesino Paraguayo. It's a peasant movement. They have a permanent commission to help the relatives of the disappeared and murdered. Someone else in the movement may have news of Renato or Eliana."

Now, that conversation seemed to have taken place days ago.

Stanek looked at his watch. Just after six o'clock. Only eight hours since he'd seen them.

Harrington had given him nothing. The old man hadn't yet been able to contact the judge; he would do so Monday morning, he said, then raised his eyebrows and added, even if he had to arrive late to the session.

The meaning of the raised eyebrows was clear. After meeting Pina and the others that morning, Stanek had arrived late for the first session of the war games. Control had not been happy. General Paredes himself had caught Stanek and had warned him to get there on time in the future. The general's foul breath had reached Stanek's nostrils, stinking of putrefaction, and the taller American had leaned back and nodded. They should have called him the Devil, not God the Father.

If Harrington missed an entire session—especially one where preventive measures were to be discussed—what would Control do then?

Scream and spit in the old man's face?

That evening, in the quietness of the United States Embassy—where the only visible presence was a Marine corporal, the duty officer—Conrad Kleemer, Counselor to the political section, used a scrambled line to telephone Colonel Hector Ibarras. Several hours had passed since Dink Denton had talked to him, hours during which he had been in touch with CIA computers in Langley, Virginia.

The head of the secret police listened to the message and then said, "I've talked to the woman. What do these others have to do with her?"

"Harrington and Stanek are working for Samcon. My contact says they claim they ran into the woman at the Club Bahia Negra." The Counselor laughed. "A chance meeting—likely sounding story."

"So who are they?"

"They're not CIA—at least not that I know." His voice took on a worried tone. "Not unless someone's found out what's going on. The Company might be working behind my back."

"You've told no one about my plans?"

"Not a soul. But I can guarantee there'll be no interference by my government. The Ambassador's in my pocket. He's no more satisfied with Zancon than you are." The Counselor paused. "I don't know about Samcon. That's a bit of a problem, isn't it? They seem to be tied to *El Tigre*, unless they're planning something they haven't told me about—but whatever the case I think we can deal with them when the time comes. Money talks."

Ibarras said nothing and the Counselor could not see the smile on his face. Ibarras had his tentacles deep into Samcon. Nothing to fear there. In fact, when the time came, as Kleemer put it, Samcon would be paving the way for him. He'd already promised them a massive share of future government contracts. But if this Harrington and Stanek had infiltrated Samcon from outside ... that he didn't like.

The colonel cleared his throat. "When you talk to your contact again—*señor* Denton, no?—do me a favor. Tell him to keep his nose out of our affairs."

"Don't worry about Dink, Colonel. He's DEA. He's a good ol' boy. He won't cause any problems. He's after the small fry—drug smugglers. He won't get involved in politics."

"I'm meeting with the Bolivians next week. I don't want him interfering."

"Nothing to sweat. The DEA has him on De Negri."

"I'll give him De Negri the day before I meet the Bolivians. Make him think he's shut down the pipeline into Paraguay and then sidestep him."

"Good, but in the meantime, I wouldn't put much stock in the other two—this Stanek and Harrington. I think they heard a sob story from a beautiful woman and just tried to help out."

"Thanks for your help, Counselor. As usual, nice to do business with you."

Colonel Hector Ibarras replaced the phone, then rubbed his chin pensively. The woman—Señora Lang—was a meddler; she'd be taken care of. But what about the men?

They were loose ends—and that was something he didn't like.

He spread his fingers on the desk in front of him and stared at them.

Well, he thought, there was one way to take care of loose ends.

Tie a good knot.

Sunday night, Stanek ate by himself in the restaurant of the Hotel Guaraní. Diane Lang was off with a faculty member from the Catholic University, and who knew where Dink was.

Stanek found himself blinking his eyes hard, as if they hurt, a mannerism he didn't like. Nerves, tension building up. He wasn't happy with the tenor of the war games. He hadn't come to Paraguay to help the government combat insurgency. He didn't like being a part of a program to oppress innocent citizens. Could he ask to leave early for the proposed site of the Corpus project? He wanted to start his advisory work on the dam—at least that was something positive.

When the day's war games session had ended, he'd been tired of people and had turned down Harrington's offer of dinner together. But now, he felt silence closing in around him. Hungry for a sympathetic voice, he decided he would call his sister Randi after dinner. Find out how things were going on the farm.

For a moment, he wondered what Diane Lang was doing. Probably dining at a large table in some faculty home with a crowd of animated professors. Academics talking shop. He was one himself, but he doubted he'd fit in there. They'd be talking about literature and ideas—and he'd be trying to discuss the chemical composition of a power plant discharge in Oregon or the effects of intake and outfall siting and design on thermal plumes in Alaska.

No, they just wouldn't mix.

What was she going to be talking about Monday at the conference?

The Mennonites.

Hell, if Harrington was going to miss part of the next day's morning session, maybe he would, too. Find the room where she was speaking at the Catholic University and listen in. It wouldn't hurt to learn something new.

Let the general yell. There'd be two of them—Harrington and Stanek. Share half the wrath. Divide and conquer.

Harrington and Stanek—hell, it sounded like a law firm.

Chapter Twenty-Two

The first interruption came ten minutes into Professor Diane Lang's talk. A man sitting halfway down on the outer aisle to her right stood up and shouted something she didn't quite catch. She paused for a second, momentarily disconcerted, then went on as if nothing had happened while a security guard hustled the man out of the hall.

At the time, she was in the process of analyzing the themes of Menno Simons' most important book, *The Foundations of Christian Doctrine*, published in Holland in 1539. She'd already commented on the influence of the early Swiss Anabaptists, tracing their contacts with Melchior Hofmann. Like Menno Simons, Hofmann was a Dutchman. He'd met the Anabaptists—a radical group composed of Konrad Grebel, Felix Manz, George Blaurock, and Simon Stumph—in Strasburg, and returned to Holland to baptize over three hundred people in Emden in 1530. Among his converts were two brothers from Leeuwarden—Obbe and Dirk Philips, the men who in turn had converted Menno Simons.

Diane was intrigued by how these men had arrived at their ideas, ideas familiar to her from her own upbringing. Her parents had attended an Evangelical Free Methodist church and had raised her in a strict Protestant environment. In his later years, as his banking interests came to the fore, her father had fallen away, and she herself had long ago rebelled against most of the church's strictures—no rock-and-roll (everyone knew that meant sexual intercourse), no makeup (she used to sit in the backseat of her boyfriend's Chevy after Sunday evening meetings, smear on thick, red lipstick, and then make-out to hot tunes on the radio while the other kids played ping-pong in the rec room), no jewelry, no coffee, no alcohol (for years, as a kid, she thought filthy lucre meant filthy liquor), no smoking (she'd tried menthols for one year in college and then gave them up), no movies or television, no masturbation, no sex before wedlock (forget those last two prohibitions!), and so on and so forth.

"For Menno Simons, the New Testament taught that Christians must live a life based on love. Any institution that operated on the basis of force was anathema. No follower of Christ could participate in the taking of human life. Christians, Simons preached, must abstain from the military, the police, and the magistracy."

She was about to turn a page when another commotion broke out. A man was on his feet on the other side of the room near an exit, calling her dirty names and shouting some nonsense about Yankee imperialism. Her face turned pale. The attack was directed at her, not at the University—it was personal.

She felt like a fist had punched her in the belly. Yankee imperialism. What did that have to do with her and Menno Simons? She was a professor of German studies and Menno was a sixteenth-century religious reformer. Why disrupt her talk and not that of any of the other participants? She had nothing to do with U.S. foreign policy. Go to the Embassy if you wanted to protest imperialism.

While she watched in stunned silence, two priests pushed the protester out the exit and followed after him. She could hear shouts from the courtyard. She looked behind her nervously, to the elevated podium where five men sat, renowned scholars from Europe, the United States, and Latin America. Executive officers of the International Association for the Study of German Language and Literature, presiding over the day's session. The president, a professor emeritus known to her only by name and reputation, raised his pale eyebrows as if to ask her what she had to do with the ruckus, then with a sour look on his face nodded for her to continue.

She started again, her mind a flurry of activity. Her voice, which had been whispy and tremulous from the start, had grown hoarser. She stopped and took a sip of water from a glass on a shelf below the podium, being careful not to swallow down the wrong tube and choke. Her composure was badly shaken.

It was not the first time she'd given a speech that turned out to be a disaster. What aggravated her was that she'd been nervous from the start—in front of people she didn't even know!

That seemed to bother her as much as the interruptions. By now in her career, she walked into classes the first day of the semester and spoke with assurance from the start. But a public lecture was a different matter. She never knew until the moment came how she would react. She would introduce a German film at one of Yale's foreign film festivals and find her voice shaky; she'd speak at one of Columbia University's colloquia before local and foreign scholars and find it was a snap, her voice strong and firm. Sometimes she'd be nervous ahead of time, then calm during the presentation; sometimes it turned out just the opposite. Who knew why?

As she read her paper, with her mind uncontrollably divided between past and present, she remembered her first major speech in high school.

She was valedictorian of her class and spoke at graduation in front of over six hundred parents, including her own. The school's forensics teachers had helped her in advance, giving her hints on breathing and rhythm, suggesting a pattern for her eyes to follow so all in the audience would feel she was speaking to them, letting her practice in front of their beginning classes.

That was something she enjoyed—the practice sessions in the Freshman and Sophomore speech classes. The students met her with smiling faces and looks of encouragement. They positively beamed when she made a small joke, they listened attentively, they looked up to her as a Senior, they gave her so much energy that she felt buoyant. But when the time came to speak in the school's vast auditorium, she panicked. Halfway through the talk—on nature and art as sources of inspiration—her memory failed her. She'd forgotten to turn the note cards stacked on the podium as she went along, and now she couldn't find her place. The silence grew. She tried to think of a joke, she pondered tossing the cards in the air and saying, what the fuck. That would shock them. But she could see the faces of her father and mother, waiting expectantly for her to continue. And then she found her place, just a line was all she needed and she was rolling again—but the quaver never left her voice. Everyone else on the program had seemed so self-assured. Would she ever feel at ease in front of a crowd?

She scanned the audience in the lecture hall of the Colegio de la Providencia. The Catholic University had no central campus of its own and the conference was being held in one of the college's buildings near the bay. With the exception of local students, almost all in the audience were fellow participants, colleagues from around the world. The tables where they sat, on a series of gradated levels that dropped down, like the seats of a Greek theater, to an oval pit, were equipped with microphones for the question-and-answer period and with headsets. Simultaneous translations were available in three languages—German, English, and

Spanish. Diane, herself, spoke in German, more haltingly than she would have wished, her mouth dry, her accent stronger than normal.

God, she thought, hearing herself speak, she sounded like a graduate student! Words tumbled out of her mouth like the backfire of a faulty muffler.

She prayed for the end of the talk. She was three-fourths of the way through, working toward her conclusion.

When she glanced up for a moment, Walter Stanek, in the top row, was staring at the bottom of one of his shoes, one leg crossed over the other. Was he embarrassed for her? She'd seen him come in late—the sun bright behind him for a moment—and take a seat high up at the top of the lecture hall. He had the earphones on his head, listening, she supposed, to the English translation.

What was he doing here? The last she'd heard he had another disaster-prevention session to attend. Had Renato or Eliana shown up at the Sosa's?

Distractions. She skipped a line in her speech and had to go back and correct herself, blushing at the error.

Pay attention to what you're doing!

She heard a bang that sounded like someone had dropped a book. A shout. A sudden commotion.

She lifted her head, startled by the outcry. Several professors were on their feet, gesticulating wildly. And then she saw it—a cloud of smoke billowing up from one side of the room.

Before she could react, a round object rolled down the middle aisle and exploded near the podium. A loud puff, an expanding mass of smoke. She could smell it then—a stink bomb.

There was a scuffle near the back of the room. Through the smoke she thought she could see Walter Stanek grappling with another man. A chair went flying to the side, kicked by one of the men. Someone had hit a microphone switch at one of the tables. She could hear the huffs of the men, exhalations of breath as fists met body parts. A shirt being torn. The table slammed over then, dropping to the level below, microphone screeching before it went dead.

She felt a hand on her arm, turned to see a nun who'd come out from the wings of the stage.

"Por favor, profesora, venga usted conmigo. Está demasiado peligroso aquí."

For a moment, Diane refused to turn away. Anger flared. "Hooligans," she shouted into the microphone. "Fascists! You have silenced me, but you will never silence the people of Paraguay."

"Come," the nun pleaded. "These men are violent."

Diane turned to follow her. The five officers of the association sitting behind her had already left the room. "Have you called the police?" she asked. She was still angry. "This is indefensible in an institution of learning."

"We are used to it, *profesora*. The police can do nothing to help. This is a sanctuary. We refuse to allow the police on our grounds." She dipped her head in a gesture of chagrin. "But sometimes they come anyway. Sometimes we think it is the secret police themselves who disrupt us." Her voice was full of mortification. "But how are we to know, *profesora*?"

Diane followed the nun down a corridor and into a small office with no windows. The nun pointed to a chair, but Diane shook her head. "I have a friend back there in the audience, Sister. Is there any way to get to him?"

"A friend?" The nun cocked her head in surprise. She was a small woman with a pinched face and dark pockets below her eyes. "The hall will have been cleared by now ... He may be in the courtyard." She sounded reluctant to check.

Diane looked worried. "He was struggling with another man."

The nun wrung her hands. She had pale skin and swollen knuckles with splotchy red highlights, a floor scrubber's fingers. "It's best to stay here for now, *profesora*. There's nothing you can do to help."

"Can you send someone to look for him?"

The nun hesitated. "What does he look like?"

Diane gave a brief description of Stanek. He was probably the only man in the audience wearing corduroy pants and a pullover T-shirt. "Brown corduroy," she said in English, not knowing the correct word in Spanish, "a rough material with ridges." She ran her fingers through the air. "Lines running down."

The nun was confused.

Diane went back to Spanish. "A blue T-shirt," she said, "with a pocket."

"Wait here," the nun said. "I'll see what I can do."

"Who were those assholes?"

Stanek laughed. "At least you're calling *them* the assholes and not me. I figured you'd think *I* was somehow responsible."

She stared at him. "This is not funny."

He wiped the smile off his face. "Sorry. I don't know who it was. There were three or four of them. You were right when you called them fascists. They had some friends outside spray painting the walls with swastikas and black streaks like a triple wave."

"Black streaks?" Diane turned to the nun, a question in her eyes.

"*El Tigre*," the nun said. "They support the dictator."

"Were you fighting with one?" Diane asked Stanek.

He shrugged. "Two of them. Got in a few good blows to the ribs. Had one of them leaning over like a busted stake. His friends had to carry him off."

There was a glint in her eyes. "Good. He deserved it. I'd hate to think they can do this with impunity."

"The university's lucky they tossed stink bombs and not dynamite or a hand grenade."

They were speaking in English, the nun staring back and forth like a bird entranced by a pendulum. She didn't appear to understand a word.

"The nun says it might have been the police," Diane told him.

Stanek shrugged. "Does it matter? Like you said, they're assholes."

"But why me? Saturday, Dink said one of them was coming at me with a knife."

"That student of yours you mentioned—the girl—"

"Rosa."

"Right. She must have done something bad and they think you're involved with the same people. Internal security. They hassle anyone who tries to topple the regime."

"Christ, I'm just a professor of German. Do they really think I'm going to help someone overthrow the government?" She tossed her paper on the desk in frustration. "That's ridiculous."

"That's paranoia, you mean. You might as well forget logic. They perceive you as a threat. They have no idea who you might represent. You could be a go-between for outside forces for all they know."

A young man in a cleric's collar appeared at the door to the office. "Sor Juana would like to see you, *profesora*. She's in her office."

Stanek turned to her. "Who's she?"

"I talked to Professor Aguirre yesterday and he put me in touch with one of the Sisters of the Good Shepherd. They're responsible for the Women's Correctional Institute. From what I gather, they teach courses in domestic science—sewing, nutrition, things like that. Anyway, they think Eliana may have been taken there. They have a section for female juveniles."

While they were being escorted to the administrative wing of the college, Diane asked Stanek about his disaster-prevention program. "Weren't you supposed to be there this morning?"

"I stopped by for ten minutes before it got started," he said, "and then skipped out. Harrington wasn't there either. Off talking to that judge like he promised us, I think. I figured if he wasn't going to make it, then neither was I." He grinned. "Share the punishment. If they want to dock my pay, fine by me."

The sister met them in another small office with a leather sofa facing a plain wooden desk, much scarred. The desk held an Olivetti typewriter, a phone, and stacks of paper. To the side was an ornate, marble-topped table with a chess board on top and a map of Paraguay on the wall. Behind the desk hung an unframed, board-mounted depiction of a sorrowful Virgin Mary, eyes downcast.

Sor Juana listened intently as Diane explained again about Eliana's arrest. "There's no question the police took her," Diane said. "I saw them shove her into the truck myself. And her mother says she hasn't shown up at home."

The sister said the nuns who went to teach at the Correctional Institute often never knew the names of the female prisoners. They were faces in a classroom. "We will need a recent photo," she said. "But even then it may be difficult. The girls are sometimes beaten and their hair is cut."

"Then let me go," Diane said. "Put me in a nun's habit and let me go with one of the other teachers. I know what she looks like. If she's there—if I see her in person, the police can't deny they have her."

Sor Juana shook her head, aghast at the thought. "Impossible," she said. "Too dangerous—and you are not a nun. You have not taken our vows. You belong to no religious order. We could not do this, even if you were her mother."

A hint of chastisement there, Diane thought. Presumption on her part that she should ask to go and not Pina. But she was just trying to help; it didn't matter who went—as long as someone who knew Eliana looked for the girl.

Sor Juana was still shaking her head. "The guards know who we send. We would be discovered and the Order would suffer."

"The guards recognize the nuns in their full habits?"

The sister nodded. "We send the same people for many years." Seeing the frustration on Diane's face, she stopped and lifted her hands apologetically.

Diane closed her eyes for a moment to calm herself. Getting angry would not help. "Can't you do something, Sister?"

"We can pray … we can ask the Holy Father for his intercession."

Did she mean God or the Pope? Not being a Catholic, Diane wasn't sure. She leaned forward and said, "If we don't do something immediately, this girl may disappear forever."

The sister was startled by the passion in Diane's voice. She stared at her a moment longer, compassion in her eyes, then put her hand on her chest and took a deep breath. "Perhaps we could arrange for a special visit …" Her head wobbled like a child's top on its last spin, and her hands fluttered on the desk. "We could take you in as a nutritional expert from another country in Latin America."

"But I don't look Spanish." Maybe Pina should be the one to go. But she had José to take care of, and someone should be there if her husband returned.

"Then you are an expert from America, come to see how we rehabilitate our prisoners."

Diane reached forward and grabbed the nun's shaking hands. She could feel her own heartbeat pick up in renewed hope. "Would the authorities permit that?"

"I know the director of the Institute." The nun shrugged and freed her hands, clasping them in prayer. "A personal appeal. He is married to a cousin of one of our charges."

"Would I wear the habit?"

Sor Juana hesitated before nodding. "God forgive me, it's the only way."

Diane turned to Stanek. "What do you think, Walter?"

"You want my opinion?" he said. He'd been listening to the conversation in disbelief. "Forget trying to get *into* a Women's Correctional Institute and start thinking about getting *out* of the country—and fast. The police already know who you are—and it doesn't look like they take kindly to you. You're worried about Eliana and your own life is at stake."

Their eyes locked for a moment, then Diane said, "Walter, I have a daughter who's just about Eliana's age. If she disappeared, I'd want help from anyone who could give it."

"And if you disappear, what about *your* daughter?"

Diane shook her head with conviction. "I won't disappear. No one at the Institute knows me. Can you imagine me in a nun's habit? Even you wouldn't recognize me."

A crooked smile crossed his face for a second. "I don't know about that," he said. She was too good looking to go unrecognized.

"What color are my eyes?"

"What?" He tried to look but she had covered her face.

Hell, he never noticed eyes. "Brown."

She dropped her hand, a smile of victory on her face. "That settles it then. My eyes are light blue. Even you wouldn't recognize me. If the sister can arrange it, I'm going in."

Chapter Twenty-Three

It was when he turned away from the bar of the Excelsior Hotel that Harrington noticed the men—at least ten, maybe fifteen, all dressed in business suits. They appeared to have filtered out of the Golden Room, where a large wedding reception was being held. Like everyone else in the crowded lounge the men were shouting and gesticulating as if in animated conversation, only these men held no drinks in their hands.

Harrington looked for the judge, who had asked him if they could meet here. He was nowhere in sight. Probably held up in court.

One of the men in the group from the Golden Room stopped in front of him and said, "Are you *señor* Harrington?"

Ah, the judge had sent someone to find him. Harrington stretched his neck and adjusted his bow tie. "Yes, indeed, I am. Jolly good of you to have picked me out. I say, don't tell me the judge can't make it?"

The other men surrounded him as he spoke, tightening the circle, blocking his way out. He saw it then in their faces, a ferocity that sent a chill up his back. A half-smile appeared on the lips of the man who had tricked him.

Harrington's jaundiced eyes registered a quick understanding of the situation. He knew who they were and what they wanted. Too many of them for anything but the worst. He looked for help from someone who might know him—another judge he'd bribed, a businessman, a lawyer who might have argued a case for Samcon, a banker. But the men pressing in on him cut off his view.

Suddenly, before he could react, hands closed around him from behind. He opened his mouth to scream: he wasn't going to be easily taken—not him; if these men got him alone, he was dead—and he couldn't stand the thought of torture first. But when the scream was still deep in his throat, another man jammed a thick wad of cotton in his mouth and yet another slapped a piece of tape over the cotton. A quick taste of hot, salty blood.

They were moving him through the room then, laughing and talking over the music, a solid force like the prow of a barge cutting upstream. Happy revelers parted to each side, oblivious to his plight.

He tried to jerk free, but pressure was applied to his neck until he nearly passed out. Two men supported him between them.

At the elevator, he managed to kick one of his abductors, moaning through the cotton as he struggled to catch someone's attention. And then they hit him. Hard. In the belly.

Vomit rose in his throat. He gasped for air and couldn't get any. Panic overwhelmed him. He was choking to death on his own vomit. Acrid drops of stomach acid burned through his septum and leaked from his nostrils.

And then, with a last jolt, his heart simply stopped beating. Every fiber in his body jerked as a massive electrical discharge fired through his brain. An explosive flash and then darkness, as if a light bulb had shattered on cement. And just as quickly, his body collapsed.

One of the men punched him in the kidneys to see if he was faking, and then, when that received no response, another searched for a pulse. The man swore, and looked up at the group. "A coronary." It was not the first time this had happened.

"Quick, into the restroom," ordered the *jefe*, gesturing to his left up the hallway.

Inside they removed the tape.

"Take out the cotton."

An agent removed the wad with the tips of two fingers. "*¡Qué hedor!*" He plugged his nostrils with the other hand and dropped the cotton into the toilet.

"It's not the vomit," the *jefe* said. "He's crapped his pants."

The men laughed.

"Another piece of *mierda*." The *jefe* shook his head in disgust. "When we get to the car, throw him in the trunk. Adelmo, you know where to dump him."

"Yeah," one of the agents said. "In a ditch, with all the other dog shit."

"Who you working for, anyway, Stanek?" An angry Raymond Kohlbert had cornered him just before the start of the afternoon session at the Colegio Militar.

"You know who I'm working for." Stanek didn't care for Kohlbert's tone of voice. It reminded him of his dad's when Walter was a boy and had done something he wasn't supposed to. Made him feel defensive. "Samcon."

"Sometimes I wonder. You fucked up with the package, didn't you?"

Stanek's head came up. "What do you mean?"

"The stamps."

Stanek's cheeks reddened. He didn't know what to say. Who cared about the stamps? He felt again like a kid called on the carpet, and at forty-three he didn't like the feeling. Next they'd take him out to the woodshed and tan his hide.

Kohlbert stabbed a finger at his chest. "That was just the first fuck-up. You've been late and you've missed a session."

The Samcon agent's stubby boxer's ears were red with anger and the age spots on his forehead stood out like glowing cinders. Kohlbert had just returned from São Paulo that afternoon and was still dressed in jungle fatigues, but his clothes, despite the heat, looked freshly pressed. A military manner in his bearing. Crisp and official. Stanek almost felt like he should be saying *Yes, sir,* and *No, sir.* Instead he just listened.

"You're finished with the war games, buddy. General Paredes warned you yesterday."

"I'm fired? Good, no one told me I was going to be working with a bunch of right-wing fanatics." Stanek felt impatient and Kohlbert irritated him.

"You're on a one-month contract," Kohlbert said, his voice tight. "You don't get out of it so easy. We're sending you to the Corpus project tomorrow. You can do some work for once."

"What about Harrington? I haven't seen him all day."

"You let us worry about Harrington. And what's with this stupid comment about fanatics?" Kohlbert thrust out his chest like a general chastising a soldier. "Samcon's a business. All we want is stability. General Zancon provides that. If you think the left-wing rabble-rousers in this country have the answer you're crazy. Those subversives don't know what they're asking for. You know what happened when the leftist leaders in Guatemala nationalized the United Fruit Company in '54, right?" The small muscles at the corner of his mouth were twitching. "We fucking overthrew the government. Backed the revolt by Colonel Castillo. And we did the same thing in Brazil in 1964."

"And that's your idea of the way to do things?" Stanek looked incredulous. "I thought by now people were a little smarter."

Kohlbert's eyes narrowed. "I'm telling you a revolution is what we're trying to prevent. If we let the people destabilize the regime, we're going to open the door to anti-American forces in this country. No one benefits from that. If they'd had a stable government in Guatemala or Brazil, nothing would have happened."

Stanek shook his head but didn't say anything. He'd wanted to ask Kohlbert if Harrington had gotten through to him about the Sosas. Fat chance of that now. It was people like the Sosas that Kohlbert hated. The old man would have turned them into the police himself—and long before now.

He watched as Kohlbert ran a hand through his grizzled hair, his face growing less rigid. "You're an academic, Stanek, not a businessman. You have to understand where we come from. The market down here is expanding faster than almost anywhere else in the world. To survive, corporations like Samcon have to adapt to changing circumstances. The government erects tariffs against us, so we jump around that by setting up local subsidiaries. They demand an equal voice, so we give the okay to a joint venture. If they create a monopoly in an area of interest to us, we try for a licensing or managing arrangement. But you get a bunch of revolutionaries in there and all hell breaks loose. Then we have to intervene."

"You're like a virus," Stanek said. "Once you've worked your way into a host country, they never get rid of you."

"That's right," Kohlbert said. "And the hotheads in this country won't ever find an antibiotic that we can't get around. But look at it from the other side: we're providing services to an underdeveloped country. The people benefit from that."

He clapped Stanek on the back, as if things were okay now that they'd had a frank talk. "If you were a businessman coming down here with a company, you'd want to know what the political hot spots were, right? You'd want advice on potential threats. These so-called national liberation armies are a bunch of hogwash. They're only going to make things worse. We've got to support the forces of order."

Stanek nodded as if he understood. Kohlbert wasn't going to change, not at his age. "How do I get to the site of the Corpus project tomorrow."

Kohlbert smiled. "In one of our Cessnas. I'll have you flown in to a military base near the dam site. The army'll put you up while you do your work. I've arranged everything with General Paredes. I want you out at the air field by eight tomorrow morning. I'd fly you myself but I have some business to take care of."

"You said the air field. Do you mean the international airport?"

"No, there's a base just south of the airport with its own runway. Take a taxi. You want Avenida General Genes. You'll see the Comando de Aeronautica before you get to the airport. Tell the driver to turn left on Carmelo Peralta."

"Here, let me write this down," Stanek said.

"You can't miss it." Kohlbert's tone was crisp and efficient. "You take another left at any of the next three roads. If you pass a swimming pool you've gone too far. You'll see a row of hangars by the aeronautical school. I'll have a pilot standing by."

That evening, Stanek accompanied Diane Lang by taxi to the Sosa residence. Pina had just put José to bed and was sitting in the living room talking to several other guests who had dropped by to see how she was doing. Pina introduced the two Americans and explained their involvement; they were friends who could be trusted, she said.

The Paraguayans absorbed that comment without expression, but soon, as their initial wariness diminished, they began to talk about their work.

One of the men had just come back from reorganizing a unit of the Asamblea de Campesinos sin Tierra—the Assembly of Landless Peasants—in the Cordillera Department near Emboscada, where the union had succeeded in gaining control of the *junta municipal*, elected by the local residents, but was having problems with the *intendente*, who governed the area by presidential appointment.

From the conversation, it became apparent that they were colleagues of Renato Sosa, and, like him, were not only active in the union movement but members of an underground political party. Renato appeared to be the leader of their particular cell.

"Officially, the party's illegal," one of them said, smiling. "As foreigners, you could be construed to have broken the law just by talking to us. Especially in a group."

Stanek shrugged. "That's fine," he said. "I'm an anarchist by nature."

"And from all appearances I'm a wanted woman anyway," Diane added.

One of the men eyed her with a lustful look. "Wanted in more ways than one," he said.

Stanek didn't care for the innuendo but as far as he could tell Lang didn't seem to take it amiss. In fact, she took advantage of the moment to tell Pina what she intended to do regarding the Women's Correctional Institute. When she finished, several of the men tried to warn her.

"The director of that Institute is very suspicious of outsiders," a dark-skinned man told her, straight black hair hanging to his eyebrows and over his ears. "We tried to send in a nurse one time. To organize the women. When she pressed for improvements in their living conditions, she was arrested. They took her across the border and told her not to come back. They threatened to kill her if they saw her again."

"Someone's already tried to kill Diane," Stanek said.

The men looked at her with renewed interest. *"¿Por qué, señora?"*

Diane shook her head slowly, a baffled look on her face. "I'm not sure. At first I thought it was because I was here to talk about the Mennonites, but … it might be because of a student of mine. She was arrested and beaten by the secret police. I don't really know what she was doing, but she died in their custody."

There was a moment of silence.

Stanek turned to Pina. "Was this political party Renato belongs to doing something that threatened the government?"

One of the men laughed. "Everything we do, *señor*, threatens the government. Renato is a lawyer. He defends *campesinos* who have seized their land from the *latifundios*."

"From the what?"

"From very large landholdings. Usually controlled by foreigners. They are the *patrones*, we are the *peones*. The history of this is long. Years ago, one Argentine company—just one—purchased fifteen percent of the Chaco region. A vast area. They came in, cut down the quebracho trees for their tannin and hardwood, and then left. They have no love for the land. They strip it and move on."

Pina plucked at her blouse. An overhead fan circulated the air, which still held the day's heat. "Renato was trying to contact one of the party's leaders," she said. "A man held by the government. I think that is why they arrested him. To silence him."

"Alquijana," another man said. "Francisco Rojas de Alquijana. We no longer know where they have taken him." He took a drag from a cigarette and exhaled toward the fireplace. No one else in the room was smoking. "Alquijana is the only man who really threatens General Zancon. The people love him. For now, he is our only hope."

"General Zancon calls himself *El Tigre*," another said, "but Alquijana is *El León*." He raised his hands to his ears as if to brush back hair. "He has a flowing mane of white hair. Very majestic."

"Why was he arrested?" Diane asked.

"Does the government need a reason?" The smoker waved his free hand. "Alquijana was walking home from the office one evening. A car stopped to pick him up. An offer of a ride was made. We never saw him again."

"But he's alive," Pina said. "*El Tigre* is afraid to kill him. He would lose all the people then."

"We've heard rumors as to his whereabouts," another said. "They questioned him first at the Policía Central and then at Tacumbú Penitentiary. One of our priests—"

"Padre Guzman," Pina said.

"Yes, Padre Guzman talked to him once. But now Alquijana has disappeared again. We don't know where they've moved him or if he's still alive."

"He's not at Emboscada," the dark-skinned man said. He looked at the Americans. "Emboscada is what you would call a concentration camp. We've contacted people inside the prison there."

There was a pause in the conversation and Pina got up to serve drinks. One of the men turned to Stanek and asked him what he would be doing while Professor Lang was in the Women's Correctional Institute.

"Unfortunately, I can't do anything to help Pina. I'm leaving tomorrow morning. But I have a friend who is trying to help."

"And what is he doing?"

"He works for the same company I do. Harrington's his name. He knows a judge in the city. He promised to contact him to see if he could come up with any information on Renato. But I haven't heard from him all day. I told Professor Lang how to contact him."

"So you return to America?"

"No, not yet. I'm supposed to be here a month. I'm working on the Corpus Dam project."

"You are in construction?"

Stanek shook his head. "I'm a hydrogeologist. I'll be preparing a survey of the dam's possible environmental effects. They tell me most of the plans have been drawn up, so I doubt if anything will change, but they want to know ahead of time what might happen to the region."

"So you will tour the whole area?"

Stanek nodded. "I'll probably fly the Paraná river between Encarnación and Itaipú Dam. And then there's a lot of work to be done on the ground."

Two of the others had approached the couch where Stanek sat. Diane had moved off to the kitchen with Pina.

One of the men said, "The army has a secret military base between the Cordillera de San Rafael and the Paraná river, near Pirapo and Vicay."

"I know. I'll be staying at the compound."

"They have a garrison and a military prison."

"No one mentioned that."

"It's very hard to learn these things. We think they may have political prisoners there."

Stanek could feel the change in atmosphere. The men standing around him had grown intent, like vultures hovering over their prey.

"We have been unable to infiltrate the base. It's highly restricted. They admit men loyal only to the president."

"But you will be allowed inside?" another asked.

"As far as I know. That's what I was saying. I'll be working out of an office in one of the barracks there. That'll be my headquarters."

Two of the men turned away and began talking rapidly in Guaraní. The others listened, but looked around the room as if nothing were going on. Stanek felt uncomfortable. They were going to ask him to look for this leader of theirs—Alquijana. He was sure of it.

He hadn't minded trying to find Renato Sosa—he knew the man; the family had helped him. But Alquijana was a different matter. If these men asked him to fool around on a secret military base, they were putting his life in jeopardy. That wasn't the same as running around Asunción, trying to find out where the police had taken Renato and Eliana.

When Pina returned, the fellow who'd been smoking told her about Stanek's trip to the Corpus project.

"He'll be headquartered at the Poromoco base," he said.

Pina's eyes widened. "Renato," she said. "They may have Renato there."

By the time the two Americans were ready to leave, the group had convinced Stanek to ask around—carefully, of course—about both Renato Sosa and Francisco Rojas de Alquijana, and he had agreed for Pina's sake.

Since no one knew where Diane would be on any given day, his contact would be Pina. He was not to write or telephone, however, since that carried too many risks. If he learned anything useful, he would have to think of some excuse to return to Asunción, where they could speak with each other in person.

Stanek nodded his head without responding. It was easier to say yes and go about one's business than to get involved in the details of their security.

On the way back downtown, once again in a taxi, Stanek asked Diane whether she'd heard from Dink Denton.

She shook her head. "He told me to contact him if I needed help. He said he had business to take care of."

"Well, I hope everything goes well for you," Stanek said. "I won't be able to help from the Corpus site."

"You'll have enough to worry about on your own," she said. "Let me give you Dink's number. Who knows, you may need more help than me."

Yeah, Stanek thought, but that didn't mean Dink would jump to help him. He didn't wear a skirt.

Five minutes after she gave him Dink's telephone number, in the darkness of the taxi, she slipped her hand into his. Stanek was surprised but said nothing in response. He thought he understood why she did it—they both had need of human contact—but whatever the reason, even if only human solidarity, he liked it, liked the warmth of her hand, the softness of flesh, the sensation of skin on skin.

The funny thing was, he realized, this might be the last time he ever saw her. They were both going their separate ways.

Just when they were beginning to like each other.

Chapter Twenty-Four

Stanek had to read about it in the morning paper, a small item on page one of *El Diario de Noticias*. D. Benjamin Harrington was dead.

While the pilot prepared the Cessna for their flight to the military base near the Corpus Dam project, Stanek sat on a bench inside the corrugated-tin hangar and read the story.

Muerto un Extranjero

The body of a man identified as D. Benjamin Harrington was discovered in a ditch outside Asunción late yesterday evening.

According to observers, the man resembled other recent victims found in the area who have been tortured and then burned, but Col. Hector Ibarras, *Jefe de Investigaciones* of the National Police told reporters that Harrington appeared to have been the victim of a robbery.

Harrington died less than two weeks after arriving in this country to take a position as director of the risk control division of Samcon International, a multinational corporation with several local subsidiaries. He was a frequent visitor to our city and was well known in the business community.

Late last night, Colonel Ibarras released a statement saying that Harrington's body had been cremated at the request of his employer and "in order to provide for the peace and stability of the Paraguayan people."

According to the same statement, an autopsy revealed that Harrington died of a heart attack, "probably caused by his efforts to resist the men attempting to rob him. He was then burned by the thieves in an attempt to disguise his identity."

The police have no suspects.

By the time Stanek finished the story, the newspaper was shaking in his hands. He got up, decided he couldn't risk using his voice to ask the pilot if there was a restroom nearby, and went to look for it himself.

He found the toilet and wash basin next to a mechanic's work area and tool shed. The fixtures were stained with oil and grease, but Stanek turned on the single tap and dashed cold water into his face.

Harrington's death was a shock. Stanek could feel the trembling in his legs. He felt weak and shaky, as if from a sugar hit, an empty sensation deep in his chest that left him feeling airy and light-headed.

Harrington's death was no accident. No attempted robbery. Stanek was convinced of that. No, Harrington had been killed in the middle of the day. For trying to help the Sosas. And for that Stanek felt responsible. Had he let a simple act of kindness—his and Diane's rescue in the barrio—draw him, and Harrington, into a quagmire? The Sosas had done what any good-hearted person would have. None of them owed the family their lives.

He drank a few swallows of water, and then used the toilet. Before he was finished, the pilot knocked on the door and said he was ready for take-off.

Stanek mumbled a response, then zipped up his pants. He had to flush the toilet by reaching into the tank and lifting the lever that raised the ball. The outside trip handle was broken. *What am I doing in this country?* God, it was just like Mexico—and he'd swore that he'd never go back there.

What about Diane? Would she read the article? Would she realize the full extent of the danger? All of them could simply disappear—like Harrington. A pile of ashes tossed in the dump. Did the old man have family who cared?

Stanek left the bathroom and walked to the plane. He felt numb. The pilot gestured to a seat and continued his rundown of the checklist. Stanek fastened his lap and shoulder harness and then saw the headset.

Damn. He was hoping they wouldn't have to talk during the flight. Samcon's pilot, at least, had seemed a laconic man—a tall, lanky American from Montana named Hank Wilson—and that had suited Stanek fine. He didn't feel like talking either.

Wilson was cleared for take-off by the control tower and almost immediately they were rolling and then airborne, climbing at a steady angle and turning toward the east. Behind them, two of the air force's T-6s were making their final approach for landing.

Soon they'd left the city behind and were following the train tracks that skirted the Cordillera de los Altos. None of the mountain ranges were very impressive. A series of low hills really, with an elevation of at most three hundred and fifty meters.

Stanek could see thick woods—the *monte*—on some hills, with valleys of grassland—the *campo*—and tiny farms called *chacras* scattered here and there, each with a mud-and-stick rancho with a thatched roof. Coconut palms dotted the land in profusion, and here and there lay a larger estancia with a ranch house and outbuildings. Occasionally a village passed below them, some with a grass airstrip.

They left the train tracks at Paraguarí.

During the night, thick storm clouds had moved in over the central region—warm, humid winds out of Brazil—and the prior day's heat had failed to dissipate. The air was muggy and hot and Stanek found himself wishing for rain, for cool drops to wash away the prickly, oppressive feeling. An irrational thought, he realized. He was enclosed in an airplane. The rain would be like a downpour drumming on a tomb. He didn't like the image that came to mind. *I don't belong here*, was all he could think.

More hill ridges—the Serranía de Ybycuí. At Maciel, they crossed the train tracks, which angled south toward Encarnación. The pilot offered Stanek a banana but he declined. He sipped sparingly from a bottle of purified water.

By noon, as if in answer to his prayers, the sky grew dark and the pilot dropped closer to the ground, trying to fly under the storm. Their route lay just to the south of the Cordillera de San Rafael and the terrain undulated gently. Sporadic rain lashed the Cessna's windshield. Below them, the first breath of a tropical storm shook the dead branches of the scattered palm trees. Stanek could see a dirt road, the soil red, and four vaqueros driving a motley assortment of cattle toward an estancia. The men were hidden under ponchos.

And then the skies above them broke open and a torrent of rain sluiced down, blinding them. The wipers struggle against the onslaught.

Stanek could hear something on the radio—a report from a weather station transmitted from the military base at Coronel Bogado. It sounded like the ceiling varied from three hundred to eight hundred feet with visibilities from one to two miles. Isolated thunderstorms with tops to thirty-five thousand feet, winds aloft at thirty-two knots, gusting to fifty.

It didn't sound good to him, but he didn't need a weather report to tell it was bad. The plane was being buffeted about now, the engine noise rising and falling, but the pilot showed no signs of worry. Stanek thought about asking him to look for a landing place to wait out the storm, but the dirt roads, when they crossed them, were rivers of mud.

A landing strip appeared ahead of them, a tower to one side, two hangars. Stanek could see a row of military barracks behind the hangers and then a compound, with a fortlike structure that flew the Paraguayan flag, several other buildings, and rows of small cabins, many of them hidden in trees.

"Poromoco," Hank said, his first words in well over an hour. The pilot contacted the tower and was instructed to start his descent. To one side, a helicopter lifted off a pad and swept away to the southeast.

It was still raining when they rolled to a stop at one of the hangars, but in a few minutes the clouds passed over and the sun reappeared. Steam rose from muddy puddles and the buzz of insects lifted to a crescendo. The air was muggy and Stanek wanted a shower.

He looked at his watch. It was a little after two and he suddenly realized he was hungry. A *subteniente* was waiting for him in a jeep.

"I'll see you later," Hank said. "What time you want to tour the river tomorrow?"

"Let's start at eight," Stanek said. "I've got the rest of the today to make preparations. When do you return to Asunción?"

"I'm at your service till Friday, then I head back. How long before you're done here?"

Stanek shrugged. "I don't know. I'm on a one-month contract. That gives me about three weeks. That should be enough time for a preliminary study and the locals can take it from there."

And if he was lucky, he thought, he could write the report from Asunción. The sooner he got back to the capital and out of the army's hands the better.

• • •

After a quick meal, two military engineers, both captains, led him to a small cabin where he left his belongings. They then took him on foot to an office area in a wood-plank building surrounded by ferns with reddish-brown mossy boles. Before going inside, Stanke could see that, farther back, a dense forest of hardwood trees took over, mostly cedar and ceiba, rising slowly into the low hills to the north.

Both engineers spoke excellent English, but the *subteniente* who'd been assigned to watch over him spoke only Guaraní and Spanish. That'd be the guy he'd have to work on, Stanek thought. A second lieutenant, young and eager to please. He might know something about the prisoners. If there really was a prison here. He'd seen no sign of one so far.

Stanek dismissed the junior officer for the afternoon and sat down to begin work. He had a variety of reports and maps to pour over before initiating his own study. When he asked the two captains what had already been done, the men said that most of their work consisted of helping design the project itself, from the layout of blueprints to logistical arrangements for when construction actually began to the setting up of communication facilities.

The two men were part of the army's engineer command, composed of six battalions. In answer to a question, they explained that the battalions were dispatched as needed throughout the country. They were assigned to both military and civilian construction projects and also assisted in other civic-action tasks. None of the engineers, it turned out, were trained in the most recent advances in conservation and the ecology of natural waters. That's where Stanek came in.

What surprised him the most was that no one, as far as he could tell, would impose any pressure on him. On most research projects dealing with the generation of electricity, he had to contend with two contrasting points of view—that of industry and that of conservationists. On this project he was apparently free to put the ecological truths into perspective without reference to either politics or public relations.

When the two engineers had covered their work to date, Stanek asked for time to go over their reports and sat down at a metal desk to begin reading. At first, he had trouble concentrating, but soon work habits took over and Renato Sosa receded from his mind as the details of the Corpus project sprang to life.

For the rest of the day, he scanned data until his eyes blurred—detailed descriptions of the natural environment, sketches of the geological structures in the zone, soil analyses including permeability and evaporation rates, climatic conditions with average rainfall and temperature ranges, a study of the natural vegetation, an inventory of animal species, a summary of the economy of the region, and maps of the rivers and streams, of areas suitable for arable farming, of historical sites, of villages and other colonization zones, of the road network.

But no analysis of the environmental impact of the project or of its effect on the human population.

Still, it was a good beginning; there was much there to form a basis for interpretation, and that would spare him some time. All of the preliminary work had been done for him. Shoot, maybe he could get out of the area quicker than he'd thought. Do the study, snoop around to see if there was a military prison—but how in hell he could find out if Renato Sosa was there, or this Alquijana, he had no idea—and then back to civilization.

Such as it was.

At seven that evening, the *subteniente* returned on foot to pick him up and escort him to the officer's mess hall. Stanek tried to engage the fellow in conversation, but could not get beyond the basics.

The kid was a thin, dark-skinned Indian of medium height from Horqueta, a village near Concepción. His name was Tito Gauna, he said, but his friends called him Mamenga, which meant hornet. He was a member of the Ava-Chiripa tribe.

And that was all Stanek managed to get out of the fellow, despite his cheerful volubility. Half of what the guy said, Stanek did not understand.

At dinner, which consisted of cold manioc, fried fish, sweet potatoes, lima beans, and fresh fruit for dessert, Stanek drank too much Suabia, a honey-colored, heavy-bodied Paraguayan wine that left him feeling sleepy.

This would not be a night for wandering around the compound, he decided. In fact, when the meal was over he barely managed to stumble back to his private cabin in the darkness, with Tito at his side. Muttering his thanks, he tumbled fully dressed into his cot, and fell asleep the minute his head hit the thin pillow.

"What time do we move in?" Dink asked.

His companion, a senior DEA agent, looked at his watch out of reflex. It was nearly two-thirty in the morning. "Henderson and Palmer need time to scale a fence and disable the electronic security system." He fingered the two-way radio on the seat between them. "Once I get the word, I'll call in the boys."

The van with the other members of the assault force was parked on a side street a block away.

Dink hadn't been in on the planning. The day before, at his request, other men had taken over for him, tailing De Negri, the *narcotraficante*, while Dink helped Diane Lang and Walter Stanek. Dink had called in sick to the DEA's local safe house, using a public telephone in a *bolichero* near his girlfriend's shack. During his absence, things had moved fast. Proof of De Negri's dealings with the Bolivians had come through from a wire tap. General Zancon had given his approval. The Americans would arrest De Negri, fly him out to Miami on one of their own planes, and leave the Bolivian contacts, by prearrangement, up to their own government.

While they waited for the word from Henderson, Dink said, "Is the

Embassy in on this?"

The senior agent shook his head. "I convinced Washington last night that you were right. Too many leaks."

"Good."

Conrad Kleemer, Embassy Counselor, CIA agent. When Dink had asked for his help with the Sosas, Kleemer had wanted a quid pro quo—the identity of their drug suspect in Paraguay, claiming it was the CIA, after all, who'd put the DEA on the Bolivians' trail.

But Kleemer had nothing to do with that. The Company's information came out of La Paz and Sucre, in Bolivia. Kleemer's contacts in Asunción had come up with nothing. At this stage, the Counselor had no need to know, and his very asking had made Dink suspicious. Too many other busts had gone haywire in Paraguay.

But not this one. It wouldn't be long now.

Colonel Hector Ibarras answered the phone in his office in the compound of the Presidential Escort Regiment.

"That's right," he said. "You'll be dealing directly with me."

He listened to the high-pitched voice of the man at the other end of the line, a grin on his own face.

"I had to," he said. "The DEA's like a hungry shark. I fed them De Negri. That will satisfy them for a while." Until *I* take over as president, he thought.

He listened a second time to the angry voice of the Bolivian, then said, "You must understand my reasons. General Zancon has been pressuring the police for results. He's afraid of losing aid from the United States. Now, with this fish in their net, you will have no worries. He'll keep them busy."

A calmer voice at the other end. The Bolivian was beginning to see the advantages.

Ibarras said, "I've made arrangements with the head of the Banco

Central. Starting now we'll be able to launder up to a million in U.S. dollars a week. At our usual cut, of course."

He smiled at the reply, not only at the words, which were gratifying, but at the tone, which, finally, as he had expected, was obsequious.

The Bolivians knew, too. Before long, they would have a direct line to the president of Paraguay—Colonel, no, make that *General* Hector Ibarras himself. Just a few more steps to take, one or two more obstacles to flatten, and the good life would begin.

Chapter Twenty-Five

For two days, Wednesday and Thursday of that week, Stanek flew the Paraná river with Hank Wilson.

In November, with the start of summer, the water flow was diminishing, but the river was still impressive, at times, particularly after it left Paraguay and entered Argentina, extending as much as ten miles in width.

"Good fishing down there," was all Hank Wilson said. "Pacu and dorado." He seemed oblivious to the beauty that sometimes left Stanek in awe.

The water varied in color as the day advanced. In the early morning, it lay oyster-gray, a mist rising from its slow, quiescent u-bends and drifting over the creeper-infested trees along the banks. Rotting logs lay half in, half out of the water, and a profusion of brilliant flowers—scarlet, white, violet—added a haze to the greenery.

As the sun soared skyward, pale rose tints along the river's surface turned tangerine, then brick red. In stretches, the riverbed lay like a straight road cut through the forest, the water as red as the surrounding soil, a clay heavy in iron oxides.

After midday, with the sun blazing overhead, tumbling white water appeared, a series of rapids on a tributary, and then, in the afternoon, as they made their way back to the main channel, the serene color of blue. And after that, long, hot hours that dragged on, the glare of light reflecting off the water as if it were chrome. But as soon as the sun began its decline, the river turned from reflected gold to blue-black, sliding by like a long, thin water snake, dangerous and foreboding.

For its final transformation, just before sunset, as if to belie the threat, the rippling water glistened with cool lavender, shading finally to gray, before darkness erased it from view.

At dawn on Friday, Hank Wilson returned in the Cessna to Asunción.

Having made arrangements the night before to visit the proposed site of the Corpus dam, Stanek and the two Paraguayan engineers left the army post soon after. A military helicopter ferried the three men to Puerto Bella Vista, and from there they crossed the river by ferry to Puerto Corpus in Argentina.

The Paraná river, which had been flowing for a short distance from east to west, cut due south at that point, dividing around a small island dotted with willows and sand spits. Buoys marked the deepest channel and several freighters and tugboats moved slowly upstream against a northerly summer wind toward Ciudad del Este. Old, rusty craft, mostly flat-bottomed, plied the river on mysterious errands, crossing back and forth from one side to the other.

"A smuggler's paradise," one of the men said. "The navy patrols the river, but—" His words died away and he shrugged eloquently.

"No hay que hacerse mala sangre," the other said.

Stanek snorted. Yeah, maybe that should be his attitude. Don't let it get to you. He'd been thinking about the Sosas and Diane Lang and his own problems. But hadn't he told his sister Randi—jeez, it was barely a week ago—that he was bored and wanted a change of scenery? That he needed a little spice in his life?

So why get excited? This was what he asked for, right?

Well ... not quite. A little spice didn't mean the fear of being picked up and questioned by secret police goons or by military intelligence. A little spice didn't include being tortured or killed.

He spent the day with a divided mind, doing his job but wondering at the same time how long it would be before a dark tentacle reached out and touched him on the shoulder—or wrapped itself around his neck.

Friday night, his fourth in the compound.

He had not yet dared ask around about political prisoners. He couldn't wait much longer. Who knew what was happening back in Asunción?

They would be waiting on him, no doubt about that.

Sitting in his cabin, trying to read in the light cast by a kerosene lantern, the air hot and muggy, Stanek was surprised to find he missed his contacts with Diane and the others. Despite the initial antagonism, he and Diane had quickly established a bond that until now he hadn't realized existed. It was true, there existed an intimacy of antagonism as close as the intimacy of affection. And passing from one to the other was sometimes as easy as crossing the street. He felt a tug within him that he couldn't deny.

Hell, he even missed Dink. Now there was a character. Earlier in the week, when they were trying to help Pina Sosa, they'd seen a group of kids shooting baskets at one of the schools near the Policlínico Cristo Rey and Dink had said that when he was a kid, shooting basketballs meant blowing them apart with a thirty-ought-six.

They'd had a good laugh about that.

Stanek turned down the kerosene lamp until the flame died away. Lying on his cot in the dark, he remembered another conversation—this one with Diane, late one night in a taxi. Walter had said that at first all he'd come down here to do was a good job. But that goal had quickly changed to: do a good job *and survive!*

Diane had laughed, then grown serious. She had come down to conduct research on the Mennonites, she said, but she believed in helping people who needed it. She understood darkness and despair.

And then she told him what had happened to her once when she was just four years old and lived in Shelton, a small town near the Housatonic River in Connecticut, not far from New Haven. An older neighborhood boy, probably only in the first or second grade, had locked her in a coal bin behind a row of apartment houses where they were playing. She'd stayed there all night, wetting her underpants, sobbing in the darkness, crying until no more tears would come, her face streaked with soot.

The whole neighborhood turned out to help her parents and the police look for her, but no one could hear her whimpering and no one thought to look in a locked coal bin until daybreak.

The point of the story was, who knew what Eliana was facing? She was older, but still—being locked in a coal shed was different from being picked up by the secret police. Stanek understood what she was saying—it was the difference between fear and terror.

Then there was Harrington ... Stanek couldn't forget him—with his dishwater-gray hair and jaundiced eyes and ridiculous bow ties, his dry wit and sharp tongue, cracking his big, bony knuckles when he was nervous, hanging on to his accent and his British mannerisms though he'd lived in the States for over forty years.

Stanek smiled. That first night, at the bar in the Club Bahia Negra, when Harrington had asked which stool he should take, Stanek had pointed to either side, then made a comment about being ambidextrous, joking that it didn't matter which hand he had to use to lift a beer. "Well, old chap," Harrington had said, jerking both hands as if he were milking a cow. "I'm bisexual, too, but that doesn't mean I'll drink the foam off your lager."

Whatever that had meant; Stanek still wasn't sure if the old man had intended the sexual innuendo, or if it was a joke gone somehow awry. But they had both burst out laughing.

Now, it didn't matter. Harrington was dead.

And Randi ... what was she doing these days? Hard to imagine in this muggy heat that up there in Ferndale, not far from the Canadian border, there might be frost on the ground. Randi would be out chopping wood, preparing the log pile for winter. No Thanksgiving together, but Christmas, for sure ... he'd promised.

It didn't matter who came to mind—Randi, Harrington, Dink, or Diane. In this vast darkness, he missed them all.

On Saturday, Stanek told the two engineers he needed a break. He wanted to tramp around the woods a bit with the *subteniente* as his guide.

"If you come across any creeks, watch out for the *yacares*," one said, the corners of his mouth twisting up into a half-smile.

"What's that?" Stanek asked, wondering if the fellow was pulling his leg, expecting some story about a mythic monster deep in the jungle.

The other engineer laughed. "Alligators," he said. "If you see a bluish tint on a dark-brown bank, stay the hell clear of it. They're damn hungry around here."

Promising to watch his step, Stanek left the office and signaled to the *subteniente*, who was sitting on a metal chair outside the door. He explained in broken Spanish what he wanted to do and then stopped by his cabin for the knapsack he'd prepared earlier that morning. He expected to be gone most of the day and had packed food and a canteen of water.

With Tito out in front, Stanek worked his way toward the crown of a hill, following a twisting path through tangled lianas and creepers. Whenever the terrain leveled out, stagnant water puddled in swampy declivities and a rich scent of leaf decay hung in the air. Overhead, howler monkeys screamed in the tree tops and at one point, exasperated by the ruckus, Stanek shouted and tossed a rock into the leafy growth. Tito laughed and before Stanek could say anything drew a pistol and fired a warning shot.

"Carayas," he said. "You want roasted monkey for lunch?" He looked disappointed when Stanek shook his head. The American had packed chipa bread, apples, and grapes in his knapsack.

Stanek decided to humor him. "What else you got out here worth eating, Tito?"

The *subteniente* tipped his head, then said the words first in Guaraní and then in Spanish. "*Yaguareté*—the jaguar, *taí catí*—the wild boar, *curiyú*—the anaconda, *ñacurutú*—the owl. All very good. If you like, I'll go hunting and fix you one of them."

"No thanks," Stanek said. "I'll stick to bread and fruit."

The Indian laughed. He'd been educated in Concepción, but he still retained the tastes of his tribe. "In school," he said, "we had to read *La Voragine*. I always remember one line. 'And when dawn sheds over the forest its tragic glory, there begins the outcry of those who have survived.'"

"Let's hope that includes us," Stanek said.

Two hours later when they reached the crown of the hill—a bald spot of hard rock ringed by stunted eucalyptus, Stanek stopped and looked back toward the army post. The cabins were hidden in trees, but the turreted walls of the fort were clearly visible and beyond that the hangars and airfield. He could see one of the army's counterinsurgency aircraft as it lifted off the runway and headed south toward Encarnación.

"Rumors of guerrilla activity from the other side," Tito said, noticing

Stanek's eyes following the plane. "Our officers say they may attack from Argentina."

"Here?"

Tito shook his head. "In the city. Encarnación. Here they would stand no chance. We are too well protected. And they are not sure how to find us."

"What if some of the military turned?" Stanek asked. "Not everyone is content with *El Tigre*."

Tito shrugged. "The soldiers of this battalion are loyal. We will do what our officers tell us."

But that was just it, Stanek thought. If there was to be a coup, it would probably come from the army, led by one of their officers. He wondered if the guerrillas had been successful in recruiting any of the soldiers to their side. If the military rose up and took over on its own, the country would find itself with just another dictator. If the guerrillas were in charge, if they were successful, then democracy had a chance.

He was about to turn away when he asked about the fort, his voice casual. "Why all the guards around the fort, anyway? You'd think the president was staying there."

A sardonic smile twisted Tito's broad features. "Men who would like to be president," he said. "Crazy men. Politicians. Soldiers who refuse to obey commands. Enemies of the state. The fort is a military prison. Only *El Tigre* knows who is here."

Stanek hid his excitement. *Okay!* So there was a prison and it held political prisoners. Was that going to satisfy Sosa's friends back in Asunción? Probably not. They'd already told him they knew that. All he could do now was confirm what they already knew.

And it looked like it would stay that way. He wouldn't get inside, that was for sure. He wasn't even going to try. This was no Women's Correctional Institute where nuns attended to the female prisoners. He'd seen the guards patrolling the fort. Hard-faced men, all heavily armed. Well-trained commandoes who obviously knew what they were doing.

But every prison had to keep records. The question was where—and would Tito know.

"So they fly the prisoners in," Stanek said, nodding toward the airstrip beyond the fort.

Tito nodded. "Special units of the military police. The prisoners are blindfolded. They never know where they are. And no one has ever left."

"They must be important men."

Tito shrugged. He appeared indifferent to their fate.

"Who does the interrogation?"

"Intelligence officers. They keep to themselves."

For a moment, the conversation died. He and Tito were making their way down the other side of the hill, following a ridge that dropped to a grassy valley with a stream flowing through it.

Apparently Tito had no connection with the intelligence units, but that was to be expected. "Have you been inside the fort?" Stanek asked.

Tito shook his head. "But you can hear the screams." He stopped in a clearing to light a cigarette.

"So you never see the prisoners?"

A slow grin appeared on Tito's face. He raised his hands as if holding a rifle, smoke curling around his head from the cigarette in his right hand. "*¡Pum, pum, pum!*" he said. "Only when we execute them."

Chapter Twenty-Six

By four o'clock Stanek and the *subteniente* were back in the compound, strangely quiet under a withering sun. Even the army seemed to observe the hour of siesta, Stanek thought. Either that or they were occupied elsewhere. The fort, however, had its usual complement of guards.

Dust rose in puffs from the dirt paths between the temporary office buildings. A fine, red layer settled on their shoes. Stanek stopped outside the engineer's workroom. He gestured toward the larger building across from the fort, regimental headquarters. "Sometime soon, Tito, I would like to thank the commander for his hospitality. Can you arrange a visit for me?"

The *subteniente* hunched his shoulders, a doubtful look on his face.

"I'm a guest of your government," Stanek said. "I was talking to General

Paredes just before coming out. He said everything would be done to facilitate my work. I want to thank your commander for his help."

Tito's eyes widened. "General Bernardo Paredes?"

Stanek nodded. "And I saw Major General Alberto Campos also."

"He's the head of army intelligence."

"Yes, I know. I met them both in Asunción at the Colegio Militar."

"The major general has an office here." Tito pointed to the rectangular headquarters building across from the fort. "Right now, Colonel Samudio is the highest ranking officer available. I will talk to my immediate superior and see what he can do. The colonel is usually quite busy."

"Thanks," Stanek said. "If the colonel can spare just a moment, perhaps sometime tomorrow, I'd like to stop in and express my gratitude in person."

Sunday afternoon, the visit, as Stanek expected, was brief. At first, he wasn't sure what he had hoped to accomplish. Colonel Samudio met him in a large room that was nearly empty. He saw two desks, one with a typewriter, the other with a small bronze bust of General Zancon next to a clipboard, a nameplate for the regiment embossed on an inverted v-shaped piece of metal, and assorted papers and work materials. Four chairs were lined up against one wall. The rough wallboards were painted a bright green, the sturdy plank doors a shiny red. The air smelled lightly of varnish. There were no files or filing cabinets visible.

One detail, of no real significance, caught Stanek's eye. Everyone— from the colonel on down to the private on guard duty at the door—wore fancy imported watches with thick gold bands and large faces. Somehow the watches didn't seem to belong with the uniforms.

The colonel was a serious man, not given to smiling. His dark face was shiny with perspiration. He wore a white T-shirt under his long-sleeved uniform, which was unbuttoned at the neck. There was no air-conditioning and no fan to stir up a breeze.

Smelling his own sweat, more acrid than normal because of his nerves, Stanek shook hands and thanked the colonel for the military's aid with the Corpus project.

They exchanged a few polite words and then Stanek turned to go. At that moment, a door off to one side was thrust open and another officer stepped into the room, drawing up in surprise at the site of a civilian. Behind him, before he could shut the door, Stanek saw a narrow room with a row of gray filing cabinets lined up against the wall behind a work table and chair.

He had no chance to see if there was another entrance. The officer shut the door behind him, and Stanek, with a nod in his direction, stepped out the other door into a hallway where Tito was patiently waiting.

"Let's go," Stanek said. "I've got some work to do in the office."

For the rest of the afternoon Stanek thought of ways to infiltrate the headquarters building. He had seen it at night, a dark object in the gloom, apparently unguarded. But there were soldiers who patrolled the compound and for all he knew other measures to detect intruders. The building had sturdy doors and locks that did not look easy to jimmy.

What about windows? There had been a few. The afternoon sun had illuminated the room from behind him. But the windows had heavy shutters that were closed at night. He couldn't remember if they were locked from the outside or bolted from within. Too many other things to catch his attention for the few short minutes of his visit.

What about from under the floor? The buildings were all built up off the ground. They had to have crawl spaces. But how to get through the floor without tools? And at night, who knew what snakes or poisonous insects lurked in those hidden recesses.

He swore to himself. Should have taken some object he could have left and gone back for later when only one or two men were around. But what did he expect to do? Kill one or two with his bare hands?

Sure.

But what about it? If he could get back there alone after dark, he might be able to convince someone he'd lost something inside during his visit. But even if they let him in, what then? He knew he had no chance to overpower a soldier. He'd been in a few fights in his time—engineers on dam projects were sometimes a rowdy bunch—but he'd never been trained in hand-to-hand combat. Not like these soldiers. The idea was ridiculous. A fantasy that quickly faded when faced with reality. And even if he managed to take out someone, unless he killed the man (and he wasn't prepared to kill anyone in cold blood), how would he get away undetected?

"Tito, I was thinking."

"*¿Sí, señor?*"

"There was a frightened bat in here I had to chase out last night."

"Yes, they roost under the eaves. But it's nothing to worry about. They won't hurt you."

"Well, I'd like to leave my door open for the breeze, but I have no weapon. What if a snake tried to get in?"

Tito laughed. "You wouldn't see it in the dark. If you had a gun—" He shrugged. "More likely to shoot your own foot."

Stanek hesitated. There was no way Tito was going to hand over his own gun. And the only weapon he had was a flashlight one of the engineers had given him that evening.

He slapped his forehead. "*Mierda.*"

"What is it, *señor?*"

"I just realized I left my pocket calculator on the colonel's desk. He asked to see it and I forgot to take it back. Listen, Tito, I wanted to do some work in my cabin tonight. I can't do anything without the calculator. Any chance you can take me back there?

Tito looked at his own gold wristwatch. "At this hour—it is too late, *señor.* The headquarters building is closed and no one will bother the colonel now."

"Isn't there someone else who can help us without disturbing the colonel?"

Tito did not look encouraging.

"It's very important, Tito. I have to get the work done before I leave tomorrow."

Tito stared at him. "You leave tomorrow?"

Stanek nodded. "Just for a few days. I have to return to Asunción to talk to my superiors at Samcon. They have some equipment I need. I had it flown in from the States."

"But you have not asked for permission from the colonel, have you?"

"Well, not yet. But I thought I'd do that in the morning. General Paredes said the army would do whatever I asked."

"I don't know, *señor.*" Tito's face was a mask of confusion.

"Listen, Tito. Don't you worry about that. I'll straighten everything out in the morning. But I absolutely have to get my calculator."

The *subteniente* sighed. "Okay, *señor* Stanek, wait here, please. I will see what I can do."

When he was alone, Stanek shivered, cold sweat making his shirt stick to his back. *What in hell was he trying to do?*

The master sergeant fumbled with the key chain, holding a flashlight under one arm while he undid the locks.

"Listen, Tito," Stanek said. "It's late. I won't need you any more tonight."

Tito hesitated.

"Don't worry, *subteniente.* I'll see that he gets back to his cabin," the sergeant said. "Colonel Samudio's orders."

The *sargento ayudante* was a career soldier, the colonel's orderly, a man with streaks of gray in his hair. Stanek had seen him under the light of a kerosene lamp. A compact body with bulging muscles, a stump of a neck, a pockmarked face. Not a man to take lightly. As a commissioned officer, Tito outranked him but you couldn't tell by his manner.

Once they were inside the building, Stanek asked about lights.

"I'm sorry, señor, but the naptha generator for this building is not running tonight. We'll have to use flashlights." The master sergeant's voice was guttural. He lit a cigarette in the dark and after the brief flare of the phosphorus match, it took a moment for Stanek's eyes to adjust to the darkness. In the glow of the hand-rolled cigarette, he could see the man's bronzed face, his bushy eyebrows hanging over dark eye sockets.

The sergeant pocketed the match and led the way toward the colonel's office. He found another key on the chain, and snapped the locks, then shoved the door open. Stanek stepped inside with the sergeant following.

"I think he laid it on the desk," Stanek said, stepping to the desk with the bronzed bust of the president. His heart was pounding so hard he could barely hear anything over the roar of the blood in his head.

He ran his flashlight over the surface, recognizing the objects he'd seen there earlier in the day.

This was foolhardy. Trying to break into the file room with an armed soldier standing at his back. He had to fight down the rise of panic.

He bent over, pushing the colonel's chair away from the desk. "Is that it?" he asked, flashing his light under the desk. "Can you reach that for me?" His breathing was so shallow he could barely get the words out.

The sergeant flashed his light under the desk. "There's nothing under there, *señor*."

"By the back leg, I think," Stanek said. "My back's killing me." He placed his left hand behind his back and tried to bend over. *God, what am I doing?*

"Let me see," the sergeant said.

He dropped to one knee, left hand on the side of the desk.

Do it now, Stanek thought. And fast. Don't think, just do it.

For a second, he froze, suddenly aware that the sergeant would see the light beam change once he raised the flashlight.

The sergeant dipped his head, right hand training his own flashlight under the desk.

Stanek waited no longer. Gritting his teeth, he raised his light and smashed the back of the man's head. The glass lens shattered and the light went out. For a moment, hearing the thudding noise, Stanek was afraid that he had held up too much out of fear of killing the guy, that the sergeant was merely injured and would shout an alarm or rise to attack him. But the sergeant's flashlight rolled slowly across the floor and came to rest against the wall.

Stanek retrieved the light. His heart was pounding so violently that he had to sit down to calm himself. He massaged his chest, afraid his heart might give out on him. The veins in his neck were throbbing and his head felt like it no longer rested on his shoulders.

Damn. He wasn't trained for this. He tried to take deep, slow breaths. *Think of Randi, think of the farm, imagine the fields of grain rippling under a summer breeze.* He couldn't hold the vision. The darkness of the room closed in around him, oppressive. Too much like a tomb.

Dangerous to wait. He had to get moving. Was the sergeant breathing? Should he try and tie him up? He had no rope, didn't think he could find anything in the office. *How could I be so stupid in the first place?* But this was for Renato Sosa, for Eliana, for Pina; hell, even for Diane.

The electrical cord to the lamp.

He unplugged the cord and then tried to rip it out of the lamp base. The damn cord wouldn't give. He swore under his breath. He was wasting too much time.

He tied the sergeant's hands behind his back, lamp dangling off one end, then folded the man's field cap and stuffed it in his mouth. He had to listen to make sure the sergeant was breathing through his nose. He didn't want to suffocate the guy.

The keys. He found the chain and went straight to the side door. Please God, let the key to the file room be here, he thought, frantically trying one key after the other.

And then the lock slipped back and he was able to step inside.

How much time had passed? How long would it take for someone to notice the sergeant's absence?

He felt strangely disembodied. He struggled to hold down his panic. Sweat poured off his forehead. His shirt was drenched. The keys slipped from his hand and clattered to the floor.

Each sound crashed on his ears like smashing cymbals.

That's right, he thought, call out the guard.

None of the file drawers were labeled—and, *thank God*, they weren't individually locked. He started at the far left and opened the top drawer of the first cabinet.

Regimental records it looked like. Documents, directives, administrative reports, pamphlets, Ministry of Defense publications, circulars. Another drawer—personnel files for noncommissioned officers, duty rosters—names entered alphabetically by rank. He tried to work faster. Opening file drawers and scanning the index tabs. Blank forms. Training manuals, supply catalogues, equipment bulletins, lubrication orders, maintenance records, confidential files on the performance characteristics of the regiment's various munitions, investigative and disciplinary reports, words on index tabs he didn't know.

Damn. This would take forever. Only one file left, four drawers and he was out of luck.

Could he have missed the information? Who knew how and under what category it was filed.

Inventories, receipts. Lost, damaged, and destroyed property forms, a payroll list—these files were a mess. Stanek couldn't figure out how they were organized.

He tried to open the next drawer. It wouldn't budge. He tried the one below that. Both were jammed.

He played the narrow beam of the sergeant's flashlight around the edges of the drawers. There it was. A hasp had been welded to the front of each drawer with a slotted flap that fit over a swivel eye around the side of the unit. Padlocks.

He trained the light on his wristwatch. Eleven-fifteen. He'd been inside over twenty minutes. An eternity.

He grabbed the key chain and began trying the different keys. It took him five minutes to try every key on both locks. None of them worked.

He swore out loud and stepped back into the main office. He hoped the sergeant was still unconscious. He didn't want to have to face the man's eyes.

He needed a screwdriver—or some tool that would break either the hasp or the padlock. A crowbar would do the trick, but he wasn't likely to find one in a desk.

He saw a long, slim, blade that looked like a stiletto. A letter opener.

Three minutes later, the blade had snapped, leaving the hasp and padlocks unscathed.

Stanek paused to catch his breath. Stinging sweat dripped into his eyes. He brushed it away and massaged his hands, which ached with tension. He'd broken a fingernail and a dark spot of blood appeared at the tip.

Hell, he hadn't taken the sergeant's gun.

He rushed back into the outer office, flashlight beam stabbing ahead of him. The sergeant hadn't moved.

God, what an idiot. The man could have pulled the pistol out of its holster even with his hands tied behind his back.

Stanek unbuckled the strap over the gun and slid it out. An automatic like Tito's. A Beretta with an extended magazine. What had Tito said? Twenty rounds. A combat model.

He tucked the pistol under his waistband. Too bad he couldn't use it on the padlocks. The noise would wake the devil. And if he had to use it on a soldier he was as good as dead himself.

He was beginning to despair. But there was no turning back now. He'd knocked a man unconscious. He was going to be on the run whether he found what he came for or not.

Five minutes, he told himself. If I haven't succeeded by then, I'm leaving. He wasn't going to risk his life for a list of prisoners.

He straightened, suddenly alert, every sense tuned and focused. He'd heard something, sensed a presence.

A guard on patrol?

Had the sergeant locked the front door behind them? He couldn't remember.

He tried to still his breath, crouching behind the desk, flashlight extinguished.

There, he heard it again. Inside the room.

He flicked on the light. *The sergeant was not on the floor where he'd left him!*

Chapter Twenty-Seven

Stanek shoved himself away from the desk, rolling once and coming to rest flat on the floor with the gun extended in both hands. He'd dropped the flashlight in his haste, heard the sound of it rolling away from him.

His forefinger was jerking on the trigger but nothing was happening.

The safety!

Thank God for that. He didn't want to use the gun. What was he thinking?

He wasn't thinking. He'd panicked. Breathing loud enough that a blind man could find him.

He heard the noise of glass breaking.

The hallway! The sergeant had left the room.

Stanek scrambled around the room on hands and knees looking for the flashlight. He had to find it before the sergeant reached the front door. He could hear the muffled steps now, as the man staggered down the hallway, using the wall for support.

A sound of metal at his ear—the gun had hit the flashlight.

Stanek fumbled for the switch with his left hand, felt a second's relief when a beam of light stabbed out of the darkness. He found the door and rushed for the hallway, his feet crunching over broken glass. The sergeant had smashed the lamp but his hands were still tied behind his back. Stanek could see him up ahead, leaning against the wall in a daze.

As Stanek ran toward him, the sergeant sank to the floor, a dark stain spreading down the back of his shirt.

Blood. Stanek couldn't stand the thought of hitting him again, but the man had to be stopped.

He knelt by the body and focused the light on his face. The sergeant had passed out.

Stanek dragged the body back into the office, found another lamp with a cord and tied the man's feet together. The gag was still in place.

He saw it then—the metal rod extending from the broken lamp's socket to its base. A tool! The rod was solid metal, the cord taped to its side.

He stepped on the length of cord running from the sergeant's hands and pulled on the socket and rod with both hands, grunting at the exertion. And then the lamp came free of the cord and Stanek stumbled back and nearly fell.

The rod bent at first but Stanek, despite the elapsing time, forced himself to be patient. He worked the hasp back and forth, applying pressure, until it snapped.

A row of files, alphabetized from A to L. He spread the hanging folder for A and saw ten or twelve thin file folders.

Francisco Rojas de Alquijana.

How would they file that name? Under *R* or *A*?

Alquijana! It was there all right. Stanek started to pull the folder out and then thought better of it.

If he let them know who he was interested in, the man might die.

He closed the drawer and picked up the rod. Far too much time was passing. It would take another five minutes to break the bottom hasp.

The temptation to flee was strong. But he cared more for Renato Sosa than he did for Alquijana, a man he'd never met. Pina would never forgive him if he didn't look.

If only he could take both drawers with all the files—there were many Paraguayans who would pay with their lives for that information.

The bottom hasp was harder to break. It was difficult to get the right kind of leverage. Stanek could feel his energy draining out of him. He'd been inside the headquarters building for over a half-hour … a lifetime. His clothes were drenched in sweat and he felt dehydrated and dizzy.

The hasp broke with a resounding pop.

Stanek cringed, his eyes blinking back salty sweat. Please God, don't let anyone hear that.

Jeez, he wasn't even sure he believed in God and he'd been begging for help every five minutes. And he didn't like beggars. If you were going to ask God for help, you'd better also be keeping the line open even when you didn't need it. As far as he was concerned, the thanks had to at least equal the requests.

S's. Several Sosas. A common name. Adelberto, Benito, Domingo, Hector, Julio, Martin.

Renato!

Okay, Stanek thought. At least we know where he is and that he's still alive. Now get the hell out of here before it's too late.

Between the two hangars and the airstrip was a dirt field where the regiment's vehicles were parked. A chain link fence topped with strands of razor wire surrounded the field.

Controlled access. He could see at least two guards on duty, and others might be patrolling the perimeter.

It wouldn't do any good to sneak in, even if he could. The second he started to drive off, they'd open fire.

He tucked the gun behind his back and began to whistle softly, walking down the center of the dirt road toward the guards at the entrance to the compound.

The guards moved apart, rifles trained on him as he advanced. A single arc lamp high on a wood pole cast a timid cone of light. Generator-powered. Stanek could smell a faint whiff of *alconafta* in the heavy air.

There was a small guard booth, open on all sides where windows should have been. No one inside.

Stanek greeted the men in Spanish, then identified himself as the American engineer working on the Corpus dam project. Neither man seemed to know what he was talking about.

Stanek waved his arms. "I talked to Colonel Samudio today about getting a jeep. I need to make a quick trip to the capital for some equipment I had flown in from the States. If I don't leave now, I won't get back in time tomorrow. We're carrying out some percolation and soil infiltration tests on the drainage basin."

The guards had lowered their rifles, but seemed uncertain what to do.

"Do you have written orders?" one asked.

"I don't need orders," Stanek said. "The colonel said I had free access to the motor pool. Didn't you get the message today?"

"We just came on duty an hour ago," the other soldier said. "No one told us anything."

"Well, you can wake the colonel if you want, but don't blame me if he chews out your ass."

Both men laughed. "Eat your anus" was what Stanek had said. He was translating word for word, hoping what he said made sense.

He was going to use more Spanish in a month, he thought, than he had in the last ten years. Every sentence was a struggle. Mind working like lightning. Words coming back from years ago. He'd spent several summers in Mexico City when he was an undergraduate and had worked in the country later, on a water-treatment plant in Sinaloa and on the Rio Conchos in Chihuahu, where he'd designed several pumped storage plants capable of low-head hydropower generation. He'd be fluent again before he left Paraguay.

If he left. It looked like these two were going to take all night to make up their minds. It was clear they were surprised by his presence, but also that what he had said was convincing. They knew he wouldn't be on a secret military base, wouldn't know the colonel, if he hadn't received authorization from high up in the government.

He took a chance. "I need a jeep, men. The colonel said the keys would be in the vehicles. Can one of you bring one out? And make sure it has a full tank of gas. The colonel said there wouldn't be any stations open at night. I don't want to be sitting out in the middle of nowhere waiting for daylight."

Apparently that did the trick. Ten minutes later he had motored out of the post and was driving on a heavily rutted dirt road toward Encarnación. The city lay fifty or sixty kilometers to the south, out of his way, but he didn't want to get lost at night, wandering around unmarked roads through the hills of the Itapua Department. From Encarnación there would be a paved road all the way to the capital, another two hundred and fifty or so miles. He only hoped he had the energy to make it all the way and that he would arrive before dawn. By then, the colonel would know what had happened in his office, and the word for Stanek's arrest and detainment would reach the capital.

He reached over in the dark and fingered the automatic lying on the passenger seat to his right. And then, as if to reassure himself that he was still alive, he said out loud, "Don't get lost, Walter. Just don't get lost."

224

Chapter Twenty-Eight

Diane Lang had waited until Friday before learning from Sor Juana that the Director of the Women's Correctional Institute had given permission for her to observe the institute's classes in domestic science. Sor Juana had explained that Sister Diana was a Canadian from Quebec and that in her province the nuns were interested in running reform schools for wayward girls. The visit was scheduled for the following Sunday after morning mass.

"Why Canadian?" Diane wanted to know.

"Better that than telling them you're from the United States," the sister said. "The Canadians arouse no antipathy. If you're Canadian, it's almost as if you're from the United Nations."

"But what about my American passport?"

"You will not need a passport," the sister said. "You will be taken to the

Institute in the same van as the others. Everything has been prepared."

"And when do I come out?"

"The same day."

"But do you teach classes on Sunday?"

"Volunteer classes," the sister said. "Child care and parenting skills. Some of the girls will be visiting their families, the others are free to do what they wish. But most of them are bored. They'll come to the classes. That's the best I could do for you." Sor Juana smiled sweetly. "Now my child, it's time to measure you for your habit."

Diane had spent her free time in the Biblioteca Nacional. Her trip to the Mennonite settlements in the Chaco now appeared out of the question, but life went on. She took advantage of the free days to do some bibliographical work and to read. The library's manuscript collection, strong in Guaraní and Spanish, was sparse in Mennonite material in German, but it did contain a few early diaries and several works of literary merit. Reading the texts helped occupy her mind, and talking to Kim on the telephone each night helped ease her loneliness.

Once, she tried contacting Dink Denton, but someone at the number he'd given her said he was away on an assignment. She didn't ask doing what.

She thought of Walter Stanek and wondered if she would see him again. She had decided to leave Paraguay as soon as her mission in the Women's Correctional Institute was completed. The threat to her personal safety was too great. She would return another time when the political situation was calmer.

An image of Walter Stanek at the Sosa's residence came to mind. She'd been impressed with his calmness. Were all engineers so sure of themselves? What had struck her about Walter was how different he was from most academics she knew. He was an unassuming man, steady, sure of his own abilities. And his faults? Perhaps he was not cautious enough, too sure of his abilities. He didn't seem the sort who was willing to trust others. Too much the independent man who relied only on himself.

Or had she misjudged him?

God knows they hadn't hit it off at the start. But there was an attraction there, despite the fact each had seemed determined to ignore it.

She laughed, remembering one of Walter's responses to a comment made at the Sosa residence after the disappearance of Renato and Eliana. Renato's colleagues were talking about the American Embassy and whether or not the CIA was working to undercut the opposition in favor of General Zancon and the current form of government. Walter, standing firm in his naïveté, had doubted the existence of a conspiracy between the Paraguayan secret police and the CIA.

One of the lawyers had spoke in a mocking tone. "I admit you have a greater intelligence," he said. "You're not convinced the CIA is involved *but I am*. What will not fill a quart bottle like yours"—he pointed to Stanek's head, exaggerating its size with both hands—"will easily fill a pint bottle like mine." And he tapped his skull and then shrunk his hands down to a small cylinder, grinning the while. "My little bottle, *señor* Stanek, is filled with belief."

"Is it?" Stanek had replied, as they exchanged a measuring look. "Then how about corking it up."

She'd been the only one who'd laughed, and Walter had appeared to appreciate a kindred spirit. In some people, they both knew, conviction became a madness that destroyed them.

She wondered for a moment what Walter thought of her. She'd come across like an impassioned left-wing radical, she supposed. Spouting off about injustice and oppression. Trying to empathize with *la gente* as opposed to *la sociedad*. Maybe he thought she was filled with too much conviction herself.

But that was one of her strong points: She was committed to helping others less fortunate than herself. In her mind, generosity and self-sacrifice were still lofty ideals worth striving for.

And her flaws? She'd seen it in his eyes more than once. From his point of view she was too idealistic, too impassioned. She knew what he would say—that she needed to recognize that personal survival, not self-sacrifice, was essential to the cause of freedom. You couldn't help someone else if you were dead.

But, thinking about it again, she refused to deny her emotions. In some cases, especially if you loved someone, you sacrificed everything if necessary, even your life. She would do as much for Kim. Maybe Walter had never loved anyone enough to understand that. Under certain circumstances life was not worth living. You sacrificed to make it better for others.

Which didn't mean she was going to roll over and die! Her lips rose in a half-smile and she took a deep breath to calm the tremor that threatened to break out. She knew the risks of what she was doing. If she didn't think she'd come out alive, she wouldn't be going in. Eliana, after all, was Pina's daughter, not hers. She had Kim to think about.

Early Sunday morning, Diane underwent her transformation to a nun, marveling as each piece of apparel was laid out for her. The solemnity of the sisters who were helping her, the dark colors of the vestments, the air of sanctity in the nunnery's vestry, the wood-carved statue of Saint Veronica in the corner, all overwhelmed her.

Yet strangely, as she invested each garment—the black stockings, the habit itself, the veil, the wimple and guimpe—the danger of the task facing her seemed slowly to subside, almost as if dampened down by the hallowed garments themselves. The silver cross around her neck and each piece of cloth was another layer of protection.

Then she remembered the stories of nuns and priests who'd been shot to death in ambushes in Central and South America. Don't forget, she told herself. Nothing foolish now. Hallowed garments did not a shield make.

Concrete floors, cement-block walls, tile roofs rising to a peak, windows heavily screened, doors barred. Even the lights high overhead were covered with a protective wire mesh. The sunlight coming in from a row of high, narrow windows to the north hit the bare wood desks with the mottled effect of filtering leaves. If she looked only at the faces of the women in front of her, Diane could imagine they were sitting in the Parque Caballero, under a lofty expanse of old Aleppo pines. Only here, no air stirred, there was no municipal swimming pool, no waterfall. Instead of pine scents, she smelled the rancid odor of sweaty, unwashed bodies.

It was difficult to read the expressions on the solemn faces of the women. Indians, mestizas, lighter-skinned natives of European origin, orientals. All barefoot. None of them answered her smile when she was introduced by Sister Nilda. None of them were Eliana.

A lace-making class came first—the delicate *ñandutí* or spider's web. Diane watched as the women took their places. A frame, a needle, a spool of thread, each was checked out and carefully controlled by the sisters. The designs, she was told, were traditional—ostrich plumage, foot prints of oxen, grains of rice. Diane observed without asking questions. These women were all older than Eliana, and she'd been told that the women and girls were kept in separate wings of the Institute.

Next came a class for girls in the art of *aho-poi*—a cotton homespun cloth, hand-embroidered in a variety of colors. Seventeen girls in attendance, but no Eliana.

Three more classes came and went, women alternating with young girls. With the women, Diane was silent; with the girls, she moved from desk to desk, watching them as they worked, trying to strike up a conversation but not having much luck. In the silence of room, with the nuns looking on, few girls wished to speak. No one had heard of an Eliana Sosa.

• • •

"Sor Diana."

"Yes?"

Sister Nilda hovered at her elbow, a diminutive woman, sharp-eyed and birdlike in her movements. She tugged at the sleeve of Diane's habit, then beckoned for Diane to lower her head.

"The director has been asking about you," she whispered. "Apparently some of the girls talked and he became suspicious. You were told not to ask about anyone by name."

Caught.

Diane's cheeks turned red. She'd promised Sor Juana she would only look for Eliana. Asking questions, she'd been warned, was too dangerous. But as the day passed, when Eliana failed to show, Diane had felt obliged to do something. Desperate measures were needed if she was going to succeed. To have come this far in vain—

"I'm sorry, Sister," she said. "I had to ask."

"You must come with me immediately," Sor Nilda said.

"But what about the last two classes?"

Sor Nilda shook her head. "There is no time," she said. "The director has sent a man for you. We are trying to delay him now. The van is waiting for you."

"But what about you … and Sor Juana? If I disappear—"

"Come, I will tell the director you were recalled to the convent by Sor Juana—that you left before he asked for you. The discipline will have been imposed by us. You must get out immediately. If the guards find you—" She shook her head and pulled at Diane's arm again.

"Okay," Diane said, her heart heavy. How was she going to be able to face Pina Sosa? It had all been for naught.

They took a back staircase, a poorly lit, narrow, twisting set of wood stairs that led from an administrative office to the floor below, into a large storage closet that opened on to a back hall and a loading dock. Halfway down, they came upon a young nun on her hands and knees with a bristle brush and a bucket of soapy water, carefully scrubbing both the treads and the risers. The sister rose in surprise as the two black-robbed women appeared above her like wraiths.

Sor Nilda raised a hand in admonition, then touched her lips requesting silence. "Is there anyone down below?" she asked, her voice quiet.

The sister shook her head, eyes wide. "What is it?"

"Nothing to be concerned about." Sor Nilda gestured for the nun to back down the stairs. There was only room for one person at a time.

In the storage room, Sor Nilda sent the younger sister out into the hall. "Please see if there are any trucks at the dock."

In a few moments, the sister returned. "There is no one, Sister."

"Did you see the van?"

The nun shook her head, staring at them both with a questioning look.

Sor Nilda turned to Diane, the corners of her eyes tight with worry. "The van should have been there by now. I told Sister Taciana to request the driver immediately. He usually parks near a row of shade trees at the back of the institute. He's not expected until later, but he is not to leave the van. Something must have gone wrong." She paused in thought. "Perhaps the guards have detained him ... but they have no authority over Church affairs. We are free to come and go as we need."

"Is it safe to stay here in the storage room?"

Sor Nilda shook her head. "When they can't find you in the classrooms they'll search all the rooms." She made up her mind. "Come, Sister. We will walk."

"What about the guards?"

Sor Nilda crossed herself. "We will ask God to blind their eyes."

Blind their eyes? Diane wasn't that gullible. God did not blind the eyes of prison guards. Not even for nuns—and especially when one was a fraud.

***

They took the steps at one end of the loading dock, crossed a paved road and followed a dirt path that led between the cell blocks. A voice behind them shouted for them to halt.

Diane looked around just as Sor Nilda was telling her not to look back. "He's got a gun," Diane said. "A submachine gun."

Sor Nilda took her hand and pulled her along. "Don't look back."

A burst of automatic fire rippled through the still air. A flock of noisy birds, crows by the sound and color, shot out of the guava thickets near the end of the compound.

Diane froze. The next burst would be aimed at them.

Sor Nilda reached for her hand and stumbled. She dropped to her knees and for a moment, alarmed, Diane thought she'd been hit by one of the rounds.

"Are you hurt, Sister?"

She heard a motor in low gear and looked up to see the van coming toward them. The female driver was leaning forward over the steering wheel in obvious panic. She, too, obviously thought Sor Nilda had been hit.

The guard was running toward them and two more men appeared behind the van, taking up positions in the middle of the narrow paved road. They would not get out as easily as they'd gotten in.

For ten minutes they argued. Diane crouched in the back of the van, doors locked behind her as the other nuns talked to the guards.

"You have no right to stop us," Sor Nilda protested. "The van is Church property. We have a sister who is sick and must get to the hospital."

But the guards were unrelenting. "Unlock the doors or we'll break them open," one said.

The sister behind the wheel looked over her shoulder at Diane. "Stay down," she said. "I'm going to run for the gate."

The butt of a rifle crashed through the glass on the passenger side and a hand reached through just as the sister released the clutch and accelerated. They could hear a scream from outside, and bright blood appeared on the broken shards of glass as the hand disappeared from view.

Another burst of fire. Bullets ripped into the doors at the back of the van, a sound of metal wrenching. The van shimmied but the nun behind the wheel continued to accelerate, her hands tight on the wheel, knuckles showing the strain.

Diane heard a whack as they passed through the gate, snapping a metal crossarm from its post.

Hot bullets stitched a zig-zag pattern down the side of the van and Diane realized the nun was screaming.

"Are you hit?" she shouted.

"They have no right," the woman screamed. "They have no right."

Diane crawled forward, brushing glass off the passenger seat.

"Stay down," the nun shouted. She wrenched the wheel and the van slid around a corner, bouncing from pavement to dirt. Diane could hear a siren in the distance. And another up ahead.

"There's a bag back there," the sister shouted. "See it?"

Diane looked around the dim interior. "Yes. I've got it."

"Your clothes," the nun said, her words coming out in gasps as the vehicle bounced over the ruts in the road. To each side lay the dilapidated sheds and hovels of a shantytown. The nun hit the horn, scattering a group of kids playing stickball in the middle of the road.

"Take the bag with you," she said. "It's safer on foot. I'll keep them from stopping the van as long as I can. You can trust the people here, but get rid of the habit." She hit the brakes near an alley that reached deeper into the shantytown. "Run, Sister, run! And good luck!"

Tears welled in Diane's eyes as the van pulled away. The nun had called her sister, knowing full well she was an impostor. A young woman risking her own life to help a stranger. Gratitude overwhelmed her and then the realization that she still wasn't safe.

She ran up the alley, catching the startled faces of young and old. Poor people, most barefoot, dressed in sweat-stained, tattered hand-me-downs—sleeveless T-shirts and cut-offs. The strain of a life of scavenging etched into their faces. Young boys with dirty hands and faces and eyes old before their time—the same sort, she thought, who'd attacked Walter.

She stopped at a wood shack with a frayed rug hanging over the open doorway. An old woman sat outside shelling peas into a battered pot.

The woman looked up, eyes widening. She crossed herself and then tried to rise, spilling the peas in the dirt.

"*La muerte,*" she hissed.

"No," Diane said. "I'm just a—just a nun … a woman like you." She reached out and the old woman backed away, babbling in fear. Spit dribbled from a toothless mouth.

Frightened her half to death.

Diane straightened and cocked her head. More sirens. A high wailing sound that sent a shiver up her back. A trap. She had to get out of there before the police surrounded the barrio and started a systematic search.

Get out of the barrio—hell, get out of the whole damned country.

An empty shack. Diane stepped inside and looked around. A straw palliasse in one corner, a broken chair, chipped plates stacked in a ramshackle rack against one wall. A small back door led to a cooking pit and a beehive mud-and-brick oven on a clay platform.

No one in sight.

She opened the bag and pulled out her clothes—a skirt and blouse, her wallet with ID and money. A pair of brown loafers.

Moving quickly now, aware of voices outside in the street, she changed clothes, then packed the nun's habit and the silver cross into the bag and took it with her. She stepped into the street to find a group of boys watching her.

She smiled. "*Muchachos*, can you tell me where I can catch a bus to the center? I came to visit my sister, but she's not here now."

The boys looked around awkwardly. What *yanqui* had a sister in the barrio?

Diane opened her wallet and drew out several bills. She held up the money and said, "Who wants to help me?"

Five minutes later, with her wallet several bills lighter, she was on a crowded bus headed for Plaza Uruguaya, sharing a seat with an old woman and two squawking chickens held upside down with their feet tied together.

That could have been me, she thought. Poor Kim, that could have been me.

Never again.

She had her own daughter to think about.

Chapter Twenty-Nine

Stanek drove all night with no sign of anyone in pursuit. At one point, early in the morning while it was still dark, he came upon a military checkpoint near San Juan Bautista, the headlights of the angled jeeps coming into view around a bend in the highway.

He braked as soon as he saw the vehicles, but it was too late to take evasive action. Heart thumping, he reached for the automatic on the seat to his right. His thumb gently released the safety. Before he could come to a complete stop, however, the two helmeted soldiers, submachine guns at port rest, waved him through without asking any questions. Looking for smugglers in civilian trucks apparently. He lifted his foot off the brake and rolled by them with his head dipped, left hand raised to cut the glare of the headlights.

As dawn approached, he looked for signs of life in the villages along the highway. He had moved from the larger vistas of the campo—broad grassy plains with small islands of woods, to rolling hills. Every now and then he caught a glimpse of a blue haze in the distance—a range of hills that surrounded the region like a low rampart.

If he could find a telephone in one of the *aldeas*, he would risk a call to Pina Sosa, telling her in a kind of code that both Alquijana and her husband were in the Poromoco stockade. If the leftists were going to mount an operation to rescue them, the sooner they moved the better.

But he would also have to warn them of the considerable obstacles. It would take a major assault in maximum stealth if they were to have any hopes of succeeding.

In San Lorenzo, a village just a few kilometers from the outskirts of Asunción, he passed a Nueva Asunción bus and accelerated to put some distance between the vehicles. It might be dangerous as an American to drive directly into the city in a military jeep. Better to be one face among many.

The suburbs were in sight. He entered Fernando de la Mora and looked for a side street where he could leave the jeep and get back to the highway in time to flag down the bus.

Up ahead he saw the marquee for the Cine Terraza—as good a place as any—and pulled off the highway to the left. He parked the jeep just around the corner on Calle Rivarola.

No sooner had he taken his seat near the front of the bus then he saw two military troop transports pull to a stop in the middle of the next intersection. He saw the road sign to the right. *Capital* in large white letters on a dark blue background. A roadblock at the boundary between departments.

Armed troops were disgorging from the transports as the bus pulled into the intersection. None of the soldiers seemed prepared to stop the vehicle—they were pulling barricades from the backs of the trucks and the bus passed by, moving under a green light, the first traffic signal Stanek had seen in some time.

He breathed a sigh of relief. That was close. If only he didn't stand out like such a gringo—American loafers, short-sleeved polo shirt, corduroy pants. His bag with the rest of his belongings was back in the officer's cabin at Poromoco.

As they approached the center of Asunción, he became aware of the increasing presence of the military. There were soldiers at each corner, with jeeps and trucks parked along the streets. No tanks in sight, but an armored personnel carrier circled the Plaza Uruguaya.

If the soldiers stopped every bus and asked the Anglo passengers for ID, he was screwed.

He turned to the young woman sitting across the aisle, leaning over to attract her attention. For a moment, until she realized he was a foreigner, she appeared prepared to ignore him.

"*Señora*," he said, "why all the soldiers?"

"*¿Quién sabe?*" she replied, shrugging her shoulders. "Perhaps a rumor of a coup attempt. Perhaps an exercise."

A state of siege, he thought, a net slowly tightening around the prey. He felt like a scrawny rabbit, scared out of its mind, waiting for the hounds to pounce and tear it to shreds.

Well, a rabbit—even one reduced in fear to pure instinct—had its wiles. And in this case, the rabbit had a gun.

He laid a hand over his stomach, pressing the cold steel to hot flesh.

"*Señor* Stanek, *la profesora está a salvo*. Where are you calling from?"

Good, Diane had made it out of the women's prison. But now was not the time to exult. He said, "I have only a minute, Pina. Tell the others that I found both men. Understand?"

"Renato?"

"No more on the phone, Pina. Can I come see you now?"

"Not here, *profesor*. The house is being watched. Tell me where you are.

I will send someone to pick you up. They will take you where it is safe."

Stanek hesitated. If the Sosa's house was being watched, who knew about the phone? "Listen, Pina, don't say anything for a moment. Don't answer this question out loud, okay? Remember where we met with Dink and Diane that Sunday morning? I'll be there an hour from now, okay? Send someone I know—one of the men I met at your home."

"I understand," Pina said. "An hour from now."

Stanek was wearing a straw hat and an unbuttoned dress shirt at least two sizes too big, both bought from street vendors on the Calle Bogado just beyond the train station.

He stopped in front of a truck repair shop and tried to catch his reflection in the grimy window. He didn't want the gun to show. He was aware of its bulge beneath his belt. He buttoned the bottom two buttons on his shirt and let the rest billow out. Now to find an *almacén* for a pair of sunglasses.

He looked at his watch. Fifteen minutes until he was due on the steps of the Catedral Metropolitana. What else could he do to disguise himself?

Stanek recognized the man but couldn't remember his name, middle-aged with a prosperous air about him, thinning hair parted on the right, a double chin, dressed in a business suit and driving a Fiat sedan.

"Heriberto Sanchez," the man said. "Get in."

Behind the Fiat, a taxi laid on his horn, the driver hanging out the window. Crossing between the vehicles, Stanek caught a glimpse of an unshaven face, a threatening gesture. *"A la puta,"* the driver shouted. Stanek ignored him.

"Muchas gracias," he said as he got into the car. "I can't believe how many soldiers there are." He reached for the seat belt as the Fiat pulled away.

Sanchez nodded. "We have been betrayed," he said. "We are launching our attack now—before it is too late. Escobar wants to see you immediately."

"Escobar?"

"Our commander."

Great, Stanek thought, someone else to hassle him.

"They know I know something," Stanek said.

The faces of the three men across the table reflected no comprehension. Escobar and two assistants.

"Listen, I had to knock a man out and left him tied up in the headquarters building. I had to destroy the file cabinets to get them open. They have Renato Sosa and Alquijana. But who knows for how long now? They're going to know you're coming."

Escobar cleared his throat. "We may catch them by surprise," he said, his voice raspy. He was an imposing man, an ex-army officer with a swarthy complexion, full black beard and bushy mustache—and broad thumbs for squashing spiders and cockroaches. "I have ordered our forces in Posadas to cross the river and attack from the south. We hope to move more men from Caazapá and Villarrica. A pincer movement."

"But force won't do it," Stanek said. "The soldiers will be prepared."

"We are launching diversionary attacks throughout the country with major emphasis on Asunción. They will not expect an attack at so remote a base."

"Listen," Stanek said, tapping his knuckles on the table. "You don't understand. Ten days ago I took part in a government-sponsored project. A series of war games to prepare for just this type of scenario. They know you're going to attack from Posadas."

Escobar frowned, the ridges in his forehead deepening. "They know? And what will they do to stop us?"

Hell, how was that handled? Stanek rubbed his cheeks. The Minister of Defense took care of that contingency. The man from the Pentagon. But what had he done? Called in the Interior Minister, wasn't it? Took advantage of the secret police; they had undercover agents in the exile forces who would liaise with the military.

"I believe they have infiltrators among the guerrilla forces," Stanek said. "Secret police who will inform the army regiment at Poromoco where your men are and when they'll attack. The army will wipe you out with superior force. I strongly advise you not to have those forces cross at Posadas."

The three men talked among themselves in Guaraní, then Escobar turned to Stanek. "We have Professor Lang here with us. She says she has a friend who used to be a helicopter pilot—a Señor Dink Denton. She said you could vouch for him."

Stanek stared at the men. Apparently they were going to ignore his advice. Disaster. He took a deep breath. What did he know about Dink? Next to nothing. For all he knew, Dink could be a conduit straight into General Zancon's office—or into the CIA's. The guy had said he had a friend in the Embassy.

The men were waiting for an answer.

Stanek shrugged. "I don't know him as well as Professor Lang ... but if she said he's okay, then he's okay with me. What do you need him for?"

"We have access to three air force helicopters," Escobar said. "But we only have one pilot capable of flying them. We need at least two—one to attack the compound, the other to swoop down into the fort."

Swoop down? These guys had no idea how hard that was going to be. "For Alquijana?"

"Exactly."

Stanek tapped his fingernails on the table, lost in thought for a moment. "Will he know you're coming?"

"If Renato has talked to him, he will recognize what is happening. If not"—Escobar shrugged—"we do our best."

"He's that important?"

Escobar leaned forward, both elbows on the table. "Once he's free and can address the people by radio or on TV, many of the soldiers will turn to our cause. No one is happy with General Zancon. We expect the Four-teenth Cerro Corá Infantry Regiment to support us—along with troops of the General Brugez Artillery Regiment in Paraguarí and a motorized cavalry brigade at Campo Grande. We hear even the secret police are against Zancon. Colonel Ibarras has made no secret of his ambition."

"But he won't fight for Alquijana."

Escobar laughed. "No, he won't. Ibarras will only fight to find and kill him. He is not afraid of General Zancon. *El Tigre* will be no match for his treachery. *El Tigre* is a stray cat with illusions of grandeur. He thinks he's cruel, but he's merely rapacious. He is not the beast he imagines himself to be. Ibarras, who is a true beast, will destroy him like that." Escobar snapped his fingers.

"But Alquijana—that is a different matter. He is a man of great cunning and great eloquence. *El León*. A man of tremendous popular appeal. Against him, the colonel will stand no chance. He will be seen for the greedy, grasping man that he is. More dangerous than Zancon, yes, but not a leader. If Ibarras comes to power, the people know it will be with the aid of the *narcotraficantes* from outside this country. With Ibarras as president, we our ruined."

Escobar leaned forward, his glistening black eyes locked on Stanek's. "General Zancon allowed the secret police to torture his enemies, but he never had the guts to lift the rod or attach the electrodes himself. Ibarras has the guts—and not only that; he also has the intelligence to create a systematic reign of terror far worse than what we have seen so far. So, you understand, correct?"

Stanek nodded wearily. "I understand," he said.

"Good. Then you see, it does not matter if the government wipes out our forces from Posadas—if they kill every man and boy who attacks from Caazapá and Villarrica." Escobar pounded the table with a clenched fist. "It does not matter provided we are successful. No matter what the cost, *Alquijana must be saved*."

Stanek leaned back, away from the man's intense stare. He took a deep breath. "Good luck," he said. "I wish you the best. I'm going to contact the company I work for and then I'll be leaving your country. If I'm lucky, no one will notice me in the confusion."

Escobar snorted and then shook his head. "General Zancon has stopped all commercial flights into and out of the country. The border checkpoints are closed. The port has been shut down. For the time being, you are stuck here like everybody else."

"But how do you know Dink will even do it?" Stanek waved his arms in frustration. "I mean, the guy could be out of the country by now."

"I called him last night," Diane said. "He took me in until Pina could send someone to bring me here."

The two Americans were talking in a bedroom of one of the opposition's safe houses, located on Blas Garay near the Adriano Irala stadium, three blocks from the main road leading south to Lambaré. Stanek leaned back into the headboard. Diane sat in the middle of the bed to his left, legs crossed beneath her. He could reach out and touch her if he wished.

Stanek's happiness at their initial embrace was rapidly dissipating. He had kissed her on the cheek and she had responded with a hug that warmed them both. He'd forgotten how damn good-looking she was, how vibrant with life. And he'd sensed something in her eyes he hadn't seen there before, a gaze that had quickened his heart. Despite the obstacles and the danger they faced, she had an inner heat—whether from energy or eagerness he couldn't tell—that was contagious.

"It's the only way," Diane said. "Dink can fly us to the border at Encarnación and then help the guerrillas. They've promised to pay him ten thousand dollars. He's a commando at heart, Walter. When they talked to him about flying one of the helicopters, he looked like a kid with a new toy. He'll fly the attack copter and the Paraguayan pilot will drop into the fort to pick up Renato and Alquijana."

"Where are these helicopters, anyway? Are you sure they're in the hands of the guerrillas?"

She reached out and touched him on the arm. "They're at the air base at Luque, just outside the capital. Dink's checking them out."

"Hell, that may be where I flew out of here with Hank Wilson, Samcon's pilot."

"Does it matter?" She withdrew her hand.

"I guess not." He missed the warmth of her touch. He could feel the heat radiating between them. God, she was beautiful. But what did she see in him? A friend in need? Someone you shared a momentary closeness with and then just as easily said good-bye to? Thrust together by chance for an odd instant in an odd place.

Diane uncrossed her legs and lay on her side facing him, her head propped up on one hand. The gesture had an air of shared intimacy and he found himself breathing harder. Her blouse was stretched tight across her breasts.

"Dink talked to his friend at the Embassy to see if the U.S. could help," she said, "but they told him to stay out of it. If we want to get out of here, this is our only chance."

He took a deep breath, then nodded. "Okay, Diane. It's just that I think I should talk to someone at Samcon first."

"Do you trust them?"

He hesitated. "Not as much as you trust Dink. I'll try to contact their head office in Houston first."

Diane shook her head. "You can't, Walter. I tried to call my daughter. The international lines are down. We're cut off."

"I'll call Kohlbert then. I don't trust the bastard but he can't do anything over the phone. I'll try to find out what they know and what they're doing to protect their other employees."

Diane reached for his hand. She'd already told him that as a security precaution no one could telephone from the safe house. "I don't like you going back out on the streets, Walter."

"One of them will go with me. They don't want anyone compromising the safe house."

"Be careful, okay?" A wry smile creased her cheeks. "I don't think I can take any more stress."

Stanek snorted. "Me neither. My sister warned me about this just before I came down—and I told her I needed a vacation!"

They both laughed, then grew serious, sitting in silence for a moment, hand in hand, before Stanek finally stood.

"Nothing to worry about," he said. "I'll talk to Kohlbert on the phone and that'll be it."

Chapter Thirty

Colonel? Conrad Kleemer here. At the Embassy."

"*¿Qué tal?* Let me be the first to tell you that I am now a *general de brigada*."

"I talked to our boy from the DEA again and—what? You were promoted?"

"Yes, a sop that will only wet my appetite. The president thinks that a *Jefe de Investigaciones* will be satisfied with a higher military rank." Ibarras snorted, then spoke with scorn. "I left the army long ago—in all but title. My allegiance is to my men, my own department. The fool."

Ibarras paused, aware that he'd shouted, pounded his fist. He took a deep breath, flexing his free hand to calm himself. "And what did your friend at the DEA tell you this time? Are they happy with the fish we fed them?"

"Congratulations on the promotion, General. Ah ... we didn't even talk about that. He's trying to get out of the country."

"Why the rush?"

"I got the feeling it wasn't just for himself. He asked if we had a plane we could spare. When I asked him why, he said he needed to fly some friends to Encarnación."

"Give him the plane. We will stop them at Encarnación."

"But that's at the border. He can cross the river to Posadas and set down in Argentina."

"If he tries, we'll shoot it out of the sky."

Conrad Kleemer hesitated. "Listen, Colonel—I mean, General, I've already told *señor* Denton we don't have access to a plane for private business. I just called to let you know—he asked me about Alquijana."

El León. A moment of silence from the other end. "Are you sure? By name?"

"Yep, knew who he was and everything. Said something about him being in a military base at Poromoco. Heard of it?"

Ibarras swore. "So that's where Zancon is keeping the bastard." He paused, thinking. It would be difficult to get his men—men loyal only to him—into that base. But they could get damn close, they could be waiting, they could be watching from the surrounding hills.

"Listen, Counselor, this DEA agent has to have contacts in the opposition. No one else cares about Alquijana." He grunted. "*El León.* I want him for myself ... but who says I have to get him first? Let the guerrillas try to bust him out. We have agents in their ranks to inform us of their progress. They accomplish one of two things—either they get Alquijana killed or they succeed in freeing him. And if they succeed? Then my men take them all."

He'd send an elite team from his network of paramilitary forces, men trained in counterinsurgency by the CIA. They'd hide in the hills around the base and show the regular army how it was done.

Hell, he thought, he'd go there in person and do it himself.

The orders had been given, passed down the line to his staff. In a few hours he would join his men in the field, but now he had something else to attend to.

Hector Ibarras looked at the report on his desk. Outside his office in the compound of the Presidential Escort Regiment a helicopter lifted off its pad and circled away over the city. A smile came to his lips as he stroked his thin mustache.

The president himself had telephoned less than an hour ago, asking that his protection be increased. Ibarras was sending a squad of hand-picked men, loyal only to him, to guard the president, who was working in his office in the Government Palace. When the time came and Ibarras gave the word, they would arrest the man. It would be that simple.

His smile turned to a frown as he reread the report on his desk. That damn woman. Meddling again. He'd known from the start she was involved in this. The file provided by the Embassy had told the story. Fine, she'd stuck her neck out too far this time.

He looked again to find the name of the girl the *yanqui* was trying to help. There it was—Eliana Sosa. His men had arrested the girl and her father, only to lose the father to army intelligence. Expropriated by Major General Alberto Campos on General Zancon's orders. But the army's agents hadn't known about the girl. She was still in his hands. No longer needed.

He picked up the telephone and dialed the number of the Policlínico Policial, then asked to speak to the director.

"Listen, *amigo*, I have a gift for your boys. A favor for their fine work. You have a girl in one of your cells there—Eliana Sosa. Give her to your best interrogators." A pause. "No, no. There is nothing to learn from her. Tell them to have fun—that she is a gift from me."

"A gift?"

"Yes, to do with as they wish … oh, and see that she doesn't survive."

There was a moment of hesitation at the other end, then the director came back, speaking quickly. "Very well, sir. Understood. Anything else we can do?"

Ibarras thought for a moment. "Yes, in this case, *Director*, I think there is." His voice had a careless tone. "I see no reason to dispose of what is left of her in the usual way. Drop the body in front of her parent's home tonight. They'll get the message."

With the phone back on the hook, Ibarras picked up a banana and began slowly to peel and eat it. Now for the woman. The *yanqui*. He'd given the order that morning. Find her and bring her to him.

This one he'd enjoy for himself.

Chapter Thirty-One

"What did they say?"

Stanek looked at Diane. They were alone at the moment, standing in the patio of the safe house on Calle Blas Garay, the external lights extinguished. From just over the tiled rooftop, a full moon shed its warm illumination onto the patio.

Around them rose the walls of a two-story building with a corridor open to the air. The guard who had patrolled the corridor earlier had gone inside with his companions. An air conditioner hummed from one of the windows facing onto the balcony. Nearby, a small fountain trickled recirculated water over mossy rocks and into a series of small pools. A fig tree, a medlar tree with ripening fruit pods, two miniature fan palms, and lush tropical flowers surrounded the pools. The safe house was the home and clinic of a wealthy doctor.

"Kohlbert was surprised I was back in Asunción. I don't think the army's told Samcon what happened on the base."

"I don't understand that." She was standing close to him, their voices low.

He shook his head. "I can't figure it out, either. Even if I killed that guy in the headquarters building, my assistant Tito knew I'd gone in with him. I had to be responsible—unless they think it was someone else who took me as hostage. But even then you'd think they'd tell Samcon."

"They may be too busy. Escobar said the guerrillas have crossed the river and are massing to the south of the base."

Stanek nodded, deep in thought. "I didn't like what Kohlbert said. He was angry about my leaving the Corpus area. I told him there was a revolution going on but he didn't want to listen. He threatened me."

"He can't do anything to you, Walter." She touched him on the arm.

"I don't know. He mentioned my sister."

"I didn't know you had a sister." She leaned toward him, attentive.

Stanek nodded. Diane's face was barely visible in the darkness—a round pale oval surrounded by dark waves of hair that blended into the night. He wanted to put his arms around her waist, but something held him back.

"A younger sister. Her name's Randi. She lives in Ferndale, Washington. Kohlbert knew that. He'd talked to the guy who hired me in Houston. I don't know. Maybe it was only me he was threatening. He kept talking about my insurance policy. I listed her as a beneficiary." He slapped his leg. "That's how they tracked her down. I had to list her name and address on the insurance form."

"I don't see why they would bother her."

Diane's head was tipped up to him. The moonlight shone in her eyes, her red lips dark against pale cheeks, her hair lustrous.

"You're probably right. I'm getting paranoid."

They touched hands, swaying toward each other. Her white cotton skirt, its floral print invisible in the darkness, wafted around his legs. The light breeze brought a moment's respite from the heat. He leaned toward her, feeling their legs touch along the thigh, and then she was in his arms, her hands rising to embrace him around the neck, pulling his head down for the kiss.

Stanek felt a tremendous release of repressed emotions, as if the sluice gates of a blocked dam had suddenly let go, a rush that drained the tension from his body. He could feel her heart beating against his chest, smell the fragrance of her hair. They kissed again, longer this time, open-mouthed, their tongues touching, their bodies pulled tight against each other. Her soft, wet mouth intoxicated him.

When they finally broke apart and laughed, happy the initial awkwardness was past, giddy at the emotions washing over them, Stanek said, "This is the first time I've ever kissed a nun."

Her peal of laughter brightened the night air, filling him with pleasure.

Diane's hands dropped to his chest and then slid around to his back. He pulled her body into his, crushing her breasts against his chest, the touch sending a quiver through both of them. He kissed her cheek and then her neck, nibbling and sucking as her breath quickened in his ear.

Diane opened her mouth. "How about we make it another first for both of us?" The words came out in a whisper, heavy with passion. "I've never made love to a hydrogeologist."

He could see her smile, the shine of white teeth and then the mouth opening for another kiss.

He reached down for her skirt, lifting the fabric until his hands felt flesh, sliding underneath and moving up the insides of her thigh toward her soft mound.

When he touched her there, she gasped and drew away from him for a second, then leaned into his hand as he caressed her through her underpants. His fingers found the elastic and slipped inside and she moaned.

A few moments later, her voice catching in her throat, she said, "Let's lie down, Walter. There's a bench over there." She pointed toward one of the pools, where a fan palm brushed against a wrought-iron bench lined with tufted cushions. Moonlight struck the flagstones leading to the bench and the pools of water, casting a silvery sheen over the courtyard.

On the bench, as the moon rose higher into the clear sky, growing smaller and harsher, their warm bodies met in another embrace. They made love then with a need that drove them to forget their surroundings, a desire that was almost desperate, a sense of urgency that only at the end became release.

"Why did it take us so long?" Walter asked. "I didn't realize how much I wanted you." They were sitting side by side on the bench.

Diane laughed. "We just met," she said. "It's only been a little over a week."

"It seems forever."

"That's the truth." She reached for Stanek's arm. "My underpants are around here somewhere."

"Gee, I was hoping I could keep them."

She laughed, then took the panties from him and slid them on.

Stanek reached for her waist. "Can we make love again?"

She laughed, then nodded and kissed him on the nose. "In the bedroom this time … and slower."

Stanek grinned, then shook his head, marveling at the ease with which they talked. "I can't get enough of you," he said.

She slipped into his arms again, luxuriating in the sensation.

"You know," he said, looking into her eyes as the moonlight touched them, "I thought it was just physical attraction at first. You have this inner glow. Desire came so fast it surprised me, especially when we didn't hit it off right at the start. I still felt this attraction—almost against my will.

But it was hard to resist. You're the most beautiful woman I've ever met. And then I was afraid the love I was starting to feel for you was just—"

"Just the circumstances?"

He nodded. "You wondered, too?"

"For a while ... but then I realized this wasn't normal."

Stanek laughed.

"No, I mean the pressure of events ... I learned a lot about you—your character, your personality. The physical attraction was an added benefit." She poked him in the chest. "Usually I fall in love with wimpy intellectual types."

"So I'm not wimpy or intellectual."

"Walter, you're strong, courageous, loyal, down-to-earth, handsome, *and* smart. For me that's a rare combination."

"No one ever told me I was handsome before. You must get tired of people telling you how smart and beautiful you are."

"You never get used to it," she said. "Besides, you've only told me once."

He laughed. "Let's go inside and I'll tell you a few more times tonight."

Tuesday morning. The sound of Dink's voice in the patio.

Diane came back into the bedroom. "I've talked to Dink," she said. "He says the international lines are working."

"Are you going to call your daughter?"

"Kim?" Diane shook her head. "If I call her and tell her the truth, she'll only worry. Besides, she thinks I'm in the Chaco and out of touch until the end of the week."

"I promised Randi I'd call her on Fridays and I missed last time. She'll be worried if I don't get in touch with her."

"They may not let us out of here in the daylight. Dink's the only one no one's looking for."

Stanek turned toward her. He'd just finished shaving at a small basin. "I don't see why Dink is doing this. What's he got to gain?"

"Plenty," she said. "He loves excitement—and they're paying him a lot of money."

"He said he didn't care about money."

She nodded. "He's heard of Alquijana. He said with him in power, the government will turn a deaf ear to the Bolivian and Peruvian drug lords. Alquijana will clean up the smuggling and money laundering by government and military figures."

"I didn't realize Dink was into politics."

"He hates drugs. That's all he can talk about—the *drogadictos* and the *narcotraficantes*. I used to think he was one himself."

"Alcohol's his drug."

"At least it's not illegal."

"Is this our first fight?"

Diane laughed. "Walter, you're jealous, aren't you?"

A sheepish grin answered her.

She shook her head, so finally he said, "I've seen Dink eyeing you—licking his lips with lust."

"Walter, everyone could eye me with lust and it wouldn't make a bit of difference. *I love you.* It's who *I* look at that matters, not who looks at *me*. Now let's go down there and see if you can get through to Randi."

An answering machine. Stanek couldn't believe it. Randi had joined the modern age. He stumbled for a moment, then said he was okay and would call back later with a number where she could reach him.

"Everything okay?" Diane was waiting in the Fiat with Heriberto Sanchez, the man who'd picked up Walter the day before. The windows were rolled down, but it was still hot. The sun reflecting off the window of a *confitería* blinded her.

"I didn't talk to Randi," Stanek said. "She has a new answering machine.

I couldn't leave her a number. I'll have to call back later."

When they reached the safe house and went up to their bedroom, Diane said, "What about a hotel in Posadas? We should be there by tomorrow or the day after that. I have a guide book that should list some places to stay. We can choose a nice hotel, get the phone number, and leave it for Randi. She can call us there."

Pina Sosa had kept Diane's suitcase for her. She walked over to it and found the guide book. Walter had left his things behind in the officer's cabin at the Poromoco base. They would have to buy him some new clothes at the first opportunity.

"How about the Hotel Continental?" she said, finding Posadas in the section for Argentina. "On Avenida Simon Bolivar. It'll give us a place to meet if we're separated. The telephone number's 36-673."

"Let's get Heriberto," Stanek said. "I'll leave the number for Randi."

An hour later, Sanchez took them to another telephone, this time at the Club Atlantida, a few blocks from the safe house. The men used a back entrance to leave the house, avoiding the clinic on the first floor, where the resident doctor treated his patients.

The machine again. Randi must be out working in the fields or the barn, Stanek thought. He left another message, not telling her that the Hotel Continental was in Argentina, but leaving the country prefix with the telephone number. Better to tell her in person why he was leaving Paraguay. Let her dial the number thinking he was in Asunción. No reason to alarm her.

"Look," Stanek said, "shouldn't we be watching TV or something to see what's going on?"

"A black-out," Dink said. "Only one government channel is on the air. Broadcasting propaganda for General Zancon."

Escobar stroked his thick, black beard. "Before long," he said, his voice deep, "we hope to put even that off the air. And if we get Alquijana, we have a studio prepared for a clandestine broadcast in one of the TV stations friendly to our cause."

"What we should do," Sanchez said, "is go over the plan for tonight."

Across the table, a thin, ascetic man with eyes that were totally calm cleared his throat. He turned to the three Americans, who were grouped at one end of the refectory table in the doctor's formal dining room on the second floor of the safe house. "We've been working on the plan for some time. We knew our objective, but not our target. Now we have both."

"But there's a problem," another man said. He was a twisted fellow with one shoulder higher than the other, head tipped at an angle as if he were seven feet tall and afraid of bumping his head. "We can't get both of you in the chopper with *señor* Denton. We need the space for our commandoes. One of you will have to go by truck."

Diane looked at Dink and Walter, then back at Escobar. "But that's too dangerous," she said. "The police are looking for me, and the army's looking for Walter."

Escobar sucked at his lips for a moment, then shrugged. "We need Professor Stanek in the lead chopper. He is the only one who knows exactly where the base is. We need to follow the same route he took or we may run out of fuel. These are old helicopters and they are not the most efficient."

"Hey, wait a minute," Stanek said. "I've already told you everything I know."

Escobar sat back in his chair, both arms on the table. "True, but words are not always enough. You've flown into the base, you've seen the landmarks, you'll recognize the terrain."

"Not in the dark."

"We may attack at twilight. If not ... under a full moon, flying low—" Escobar shrugged. "You should do okay. We need to come in fast. You know the layout of the hills. You have a trained eye for these things."

Stanek's voice hardened. "I never volunteered to go in with anybody. Dink is supposed to drop Diane and me in Posadas before you go in."

Escobar shook his head. "No time for that. Too far south to go there and come back. Too dangerous. We'll get both of you to Posadas after the raid."

"Look, Dink may be crazy, but I'm not. There's no way I'm going back to that base."

"Then we take the *profesora*." Escobar's voice had taken on a threatening tone.

"And if she refuses to go?"

"You have no choice in the matter, *señor*."

Stanek looked at the two men across the room with submachine guns. Standing guard.

"I'll go," he said then, "but only if you promise you'll get Professor Lang safely out of the country."

Escobar turned to Diane, who had watched the exchange in stunned silence. "You have my promise, *profesora*."

Sanchez leaned forward and rubbed his hands together in a placating gesture. "To return to the helicopters. As it is, they will not have enough fuel. We would like for you, *profesora*, to ride in a secret compartment of a gas truck. The truck will be leaving Asunción in—" he looked at a pocket watch, gold chain dangling—"approximately one hour. You will stop at Maciel, that's a small village located along the train tracks that señor Stanek followed on his way to the base. The driver will take care of everything. The rendezvous has been arranged. You will have a chance to get out of the truck and attend to your needs before we get there."

He paused. "And once the two helicopters are refueled, the truck will proceed to Encarnación. You will be met by a boat and taken to Posadas."

"Where Professor Stanek will join you later," Escobar added.

• • •

Alone in their bedroom, Stanek helped Diane pack. Most of her clothes and her research notes, such as they were, would be left behind. Escobar had promised to have Pina mail the papers to Diane at her address in New Haven.

"Fine friends you've got," Stanek said, unable to keep the bitterness out of his voice. "They're using us. For all we've done, we mean nothing to them."

He could see the hurt in her eyes. "I'm sorry," he said. "It's not your fault. I didn't have to get involved if I didn't want to. It's just that I'm worried about us. I don't like being separated."

"We both got in over our heads," she said. "We tried to help an individual—a family, and it grew from there."

"We're no longer even dealing with Pina—or the Sosa's friends for that matter. Other people have taken over and I don't like it. People who have no real concern for our safety, who feel no sense of obligation for what we've done. They think we owe them because they're letting us stay here."

She nodded. "If we wanted to leave on our own, they wouldn't let us. I'm sorry, Walter. I don't like being apart either. I'm more worried about you than me. You've got to get Dink to drop you outside the base before the raid begins. If he's shot down, at least you'll have a chance on foot." Walter reached for her and the two hugged for a moment in silence. "You could blame me, I guess," he said. "If you hadn't followed me out of the Club Bahia Negra, you'd never have met the Sosas."

"That's true," she said. "But then I'd never really have met you, either, right? I'd have always thought of you as that aggressive asshole who wanted to dine first."

He laughed. "I had to come to Paraguay to find the woman of my dreams."

Dink was calling for them from below. They were both going to accompany her to the airport where the gas truck was waiting.

She stepped back, an impish look on her face. "Is that what I am, Walter—the woman of your dreams?"

He grinned. "Well, awful damned close to it."

But the truth was, he realized, as she preceded him down the stairs, aware already of an emptiness inside at the thought of their impending separation, she was a hell of a lot nicer than any dream woman.

Chapter Thirty-Two

At first, the head rolled awkwardly.

It hit each of the top three steps with an audible whack, like a wet sponge smacking a tile floor, followed by a soft squishy sound as the fleshy tissues absorbed the blow. Bright red blood splattered out of the broken veins and arteries at the neck.

Slowly it picked up speed as it rolled down the pitted stone steps that led from the estancia's terrace to the base of the hill. The head bounded higher, missed a step or two, then began to hurtle down toward the soldiers waiting at the bottom. Pieces of flesh ripped loose, the skull cracked, teeth shattered and flew.

When what was left of the pulped head hit the dust at the base of the hill and rolled to a stop, newly promoted Brigadier General Hector Ibarras stepped to the edge of the flagstone terrace and thrust both hands into the air, the executioner's sword clenched in his right fist.

The paramilitary forces at the base of the hill responded with a mighty cheer.

A flock of scarlet tanagers shot out of a bitterwood tree behind the men and stormed overhead, sweeping twice before settling down in a clump of wild orange trees and thorny scrub at the far end of the clearing.

When the shouts died away, the general dropped his arms and spoke to the upturned, sweaty faces of his men. They had just routed a guerrilla force that had crossed the Paraná river to the north of Encarnación, driving most of the rebels back into the river, where they were swept away or gunned down.

"*Compañeros*, today I give you Comandante Oliveros, the leader of the guerrilla forces in Argentina. He had a Spanish name but he was a *yanqui* soldier recruited by our enemies."

The men erupted with jeers, hoots, and whistles.

Ibarras, a thin smile on his lips, waited until they were silent again.

"Like the others—our traitorous countrymen who do not deserve to be called Paraguayans—he was no match for us."

Another cheer.

"And tomorrow—" Ibarras struck the blade of the sword on the stone parapet, edge first—"or the next day—" another blow rang out, chips of rock flying—"or the day after that—" this time sparks flew—"no matter how long it takes—" here he thrust the sword point into the crumbling stone—"I will give you this so-called resistance leader that the Comandante came to help—Francisco Rojas de Alquijana."

A new tumult swept up the hillside, washing over the *jefe* with a physical force that energized each tingling cell, swelling his chest with pride and lifting him up until he seemed to float above the assembled troops.

Ibarras laughed, intoxicated by the sense of triumph. In a few days, he would stand in the Plaza de los Héroes to be proclaimed *Presidente de la República,* and a whole nation would rise up and greet him with a roar.

When his men had quieted down, he extended his right arm, pointing at the severed head far below.

"A souvenir," he shouted. "Something from the *norteamericanos*."

The clamor swelled and Ibarras laughed again. Feeling giddy, he stepped away from the edge of the terrace and turned to the police officers grouped around what remained of the dead Comandante. He kicked the body, a sneer on his face, then wiped the drops of blood off his black leather boots, using the pants of the man he had just executed.

He turned to one of the men, his chief assistant, a thin man with nervous eyes. "Jorge, is the helicopter ready? I'm staying here with the men. Make sure this maggot's passport is in his pocket and drop him in front of the American Ambassador's residence tonight. He needs to learn what happens to *yanqui* meddlers who pick the wrong side."

Raymond Kohlbert looked around the conference table at the other men from Samcon. Six of them, counting himself. Four had just flown in from regional offices in other South American countries, the fifth, a senior executive, from corporate headquarters in Houston. All of them came from different backgrounds but all were leaders in their respective fields, whether heavy industry, international banking, the import and export business (wood products out, pharmaceuticals in), construction, oil, armaments. Only one man, from Caracas, was younger than fifty.

Sam Kerson, an investment banker out of the Buenos Aires office, said, "Let me see if I got this straight. We all know Samcon has influence in Washington among certain financial circles. If this Ibarras takes over you can guarantee those companies will have an edge on doing business here?"

Kohlbert nodded. He was nominally chairing the meeting since it took place in his bailiwick, even though the man from Houston was his corporate senior. "I've spoken to him personally. Samcon has given Ibarras a lot of help over the years, particularly over the last two years when the situation here started to deteriorate. We made arrangements for some of his men to be trained at Fort Benning, Georgia. We facilitated the importation of arms and aircraft for counterinsurgency operations. We even loaned him money to start an exchange bank for his nephew. Once he's in power, he'll give the go-ahead to anyone we want. Development projects, contracts for supplies, oil exploration licenses, a whole range of opportunities will be offered to our people and our friends."

"And the danger if Ibarras fails?" Kerson again, eyebrows knitted. The only doubter in the lot. Kohlbert repressed a sigh. Were all investment bankers this conservative?

"There're always risks in business. In this case, I'd say the odds are high for success."

"And what will failure cost us?" Thurston Walpole, the man from Bogotá.

Kohlbert turned in his direction. Behind Walpole, a long strip of brocaded damask ran from floor to ceiling, one of the room's odd decorative features, its pale rose and lime-green pattern illuminated by an Art Deco wall sconce. Samcon's offices on Calle Iturbe had once been the office of an Austrian aristocrat, who had come to Asunción to make his fortune as a decorator. A fitting backdrop for Walpole, a New Englander with pretensions of nobility. Even his Spanish was full of annoying Castilian lisps.

"The cost of our failure?" Kohlbert shrugged. "Not much. We set up the disaster-prevention program to make General Zancon think we were supporting his regime. We've made it clear we don't want the opposition to gain power. But our counterinsurgency plans will also serve Ibarras. If he fails, Zancon has no reason to suspect us. It's the opposition we have to worry about. Their most charismatic leader is a man named Francisco Rojas de Alquijana—a real favorite of the peasants. He hates foreign corporations and the multinationals on principle alone. Fortunately, he's locked up in one of Zancon's prisons. And if he gets out, Ibarras will see that he's assassinated."

"I don't think we should be involved with assassinating heads of state." Walpole again, his nasal voice sarcastic.

"We're not assassinating anyone. And Alquijana is not a head of state. What we're doing is supporting the government's counterinsurgency operations."

Sam Kerson, the banker, said, "What about this fellow who was giving you problems?"

Damn. The man heard about everything. Probably had talked to Gonzalez on Control, the one member of the Trinity who came from the business sector, ex-president of the Banco Central. Sam Kerson had worked with Gonzalez before.

"Stanek?" Kohlbert tossed one hand in a gesture of indifference. "An insignificant matter. We'll take care of it locally."

The senior executive from Houston said, "You've already involved Greg Brown." An edge to his voice.

Kohlbert shrugged. "Greg hired him. I figured he could help—but like I said, consider the matter taken care of."

"I thought you'd lost touch with Stanek." A trace of accusation in the tone.

Kohlbert hid his annoyance. He didn't like talking about problems of this nature in front of the others. He knew how to take care of Stanek; it was all a matter of getting approval from the senior executive. Veiled words, an unexpressed but unequivocal understanding.

Kerson said, "He's gone rogue on you, Raymond."

Kohlbert looked around the table. "Gentlemen, there's no need to worry. Stanek can't do anything to hurt us. Greg Brown said the guy's been in regular contact with his sister in Washington state. When he telephones again, we'll use her to find out where he is."

Walpole said, "Back to Ibarras. Can he handle this insurrection? I've heard reports the guerrilla forces are preparing to attack strategic targets."

"With the training we've provided, yes. He has well-trained paramilitary forces scattered throughout the country. A revolution from the left actually serves him well. We've even tried to help in that regard—isolated events of sabotage to turn the people against the left."

"We don't need destabilization."

"No … but we can't stop the left on our own—and they are a threat to our continued existence in Paraguay."

"In all of Latin America," Kerson said.

Kohlbert went on. "When Ibarras succeeds in putting down this latest uprising, he will appear as the strongman who saved his country from weaklings like Zancon. The people are used to dictators in Paraguay. They know a strongman like Ibarras can pull the country out of its chaos."

"And what about the military? Why are you so sure they will fail?"

"It's not that they'll fail. The military will be fighting along with the secret police and other paramilitary forces. But once Ibarras arrests Zancon, the army will capitulate."

"And General Paredes?" God the Father, head of Control, top man of the elite 1st Army Corps.

"I've spoken to the general at great length before and during our war games. I'm convinced he has no presidential ambitions. He may not like what happens but he'll support Ibarras once he's taken over."

The man from the head office in Houston cleared his throat. "Well, at the appropriate time you might let him know Ibarras is our man as well." Approval in his voice.

Kohlbert hid a smile. "Will do," he said.

"And while you're at it, make sure you bury any problems."

The two men—Kohlbert and the senior executive—exchanged the look Kohlbert had been waiting for. The order had been given, no doubt as to its message. He nodded once, the silent response resounding through his head: *Ja wohl, Kamerad.* That would be a pleasure.

Chapter Thirty-Three

Diane lay behind the driver across the back of the cab in a tool box with a false bottom. A row of holes with wire mesh screens, the size of a tailpipe, were cut out the back of the tool box and the cab. But once they started moving, there was no forward draft of air and in the dark confines of the box she felt claustrophobic. The smell of exhaust that permeated the cab, from a faulty muffler it seemed, nauseated her. The veins in her temples were pounding.

Please God, not another migraine.

Why hadn't she thought ahead? She could have taken something as a preventative.

In an attempt to distract herself, she let her mind run over recent events.

Walter and Dink had accompanied her to the airfield at Luque to see the helicopters. The gas truck that pulled up at the hangar was an old Mercedes Benz diesel, its frame rusting away, the logo of the gas company long ago effaced. While Pablo, the driver, topped up the two helicopters they would be using, Diane watched as Dink went over the equipment and tried, in a running monologue, to explain to Walter the principles of helicopter flight.

That was hours ago now, hours during which she'd grown progressively queasier. The lack of ventilation, the vibration of the chassis, the slamming back and forth as Pablo changed gears, the darkness, all made her feel she was on a nightmare carnival ride. She tried to bang on the sides of the tool box with her fists but the sound she made was masked by the truck's other noises. If Pablo didn't stop soon she would vomit—and there was barely enough room to turn her head to the side.

Please let me out of here!

As if in answer to her prayers, she felt a sudden deceleration, heard the squeal of brakes and the tools above her head shifted in the metal tray a few inches above her body. The braking continued, a long, slow process that left her waiting for the sounds of a collision.

Motionless. Nausea settling in the pit of her stomach. Waves slowly subsiding.

What now? A police roadblock? An accident?

A moment later, the tools shifted again and Pablo's face with its deep ridges appeared. A peasant's face, weathered by the sun and wind and probably by torture at some point, scars on his upper lip and at the outer edge of one eyebrow. Tufts of black hair sprouted from his ears. But at the moment, no sight was more gratifying.

Pablo slid the tray of tools out of the box.

"A chance for air," he said, helping her up, his face expressionless.

She had tried to assay that face at the hangar, wondering if he was a man to be trusted, but it was a difficult face, pain hidden there. She could find no compassion in his eyes, no feeling of shared kinship, no willingness to see her as anything other than a hazard to the success of his mission.

The truck had stopped at the side of the road in what appeared, at first glance, to be a deserted stretch of countryside with no sign of habitation.

An anxious moment, the quick thought that she was defenseless, that Pablo might attack or abandon her. A charge of adrenaline. If he moved toward her she'd be ready.

But then she saw a small wooden shack with a corrugated tin roof—a *chipera*, and behind that the wood-fired kiln of a tile factory no bigger than a one-car garage. She took a deep breath to calm herself. So far so good—she was alive and heading toward the rendezvous with Walter.

They ate on their feet, crescent-shaped rolls of *chipa* bread washed down with glasses of cold *mosto*, chilled sugarcane juice. Chunks of melting ice, brought from the nearest city, floated in a large washtub along with the plastic containers of juice.

A barefoot woman with missing teeth served them, her red dress unbuttoned to the middle of her chest, her dull black hair pulled back and tied with a strip of cloth. Suffering to make an existence out of nothing, too overburdened by life to want to talk, too sullen.

While they ate, protected from view by the kiln, a bright red bus rolled by but traffic on the whole seemed sparse. She used the outhouse and Pablo after her, and they were back on the road. Diane had wanted to sit up front but Pablo said no, it was too dangerous. He couldn't risk not getting through to the landing zone to refuel the helicopters. They'd already passed several military convoys. The next one might stop them.

Back in the coffin, fortified with Tylenol and aspirin.

What were Dink and Walter doing now? The plan called for them to take off in the helicopters three hours after the departure of the truck. If all went well, they would arrive at the landing zone in late afternoon or early evening. The assault on the Poromoco compound would take place at twilight, with darkness settling in. Escobar had promised that guerrilla forces would attack military outposts in villages to the north and south of the base several hours before the rescue mission. The intention? To draw troops away from the area. Those left behind would not be expecting an attack from the air.

She tried to distract herself with thoughts of home, but visions of Kim—alone—were suddenly too painful. She thought about Walter then, reliving in her mind their hours of lovemaking, blocking out the smells of exhaust, the rumbling of the motor, the stiffness of her body.

And then, when those moments had been exhausted, she let the trip to Luque airfield that morning occupy her thoughts. She went over the scene, moment by moment, seeing again the colors, feeling the textures—her hand on Walter's back, listening once more to the two men as they talked.

After they were passed through a back entrance by the lone guard ("Our man," Escobar had explained) and reached the hangar, Walter had stared at the helicopters with a horrified look on his face. "What are they, Dink?"

Dink had laughed. "Hard to tell. They've redesigned the shit out of this one." He was looking at a modified gunship. "Probably done by the Brazilians and then passed on when they got better ones."

Dink walked up to the copter, eyeing the heavy armament. This was the bird he'd be flying. "It looks like they tore an old Cobra apart and glommed it on to this bird. Your typical attack chopper usually has room for just two people. This one's got a passenger compartment along with the weaponry. Not your normal gunship."

He unlatched and slid back the side door. It looked like there was room for at least ten or so guerrillas.

"Relics," Dink said. "Civilian aircraft originally. See that—" he pointed to a large chopper nearby—"Made under license in Italy by Agusta. Looks like some version of the Bell 250 but that's gotta carry at least fifteen passengers." The bird they'd be escorting. The one they'd provide cover fire for during the assault, their own men dropped off outside the base to provide a diversionary movement while Dink hovered over the fort, strafing any forces who tried to intervene.

"But this one—" Dink patted the Plexiglass of the gunship's cockpit—"this one's for us, Walter. Like a whore with lots of make-up. See these wings jutting out to each side?"

He pointed to a metal framework extending from the fuselage, just aft of the cockpit. "They added these later—for the armament. Must've been one hell of a job."

Walter had wanted to know what all was there and Dink had talked of miniguns, each with four thousand rounds of ammunition, of 40mm grenade launchers, of rocket pods with seven rockets each, of 20mm canon.

"They can all be fired by the pilot, but it'd help if I had a gunner." He punched Walter on the arm. "You're riding in the cockpit with me, Cowboy. Ever fired a turret gun?"

"I've never fired anything," Walter said. "Except a .22 when I was a kid."

"Well, there's a first time for everything. Let's get inside. I'll show you how she flies."

Diane had watched as Dink went over the instrumentation.

"Why you telling me all this?" Walter wanted to know.

"In case you have to fly. In case my butt is shot out from under me and you're the only one in the cockpit still alive."

"Shit," Walter had said. "This is too complicated. Just give me a pistol so I can blow my brains out before we hit the ground."

Dink laughed. "Forget the instruments," he said. "The controls are simple—it's just getting used to them that takes time."

He put his hand on the collective-pitch lever to the left of the pilot's seat. "Pull up on this and you go up—we call it the 'lever' or the 'collective'—it changes the pitch of the blades, the angle of attack. You're in luck, this one's got an automatic r.p.m. control. You got a throttle at the end of the lever here, this twist grip, but it's only used for manual adjustments. All you gotta do is lift up on the collective and the throttle opens—feeds a richer fuel mixture to the engine. Push down and the r.p.m. drops. Got that?"

But that wasn't all of course. There was the cyclic-pitch stick between the pilot's legs and the two rudder pedals at his feet.

"With the stick, you got a free range of motion," Dink said. His biceps bulged as he gripped the corrugated-rubber handle. "Nice and easy does it, okay? You push the stick forward, you go forward. What happens? The main rotor changes its angle of attack and the nose drops, so you lift up the collective to increase the lift and the r.p.m. You got to adjust them both to climb or to keep level flight."

"What about the pedals?" Walter asked.

"We sometimes call these the yaw pedals," Dink said. "You step on the left rudder, the nose turns left, you step on the right pedal, you go right. They control the tail rotor—that's for the torque. Keeps you from spinning around in a circle."

He paused for a moment, looking at Walter to see if he understood.

"I don't know if I can remember all this," Walter said. "I hope you were joking about me flying."

Dink shrugged, his expression serious. "It's your life, man."

He looked back at the instrument panel. "See this—" he tapped a dial. "The slip indicator, or ball. Tells you if you're skidding or slipping sideways, which cuts down on your fuel efficiency. You use the rudder pedals to keep the bird straight."

From the ground, listening to Dink's instructions at the open cockpit door, Diane had asked a question. "What controls the speed of the tail rotor?"

"You don't have to worry about that," Dink said. "The tail rotor's driven by a take-off drive from the main-motor gear-box—"

"Whoa, wait a minute. In layman's language."

"Okay," Dink said. "In lay-*woman's* language."

"Do I detect some sexism there?"

Dink shrugged. "Walter got it, didn't you?"

"Walter's an engineer," she said. "I teach German."

"Well, let me put it this way, the tail rotor's hooked up to the same engine that drives the main motor. You turn one up, the other follows. If they both fail, you still got what we call an autorotation landing. I think this is going to be a little beyond Walter, too, but the pilot can keep the blades turning without an engine."

And for the next five minutes he'd gone through the procedures—the change of pitch on the blades, the long, slow glide, how to prevent drift, the sudden increase in pitch at just the right moment, the flare-out and landing.

When he'd finished with that, he'd taken Walter back to the beginning and they went over the whole thing again—from take-off to hover to level flight to banked turns and landing.

And then the instruments again, even though Walter had said he'd never remember. "The rest," Dink concluded, "I'll show you in the air."

In the back of the gas truck, enclosed in what felt like a metal strait-jacket, Diane whispered, "Good luck, guys."

If Walter had to fly, they were going to need it.

Around four o'clock in the afternoon, the gas truck left the main highway at Caacupú and headed east on dirt roads toward Maciel. The air in the tool box turned stale and gritty. The screen mesh over the vents could not keep out the dust. A fine swirling powder seeped in, coating Diane's face and congesting her lungs. She couldn't hear her own coughing over the noise of the straining gears.

She thought Pablo was shouting something, but she couldn't make out a single word.

At Maciel, Pablo left the dirt road, following a track that cut across a wide grassy expanse toward a grove of coconut palms. They skirted the grove on the left, dropping into a slight depression where the truck was hidden from view. Pablo pulled to a stop and helped Diane get out.

On a hill in the near distance stood the remains of a deserted estancia. That would be Dink's initial marker. From the air, the farm was within five minutes of Maciel and Maciel lay near the train tracks that Stanek had followed with Samcon's pilot. Dink had been sure he could find the farm.

Diane tried to clean her face with the edge of her skirt, but her clothes were coated with a film of red dust that smudged when she brushed at it. There was no water for washing. Pablo had only enough for drinking.

For an hour, as dusk fell, she was kept busy gathering wood for a bonfire, another marker to guide the two choppers if they were delayed. When she finished, Pablo unhooked the hose on the truck and doused the wood with fuel, then moved the truck to a level spot at a safe distance.

The wait at that point was no more than forty minutes. The first indication that someone was coming was a faint on-again, off-again whapping—a sound that rapidly grew to a heart-thumping reverberation as the two choppers came sweeping in barely a hundred feet above the ground.

The transport chopper was down first, settling on skids, the fuselage almost hidden from view in an upburst of dust. And then, not far away, Dink came in, and as soon as the attack bird touched down, the cockpit doors flew open and Walter's face appeared. He hadn't spotted her yet.

Armed men piled out of the sliding door behind him, taking up positions on the perimeter. One man took off at a run for the crest of the depression, to keep an eye out for anyone approaching on the ground. The bonfire Pablo had lit ten minutes earlier sent a thin stream of black smoke into the sky.

"Douse the fire," Escobar yelled. He was riding with the men in the transport chopper.

The guerrillas scattered the fragments that were still burning, kicking dirt on the dead limbs to extinguish the flames.

Diane was trying to yell for Walter, but her voice was lost in the confusion. Running men blocked her way, and she knew the closer she got to the helicopters the louder it would get.

Behind the choppers, the sky turned a brilliant orange as if there were a fire at the horizon. The sun was about to set.

Escobar was shouting at Pablo to hurry and Dink was helping the man as they attempted to refuel his bird first. Dink would take off once his tanks were full, to give him time to drop the diversionary force near the airstrip and vehicle park, before the other transport chopper dropped into the middle of the fort. Dink was hoping the military would think both birds were theirs, even though they'd both be maintaining radio silence, and that no antiaircraft fire would greet them. Once the transport chopper was on the ground inside the fort, he would hover overhead, directing rockets and canon fire where needed.

And then Walter spotted Diane, face bursting into a grin as he began running in her direction, a dark shadow against a sky suffused now with the color of blood, the air loud with the noise of men preparing for war.

When he reached her, with an embrace that took her breath away, all she could see were his eyes and all she could hear, as everything else died away, were words of love and the pounding of their hearts.

Chapter Thirty-Four

War—that's what it was, a furious assault that rocked the senses, cries of confusion mingled with horrible screams of pain, gut-wrenching fear, madness.

The attack chopper had dropped down on a hornet's nest and now angry bullets were whistling overhead, ripping into the chopper at Stanek's back.

His fault—*and the mission hadn't even begun!*

He lay prone, one cheek pressed to the hot earth, eyes squeezed shut. The chopper's downblast buffeted him. His fingers clawed dirt. A scream for help erupted from his throat and died in the roar. Bullets pinged into the metal, a sharp tearing sound audible over the thumping of the main rotor.

One of the guerrillas had fallen beside him, trying to help, the side of his head gone, a single eyeball fixed on Stanek with a gruesome stare, lashes burned away.

Stanek rolled onto his back, throat dry as the chopper rose into the air above him and faltered. An eyelid slivered open, a thin slit that showed a blur of red dust. He found the rifle that had bounced across his shoulders when the first guerrilla fell, an AK-47. He held the weapon to his chest, barrel pointing over his head, and began to fire. The percussion deafened his ears to the thunder around him. Guerrillas were firing from both sides of the chopper's passenger compartment and several were on the ground, at least three of them down for good.

Dink shouted something from the cockpit—words indecipherable, jaws contorted in pain. The chopper rose ten feet and settled there unsteadily, hovering in the downdraft's cushion. The cockpit door flapped open and then ripped free in a hail of fire.

The chopper began to yaw, out of control Stanek thought. He wondered if the blades would cut down through him before it crashed. But suddenly the turret gun spouted flames and he saw through bleary eyes what Dink was doing, letting the tail end spin round in a slow circle, cutting a widening swathe as the chopper turned again and again. Dink had already told him once: Without a gunner aboard, the only way he could fire the turret gun was from its fixed position.

Do it, buddy! Wipe out the fuckers!

The yawing stopped suddenly and a grenade launcher puffed. Shock waves rippled over the ground a moment later. Precious ammunition, needed for the attack on the fort, wasted because of Stanek.

A mistake. His fault. He'd convinced Dink to drop him off before the attack on the fort, only five kilometers away now, over a slight rise in the lower reaches of the cordillera. From the air, they'd spotted a dirt road where Stanek could hitch a ride to safety. He'd done his job, now he wanted to find Diane and get out of the country.

"Lucky dog," Dink had said fifteen minutes earlier, speaking over the intercom, his words sounding tinny in Stanek's earphones. "She's one hell of a woman, Walter. If I didn't have a chick waiting for me in Chacarita, I'd be jealous. The guys said you did it in the courtyard last night. Put on a real show. Pretty good for an old man like you."

Stanek's head swung around, finding Dink's. Shit, someone had seen him and Diane making love the night before. He didn't know what to say, didn't like Dink talking about it. It sounded tawdry in his mouth.

"Hell," Dink shouted, slapping his own leg with his left hand. "I had one like that in the Parque Caballero. Girl turned her back to me, lifted one foot on to a park bench, and arched her butt. Wasn't wearing any undies and had a skirt on short enough for a two-year old. Took her from behind." Stanek didn't want to hear this, but Dink roared on. "Cute little ass—hairiest cunt you'll ever see. Couldn't ask for better."

Well, Dink had other things on his mind now, that's for sure.

He'd set the chopper down in a clearing near the road, coming under intense fire seconds after the skids hit the dirt. For a moment, Stanek hadn't known what was happening, then he'd seen the bullets ripping through metal, guerrillas peeling out both sides of the chopper, afraid it was going to come down—and he'd hit the dirt himself. Dink had been hit then. The chopper pitched, blades snicking into a tangle of blackberry vines to one side.

But now the bird was under control, settling back to the earth, Dink screaming for Stanek to get in.

He stumbled for the door, rifle in one hand, and piled in, grabbing for the seat frame as the chopper pitched into the air and keeled to one side. The shirt sleeve on Dink's left arm had been ripped away, his skin peeled by a slug that had punched on through the Plexiglass screen. Hot air rushed in as they skimmed above the ground, following the contours of the hill, skids barely clearing the tree tops, sun just below the horizon.

Stanek struggled into the shoulder harness, trying to get buckled in, rifle still clasped in his hands. Nothing to shoot at now, the ambush site falling away behind them.

"You're hurt," he shouted, slipping the headphones and mike over his head.

He could hear Dink's labored breathing.

"Just nicked. Goddamn motherfuckers. How many they'd get?"

He'd been too busy flying to count.

"We lost four men," Stanek said. That left only six to launch the diversionary assault.

And what about the other transport chopper? If it went in too soon, the attack chopper wouldn't be there to help. No cover fire.

"It's no use," Stanek yelled. "We've lost the element of surprise."

"Can't stop now. That wasn't the army. Para-military uniforms. I've seen them before. Police combat units. Did you see that convoy coming up the road?"

How in the hell had Dink had time to look at the road.

"I missed it."

"*Policía*. Big letters on the side of several vans."

"They'll be in radio contact with the base."

Dink shook his head. They'd crested the hill and he could see the base ahead, the fort and the officers' cabins still hidden in trees, but some of the outbuildings and the runway sweeping into view in the dusky air.

"We got to go in," he shouted, pointing off to his left.

Stanek saw it then, the transport chopper, coming in hard and fast from the northwest.

Dink was swearing. "No time to set these guys down."

There went the diversionary force—the attack on the vehicle park.

"You're bleeding, Dink."

"Can't feel a thing. There's a First-Aid kid down by your feet."

Stanek unlatched the kit and found a supply of bandages and tape. He had to unbuckle his seat belt to reach Dink's arm, as the pilot twisted toward him, left arm extended. Stanek slapped on a gauze bandage and wrapped it tightly with a strip of tape.

"That'll have to do," Dink said. "We're there."

Stanek turned around and grabbed for the buckle of his shoulder harness, snapping it back into its holding clip.

Oh shit! A fireball erupted from the direction of the fort.

"What is it, Dink?"

"The other bird's gone down," he said. "We're going in to get them."

Jesus Christ! From the sound of it, they were going to be cut to shreds!

Chapter Thirty-Five

Grenade launchers, rockets, canon fire, the turret gun, Ak-47s, Chinese SKS rifles, and other assorted weapons blasting from both sides of the passenger compartment: They came in firing them all, blowing sections of the stockade to pieces, hitting a tower, a guard post, several interior buildings, an elevated cistern, vehicles, men.

Answering weapons blazed from the ground below as they dropped toward the fort, several hundred feet out yet, a few men in army uniform shooting up at the chopper as they ran across a yard to safety. A steady stream of bullets, a vicious crossfire, came ripping through the air as they circled in, Dink preparing to flare out at the last moment in a controlled crash landing.

But they weren't there yet. Time slowed as the mind absorbed details.

A pall of black smoke drifted across the prison grounds. The fort's layout was visible for the first time—a large rectangular stockade with at least seven buildings running along the walls on the inside, a fortified entrance for vehicles, a mechanics' shop, a log wall for executions at one end of an inner yard the size of half a football field, other buildings grouped at one end—barracks, a mess hall, a quartermaster's Quonset hut, officers' quarters, a small parade grounds.

As they swooped in, well before touching down, they could see the transport chopper burning with the bright glow of phosphorus, its main rotor twisted and bent. It had come down hard but it looked like a few men had made it out. Stanek could see several huddled by the wall used for executions, exchanging fire with soldiers in one of the guard houses, and another group had made it as far as the first cell block.

A handful of prisoners streamed out of the building. Barefoot men, dressed in filthy civilian clothes, faces bearded and ravaged by deprivation. They ran across the yard, heading toward a break in the stockade wall, split open by one of Dink's rockets. One prisoner stooped for a rifle lying near a fallen soldier and went down hard himself, blood flying as bullets chewed through the upper half of his body.

Hard anger burned through Stanek. He emptied a magazine through the open door of the chopper, firing down in the direction of the guard house, fighting the rifle's upward kick and the quick drop of the helicopter.

"Wait till we're down," Dink yelled. "Save your ammo." One of the guerrillas tossed Stanek a fresh clip. There were no more to spare.

Fifty feet from touchdown, with bullets punching into them, Dink fired the smoke grenades, then came down hard, the skids bouncing. Guerrillas tumbled from the passenger compartment, fanned out and sought protection.

"What the fuck do we do?" Stanek yelled. "I've got to stay with the bird," Dink shouted. "Look for Alquijana."

Look for Alquijana.

This was insane. They were all going to die in this stinking fort.

Stanek hit the ground running, dodging unseen bullets, waiting for the heavy heart-stopping thud, the impact and shock that would mean he'd been hit. Acrid smoke from the burning transport chopper drifted across his path, stinging his eyes. He coughed and ran lower, holding his rifle in one hand, moving too fast to try to fire.

A wood-plank building appeared and he slammed to the ground and rolled up against the wall for protection. Tried to catch his breath, tried to see what was going on, the soldiers holding their ground, firing from behind the protection of vehicles and buildings.

At least, coming in, the base around the stockade had looked emptier than before when Stanek was here. In that respect, Escobar's plan appeared to have worked; the majority of the troops had pulled out to fight the rebels north and south, but the contingent left behind seemed determined to defend the prison, and they were in greater number than expected, pouring steadily out of several barracks at the other end of the fort.

More prisoners had broken free and were fleeing in all directions. Confused by the battle around them, they died as whistling bullets found their mark. A group of five or six tried to rally the others, then charged one of the guard houses, not a weapon among them. Stanek watched as each man fell before he could reach the building, cut down by a furious hail of bullets that erupted from the windows and open doors.

He crawled toward the rubble of the cistern, yelling Renato Sosa's name, voice drowned out by the tremendous roar of weapons. Someone had to get to the remaining cell blocks where the prisoners had not yet broken free.

At the far side of the compound, the roof of an underground structure burst into flame. One of the guerrillas had hit it with a grenade. Stanek jumped when he realized what the building was. An ammo dump.

Get the hell out of there! Running in a crouch, eyes wide in panic, Stanek heard an explosion to his left, hit the ground, then saw that Dink had swung the chopper around and fired a rocket square into the stockade's largest building, some type of prison headquarters it looked like.

Good! Blow the bastards to hell!

A moment of exultation and then a sight that sobered him, as he crawled for protection behind a canvas-topped truck blown on its side by an earlier explosion.

The few soldiers who'd survived the rocket blast ran screaming from their shattered headquarters, weapons left behind, clothes on fire. Some hit the dirt and rolled, writhing in pain, others ran blindly until overcome by the flames or dropped by a stray bullet. A prisoner grabbed a pistol from the belt of a man on fire, then shot him in the face and headed for the main entrance where another contingent of soldiers was holed up, the troops unleashing a withering stream of fire toward the prison cells.

At the moment, the guards were more concerned about killing the political prisoners than stopping the guerrillas who were attacking to free them.

Bastards. The hardcore guard. Every last one of them deserved to die for this.

An orange ball of flame, a shock wave. Ammunition shooting into the air. The roof of the sunken ammo dump had burned down and ignited the fort's stores of ammunition. Hot air scorched his lungs as Stanek rolled around the overturned vehicle, crawling toward—toward what he wasn't sure. He'd lost his sense of direction, felt like a rat in the middle of a maze, scurrying around waiting for the bullet that would end it all.

Stanek saw them then, shrouded in blue-white smoke, a group of men running across his field of vision. Long shaggy hair, unkempt, some of them shirtless. He spun around and saw the attack chopper again. The prisoners were angling toward it, protecting in their midst a frail man with a leonine head and a mane of white hair.

Alquijana! All right!

They'd come from the mess hall, were trying to make it across the northern end of the open field, moving through acrid smoke tossed up by the downed transport, one bending down for a weapon lying next to a dead guerrilla—one of the Chinese rifles with a plastic buttstock—several of the others firing wildly with guns they'd already confiscated from dead or fleeing soldiers.

A belt-fed light machine gun clattered off to the west and the men hit the ground, crawling forward into choking, black smoke, seeking protection from the fusillade of heavy caliber shells. A zig-zag pattern of hot lead churned up the dirt behind them.

The old guy would never survive.

Stanek could hear screams as impacting bullets slammed into the men, and then, at the far side of the cloud of smoke, thirty feet from the attack bird where Dink hovered firing into the officers' quarters with the canons, he saw Alquijana come stumbling into view. A guerrilla appeared beside him, pulling him toward the chopper, which was settling back to the ground.

Stanek fired a few rounds in the direction of the machine gun, trying to distract the soldiers while Alquijana was in the clear. A quick burst and then a change of position, rolling away and spinning around, hugging the ground behind the body of a dead guerrilla in tattered Levi's. Two other prisoners stumbled out of the transport chopper's acrid smoke, following Alquijana. The attack chopper's main rotor cleared a small hollow in the pungent fumes. The guerrilla pulling Alquijana dropped down to provide covering fire.

The old man had made it! Two of the prisoners shoved him into the passenger compartment, then turned away to rejoin the fight. Brave men, willing to sacrifice their lives to help their fellow prisoners.

Where the hell was Renato Sosa?

The guerrillas had wanted Alquijana—and they'd got him, Stanek wanted Pina's husband and didn't know where to look.

A change in pitch—the sound of an engine accelerating.

Don't go, Dink!

The chopper lifted slightly, fusilage swaying as Dink attempted to bring its weapons into the fray.

Stanek heard other men yowling as they attacked the cell blocks, screamed himself for Renato.

The only answer was the sound of bullets and the explosion of grenades.

He had to move, wouldn't accomplish anything huddled behind a dead man. He started to turn away from the chopper, which had come down again, then saw a man in knee-length tight pants drop out of the back and begin running for cover, Dink's gun in his hand. A final prisoner—one of Alquijana's escorts—unwilling to abandon his friends, ready to fight now that he had a weapon.

Stanek fired a burst to give the guy a hand, then moved away, eyes peeled for the lawyer.

Come on, Renato! Where the hell are you?

The chopper'd have to leave soon; they couldn't risk losing Alquijana. Dink was hanging in there, but only by the skin of his teeth. The bird was riddled with holes, and Stanek had seen smoke beginning to drift from the engine cowling, had heard the labored sound of the engine, a wheezing cough, the first sign of a death rattle.

Where the hell was Sosa?

Stanek scanned the terrain, working his way down the eastern wall of the stockade. He skirted buildings, ducked under small arms fire, hit the dirt at the sound of heavy weapons, got up and ran again.

The battle was far from over, but at least it didn't look as if the guards, outnumbered by their escaping prisoners, would get any reinforcements. Still, the soldiers had fallen back to defensive positions at the southern end of the stockade and were taking a heavy toll in lives. The prisoners were fighting now with their hands and whatever else they could pick up

Chapter Thirty-Six

We're on fire," Dink yelled. "Hang on, we're going down!"

The chopper was twisting through the air, beginning its fatal spiral, engine dead, Dink struggling to control the craft as autorotation took over. Smoke billowed out of the cowling, sweeping into the open passenger compartment as the chopper spun lazily.

Stanek had his arms around Renato Sosa, the lawyer's legs dangling out the open doorway. He could feel his own slide toward the edge and dug his heels into the metal floor, saw a man with a red bandana tied around his neck reach for him with one hand, felt the hand grip his belt.

Come on, Dink, set this thing down before we explode in midair.

Streaks of fire shot through the craft. One of the guerrillas screamed as flames reached him, licking at his hair and face. They were above the trees now, green canopy below their feet, no clearing in sight.

Another scream and a man bailed out as flames engulfed him.

Oh come on, get this thing down before we all burn to death.

Flames were licking at *his* back now, and the hand on his belt fell away as another man pitched out the door. Too high to jump, still too high. Only five of them left now—Dink and Alquijana in the cockpit, Stanek and Renato Sosa and a stocky guerrilla with a bandolier around his chest in the passenger compartment.

And then they were down, the main rotor blades shattering as the bird dipped into the trees, smoke pouring from the engine compartment, the cowling ripped away, the tail buckled like a broken match.

Blackness.

They were down—at least he thought they were. Too dark to see a thing. Still alive, Diane!

Dink's voice came to him, faint and far away, and then stronger.

"Let's get the fuck out of here."

Stanek opened his eyes, saw forest around him, the night not yet entirely black. Alquijana was moving away through the trees, white hair like a beacon, the stocky guerrilla leading the way.

Stanek looked down at his own body, realized he was leaning against a tree, dazed by the final collision with the earth. He still had trouble concentrating. Too much to absorb. *His hands were empty.* No sign of Renato. Hadn't he been holding him? He tried to get up, pushing himself to one knee while his head cleared.

"Where's Renato?" he shouted, fear in his voice. Had he done this for nothing?

A gruff voice answered him from behind. "Who the fuck do you think I got over my shoulder? You goin' to sit there forever? You'd think this was an insane asylum and they'd told you to beat your meat all day."

The grin hurt. Stanek got to his feet and turned, saw the lawyer slung over Dink's back. A wave of dizziness swept over him. He touched his head, felt the sweat dripping off his brow. He had a knot forming over one eyebrow. No blood that he could feel. Had he been out of it for a while? He thought he'd been conscious the whole time, but now he felt like his senses were returning to his body from far away.

He stared at Dink. "Shit, I can't tell who's bleeding worse—you or Renato."

"If we don't get the hell out of here, in a few minutes it won't matter," Dink said. "We came down by the road and I don't aim to fall into another ambush. They got just enough light to pick us off like sitting ducks."

The light had finally left the sky. For the last half-hour, seen straight overhead through gaps in the trees, it had been dark blue turning to black. They were moving up a slope and as they came out on a rise where the trees fell away, they could see a thin line of washed-out turquoise at the western horizon. While the others rested, Dink shimmied up a tree to see what he could before blackness took over.

Stanek looked at his watch. After ten. He was dead tired. Adrenaline exhaustion, energy seeping from him like wine from a spilled bottle. They needed time to recuperate, food to eat, water to drink. They needed to find a place where they were safe before they got lost—hell, they were already lost—before total darkness overcame them. He didn't feel like hiking through a jungle, even if in time they would have the moon to guide them.

The air felt cooler, less dusty. He tried to wipe the grime from his forehead, grimaced when his hand touched the knot there. His eyelids felt gritty, red-rimmed sandpaper rubbing at his tired eyes, no moisture there, too dry for tears.

His head fell to his chest. Too damn old for this. Forty-three, going on forty-four. Hard to keep his eyes open. Running around with guerrillas in their teens and twenties. Even Dink was only thirty!

The guy was back, kicking Stanek until he looked up.

A shake of the head. "No sign of life, no roads in the area. We gotta keep moving."

Stanek nodded toward Alquijana. The old man had lain down and apparently fallen asleep. "What about him—think he can he make it?" At least there was one guy older than him.

Dink shrugged. "He's stronger than you think—up here." He tapped his skull. "A man of the mind, not the body. A man of principles and ideals, not a man of action. He survived prison for a long time, he'll survive this."

"And Sosa?"

Dink had stopped at one point to bandage the lawyer's thigh, tearing off a strip of his shirt as a loose tourniquet, catching up with the group a few minutes later. The stocky guerrilla with the bandolier was in the lead. Lot of good the bullets did—he no longer had a weapon.

"He'll be okay," Dink said, "long as the wound doesn't get infected. It'll hurt for a while but nothing seems broken. Went right through the fleshy area in his thigh. He lost a lot of blood."

"We need to get him to a doctor."

Dink looked at him. "I thought you were a doctor." Voice sarcastic.

Stanek's head tipped up. "Ph.D., you mean."

"Worthless piece of shit, ain't it?"

Stanek tried to grin. "Yeah, most of the time."

A golden moon had risen, resting now on the tree tops like an ancient bronze shield. They'd left the thicker jungle behind—the tangled lianas and swampy pools, the swarms of hungry mosquitoes. The land was still forested, but dry, reminding Stanek of the woods in Oregon and Washington: a soft, dry layer underfoot, a lack of brush, the pitchy scent of hardwood trees he couldn't identify. There were no native pine or fir trees in Paraguay.

He wondered what silent shadows moved in the dark.

They stopped twice for brief periods to rest, following the trajectory of the moon when they were in motion, hoping to stumble upon a road or an estancia.

Near dawn, Stanek felt a tension in the atmosphere as if a storm were brewing to the west, although there was no wind, not even a soft breath on his face, and the dead fronds on the scattered coconut palms hung lifeless, awaiting the day's relentless heat.

He concentrated on putting one foot in front of the other, happy that Dink seemed willing to carry Renato by himself.

First light, a soft glow of yellow to the east, then a sudden incandescence, another day, the sense of building heat ... tiredness.

Awakening life. First the birds—the quick flash of a ruby-throated hummingbird, the cawing of white cranes passing overhead, the harsh screech of an *ara macao* in a dying banana tree.

Slowly they left the forest behind, trees dwindling to an occasional shrub or a thicket of brush, clumps of tall, yellow cortadera grass taking over. With the sun came the stirring of a breeze, a hot wind that soughed through the dry grass with a rustling noise like the distant hiss of truck tires on asphalt or like a river rushing downstream through smooth rocks.

Stanek was thirsty. No one had a canteen. They'd drunk from a stream at one point in the night, shallow water trickling over a bed of rocks.

The grass bent under the hot wind as the sun stretched up into the sky. The heat pressed down on their heads and necks like a hot iron, a heavy griddle that weighed them down like the grass. They came across a pool of muddy water, found animal prints—deer, egrets, foxes. Clouds of yellow butterflies rested on the mud, peaked wings rising like cathedral arches or hands clasped in prayer.

A pungent odor of fresh manure tweaked their nostrils.

"Cattle," Dink said. "Should be an estancia nearby."

Renato was talking, his speech delirious.

"We can't drink this mud," Stanek said. "We need to find water fast or some of us won't make it." He gestured to the lawyer, slumped on the ground at Dink's feet, eyes staring vacantly.

Alquijana spoke then for the first time, addressing all of them for a moment before giving orders in Guaraní to the guerrilla with the bandolier strapped around his chest. The man nodded and began smearing mud on Renato's forehead.

Stanek hadn't understood everything, but he recognized the strong inner force that resonated in Alquijana's words. His manner was that of a born leader, a man of energy and passion. All of them would survive, he'd said, and the nation would survive along with them. They had earned the thanks and appreciation of all Paraguayans who wished to live in liberty.

Dink raised his eyes in embarrassed exasperation, as if motivational talks were all they needed.

"There has to be an estancia within reach," he said. "Some water troughs the cattle use when these ponds dry up. Let's keep at it."

They came across the dirt road near midday with the sun scorching down from high above. Renato Sosa drifted in and out of consciousness. The air was muggy and sweat dripped from their foreheads as they sat down to rest.

"A car," Dink said, sitting up, eyes in the distance.

They listened for a moment as the sound of a motor grew in volume.

"Into the grass," Dink said. "It might be the army—or the police."

Alquijana spoke to the guerrilla with the bandolier.

He slipped it off his head and stepped into the road.

Within minutes, a battered Ford that looked like an old '40 with the chrome stripped came into view, one man behind the wheel. The car rolled to a stop and the driver opened the door and stepped out, slipping a wide-brimmed straw hat on his head. A *hacendado* from the looks of him, a rancher, wearing the loose baggy trousers called *bombachas*, on his way to the next village, he said.

He hadn't heard the news of the revolution, and his eyes widened when he heard the name of the white-haired man.

"My car is at your service, *señores*," he said. "An honor."

"Do you have any water?" Alquijana asked.

The man opened his trunk and passed around a plastic bottle of warm water.

"Listen, Walter," Dink said in English. "We can't all go. What say you and I find out where the closest farm is and head there on our own. These guys can get to the next village and then back to Asunción on their own. If we're spotted, we'll only make it worse for them."

"You think they'll get through okay?"

"In this confusion ... yeah. They can stick to the back roads until they pick up an escort. Alquijana has tremendous popular support, even among the military. They'll make it."

"Okay, buddy, it's just you and me."

Despite the heat and his exhaustion, Stanek breathed a sigh of relief.

Mission accomplished. Now it was time to get the hell out of there.

With the driver's directions to guide them, they came upon an estancia an hour later. Alquijana and Renato and the rest had gone on ahead in the Ford.

Dink talked to the farmer in halting Spanish, then pulled up his shirt and unzipped a money belt Walter hadn't seen before. The farmer accepted a wad of guaranies, then led them to a shed where an old truck sat.

"Look for something to hide under," Dink said, "a tarp if you can find it. He's agreed to drive us to Encarnación."

Sunset, Thursday evening, the third week of November.

Stanek hadn't ever seen a more welcome sight—freedom. Across the wide Paraná river, its flat surface glowing with reflected light, sat the town of Posadas, Argentina. From where he and Dink stood, next to a battered donkey engine that sputtered away as it pumped river water into an irrigation canal, they could see on the other side a tall communication tower and several high-rise office buildings and apartment houses, all built on low hills that were dotted with trees. To the left, in the distance, rose the pointed twin steeples of a church.

"How do we get across the bridge?" Stanek asked. "They'll be looking for foreigners." He wanted to ask Dink if he thought Diana had made it, but knew the question was stupid, a sign of anxiety that Dink could not dispel, even with a lie.

"We don't," Dink said. "We do it the old fashioned way."

Stanek looked askance. "Swim?"

"Hell, no. We wait till dark and bribe one of these fishermen to take us over."

Chapter Thirty-Seven

Stanek could smell the scent of gardenias in her long, thick hair; and the soft curves of her body in his arms made him feel weak inside, the surrounding world forgotten. They kissed and he was aware, as he pulled away to look at her, of a deepening in her eyes—pools of blue light that drew him in—and of a quickening in her breath. Her nipples had grown hard against his chest and his own body was reacting to the touch.

Another kiss, longer and more passionate, and then they looked at each other again and this time they laughed.

"Come," Diane said, taking him by the hand. "We'll embarrass ourselves if we try to do it here."

Stanek couldn't wipe the grin off his face. Dink had gone off to hunt down a doctor to patch up his arm; a deep gash along the biceps had turned purple and needed to be cleaned and stitched. Walter and Diane were standing in the lobby of the Hotel Continental. Her room was on the fifth floor.

"I can't wait," he said. "But one thing first—I need a shower."

He watched as she bunched her hair and piled it on top her head and then leaned back against the bed's headboard. Stanek had taken a hot shower, washing away the sweat and the grime of the past forty-eight hours, and then they had made love with a passion that shook them both, each unable to believe that they were safe.

They had told each other their stories while Stanek showered, words rushing out in a flood. Now, facing her on the bed, Stanek felt a warm glow spread through his tired body as she leaned back, arms behind her head, hair falling again to her shoulders.

He couldn't get enough of her face. Her intelligent eyes sparkled with the banked fires of passion; there was an inner warmth there, a zest for life that animated all her features. Her cheeks were rosy and as she opened her mouth in a smile, her whole being radiated a happiness that made him feel like a young kid. Waves of dark hair tumbled down to frame her face as her hands reached behind her to adjust the pillow.

His breath caught in his throat as he watched the lift of her breasts, the nipples jutting forward. He bent toward her and kissed them again, and she pulled his head down and into her, her body warm and pliant.

"God, Walter, you're ready again."

He looked up, grinning at her. "Do you think Dink'll mind if we make him wait a bit longer?"

"I forgot," she said as they were dressing. Stanek had asked the bellboy to bring up a clean shirt and a pair of pants that would fit him. "There was a message at the hotel for you when I got here. Randi called. She got your message with the phone number for this place."

"Randi? Good." He straightened. "What'd she say?"

"It was only two lines. She said she'd try calling again this Friday, sometime between seven and eight in the evening."

"So I guess we have to hang around this place for at least a day," Stanek said. Neither one of them had talked about what would happen now, about the future, but he had had a lot of time to think about it over the last few days. He didn't want to lose this woman.

"I don't mind staying," she said. "The two of us. We can call Pina and see what she's heard."

"Good idea. In the meantime, we better go get Dink. He's probably swearing up a blue streak by now."

Dink said, "I've decided to go back."

They'd taken an open horse-drawn cab to pick up Dink at the waterfront clinic, a chilled bottle of white wine and three glasses with them. The air was warm and filled with perfume, the night dark like black velvet studded with diamonds. On the way back, Dink sat opposite them on the *strapontin* and pretended to look sour at their obvious happiness. And then, relenting, he'd talked of his own girl, Amada, back in the shantytown of Chacarita on the fringes of Asunción, eyes turning inward as he remembered the way she moved and talked, her little mannerisms, the sexy air she had.

And that's when he told them he was going back.

"It's too dangerous now," Stanek told him. "The roads are unsafe. Too many police."

"Hey, it's not me they're looking for; it's Diane—and maybe you."

"I wouldn't be too sure about that," Diane said. "All it would take is for one of the rebels to brag about what you did in the helicopter."

"Well, I'm not going to be driving there, anyway. I got me a buddy with a plane here in Posadas. I'll fly back."

"And land where?"

"An air strip," he said. "The fucking international airport ain't the only place to set down." He paused, reaching for the bottle of wine they'd opened, pouring himself a second glass. "You know what she told me once?"

"Who?"

"My girl … Amada. She said, it doesn't matter if you're rich or poor—life is garbage. It's just that the rich can afford to put a lid on the can." He stared at the wine glass, lost in thought for a moment. "You know, I never minded the squalor of the shantytown—actually I liked it. I felt alive there, in touch with reality … but you know, it is squalor and it is poverty and no one deserves that. I got ten thousand dollars for flying that chopper—"

"If you get paid—"

"I've got half already and when I get the rest I'm giving it all to Amada."

Walter and Diane looked at Dink for a moment before Diane spoke. "Dink, you could mail her the money."

He shook his head. "You don't understand. I miss her. I'm going back to stay."

"But what's there to live for in Asunción?" Stanek asked. "Get her out of there. Go back to the States."

Dink licked his lips. "There's something I haven't told you guys. I work for the DEA. We set up a station in Asunción in the late nineties. I still have a job to do here."

Stanek grinned. "Dink, you're a narco? Diane thought you might be a dealer."

"I did not. I just wondered—" Her voice fell away and then she laughed. "Well, Dink, you said you flew all over the place … did a little bit of everything. What was I supposed to think?"

"That's okay," he said. "I always thought you worked for the CIA."

They had a good laugh over that one.

A gauzy moon had lifted over the horizon. It hung above the hills, swollen and weighty, looking as if it might settle back down and disappear.

"The moon's beautiful tonight," Diane said. "It makes me miss home. Autumn moons in the mist."

"It'll be cold in New Haven," Stanek said.

"Yeah, and don't forget," Dink added, "the moon is dead. It's the sun you should be missing ... something that's alive and hot."

Diane smiled, a mischievous look in her eyes. "Like Amada, I bet."

"Right," he said, "now you're learning. Like Amada."

That night, in bed with Walter, who had fallen asleep in exhaustion, a delayed reaction to the events of the last two days, Diane felt as if she were lying in the center of the universe, immersed in the very plexus of life ... centered and calm, yet plugged into an immense source of energy that required her only to flip the switch for the current to flow. A fullness of being she had never felt before—not with her first husband, not with Russ, not with any other of the men who had courted her with their witty repartee.

That was something she liked about Walter—he hadn't come on to her like most men his age, especially single men. They always thought they had to be clever. But Walter—Walter was himself. He didn't have any set speeches, any memorized lines; he just *was*. He went on talking and thinking and acting in her presence just as he did around anyone else. There was no screen of gilded words between them.

Unlike some men, he had no trouble telling her he loved her—but he hadn't needed to—it was evident in his eyes, it came off him like a physical force, an invisible wave that linked the two of them and wouldn't let go.

He had already told her that—told her he would never leave her again, that his job didn't matter, he could find another one in Connecticut. He'd seen New Haven once, engineers were always in demand, he would apply to Yale and other universities in the area. And if they wouldn't hire him, some company would. He was tired of the desert. Dink could talk all he wanted about the sun and how alive it was—the sun was damn hot! He was ready for a change. He wanted to be near water.

"I can take you sailing," she'd told him. "Or do you get sea sick?" A smile crept into her cheeks.

"Hell, no," he replied. "Water's my job."

And it was, now that she thought about it, whether he called himself a geological engineer or a hydrogeologist. She couldn't wait to have him meet Kim.

She smiled, looking at Walter's rugged features in repose—his thick tangled hair, gone uncut the whole time he'd been in Paraguay, his strong face with its forceful chin, lightly cleft, the smile lines in his cheeks, the lips that she loved to feel caressing her body. A strong man, someone Dink might call staid compared to him—but it wasn't wildness she wanted. Stanek was a man of passion, too, a man of convictions and inner strength, someone you could depend on.

"They've found Eliana's body," Diane said.

The two men looked up in shock. They were sitting at a table in the Hotel Continental's restaurant, eating breakfast. Diane had gone to the reception desk to make a long-distance call to Asunción.

"She was tortured and then killed." Tears formed in her eyes, as Walter stood to embrace her and Dink slapped the table in anger. "So young and so innocent," she said, her voice quavering.

Walter hugged her to him, feeling her body tremble. After a few moments, he asked, "Where did they find her?"

"Someone dropped her body in front of the Sosa residence the night before last."

"Secret police," Dink said. "The bastards."

"What about Renato?"

Diane wiped at her eyes. "Pina hasn't told him."

"Then he made it back?"

She nodded, sniffling. "He's in the San Lucas hospital … he's going to be okay." Okay, *physically*, Pina had said—but what about deep inside … in the heart?

There, where it really mattered, he'd never be okay.

Dink spent the afternoon tracking down his friend with the private plane, an archeologist who was working on the red sandstone ruins at San Ignacio Miní, a Jesuit commune founded in the early seventeenth century and located forty miles south of Posadas.

At noon, Walter tried calling his sister in Ferndale, Washington, but no one answered, not even the machine. After lunch and a shopping trip to buy Walter a change of clothes, he and Diane walked to the tourist office on Avenida Colón and made arrangements to fly out the next morning, first with Austral to the international airport at Buenos Aires and then on to Miami that same day with Aerolineas Argentinas.

Then Walter made a long-distance call to his credit union in Tucson, wondering if Samcon had paid him like they were supposed to. Greg Brown had told him Samcon would deposit thirty thousand into his account on Friday, November 6, the day the war games sessions started in Asunción and that the second installment would be deposited two weeks later on the twentieth. Which meant the money should have gone in that morning.

The customer service representative at DM Federal Credit Union read him the amount of the deposit into his money market account and then his balance—well over sixty thousand dollars.

All right! They'd paid! That meant Randi would get the new John Deere tractor he'd promised her—and the rest would tide him over, along with some money in other accounts, until he could get set up in New Haven.

"I'm probably fired," he told Diane, "but I got paid for the whole month."

"You earned it," she said.

"Yeah, but I don't know if they'll think so. I'll probably have Greg Brown on my doorstep when I get back, asking for a refund."

Dink returned later that evening, while Walter and Diane were in their room, waiting for Randi's promised call. He told them he was heading out to a local airstrip to fuel and check out the plane, a four-seat Cessna Cutlass with retractable landing gear, but that he'd be back to share a late dinner with them before leaving. He was going to make the trip at night.

At seven-twenty, the harsh sound of the telephone startled them both, a strange ring full of vibration. Stanek had wondered if Randi would get through.

He picked up the phone, heard her voice and grinned. "Damn good connection, Randi. How you doing? Give Buck my greetings." He couldn't hear the golden retriever but knew he was probably sleeping in his box by the refrigerator in the old farm house.

"I'm coming down to visit you," she said, her voice brimming with cheer.

"Wait, Randi! No! Look, I didn't tell you everything—things are bad here." He rushed on. "I can't explain on the phone but don't come!"

There was a pause and when she came back her voice had lost its cheerfulness. "Walter, this was a joke—"

"Thank God," he muttered. She was safe. He moved the mouthpiece out of the way and said to Diane, "She was joking about coming down."

Diane raised her eyebrows.

"Walter, you don't understand. I'm calling from the Petti—the Silvio—oh, what is it here? … the international airport. I'm in Asunción! That was sweet of you, Wally, sending the money for the ticket. I missed you, too."

"Randi, I didn't send—"

"Wally, my ride's here. I have to go. They said I'd be seeing you in fifteen minutes, anyway."

Fifteen minutes. What ride? "Randi, wait! Get back on the plane! Randi—"

But she'd already hung up on him.

"What is it?" Diane asked, alarmed by how pale he was.

For a moment, he couldn't speak. He swallowed, a hard knot in his chest. "They got my sister," he said.

Chapter Thirty-Eight

The question is," Dink said, "who's got her? Ibarras or someone from Samcon?"

Walter stared at the shorter man, at the impenetrable dark eyes under his thick black eyebrows. "Now you're really scaring me," he said. "I never thought of the secret police. I was thinking Kohlbert. He's the one who talked about my sister. He made a veiled threat when I came back to the capital from the Corpus project. I tried to convince myself it was me he was threatening. Someone at Samcon told him about my sister—Greg Brown, the guy who hired me."

"But what do they want from you?" Diane looked frustrated. "You did what you could. Do they expect you to work in the middle of a revolution?"

Their eyes locked in a measuring, speculative embrace before Stanek shut his eyes and tipped his head back, trying to take a deep breath to calm himself. "I don't get it." It made no sense. If Kohlbert did anything to harm Randi, he'd kill the guy.

"Maybe they were just being nice," Dink said. "Maybe they thought you were missing your family."

No one said anything to that.

"Okay—" Dink scratched his forehead. "We get her back."

Stanek's eyes narrowed. "What?"

"We leave Diane here and you and I fly back tonight. Tomorrow we'll shake down this Kohlbert. I'll rattle his balls and we'll see what comes out of him. He won't hold out long in my hands."

"I'm not leaving Walter," Diane said, slipping her arm through his.

They were standing on the street in front of a restaurant. A ruddled light fell from a neon sign overhead, casting twisted shadows through the branches of a lapacho tree with brilliant violet flowers. Dink had called from the airstrip and told them to meet him at *El Tío Querido*, an eatery recommended by his friend, the archeologist.

"If he goes, I go. Walter, we made a deal, right?"

A young girl in sandals walked by on the uneven cobblestone street leading a mule by a rope halter, two large wicker baskets anchored to each side of the beast.

"I have to go back, Diane. My sister doesn't know what she's getting into."

"I know you have to go. I wouldn't forgive you if you didn't. It's just that I'm going, too."

"Maybe it's me they want."

"I wouldn't doubt it," Dink said.

Diane swung around to face the shorter man. His chest muscles bulged inside his tight T-shirt. "You said you'd help."

"Hey, I wasn't trying to back out. Just wanted to make sure everyone understood what the stakes are."

"The stakes are my sister's life," Walter said.

Dink nodded. "Okay, let's go get her."

The single-engine Cessna Cutlass had two fuel tanks in the wings with a total capacity of 235 litres—sixty-two U.S. gallons—and a maximum range of 829 miles on the recommended lean fuel mixture, with an allowance for starting the engine, taxi, take-off, climb, and forty-five minutes of reserve.

"Plenty to get us to China and back," Dink said, scratching his arm where the doctor had taped a dressing over his wound.

"Your arm bother your flying?" Stanek asked. He didn't want another lesson on flying, didn't want to have Dink tell him half-way through the flight that he'd have to take over and land the plane.

Dink looked at his arm as if he wanted to rip off the wide strip of tape holding the dressing in place. "No, but this bandage is going to drive me crazy. The doc said to leave it on till Monday morning. Don't know if I'll last that long." He turned back to the plane's console. "Listen up, Walter, and I'll run through a few of the features."

But Stanek was too nervous to absorb much as Dink spelled out everything the plane could do. About all he could remember was that this particular model had the avionics package of a Skyhawk II, whatever that was. He'd let Dink handle it.

They were cruising at 130 knots under a clear sky at 1,500 feet, the ground below barely discernible in the darkness. A river appeared below them, a sheen of moonlight reflecting off its surface.

"The Rio Tebicuary," Dink said, consulting a chart spread out on his lap in the dim light of the console. He'd plotted his course in Posadas, marking the checkpoints with circles. "It runs to the east into the Paraguay river. We angle north from here." He turned the plane to a new heading. "Record the time."

Stanek looked down at the navigation log and read the information Dink had already filled in. They were on the third leg of the trip, just over a hundred miles from Posadas on a straight line, but they'd zig-zagged back and forth on short hops for security purposes, covering nearly three hundred miles all told. Still, there were only sixty-nine statue miles left in the "distance remaining" column. He looked at his watch and wrote down 3:25. This was going to be one fast trip compared to the chopper ride. If all went well, they had less than a half-hour to ETA now.

The closer they got to the capital, the more nervous he became. They had filed no flight plan and he expected at any moment to be shot down by the Paraguayan air force. He tried to remember the air force's equipment and where their bases were located, knowing it had been listed in the handbook provided to each participant in Samcon's war games. He thought he recalled something about a squadron with the country's only combat planes being headquartered at Campo Grande, but he seemed to recall that the planes themselves were based at the Silvio Pettirossi international airport outside Asunción. Too damn close.

Had they been picked up the second they crossed the border? Were they being tracked on radar? Dink still hadn't told him where he expected to set down. Maybe it was time to ask again. But when he did, all Dink said was, "We'll see when we get there."

"Damn it, Dink, this is a soccer field." The lights of the city were bright, the landing gear was down and locked, the Cessna at approach speed, airspeed in the dial's yellow arc, creeping toward red.

"What we call a *campo de football*," Dink said in a rousing voice. "You awake, Diane?"

"Are we there?"

"We're flying right up their butt. See that dark patch off to the right. The *Cementerio del Sur*. That's where we meet if anything goes wrong." Velocity dropping perilously close to stall speed.

"What about the plane?" Walter asked. "They'll confiscate it."

"I asked my friend in Posadas to report it as stolen. He'll get it back. I paid him a little extra for his trouble. Said to tell the police they should look in the capital of Paraguay." He laughed out loud. "They won't have to look too hard, will they?"

Ground coming up fast.

Dink rolled his shoulders, grin frozen on his face as his concentration turned solely to the landing. "Hang on to your stomachs," he whooped, "we're going in."

The nose of the plane dropped at an alarming rate. Stanek reached for the console to brace himself, feet pressing into the floor as if to hold the ground away. "You're not going there, are you?" Voice filled with disbelief. "We just passed two fields that were twice that big."

"Yeah," Dink said. "One's next to the penitentiary and the other belongs to the army's *Comando de Ingeniería*. Maybe those guys are buddies of yours, but they ain't friends of mine."

And from then on things moved too fast for talk.

The two soccer fields Dink had overflown were large ovals surrounded by bleachers. This field was a rectangle, maybe half the size, with streets all around and buildings on the far side of the streets.

They came down into darkness, the playing field invisible, bounced once hard, Dink struggling to control the wheel, brakes digging in, doors opening before they had come to a complete stop.

Ahead of them lay an unlit street with no traffic, cars parked on both sides. Already, in the distance, they could hear sirens, coming from the direction of the Cantera Tacumbú to the south.

Walter and Diane reached the street first and turned to the right, toward the cemetery, but after one block the street came to a dead end. An arroyo lay to the right and for a moment, they hesitated, wondering if they should leave the streets to hide in the underbrush along its banks.

They heard steps behind them and turned to find Dink, breathing hard. "I know this area," he said. "There's a street five blocks to the north that's a diagonal. They'll try to cut us off. We have to go that way, find a cross street to the cemetery."

"What about the arroyo?"

Dink shook his head. "Dogs'll find us." He looked around. "Know how to hot-wire a car?"

"Never really done it," Walter said.

"What'd they teach you in college, anyway? They stop after the lesson on tying your shoestrings?" He tried the doors on a stocky, four-door sedan. "Locked." He walked around to the driver's side.

Diane could hear sirens coming from two directions now. "We can't stand here forever, Dink. They're going to cordon off this whole area."

"Well, shit." He stepped back and kicked in a window. "Get in," he said, unlocking the back door. He brushed glass off the front seat and bent under the dash. "Keep your eyes open. Someone might have heard that."

He rose up for a second and tossed a small pistol to Stanek, then bent back to the ignition wires he'd pulled loose.

"I didn't know you were armed," Stanek said. Dink had lost his pistol to one of the guerrillas during the assault on the fort.

Dink laughed. "Found it under the dash. Maybe we should keep looking. Might find us an Uzi and do us some real good."

He straightened and in a minute had the motor running. The sirens were closer, echoing in the streets. Scattered lights appeared in the apartment houses across the way. The sedan looked too slow to try to outrun a police car, and the small pistol he'd found seemed like a toy.

"What is this?" Stanek asked, trying to see it in the dim light. He'd taken the front passenger seat.

Dink laughed. "Pellet gun." He pulled away from the curb.

Diane said, "What are you so cheerful about?"

"Life," Dink said. "Suck it dry." He looked back at her. "We're alive, aren't we?" The car accelerating.

Stanek snorted. "Yeah, well, let's try and keep it that way." He tossed the gun out the window on his side. "Where you heading?"

"Off to see my girl. Want to come along?"

"Watch out!" Diane screamed.

A car had surged around the corner ahead of them, tires squealing, body lifting on its chassis, blue turret light flashing.

"Shit."

Dink hit the brakes for a mini-second, saw there was nowhere else to go and headed straight toward the police car, swerving into the wrong lane, accelerator pressed to the floor.

"Get down," he yelled.

"What are you doing, Dink? You'll get—"

Stanek jerked as a bullet slammed into the front windshield near his head, glass shattering inward. Reflexively he squeezed his eyes shut, hands rising toward his face as the shards splattered back. Another bullet punched into the body of the car.

"What the—"

"Stay the fuck down!" Dink jerked the wheel and a horrible sound of rending metal filled the air. They ripped along the side of the police car, two seconds maximum, but it seemed to last forever.

Behind them, through Dink's open window and over the sound of the motor as he continued to accelerate, they heard a collision.

Stanek looked out the back window, saw the police car on its side against one of the shuttered storefronts along the street. His ears were still ringing from the shriek of metal on metal. Diane was lying across the back seat, body half on the floor.

"You okay, Diane?"

"Next time I drive," she said. "And we fasten our seat belts."

"Have some pisco brandy," Dink said, holding out the bottle, "from

Peru."

Walter and Diane were sitting on a broken-down couch in the living room of Dink's girlfriend's house. Amada was in the kitchen nook fixing a snack.

The house was more solid than some in the barrio—adobe walls, wood roof, no glass in the single window, a wooden jalousie to shut out the flying insects, a bead curtain over the open doorway leading to the kitchen, a separate outhouse.

Opposite the couch, rolled up against the wall like a futon, lay a mattress with a thin sheet tucked around it. Fifteen minutes earlier, the mattress had been stretched out on the floor and Amada had been sleeping there.

They'd left the battered sedan along the Avenida Costanera, having shot straight up Calle Yegros to the Diagonal Cabanas where they had angled to the east as the sirens died away behind them. From there, they'd worked their way toward the Hotel Terraza and the shantytown in the mud flats overlooking the bay. Only once, along the route, did they have to pull over and hide, ducking down in their seats as a police van shot by. The last few blocks into the shantytown, they'd walked.

Diane and Walter had tried to apologize for the intrusion, but Dink had brushed aside their efforts, saying it was a Sunday and they could all sleep in later; they had the whole day. Stanek had already told him that he doubted anyone from Samcon would come in to their Calle Iturbe office on a Sunday. Still, they had talked about staking out the building just in case.

Amada, a perky creature with jet-black hair cut short around the ears and strange, dark-gray eyes that reminded Stanek of diorite, came back into the room with a plate of warm fruit and a bowl of salted pumpkin seeds. Given the hour, five-fifteen in the morning, she was surprisingly alert.·

After topping up their glasses with brandy, Dink put his arm around

Amada, who was four or five inches shorter than him, not much over five feet, a thin stick next to his muscular body.

"Amada works in a fish market," he said. "Hates the stuff, unfortunately. I'd offer you a big steak, but she's also a vegetarian."

Diane said, "Dink, we don't need food. We need sleep. We can find something to eat later." They were all clearly exhausted, going through the formalities of conversation with a half-hearted attempt to be polite. "How can you sleep after all that?" Walter asked. He still felt keyed up.

"If I lie down on this couch, I'll fall asleep inside of two minutes," she said. "I may be a woman of thirty-two, Walter, but I sleep like a kid of twelve."

"I wish I was so lucky. I haven't been sleeping well for two months."

"What? Last night in the hotel, you fell asleep before I did."

Stanek pondered that, then grinned. "Come to think of it, I've been sleeping like a log ever since I got here. Only it's been two to four hours a night."

Dink swallowed the last of his brandy. "Well, you two can have the mattress. I'm taking Amada with me."

Stanek turned toward him. "Where to?"

"The DEA station. I've got to report in or they'll think some *narcotrafi-cante* took care of me for good."

"At this hour?"

"We have a twenty-four operation. I won't be gone long. You guys just sit tight and if the police come, well, you know what to do."

"We do?" Stanek said.

"Yeah, tell them to get the fuck out of here or I'll be back to kick 'em in the butt."

Chapter Thirty-Nine

Ten a.m. The sun bright, the heat building up, the mattress drenched in sweat. Walter rolled over and came awake, his head feeling like it weighed a ton. With his eyes shut, he could hear the angry buzz of insects, the cries of children playing, sounds of far-off traffic. His head seemed filled with fuzz.

Diane stirred, groaning. "God, it's hot."

It was an effort to open her eyes. She looked at Walter. The heat was making both of them groggy. Voices outside—someone was approaching the house.

"Dink's here," she said.

Stanek exhaled a deep breath and sat up, yawning. He could hear Dink's voice then, outside the door, a bellow announcing his presence.

Bright light splashed inside as the door opened, blinding them. Dink left the door open for air and it took a moment for Diane and Walter to see. Dink had a plastic net bag stuffed with food.

"I got us another car," he said.

Amada opened the jalousie over the window. A hot breeze wafted through the room. She took the food from Dink and went into the kitchen nook to prepare lunch.

"Any trouble in the streets?"

Dink shook his head. "Deathly quiet. Had trouble finding a market that was open. Everybody's locked away until they know what's going on."

"What happened to the military?" Diane wondered.

Dink shrugged. "They've cleared out, too."

Stanek rubbed his forehead, trying to come fully awake. His tongue felt like an old sponge left out to dry. "Where'd you get the car?"

"It's one of ours. Government loan, you might say."

"Did you talk to anyone who could help us?"

Dink flopped down on the couch, the strain of the past twelve hours showing on his face. "Officially, they can't get involved. If I asked for help, they'd send me to the Embassy—and I don't trust those bastards. Samcon's too well connected. We don't have any proof they have your sister."

"They have her," Walter said flatly.

"We go to the Embassy and they make waves and she may disappear for good."

Stanek didn't respond, and after a moment Diane reached for his hand.

Dink took a deep breath. "I did talk to another agent who's a good buddy of mine. If we need him and he's available, he'll help. But the first thing we have to do is find someone from Samcon, and then find out where they're keeping your sister. Let's eat and then we'll go stake out the office. We can't plan anything until we know more."

• • •

Long, hot hours in the sun, the glare on the windshield like a lance in the eyes, three of them slumped down in the car, Amada up the street near the Franciscan school.

The towers of Radio Caritas were visible off to the right, and a few people came and went, hurrying down the streets, heads bent as if to ward off the world around them.

Dink fiddled with the radio in the car, trying to see how many stations were on the air, but all he could pick up was a high-pitched whine.

The office on Calle Iturbe was a modern four-story building with square pillars supporting the upper levels, an open walkway on the ground floor, and reinforced glass doors set back from the sidewalk. Torn political posters defaced the pillars. Samcon's corporate logo was on a bronze plaque by the entrance. The windows on the upper levels were covered with Venetian blinds. To both sides of the building they could see shuttered stores—a *confitería* with displays of bottled candies and an appliance store with radios and cassette players in the window and a Phillip's sign overhead in neon.

They had gone over a rudimentary plan. If Kohlbert showed up, by himself or with others, they would let him enter the building. A snatch in broad daylight was too risky. If he came out while it was still light or there were too many people around, they would follow him at a distance in the car.

The idea was to catch him by surprise, hopefully alone, then get him to Amada's place where Dink could work on him. Stanek had seen a few of Dink's supplies—a black sack with drawstrings lay on the front seat between them, to cover Kohlbert's head after Dink incapacitated the man—and a kit in the glove compartment with several ampules and a syringe. Once Kohlbert was in the car, he would be sedated.

"And I got a few more things in the trunk if I need them," Dink had said.

If they were successful with the snatch, Dink would have to work fast—disorient Kohlbert from the start, work him over a bit, apply a few physical measures to see if he would break. And if he didn't, Dink had chemicals that would do the job—more dangerous, with possible side effects and unforeseen damage.

Near four p.m., traffic picked up for about twenty minutes, then thinned out again. No one approached the front doors to Samcon's offices.

Six p.m. Streets deserted now. Sky still high and bright, a washed out blue. A car drove by … moving slow.

"Did you catch who it was?"

"A woman. Looked Paraguayan."

At seven, Amada sauntered up the street, hips swaying. "Look at that cheeky thing," Dink said, laughing. "Not your ideal undercover agent."

Diane opened the back door and Amada slid in beside her.

"Here," Dink said, handing her a bottle of water. "What do you think, Walter, any chance he'd show up at night?"

Stanek shrugged. Most of the time, from what he'd seen during the war games, Kohlbert wasn't even in Asunción. "You guys can go. We should have done this in shifts."

"One person watching won't do us any good," Dink said. "You going to follow him on foot if he's in a car?"

"We could go eat and come back," Diane said. "Use the bathroom."

Stanek had turned around, arm up on the seat to look at her. "God damn," he said, sitting upright for a second and then ducking down. "He's coming up the street behind us."

Dink looked past him to the outside mirror on the passenger side. "He's walking a fucking dog."

Stanek's heart was thudding in his chest and he took a deep breath, trying to calm himself down. Kohlbert didn't look like a guy who'd just kidnapped a woman … but he had to know something. Must live in the area. Maybe Randi was nearby, being watched by someone else.

———

In a few seconds, Kohlbert would be alongside them. They had to act quickly or the opportunity might slip through their fingers.

"I say we take him," Stanek whispered. "Now."

"I'll stop him," Diane said. She'd opened her door, directly behind Dink on the driver's side of the vehicle, and was out of the car before anyone could respond, in the street and moving away from Kohlbert.

"Shit," Dink hissed. "We should have used Amada."

Fifty feet up the street, Diane cut between two cars and stepped up to the tiled sidewalk. She looked at a piece of paper in her hands and then up at a sign reading *Sastrería Ribera*. Eyes back to the paper, frustrated gesture, half stamping her foot, one hand on her hip, looking around as if she were lost. She moved further away from Kohlbert, then came back a few feet, moving closer to the car, muttering to herself.

Kohlbert was alongside them. They couldn't see the man, hunched down as they were in the seats, but they could hear the dog barking. A dalmatian, female. She'd been yanking at the leash when Stanek had first spotted Kohlbert.

That was all they needed, he thought. A dog to pull the guy over to the car window where he could look inside and see them.

"Come on, Suki." The voice barely ten feet away. "Get away from there. You're just smelling her perfume."

Shit, Kohlbert had seen Diane get out of the car; did he notice that it was from the back seat?

Stanek's neck was beginning to ache. His feet were jammed up under the dashboard and his spine was bent. He stared up at the front windshield, waiting for Kohlbert's face to appear. All he could see was the sky overhead, changing tone, the blue deepening. It would soon be dark.

The dalmatian's yapping had changed in intensity. Stanek slid up and saw that the dog was now straining toward Diane, pointed tail slightly elevated, wagging furiously. Good, two things to keep Kohlbert's attention riveted in that direction.

Dink's door slid open. "Out my side after me," he whispered, crouching at the door panel.

Stanek slid across the car and out the door on his hands and knees. "Got the bag?"

Damn. He looked back and saw it on the floor, reached in under the steering wheel and snagged it.

"Stay here until you see me take him," Dink said, "then get the hell up there. We're going to have to carry him to the car."

He moved forward silently, using parked cars for protection. Kohlbert was nodding at Diane and she was saying something in Spanish, asking a question.

Oh shit, the dog—the dalmatian's head was swinging around. Dink had come up on the curb, was moving fast, his tread soundless, but somehow the dog had sensed his presence, was ready to bark.

At the last moment, Kohlbert realized that something was wrong. He started to turn, eyes widening, just as Dink chopped him behind the neck. The way the man collapsed, Stanek was afraid Dink had killed him, severing his spine with the force of the blow. The dalmatian had grabbed hold of Dink's pants, released them to attack again, got him in the leg. Stanek was running toward them, black bag in one hand, yelling at the dog.

Dink dropped to one knee, pain flickering across his face as the dog bit deep into flesh. His right fist crashed down on the dog's skull and the animal yelped and slunk away.

Stanek slowed to a walk. "Easy girl, take it easy." His voice soothing.

The dog whimpered in response, crouched on her belly. Dink's blow had stunned her, and she appeared disoriented, shaking her head as if it were misaligned.

Dink rolled over away from the dog, grimacing, grabbing for his leg. "Get the bag on him," he hissed through clenched teeth, then swore at the dog, a long stream of words to hide his pain.

Stanek slipped the bag over Kohlbert's head and drew the drawstring tight, making sure the breathing hole was near Kohlbert's mouth.

"I'll get the car," Diane said. She took off running. Dink had left the keys in the ignition.

He was trying to stand, still swearing at the dog under his breath, eyes glaring. Amada was there then, trying to help, slipping under Dink's arm to support his leg.

"Got to take it, too," Dink said. He meant the dog. "Can't have it found on the street."

"Get in the car," Stanek said. "I can drag Kohlbert over."

Diane had pulled alongside and came to help Walter as Dink limped to the front passenger seat.

So far, no one seemed to have noticed, the barking had attracted no onlookers, no one had raised a cry of alarm.

The dog growled when they lifted Kohlbert but made no move to attack.

Once Kohlbert was sprawled over the back seat, Dink turned around from in front, syringe in hand.

"I don't know," Diane said. She'd moved back to the driver's seat. "You hit him pretty hard. If you sedate him now, it may take hours before he can answer questions."

Dink hesitated, then put the syringe back in its case.

"I'll watch him from back here," Stanek said, "with Amada."

Diane took her foot off the brake.

"Don't forget the dog," Dink said.

"Diane, I need the key for the trunk." Not enough room inside.

She had to shut off the ignition to unlock the trunk. It seemed they'd been sitting there for fifteen minutes. If they didn't hurry someone would see them. For all they knew the police had already been called.

Stanek approached the dog with care, talking to it and patting his leg. The dalmatian came out of her crouch, unsteady on her feet. "Come on, girl," Stanek said. "Come on. It'll be okay."

At the rear of the car, the dog resisted, pulling away in fear at the sight of the open trunk.

"Jesus Christ!" Dink said, his head stuck out the window. "Get it in the back with Kohlbert."

For a moment, seeing the fear in the dog's eyes, Stanek felt sorry for the beast—it was just doing its job when Dink clobbered it—but then he saw a picture of Randi in his mind and what remained ahead of them to do was all that mattered.

He eased down by the dog, reached out to pet her and then grabbed the collar. He had to tug the dalmatian toward the back seat, its rump sliding along the pavement, and he couldn't help thinking, you stupid bitch, your master's in the car.

Amada had pulled Kohlbert into a sitting position and was holding him there, his head slumped forward on his chest. Forget the trunk. No way the dog would stay quiet in there. Stanek followed the dog into the car, hitting his head on the roof panel. The second the door was shut, Diane gunned the motor and the tires gripped the hot pavement with a brief squeal. The dalmatian stumbled and sat on Stanek's feet. It looked up at him, suddenly meek, head cringing as if it had done something bad.

"That's okay," he said. "You're okay, girl." He stroked its head. "Everything's going to be all right."

Yeah, *right*, and they were all one big happy family.

For a Nazi-lover, Kohlbert broke with surprising ease.

Dink had made Amada and Diane wait outside in the car, afraid, he said, that some of the kids in the barrio might steal the tires off the sedan, but knowing the two women would have no stomach for what had to be done. Amada had filled a pan of water for the dalmatian, which was panting hard in the heat and clearly nervous without her master.

The wait was less than an hour.

Before Dink revived Kohlbert with smelling salts, Stanek told Dink about Kohlbert's fascination with the Luftwaffe and his contacts with the ex-Nazis living out their lives in Paraguay. He wondered if they couldn't work on that in some way.

It wasn't necessary. Kohlbert had no stomach for pain. While Stanek watched in silence, Dink told the gagged and blindfolded man what was in store for him and then stripped him and worked him over for twenty minutes, using his fists, matches, water, and a metal fingernail file, with Kohlbert strapped to a chair and unable to speak the whole time, even if he wanted to.

The DEA agent moved with silent efficiency, working on various parts of the body, including the fingernails, prying under them and bending them back, the whole process sending a chill through Stanek; Dink could have trained the Paraguayans. He hoped the man was never *his* enemy. Kohlbert's body was wracked with pain, and the man's jerking and twisting and muffled screams were hard to take.

After the first session, Dink stopped and rummaged through some implements, making sure Kohlbert could hear the clatter over the sound of his moaning.

"Okay," he said, rubbing his hands, "that was just the first stage of many until you either spill what you know or die."

Kohlbert's body jerked as he strained to speak. Dink grinned at Stanek, who looked away, sick to his stomach.

"You want to talk?" Dink said. "You haven't even heard a question. I don't think you're ready. Don't disappoint me. I have quite a few other things I'd like to try." He poked at one of the broken fingernails.

Kohlbert twitched about in his seat. Frantic sounds issued from his mouth. In addition to the blindfold and gag, his head was still enclosed in the cloth sack, wet now from Dink's use of water to torture him, drawstring tight around his neck.

"What we'd like to know," Dink said slowly, "is where the girl is." He didn't bother personalizing her with a name; Kohlbert would know who he was talking about. "Can you tell us that?" He tugged at the nail until it ripped loose.

A muffled shriek. Kohlbert struggled to answer, nodding his head frantically, making rough, unintelligible sounds at the back of his throat and through his nose.

"You sure you can tell us where she is and who has her and what the setup is?"

The guy was growing more frantic, and Stanek was about to speak when Dink raised a finger to his lips and shook his head. He'd already told Stanek he didn't want him speaking in Kohlbert's presence. The less the man from Samcon knew the better.

"I'm going to take the gag out now," Dink said. "I'm very disappointed. I'd really like to try a few other things I have here. Of course, if I don't hear what I want to hear—if it doesn't turn out to be the truth, well, then—" His laugh was devilish.

Kohlbert broke the second the gag was removed, sobbing as he told them what they wanted to know. Randi was being held in a house in the San Antonio district, on Calle José Montero near the Shell and Esso gasoline storage yards. During the night shift, there was only one man to watch her, on the ground floor. The house had two stories, with entrances front and back. Exterior windows on the first level were barred. Randi would be upstairs, in the first room to the left at the top of the stairs, a bedroom.

"Just one guy?" Disbelief in Dink's voice.

"She doesn't know we—that we're holding her. We told her her brother was in Posadas—that he'd been sent there for the Corpus project ... an emergency. No reason for her not to believe that. She doesn't know Stanek's in trouble."

"I can't believe there's only one guy with her."

"We didn't want to involve a lot of other people—it wasn't necessary. We didn't expect anyone to find out where she was." He paused, gasping for air, eyes still taped shut. "She doesn't know what's going on. She's still expecting her brother to show up."

"Maybe he will," Dink said, an edge to his voice. "Who's the man with her?"

"A guy I work for … Greg Brown … out of Houston."

Stanek's eyes widened. He mouthed the words for Dink: *I know him.*

"Why'd you get Randi involved in this?"

Kohlbert hesitated. His fists tightened, muscles straining against the tape that held him to the chair. He licked his lips, mouth opening and closing soundlessly. He started to clear his throat.

Before he could finish, Dink jammed the gag into his mouth. A lie about to come. He slipped the hood over Kohlbert's head and tightened the drawstring with a rough jerk.

"Thanks, pal, I was hoping for that."

The veins in Kohlbert's neck stood out as he tried to scream. His body jerked and spasmed in panic, the legs of the chair bounced on the floor. Sections of the tape binding his limbs to the chair were red with blood. "What is it now?" Dink said crossly, jerking the bag open and ripping it off Kohlbert's head. He pulled the gag from his mouth. "Ten seconds to tell me why you're using the girl or it's back to work—and this time I'm not stopping for a long time."

"T-To kill him—" Kohlbert blurted out, drool dribbling down his chin as he slobbered in fear, *"to kill them both."*

Chapter Forty

The serious work began then, more questions interspersed with threats, the promise of freedom, of staying alive, if he told the truth.

"Why kill Randi?"

"I-I didn't plan on killing the girl—just using her to get him, to get her brother, but Brown ..."

"Brown what?"

"He's afraid she'll learn something and talk—that she'll figure out we killed her brother. Brown wants to play it safe. He'll blame their deaths on the rebels."

"If you call Brown and tell him to let the girl go, what'll he do?"

Kohlbert hesitated, then spoke in a panic, afraid the torture would begin again. "He—he'd hold her until you let me go—and then he'd kill her, and then he'd come after you . . . and after Stanek."

"Is Brown expecting anyone tonight?"

Kohlbert shook his head. "Not till tomorrow."

"You're lying to me, aren't you? You want another thirty minutes in the bag?"

"I swear," Kohlbert said, the words rushing out in panic. "I'm not supposed to get in touch with him until tomorrow morning at ten."

"How were you going to kill Stanek?"

"We—Brown figured he'd show up at the office. We were expecting him tomorrow at the earliest. His sister called him in Posadas." Kohlbert hesitated. "Did Stanek telephone you from there?"

"You might say that."

"Who are you?"

"A friend—and that's the last question I want to hear from you. You speak when I ask you something, otherwise you keep your mouth shut." Dink slugged him in the middle of the chest to make the point, catching Kohlbert by surprise. When he quit gasping, Dink said, "When will you be missed?"

"Tomorrow ... ten o'clock—not until then. I live alone."

Stanek waved his hand, asking for Dink to step outside. Dink frowned but followed him out, shutting the door behind them.

"I've been thinking about the dalmatian," Stanek said, his voice low. "It can't be his dog; he flies around too much to take care of it. He's lying."

Dink looked doubtful. "I don't think so, Walter. I'd hear it in the voice."

"Ask him about it, okay?"

Dink nodded. "I'll check. Now, let's get back in there before he forgets what pain is."

Stanek reached for his arm. "Listen, Dink. I want to know why they were going to kill me? I don't understand what I did to them."

"I'll ask."

Back inside, Dink kicked Kohlbert in the shin and slapped him on the side of the face. "You awake? Whose dog were you walking?"

"My own," Kohlbert said, his face twisted in pain.

"You travel a lot, right?"

Kohlbert licked his lips, breathing heavily. "I fly my own plane."

"Who keeps the dog?"

"I pay a kid to take care of him when I'm gone. When I'm in the city, Suki stays with me." He hesitated. "Did you kill her?"

Dink pounded him on the forehead. "I said no questions. Why were you going to kill Stanek?"

Kohlbert's head wobbled, the blindfold tight around his eyes. "Brown wanted to, not me."

Dink swore and slapped both of Kohlbert's ears at the same time. The man screamed and tried to twist around in his chair. A bloody froth bubbled at the corners of his mouth.

"I said, why?" His voice harsh.

"He knew too much," Kohlbert sobbed. "He messed up the plan."

Stanek frowned, a look of perplexity on his face. He made a gesture of inquiry.

Dink said, "Yeah? Knew too much about what?"

"About us helping Colonel Ibarras."

Stanek shook his head.

"Help him what?"

"Overthrow Zancon. The general was arrested two days ago."

Dink and Walter exchanged a look of surprise.

"What made you think Stanek did anything to sabotage the plan?"

"Army intelligence—they said he was helping the rebels. He was working with a lawyer, with one of the opposition leaders—they were sabotaging Ibarras ... and the colonel was *our* man."

"What's Ibarras doing now?"

Kohlbert swallowed in discomfort. Sweat was pouring down his face and he seemed to be having trouble breathing. The day's sweltering heat radiated from the walls and the room was like an oven. "He—he's in hiding, I think … The people turned against him."

"What's Samcon doing about that?"

"Doing? Nothing … The people have rallied around Alquijana—around one of the rebel leaders. We can't do much—ask the CIA to assassinate him."

"The CIA doesn't assassinate foreign leaders."

Kohlbert cleared his throat. "Can I have some water?" No one made a move. His head dropped as if he knew the request was stupid. "It doesn't have to be the agency."

"Who's behind your operations here?"

"I am. I head the regional office. We had two generals on our Board of Directors … for local operations … but both have gone over to Alquijana." Resignation and tiredness in his voice, the confession pouring from him as if he had nothing to gain any longer from silence.

"Two generals?"

Kohlbert nodded. "Bernardo Paredes—of 1st Army Corps—and Alberto Campos—army intelligence." He exhaled a deep breath, then went on in a quieter voice as if talking to himself. "We'll have to learn to live with him … with Alquijana. We've overcome worse before."

He raised his head, eyes unseeing behind the blindfolded, panic in his attitude. "You're going to kill me, aren't you? Who are you?"

"You don't know who I am? Army intelligence hasn't told you that?" A sarcastic tone.

"No … Stanek's friend, you said."

"I did? Let's just say I work for another government agency. You got in the way of one of our operations when you fooled around with Stanek. We don't like that. You understand?"

Kohlbert was listening intently. "You won't kill me?"

"I told you you'd live if you told the truth. When you get out of here, you forget this ever happened, you forget you ever knew Walter Stanek, you got me?"

Kohlbert's head dipped in acknowledgment.

"You forget him and his sister—and we'll forget you. You fuck around with him or his family, you even send him a Christmas card, you die. You understand?" Dink poked him in the chest.

Kohlbert raised his head. "I understand. We forget everything."

"Right, you go on doing business, you go on living. No one's going to hassle you. You got your dog … Suki … she's in better shape than you."

"Thank you," Kohlbert said, blubbering. "Thank you."

Diane grabbed Dink's right hand, which was picking at the bandage on his left arm. "Dink, leave that alone. You know what the doctor said. You can last another day."

"Fuck another day. The doc said Monday. Come dawn this sucker gets ripped off." He gently scratched at the wound through the bandage. He'd already torn off both edges of the tape, narrowing the bandage. The itch was harder to take than the damn bullet in the first place. Amada had wanted to redo the whole thing, telling him the best remedy was a paste made from the ashes of alligator skin. He'd decided he could stick with the antibiotic cream under the bandage. But it was driving him crazy.

Stanek looked at his watch. "Morning isn't that far off," he said. "It's just after one-thirty. We've got to figure something out." Kohlbert had given them the address of the house on Calle José Montero where Randi was being held. Greg Brown would be there watching her. Stanek wanted to get her first, make sure she was safe, then go after Greg Brown to see he left them alone. Kohlbert had got that message; Brown needed to get it, too.

Dink nodded, fingers drumming on the roof of the sedan. The dalmatian, spots visible under the dim glow cast by the dome light, was lying on the dirt outside the car, chewing on a bone Amada had found for it.

Diane sat on the back seat, legs outside the vehicle, dark hair damp near her temples. In Posadas, she'd changed from a skirt and blouse to a pair of jeans and a pullover cotton shirt, but the heat was still oppressive. Amada sat on the hood and Stanek had crouched to pet the dog.

After a moment Dink said, "The principle is you hit them hard and with maximum force—plenty of noise and confusion. You overwhelm their senses, use stun grenades if you've got them. You make them think resistance is futile."

"Dink, you're talking about a drug raid, you're talking about a force of ten or fifteen men. This is my sister. There's only one guy in there with her—and there're only two of us."

"Hey, damn good odds."

"I don't want my sister hurt—I don't want there to be the slightest chance that something'll go wrong. If Brown knows we're coming, he may kill her before we—" His voice died away.

"You think Brown's going to let her walk out of there? You think he's going to be asleep when you try to get in? You want to try something tricky and have him smell it coming?"

"Look—" Stanek paused for a moment. "The guy's been careless so far. He's made several incorrect assumptions, including the fact that I wouldn't get here until later. He hasn't prepared—"

Dink thundered, "Wait a minute. How do you know he hasn't prepared? That this isn't *exactly* what he expected? Maybe he's waiting for you to show up. You know, you're his primary target, not Randi. She's the bait. Kohlbert set the line. And you're going to take the hook and let Brown reel you in."

Diane said, "What he's saying, Dink, is he's tired of violence. He wants Randi alive."

"Hell, so do I. That don't mean we leave our guns in the glove compartment. You can bet Brown will be carrying. We can't take a chance with her life or with ours." Dink had picked up a revolver from the DEA station for Stanek, and had retrieved one of his own pistols from Amada's house, a 9mm automatic. They wouldn't be going in bare-handed.

"I wasn't trying to say we don't carry the guns," Stanek said. He felt a heavy weight of tiredness deadening his mind. "We've got to figure out the best way to get in, is all."

Dink snorted. "Well, you can't just knock on the front door and expect him to answer."

"Maybe you could," Diane said. "If he saw Walter, he'd open up. You could be waiting next to the door, Dink."

"Yeah, and he kills Walter before I can kill him."

"We're getting nowhere," Stanek said. "I say we go to the address and case out the place, then make up our minds how we can get Randi out of there."

Dink straightened. "Okay. We take Kohlbert with us. In the trunk. If—make that, *when* we get your sister, we drop him off. Let him convince Brown what'll happen to him if he tries to fuck with you guys later."

Diane said, "He'll suffocate in the trunk."

"Not if we open the lid every fifteen or twenty minutes. That'll give him plenty of fresh air. Diane, you can time it. Remind us if we get preoccupied."

"He should be arrested for what he's done."

"Yeah, and what about us?" Dink said. "We haven't exactly followed the law. If we had something concrete to turn him in on, I'd take him to the proper authorities. But we can't even prove he kidnaped Walter's sister. From what Kohlbert said, she still thinks Walter's going to walk through the door and hug her. She probably doesn't even realize she's being held."

"But I didn't send for her," Stanek said.

"No, but like I said before, they can always say they did it to reward you—a nice bonus for your work on the Corpus project. A surprise."

Stanek was tired of arguing. "What about the dog?" he asked. "We can't leave her."

"Then you handle it. Diane can sit up front with me."

Amada slid off the trunk. "What do I do?"

"You stay here," Dink said. "We've got enough people to worry about as it is."

The rectangular house looked like a territorial prison in the old West—a bare two-story facade with peeling white paint and with iron bars over all the windows, which were lined up in a row on both stories and had interior shutters. There was no inner courtyard, and the back yard lacked vegetation.

The area as a whole was rather seedy from what they could see in the night, with some illumination provided by the bright lights at the oil storage facilities across the street. The Esso and Shell complexes were large, several blocks long running east and west, with two or three massive storage tanks and dozens of smaller ones. It was an industrial area with homes that had once been nice but had fallen into disrepair.

On the side of the house facing east, away from the oil tanks that lay on land that sloped gently to the west toward the river, they could barely make out an exterior balcony on the upper level, wide enough for a row of flower pots but not much else—more decorative than functional.

"Jump up and grab on to that and you'd probably pull it from the wall," Dink whispered.

It didn't matter. The upper windows had the same bars, all attached to a framework that was screwed into the wall at the corners of each window, and the same interior shutters. If they had a screwdriver they could have worked at dismantling the barrier … but even then, Greg Brown would hear them.

Stanek licked his dry lips. "What about the doors?"

The two men were crouched behind an ancient palm tree. It's branches had been trimmed as it grew and now, with age, chunks of the dead

335

remnants were rotting and working their way loose. Dink had knocked out a piece as he leaned on the tree.

"The doors are solid wood," Dink said, his voice a whisper. "They look new."

In the scattered light, Stanek could just make out the black exterior hinges that extended halfway across both doors. There were two doors on each side of the house. "What about the locks?"

"I'll have to get closer to see. Wait here."

Dink moved forward silently, disappearing in the gloom within seconds. Stanek took a deep breath and tried to listen for sounds of activity. The city was quiet at two in the morning, no sound of traffic on the streets or voices inside houses. Most of the places in this area seemed deserted, but thin cracks of light slipped out of one of the windows on the ground floor of the house where Kohlbert said Randi and Greg Brown would be waiting.

Had Randi wondered about the area? Samcon was paying him sixty thousand for the month and this place looked like an abandoned relic. Except for the doors and windows. They looked new all right. Had Randi thought of a prison when she saw the place? Had she had any misgivings?

Dink was back, slithering in beside him. "I think I can loid the lock," he said.

"What?"

"I've got a set of picks with me. The lock shouldn't be too hard."

"What about an alarm system?"

"I doubt it. Nothing I could see anyway." He paused. "It could be wired but that's a chance we'll have to take. With Brown inside he probably wouldn't turn it on."

"What if he's awake? He'll hear you."

"We need a distraction. You could go back to the street and have Diane blow the horn, both of you do a little hollering in Spanish—late night revelers."

"That's okay if he's awake—but what if he's asleep? We just make things worse."

"Walter—" Dink's voice had grown impatient. "Don't you ever take any risks in life?"

Stanek didn't say anything for a moment. He turned toward Dink but couldn't see his eyes. "I take plenty of risks, but not with my sister's life. Besides, if you go in, I'm going also. You can take care of Brown, I'll get Randi."

"Fine, but Diane can still blow the horn and holler. Go tell her what's up. I'll be waiting here."

Diane took a deep breath. Twenty minutes had passed without a sign of the men. Time to open the trunk. Distasteful as always. She didn't like seeing Kohlbert bound and gagged—hog-tied with his eyes still taped shut and his fingers bloody. No obvious signs of beating on the body. . . but every time she saw him she thought of Renato and Eliana and of her former student Rosemarie Krupp and what the police must have done to them. Renato at least was alive.

She jumped as a form materialized out of the darkness. It was Walter. She shut the trunk. "What is it, Walter? What happened?"

"Nothing so far." He'd come around a vacant house and then up the street to where the sedan was parked opposite the chain link fence that demarcated the eastern boundary of the two oil storage facilities.

Stanek reached out to touch her. "Dink's going to try to pick one of the locks and then we're both going in. We need a distraction. Dink wants you to honk the horn and holler for a while."

"We'll wake the whole neighborhood."

"What neighborhood?" There were no other parked cars along this particular block. "The place is mostly deserted. If someone comes out, get in and lock the doors. The keys are there. If you have to, drive away and come back." He looked in the sedan. The dalmatian was stretched out on the back seat. If the dog barked, fine, another bit of noise—unless Brown recognized the sound of her bark and got ready for trouble. Not a good thought.

"I'm going back," he said. "Give me three minutes and then start in with the noise."

"Be careful, Walter. I'll be waiting."

Dink chose the back door farthest from the window with the glimmer of light. He worked on the lock with two picks, prying, twisting, probing. His pistol was jammed down behind his belt at the back of his pants. Stanek crouched beside him, revolver in hand. He didn't want to fire the gun, but if Brown got in his way and Randi was in danger, he'd shoot to kill.

A moment ago, the horn had started blowing, an on-and-off series of syncopated beeps coming to them faintly from the front of the building. Someone playing a wild tune. They couldn't hear Diane's voice.

A click, a second one, and the lock sprang open, the sound unusually loud. Both men froze for a few seconds listening for movement inside the house. Nothing penetrated the thick wood doors.

"Get it open," Walter hissed.

Dink lifted the door handle to lighten the door's weight on the hinges and pulled it open. The hinges creaked. A grimace from Dink, frightened eyes in Stanek's face. Each second they wasted, each moment of advance warning gave Brown time to rush upstairs and—

The door eased open. No time to waste. Stanek slipped through with Dink behind him . . .

Pitch black. He couldn't see a thing. He pulled up short and felt Dink's hand on his back, heard his intake of breath.

"Don't move," Dink whispered. "Furniture." He pulled Stanek to the floor. "We crawl," he said. "Feel your way. You go left. I'll go right. If you find the inner door, hiss for me. I'll do the same."

Stanek turned to the left without replying. Dink's whisper had sounded like a steam engine in his ear, loud enough to wake a drunk bum. His nerves were on fire, spots shooting before his eyes, his imagination picking out strange forms that weren't there. Dink had closed the outer door behind them and the shuttered windows admitted no light. It was going to be touch and feel the whole way.

"Psst."

It was Dink.

Stanek turned, tried to locate the sound. His shoulder bumped into something and he started to rise in panic, hands reaching out as if to catch a baby, ears waiting for the sound of metal or glass or wood to crash to the floor.

Nothing happened.

His heart wouldn't quit pounding, deafening him. He took a deep breath, tried to choke down a swallow, his throat parched.

Another hiss, closer.

He was afraid to move. He reached around him, right hand with the revolver finding a chair ... what felt like a pipe rack next to it, the smell of tobacco strong in his nostrils.

He jumped and nearly let out a shriek. A hand had touched him on the face.

"It's me," Dink hissed.

Stanek slipped his finger from the trigger of the revolver, aware that he'd almost exerted enough pressure to fire a bullet.

He could feel Dink's breath on his face, a sour smell.

"Put your hand on my back and follow me." A whisper he could hardly hear.

In a moment they were in another room, could see a sliver of light beneath a door at the far side.

Where the hell was the staircase to the upper level? Were they going to have to go by way of the lighted room?

Fine … they had to take care of Brown at some point. It might as well be now.

But there was no one in the room. The light came from a floor lamp between a sofa and a wing chair. An open book lay face down on a coffee table.

Someone had left the room without turning off the light. In a hurry? Was Brown already upstairs waiting—with a gun at Randi's head? The thought made him feel sick. He didn't trust his aim with a gun. How good a shot was Dink?

Dink brandished the automatic, pointed toward the staircase, a straight stretch to the second floor, built up against the wall, one rail.

Stanek could feel his guts tighten in fear, ears waiting for the sound of a bullet that would tell him they had been too late, had not moved quietly enough.

Maybe Dink was right—maybe they should have busted down the door and come in firing, caught him by surprise, shot him in the back as he rushed up the stairs to get Randi.

The top of the stairs, a landing, doors to each side as the upper level opened up before them.

First door on the left. No light. Stanek couldn't bear to think what was on the other side, heart in his throat.

Dink stepped away from the door, motioning with the pistol for Stanek to get his gun up.

I can't shoot, he wanted to say. I can't pull the trigger.

My God, he thought. He was just as likely to kill Randi as to save her.

Chapter Forty-One

Diane felt the cold barrel of the gun on her neck, both hands gripping the steering wheel, face frozen …

Ignition off, no time to start the car, she'd be dead if she tried.

The door behind her opened. She could hear Suki's tail thumping against the back seat. The dog knew who it was. Diane hadn't dared turn her head, knew Kohlbert could not have gotten out of the trunk. The gun shifted for a second, was jammed at the base of her skull. He'd gotten in, shut the door behind him.

A frightened glance in the rearview mirror without moving her head. Only a shadow behind her. But the gun was real enough. A friend of Greg Brown's? A guard Kohlbert hadn't told them about?

She could smell his presence, a whiff of cologne. So far, his only words had been an order not to move, a threat that he'd blow her head off.

Had things gone bad with Walter and Dink? She'd heard no shooting, wondered if the honking had drowned out the sound. Were both of them dead? And Randi—

The man with the gun prodded her, shoving her head down with the force of the blow. The gun barrel gouging at the base of her skull.

"Start the car. We're going for a drive."

A harsh voice, the words chilling ... a blackness in the mind that left her dizzy. She felt a shudder she couldn't repress start in her shoulders and run down her spine. She shut her eyes, overwhelmed by fear, unable to catch her breath. Another jab of the gun.

"Move it."

She turned the ignition blindly, heard the motor fire and start, was paralyzed by the sound. She couldn't open her eyes, couldn't face what lay ahead.

She felt the man's left hand grabbing at the nape of her neck, his fingernails digging into the flesh. Her head snapped back and a cry issued from her lips.

"If I have to tell you one more time," he said, "you're dead."

Dink's foot shattered the door and he went in high as Stanek spun around the corner and hit the floor, revolver out in front of him. Eyes scanning the room, a bed, a chest of drawers, a wood chair, a washstand.

"Under the bed," Dink said, rushing across the room. "Watch out behind us."

Stanek rolled over on his back, bringing the revolver around, training it on the shattered opening. No sound of footsteps, no scream.

The bedroom was empty.

"Come on," Dink said, hightailing it out of the room. "Check the left side."

Stanek ran down the hall, throwing doors open and spinning into darkened rooms, hand slapping for the light switch. When they'd checked the upper floor, they rushed back down the stairs and dashed through the rooms on the ground floor.

They were all empty.

"The car," Stanek said. "Diane'll be worried."

"Oh shit. How long since you've heard the horn?"

Stanek stared at him, wild-eyed. "That son of a bitch, he's got them both."

Stanek swore, hands hitting his sides. The car was gone, just as he'd feared.

"Quick," Dink said. No time to waste. "We need a vehicle. You check down that way. If you find one, fire the gun. If you hear mine, come this way. He couldn't have gotten far."

They circled the block on foot, but neither could find a car. Across the road, near the oil storage tanks, sat an old truck that looked abandoned.

"Go back and call a taxi," Dink said. "I'll try to start the truck."

"Wait." Stanek grabbed his arm before he could cross the street.

They both heard it then, the muffled sound of a motorcycle coming from the direction of the river. Beyond the oil storage fields, where the Paraguay river flowed south, sat a small *destacamento militar* and a construction site for a new dike. Earlier they'd driven by the area, passing a dark building with a sign reading *Administración APAL*. The military outpost and the construction site had also appeared deserted.

"The corner," Dink said, taking off on a run. Stanek followed.

They beat the cyclist to the corner, two people on the motorbike, heading down Isabel La Católica. A boy, with a girl holding tight, black hair streaming behind her. The boy slowed at first, surprised by the apparition in the middle of the road, then attempted to swerve around the men, trying to switch gears and accelerate at the same time. In his panic, his foot slipped off the gearshift lever and the motor, out of gear, revved up with a high-pitched scream.

Dink had the handlebars then, wrenching them to the side, toppling the two riders. Stanek came at them to see if they were all right, and the boy jumped to his feet and took off running. The girl stared up at him, too frightened to move, a puddle of urine spreading beneath her.

"It's okay," Stanek said in Spanish. "We won't hurt you. We just need the cycle."

The engine was still running and Dink righted the bike and swung into the seat. "Come on, man. We don't have time to chat with the ladies."

"Where to?" No sign of the sedan.

"Samcon," Dink said. "We've been set up. Randi's in the office. We've got to beat Greg Brown there."

Stanek was sitting behind the shorter man, right hand gripping the C-strap. "I've lost the revolver," he said, realizing it was no longer in his belt.

"We can't go back now. Hang on."

Dink popped the clutch and for the next ten minutes they tore down the deserted streets, avoiding Avenida Carlos Antonio Lopez for fear of drawing the attention of the police. Down Isabel La Católica to Dinamarca, taking the curve at over fifty miles an hour.

"We'll never make it in time," Stanek shouted. "They've got too much of a head start."

Dink's answer was to turn up the throttle.

This was suicide. Needle on seventy now. Eyes tearing, parked vehicles flashing by to each side in a blur, the cycle going airborne as they shot across Avenida Colón.

"Slow down," Walter screamed. "This is a dead end." But where the road ended there was a street running left and right.

Dink geared down, motor shrieking at the strain, the rear drum brakes smoking as he tried to slow. They took the corner in a controlled skid, coming out of it with a sudden jerk. Dink whooped and ripped back up through the gears. "Didn't know I could do that," he yelled into the wind.

Stanek didn't trust himself to speak. He tried to catch a glimpse of the street signs. They were on Calle Montevideo, heading north toward the city center. Talavera ... Troche ... Ytororo ... Bolivar ...

"Turn right at the next street," Stanek yelled. "We need to get over to Iturbe."

With advance warning, Dink did worse, taking the corner too fast and nearly losing control before they straightened out again. Muttering to himself.

Ten more blocks, a straightaway, the needle climbing, rising toward eighty miles an hour. Each time they came to an intersection, Stanek held his breath, praying that no one was about at this hour of the night. It seemed at times they were running blind, streetlights too far apart, buildings to each side mostly dark.

And then they were on Iturbe and Dink was slowing down, Samcon's address rapidly coming up on them.

Stanek looked ahead through blurry eyes and then his heart sank. The sedan was parked in the middle of the street, directly in front of the Samcon office. Brown had beat them to it.

The voice on the intercom said, "Come on up, Walter."

"The door's locked."

Dink had wanted to pick the lock, but they could see the security system was functioning. Dink had no sooner touched the door than a camera mounted high overhead had swivelled and focused in on them.

"Tell your friend to step away. I want him out in the street where I can see him. If he tries to come in when you do, both of these lovely ladies die."

Both. He had Diane with Randi. At least he hadn't killed Diane and dumped her body on the street.

Dink went into a coughing fit, body bent over, both arms wrapped around his body.

What in hell was he trying to do? Stanek wondered. Slip him the gun? Useless. The camera followed every move.

Dink looked up then, face red with the strain. "Let him in," he said. "I won't move. You got the fucking camera."

"Just remember what I said. You come with him, the chicks bite it."

There was an electronic buzz and the bolt snapped back. Stanek swung the door open and stepped inside, looked back to make sure Dink stayed where he was. Dink caught the door for a second as if to steady himself, a grimace of frustration on his face.

"No," Stanek said. "This guy'll do what he says. I have to go alone."

Dink looked up at the camera.

The metallic voice said, "Are you deaf or only stupid?"

Dink's eyes hardened. He mouthed, "You bastard," and then let go of the door.

Both men watched on opposite sides of the reinforced glass as the automatic closer pulled the door slowly shut. Stanek's heart sank. He heard the door settle into its frame with an audible thud—a final, dull sound as if the gates of hell had just swung shut behind him—and then he turned and began to climb the stairs.

Dink had got him here, but he was on his own now.

"I'm not going to sit here and talk forever," Brown said. He gestured to the right. "In the chair." Brown was standing in front of an executive desk in a suite on the fourth floor of the building, cradling a submachine gun. The sight of the weapon had hit Stanek like a blow to the solar plexus. At the slightest move, the first indication of a threat, Brown could spray the room with automatic fire. They wouldn't stand a chance.

The two women were tied up but not gagged. Both were sitting on a plush leather couch to Brown's left, tears in Randi's eyes, a beseeching look when she saw him, an angry cast to Diane's face, her eyes locked on Greg Brown and the submachine gun.

It'd take them forever to get up off that couch, soft as it was and with their hands bound behind them. His hopes of making a move on Brown had been instantly dashed. No chance. Coming up the stairs, he'd thought he could attack and risk a bullet or two, fight through that while the women rallied to help, give up his own life if it came to that.

Now it looked like they would all die. He'd been stupid, thinking he could stop this guy with superior intellect. Brown had matched him every step of the way, brought his sister here to Calle Iturbe, not to the safe house, sent Kohlbert to feed them a line, then waited for them to show up at the house, where he'd fooled them again, taking Diane while Walter and Dink ran around like chickens with their heads cut off.

Walter looked at Randi, remembering their conversation when he'd called with the news of the job and her fears, thinking of her having to drown kittens and of how much it must have hurt. A gentle kid, always looking up to her big brother for protection. Lot of good it had done her. His eyes brimmed with tears. Waves of hate, anger, regret, love for his sister and Diane, sorrow, remorse—they all rolled over him like giant combers crashing down on his head, left him dazed and confused.

Brown spoke. "You're as deaf as your friend. I said in the chair."

For a second, Stanek's eyes locked on Greg Brown's, then he snapped out of it and moved toward the chair, eyes flickering over the security monitors. Dink was still down there. He shook his fist at the camera, shouted something, and then turned to go.

Greg Brown laughed.

"What about *him*?" Stanek said quickly, still on his feet. "You can't kill us and let him get away." Brown was at least fifteen feet away. Too far to catch him by surprise, but he had to do something.

"I have other people to take care of him," Brown said. "I saved you for myself."

Do it now before Brown could gloat. Time was slipping away like water through a clepsydra.

"Oh, no!" Diane made a sudden movement, struggling to rise. Brown swung the gun toward her, his finger tightening on the trigger. "Kohlbert," she said. "He's in the trunk with no air."

Stanek had never moved so fast in his entire life. He hit Brown with a shoulder tackle at waist height, the echo of automatic fire ringing in his ears as the bullets plowed their way across the carpet. The force of the collision drove Brown into the desk, machine gun clattering to the wood surface as the breath whooshed out of him.

By some instinctual reflex, Brown's legs wrapped around Stanek as the older man fought to reach the gun. Stanek tried to elbow Brown in the face but hit the desk instead, his arm going suddenly numb. He grimaced and tried to roll, struggling to free his other hand.

Brown's fingers closed around the gun and he brought it toward Stanek's head like a club. Stanek parried the blow, grabbed and twisted a finger, heard a cry of pain from Brown and then the thud of the gun as it hit the floor.

Diane ... Randi ... their hands were tied behind their backs.

No way to get the gun—but they could run!

"Get out of here," he screamed, as he grabbed Brown's hair. Too short at the back, just enough on top to get a fistful.

The heel of Brown's hand was pushing at his chin, fingers digging into his cheeks. Stanek fought against the pressure, against the terrible pain of the nails ripping into his flesh. He heard the vertebra in his neck popping, tried to bite the kid's fingers.

No good. The guy was going to break his neck.

Stanek released his grip on Brown's hair, then slammed his fist into the man's ear. Brown's hand slipped away and both men rolled, reaching for the gun.

Stanek was farther away and had to grab for Brown's arm, the other hand finding the man's collar and ripping his shirt away. An elbow caught him in the nose, stunning him. He struggled to hang on, eyes watering, dull sensation spreading from the bridge of his nose into his brain ... a moment of gray, a black whirlpool sucking him down ... trying desperately to override the pain—to think ... he felt like a drowning man caught in a flash flood, grabbing for a branch as the muddy water tumbled him along, no longer seeing with clarity, no longer—*he had to get a better grip on the guy!* Brown was squirming away, would get the gun. It would end with a bullet through his brain.

Stanek fought against the desire to sink into blackness, to go down into silence and peace, where he would no longer feel the pain. Dimly, he knew his strength was ebbing, knew that he was losing to the younger and stronger man, a man he hated, a rich, slick-looking punk with a fancy BMW and a gold Rolex and—

He tasted hot blood, sensation coming back into his consciousness, swimming for the surface, the blackness turning gray and then white around the edges.

He saw it as if it were a vision or a dream—Greg Brown's hand closing over the submachine gun, finding the trigger, the barrel swinging around in slow motion, the round bore locking on to his forehead.

A tremendous explosion, a sound that echoed through his head as hot blood showered over him, fragments of bone and tissue flying. Greg Brown's body jerked, finger tightening on the trigger as he unleashed a burst that sprayed across the room toward the couch. And then silence ...

Chapter Forty-Two

He was on his back, could hear voices. Dink was there, slapping him in the face, laughing. Was this a dream?

He heard himself talking, but the words sounded strange and far away. "Am I hit? Am I bleeding?" A touch of panic, aware that he wasn't yet dead, that he was crossing from this realm to the next.

"Are you hit? Hell, I'll give you a hit if you want one." Dink's voice, loud and boisterous. "You got a fuckin' bloody nose. I suppose now you'll want a purple heart."

"The girls …"

"Open your eyes, you idiot." Dink laughing again.

But if he opened his eyes everything would fade—he would see only darkness.

"Walter, what's wrong?"

Diane. She was here, too. And he could hear Randi's voice. Had Brown got them all?

A hand touched him on the forehead, a soft caress, the sensation so strong that he couldn't help himself. His eyes opened. Three figures bent over him, smiling faces. God damn—this was real. This wasn't a nightmare, he wasn't dreaming, wasn't caught between life and death.

"What the hell happened?" Cold shiver passing through him, sensation returning, the light brightening.

Dink grinned. "I blew the sucker's brains out, is what happened. What were you doing? Looked like you thought this was a high school wrestling match, rolling around on the floor like you could win points for pinning him."

"Yeah, I'd like to have seen you try to make the tackle I did. Must've looked like the Super Bowl. I launched myself from ten feet away."

"Well, mudchucker, you've got some admirers here who want your autograph."

Stanek sat up, then reached for Diane's hand. Her face was lit up like a lighthouse beam in a stormy night. Damn but she looked good!

When he was on his feet, with one arm around Diane, Randi slipped into his arms and hugged him, tears streaming down her cheeks.

"Good to see you, kid," he said, kissing her on top the head. "I thought we were all goners. Have you two met?"

Diane laughed. "Yes, but the occasion was not one we'd like to remember."

"Well, let's make it better. Randi, meet my fiancée. I haven't asked her to marry me yet, but I will soon as I get her alone."

Randi looked back and forth at the both of them, wondering for a moment if her brother was pulling her leg, then broke into a grin. "Wally, I thought it'd never happen." She hugged Diane. "Diane, you must be quite a woman to get this guy to say that. I hope you'll say yes."

"Hey," Walter said. "Let me ask her first. You've got other things to worry about."

"Yeah, like what?"

"Like that Thanksgiving dinner you promised me. What is today, Monday? You got until Thursday to get it ready—if we're lucky enough to be out of here by then."

"The airport's open," Dink said. "Randi saw it on TV."

Walter looked at his sister. "Is that right? When did you see a TV?"

"Here," she said. "Last night—a news program. They said the airport was open and commercial jets would be landing by morning."

"Bringing in the journalists," Dink said. "Won't take long before they're swarming over everybody. Reporters and camera crews."

"Is the revolution over?"

Randi nodded. "The army's gone over to—what's his name?—that rebel leader."

"Not Alquijana."

"Right. They said emergency measures will be lifted at dawn today. They had a curfew last night, told everybody to stay off the streets. They've promised elections within six weeks, a free press immediately."

"What happened to General Zancon?"

"Was he the president?"

Stanek nodded and Randi said, "They let him leave. He flew out last night—to Chile, I think."

"Let's get a paper," Dink said. "I want to see what's going on."

Diane said, "They won't be out yet, will they?"

Stanek looked around the room. Earlier he'd seen a telephone on the desk. "Where's the phone?"

They found it on the floor behind the desk.

"Who you want to call?" Dink asked.

Stanek looked at Diane. "Do you want to talk to Pina?"

Diane hesitated for a moment, then nodded. "She lost Eliana. It'll be hard."

"If you can, ask if she knows what happened to Ibarras."

While Diane made the call, Stanek turned to Dink. "Dink, you've got to tell me what happened. How'd you get into the building?"

Dink grinned, then showed his left arm. The wound was bare, a bright purple gouge with a line of black stitches. "Remember that coughing fit? How I wrapped my arms around myself? I tore the fucking bandage off. Been wanting to do it all night. Thing itched like hell anyway. When you opened the door all I had to do was stick it over the bolt. The door never locked. I gave you a few minutes—too many probably. I figured you'd keep Brown occupied long enough for him to lose sight of me. I was hoping if he looked again, he'd just think I'd left for the car. By the time I got up here, you two were rolling around on the floor and it looked like he was going to blow your brains out. I beat him to it. Course my aim wasn't so good: I got him instead of you."

Stanek's eyes widened. "What about Kohlbert? Diane said he's still down in the trunk."

There was a moment of silence, then Dink said, "I went on down there before you came to."

"Diane asked him to," Randi said. "She said the trunk had been closed over an hour."

Dink stroked his jaw. "Kohlbert's eyes looked like congealed grease in a soup tureen. He either suffocated to death or had a heart attack."

"Jesus!"

Dink shrugged. "Nothing we could do about it, Walter. He took your sister. It was her life or his. Kohlbert would be alive now if it wasn't for Brown." He paused. "All the better for you. These two were in it together. Now you don't have to look over your shoulder, wondering if one of them is coming after you."

Stanek felt suddenly exhausted; the exhilaration of seeing all of them safe died away. "Where's the dog?"

"Down by the body. I had to dump Kohlbert on the sidewalk and move the car up the street."

"Shit, Dink, someone'll find him. We've got to get out of here."

Dink nodded. "Curfew's on until dawn. We've got at least an hour to spare."

"I say we've hung around here long enough."

"Yeah, maybe you're right." He looked over at Diane, who was saying good-bye to Pina. "Amada's waiting for me and I don't want to have to explain all this to the police. The situation's going to be a little tense in Asunción for a while. I say we all just go our separate ways and do what I told Kohlbert—forget this ever happened."

Stanek nodded, a distracted look on his face, his questioning eyes finding Diane's. "Was she asleep?"

Diane shook her head. "Her house is full of Renato's friends. She said the guerrillas killed Ibarras near Poromoco—too late for Eliana. Pina's taking her death hard, it's worse because Eliana suffered so much first, but she can't show it for Jose's sake. If she fell apart, he would, too. He doesn't understand why his sister had to die."

"What about Renato?"

"They've brought him home from the hospital but she said it's going to take a long time before he's on his feet. She said to thank both of you."

Dink crossed his arms, fingers palping the purple flesh, gently scratching the wound. "I'll look them up when you guys get out of here."

In the car, with Dink driving toward Amada's place, euphoria returning, Walter said, "Well, Dink, what about it? You guys want to join us for Thanksgiving on the farm? Trip's on me. Thanks to Samcon, I've got an extra sixty thousand bucks sitting in my bank account."

Dink was silent for a moment. "I don't know, Walter. I've got a good thing going here. Like I told you, I'm thinking of hanging around. The DEA's got a permanent station here. With Alquijana in power, there'll be more cooperation from the government. A bigger operation. They need me and Amada needs me—hell, I need her."

"Well, you'll miss a good spread." He turned to Diane. "I'd like the three of us out of here today. When this curfew's lifted and we can get to a hotel, let's call your daughter. Most of the foreigners have already left, so it'll mostly be people flying in and empty planes leaving. Shouldn't be a problem to get a seat today. When we get to Miami, I'll put Randi on a plane to Seattle and you and I can fly to New Haven. I want to meet Kim."

"But Walter," Randi said, "I thought you were coming for Thanksgiving."

Stanek grinned. "I am—along with Diane and Kim. You were complaining about too many leftovers. I can't wait for that cranberry sauce and dressing and gravy and turkey—and when we're done there won't be anything but scraps. There'll be four of us to share the meal—you, me, Diane, and Kim."

"Five," she said. "Don't forget the dog. You, me, Diane, Kim, *and Buck.* Won't even have to worry about scraps." Her eyes were happy.

"That's right," he said. "Can't forget good ol' Buck, can we?" He shook his head. "Shoot, with him around to lick our plates, I won't have to do the dishes now, will I?"

ACKNOWLEDGMENTS

Numerous sources were consulted for background information for this novel, but I owe the concept of "war games" as a means of disaster prevention to Dr. Martin E. Silverstein, a clinical professor of surgery and an expert in international disaster and emergency management issues. His work with the Federal Emergency Management Agency, the Department of State, and other international, federal, state, medical, and business organizations provided a direction for further research, which I then adapted for novelistic purposes. None of the specific events described in this novel derive from Dr. Silverstein or reflect his experience.

This novel was written before the publication of Lily Tuck's *The News From Paraguay* (2004), but it, too, reflects a fascination with a country famous for its dictators. Among the sources that brought Paraguay to life for me are Martin Almada, *Paraguay: La Carcel Olvidada;* Gordon Meyer, *The River and the People;* J. M. G. Kleinpenning, *Man and Land in Paraguay;* Elman R. Service and Helen S. Service, *Tobatí: Paraguayan Town*; J.W. Hillis and Ianthe Dunbar, *The Golden River. Sport and Travel in Paraguay*; and Rudolf Plett, *Presencia Menonita en el Paraguay.*

Other authors filled in part of the political background, among them Richard E. Feinberg (*The Intemperate Zone: The Third World Challenge to U.S. Foreign Policy*), Bruce Quarrie (*The World's Secret Police*), Carlos R. Miranda (*The Stroessner Era: Authoritarian Rule in Paraguay*), Scott Anderson and John Lee Anderson (*Inside the League*), Michael Grow (*The Good Neighbor Policy and Authoritarianism in Paraguay*), and Andrew Nickson

("Paraguay" in *The Latin America and Caribbean Review*, 1989).

Finally, I would like to acknowledge several general sources of information on Paraguay, dam projects, and other disparate matters, namely, articles published by The Associated Press, The Arizona Daily Star, and the Tucson Citizen, as well as issues of two journals, *ENR. Engineering News-Record* (vol. 223, no. 13, September 28, 1989) and *National Geographic* (vol. 162, no. 2, August 1982).

I should note that I have taken liberties with chronology in discussing the three major dam projects—Itaipú, Yacyretá, and Corpus Christi. Itaipú, the world's largest hydroelectric dam, was completed in 1982. The power plant is jointly owned by Paraguay and Brazil. Yacyretá, although initially completed in 1999, is not yet generating at full capacity and further construction is planned. In 2003, the dam's co-owners, Paraguay and Argentina, were still negotiating the level of the reservoir, which is scheduled to reach its intended height in June 2008. In 2001, Paraguay and Argentina hired an international consortium to conduct an environmental impact study for the planned Corpus Christi dam. Local and international opposition to the project remains strong.

As for its political situation, Paraguay today is a constitutional republic with an elected president. From 1954 until 1989, however, General Alfredo Stroessner ruled as dictator. His oppressive regime was responsible for the torture and murder of thousands of political opponents. In February 1989, Andres Rodriguez, an army general, led a coup d'état to remove him from power and set the country on the road to democracy. The military-backed Colorado Party provided several of the republic's first presidents, but suffered a major defeat in August 2000 with the election of a vice-president from the opposition Liberal Party. The most recent governments have sought to combat corruption by bringing to trial political and military figures suspected of human rights violations and other crimes. The campaign continues.

About the Author

Ron Terpening and his wife, Vicki, live in Tucson, where he teaches at the University of Arizona. He is the author of two young-adult novels, *In Light's Delay* and *The Turning*, and the thrillers, *Storm Track* and *League of Shadows*. For more information, including photo galleries, visit the author's web site at www.ronterpening.com.